JUDGMENT OF FIRE

Jy blinked, and found herself in the present again, stunned by everything she had absorbed. "I know what you intend, Moliak," she said at last. "You stole the trigger from me."

"What is the trigger?" asked Quencé.

"Let me show you," said Moliak, and the portal dome darkened an instant later. In the gloom overhead floated a holo image of the Founders' earth. "There is an ancient contingency plan," said Moliak. "Only a few Founders ever knew of its existence. I knew, and Jy knew, because she designed it. Should there come a time when there was no other answer, a code within Jy's hard-memory would be used to start a series of runaway nuclear fires."

"What does he mean?" asked Quencé.

"The Founders' earth is going to be destroyed," said Moliak. "Even the enduring work of the Makers will be obliterated, and the Bright itself will be severed into pieces!"

The explosion was sudden and soundless, the black sphere dissolving into gas and plasmas and expanding outward at the velocity of light—and someone was screaming. . . .

* * *

"Robert Reed is an emerging talent with a bright and compassionate vision of humanity."
—*Jeffrey Carver*

DOWN

the

BRIGHT

WAY

• • •

ROBERT REED

BANTAM BOOKS
NEW YORK · TORONTO · LONDON · SYDNEY · AUCKLAND

To Z.

DOWN THE BRIGHT WAY

A Bantam Spectra Book / April 1991

SPECTRA and the portrayal of a boxed "s" are trademarks of Bantam Books, a division of Bantam Doubleday Dell Publishing Group, Inc.

ISBN 0-553-28923-3

Published simultaneously in the United States and Canada

PRINTED IN THE UNITED STATES OF AMERICA

RAD   0 9 8 7 6 5 4 3 2 1

It took me years to discover that science, with all its brilliance, lights only a middle chapter of creation, a chapter with both ends bordering on the infinite, one which can be expanded but never completed.

—*Charles Lindbergh*

BOOK
ONE

•

LINCOLN

KYLE

1

SOMETIMES, WHEN I am tired and distracted, I forget—showing my age, perhaps?—and I consider my colleagues as if for the first time. They are Wanderers, authentic human beings, yet they come with many faces and no two have the same precise color and shape. Each of our species has its own talents and its own distinct intelligence and I have to marvel at them; I couldn't imagine such a multitude if I tried. All of us began as the same upright primate, roaming tropical savannas on a million identical earths, and look at us now. We have so many ways of living, and so many colors of thought . . . !

Revelations like these can fill me with such joy.

Yet sometimes, at damnably unpredictable moments, that joy dissolves into a sudden chill. A blackness is within me, for no reason what-

soever, and I start to shiver . . . and quietly
moan.

—Jy's private journal

THE FIRST sample of any new earth is a small
volume of common seawater. Its isotope ratios
and dissolved gases are studied, radioactive
traces are identified, and a tentative profile of
the new earth is compiled. Then if the sample
is relatively free of toxins, each scout, according
to tradition, wets a finger and places it on the
tongue, tasting salts as well as the bitterest
planktons.

—A scout's chronicles

She didn't play fair, Kyle was thinking. Just like a woman,
he was thinking. It was two, maybe two-thirty in the
morning, and they lay on his bed with the sheets everywhere and every window open and the breeze blowing
lazy-warm across them. Her damp body was snuggled
up against him, and she was talking. She was using her
plaintive little-girl voice, saying, "I know this is a lot to
ask. But I was wondering . . . after the rally and all?
Maybe we could borrow Janice's car, I can borrow it,
and we could go out to the new portal. Out where Jy's
supposed to stay?" A pause. A purposeful sigh. "And if
it's not too much trouble, maybe you can take me to
meet Jy? Like you can do sometimes?" *You* meaning
Wanderers. Every Wanderer. "Please, please?" she said,
somehow snuggling closer. "I'd *love* to go. Just to shake
her hand. Just once."

Kyle said nothing.

Billie bit her lower lip. "Is that okay? Could we?"

The breeze felt warmer all at once, almost hot. It
was as if someone had started the furnace in the middle
of August.

Billie was watching his face. "What's the matter?"

"Nothing."

"Is it too much?" she wondered.

"What . . . ?"

"Am I asking too much?"

He tried shaking his head. "No."

"You're sure?"

"No, it's fine," he promised. "Nothing is wrong."

She didn't speak. She just held her breath and pressed an ear against his chest, waiting.

The girl wasn't being unreasonable. How could he consider her unreasonable? A Wanderer could bring guests to meet Jy. Only it didn't happen very often, and Billie hadn't mentioned it until now. Kyle hadn't even considered the possibility, not once. *I'll just tell her it's impossible*, he thought. *She'll understand. I'll make up some excuse. I can fool her.* Only he kept thinking of her plaintive voice and her certain disappointment, and all at once he was talking. He heard his own voice and felt a strange detachment. "All right," he was saying. "We'll go and see if we can see her—"

"Jy!?"

"The Glorious One," he promised.

"You mean it?" Billie sat upright and applauded, kicked her feet and shrieked. "Really?"

He nodded.

"Oh, good good good. Good, good."

He watched her body in the yellowy glare of the street lamps. She was small and small-breasted and firm in an incidental, youthful way. Kyle was always surprised by her youth, and pleased. He started stroking her cool damp belly, wondering why he'd agreed. And what was going to happen a couple of nights from now? Did they just go see Jy as if it was nothing? Did they knock on her door and say, "Oh, hi! We were in the neighborhood. How are you?" God, he thought. Billie didn't play fair. She'd been a joy tonight, doing whatever he wanted and working him into a mood where he couldn't say *no*. He was so stupid. Sometimes he was the stupidest asshole on this earth . . . probably on every earth . . . and he blinked, hearing Billie's voice. "Is everything all right?" she was asking. "Kyle?"

"Perfect," he muttered.

"Really?"

"Sure." He shut his eyes and withdrew his hand.

Billie seemed to believe him. She started talking to herself, debating what she should wear and promising herself not to be any trouble, none at all, and wouldn't Janice flip when she heard? Janice was her roommate and best friend in the world. "I'm going to meet Jy!" She began to clap again, fast, like a child. She was going to come face to face with the most important person on a million earths, and she couldn't wait. How could she last another minute? She trembled and confessed to being excited, practically crazy, and was it okay if she told others? "Can I?" There was Janice. And her friends at work. Plus other friends, and maybe her family too, maybe . . . !?

"Whoever you want," Kyle told her. He made himself open his eyes, and he took a long deep breath. The air wasn't getting any cooler and he could feel his heart, rubbery and quick.

Billie said, "Thank you," and kissed his kneecap.

"It's sort of late," he remarked.

"Oh, but I don't think I could sleep."

"Maybe you should go home and try." He spoke with certainty, sitting up and kissing her twice before climbing off his bed. He started dressing in yesterday's clothes, Billie watching him. He felt her eyes. He could practically hear her mind working. But she didn't ask about his moods or anything else, thank God, and he sat back down beside her and coaxed her to start dressing. Maybe? Please? "You've got to work all day, don't you?"

She nodded.

"So you've got to go home sometime and get ready," he said, "and you know what happens if you stay here."

"Nobody sleeps," she responded, and she sighed.

He kissed her salty forehead and the small rounded nose and then her perfect mouth, twice on the mouth, and he stood and left the room. The air in the hallway was stale and even warmer. Or did it just feel that way? He stood in one place and picked at the eroded wallpaper. A long train was passing to the south, blaring its horns with every crossing. It was probably a coal train from Wyoming. He imagined a hundred identical hopper cars filled with the flammable earth, and he listened to the horns and the deep bass roar of the locomotives. Then Billie emerged. She was wearing shorts and a dark T-shirt, her book bag on one shoulder, and they went out his apartment door and downstairs and out the front door. He didn't lock anything; it was a quick walk to her place. They went a couple blocks in the moonlight, then behind another old house and up footworn wooden stairs to a hanging porch, and Billie fumbled for her keys. She could never find her keys in the bag, never, and Kyle was irritated by her predictability. "Here . . . ." She had the ring full of keys and found the right one, then she unlocked her door and turned back to him. She was a small girl with wiry black hair and a pretty round face with that sweet perfect mouth, and after a long moment she told him, "I'm sorry. I shouldn't have asked you." She shook her head, saying, "It was rude. I guess—"

"No, it's all right," Kyle responded. "Don't worry."

"You're sure?"

"You just surprised me. That's all."

She faltered for a moment, then confessed, "I'm just . . . I don't know. I'm bothered—"

"What about?"

"Are you angry with me?"

"How could I be angry?"

"I don't know," she admitted. She hugged herself and looked at her feet and sighed. Billie had a way of sighing with her entire body, in one dramatic motion. Nobody could seem as happy as she, or as sad. She asked, "Aren't you angry?"

"No."

"At anything?"

"I'm not."

"Then what is it?"

"I'm very tired." True enough. "Don't you ever get tired?"

She bit her lower lip, saying nothing.

"We aren't exactly the same species, Billie—"

"I know."

"I did warn you." He kept his voice flat and cool.

"Didn't I? You can't read me like you read your friends, and everyone. I'm a different sort of person—"

"'A human of a different line,'" she quoted. "I know."

"That's the way it is."

"I do understand," she insisted. Again she sighed, and she gave herself a long hug.

"I'll come see you tomorrow. At work, all right?" Kyle gave her a steady kiss, then said, "Good night, pretty girl."

She nodded.

"Tell everyone how you're going to meet Jy. All right?"

That helped. Her sweet mouth smiled, and she promised him, "They're going to be so jealous."

"Are they?"

"Oh, but they're already jealous." Billie stared up at him, proud to have her own Wanderer. "They are."

Kyle started downstairs with one hand on the wooden railing. He was careful to show nothing. He kept himself detached, his face blank.

"Bye, Kyle!"

"Good-bye."

Then Billie attempted to say the long name. Kyle-blah-blah-blah. And she asked, "Was I close?"

"Pretty close."

"Bye now!"

He said, "Bye," and kept walking. He heard the door shut and lock, and he was off the stairs, feeling tired. He came to his house and fumbled for his keys in the dark, finding them and then remembering nothing was locked. Then he went upstairs and stripped and lay on his back on the old bed, smelling his sweat and her sweat and thinking . . . what? He wasn't sure what was in his head. He lay there a long, long time without moving, eyes open and another train rolling past. The blaring horns shook the windows in their frames, and there was the solid click-click of wheels passing over some gap in the rails. Then came a bad set of wheels grinding near the back of the train. Then there was nothing. All he heard were wind sounds, ceaseless and summer-damp, and he grunted once and rolled onto his belly, drifting into a useless sleep.

2

EXPERIENCE SHOWS this to be a potentially dangerous earth. Its people evolved from hunters—always a worrisome sign—and they have a heavily spiced history of fighting among themselves. Some of their larger nation-states maintain stocks of nuclear weapons, although so far they have avoided true nuclear war . . . meaning they don't appreciate the depth of their furies. Like so many peoples who are modestly advanced, they confuse the absence of war with an authentic hard-shelled and enduring peace.
—*Final scout report*

"I'm part of a mission."

Sunshine poured into the bedroom. Kyle sat up and shook his head and said what he said every morning. It was his routine.

"I'm part of a mission," he proclaimed. "I came from a different earth, and I'm a Wanderer." He sighed and pulled a hand across his face. "I'm following the Bright until I find its Makers, whoever and whatever they might be. And as I follow I pledge to help knit together all flavors of Mankind. To the best of my ability. By purely peaceful means. Always."

It was midmorning, maybe later. Kyle stood and mopped himself with a bedsheet, then he took a quick cool shower and started dressing. Three clean gray shirts were hanging in the closet. There was nothing else. He picked one and put it on, then found yesterday's trousers and his sandals. His money was hidden under the bed. He took a couple of bills and went outside, the day cloudless and the sunshine liquid with the heat trying to scald flesh. A pair of young boys, seven or eight years

old, were riding bikes in the street, making airplane
sounds and machine gun sounds and then nothing. They
braked and stared, one saying, "That's *him*," with a quiet,
conspiring voice. Kyle felt their stares. They began shadowing him, and he did his best to ignore them. Walking
in his practiced fashion, he relaxed his arms and let his
sandals slap-slap on the pavement, his fresh shirt feeling
chilled where sweat bled through the plain gray fabric.

Kyle was tall, and he was homely. He had a large
nose mashed against his pinkish face, blonde hair growing thin, and big eyes set too close together. Yet his
mouth was tiny, his chin was delicate, and the effect was
to make his head look as if it had been built from mismatched parts.

Kyle looked thirty years old, give or take. But he
moved like someone who might be thousands of years
old. That was his intent. There was something careful
and steady and enormously patient about the way he
walked, as if he possessed some profound and hard-won
appreciation of time. People noticed his motions at a
distance. They saw his telltale clothes—the Wanderer
uniform—and when they came close there was the oddly
proportioned face, centered on those big eyes. He had
wise and intense Wanderer eyes, and he knew ways to
use them.

The boys were pedaling closer.

"He won't hurt," muttered one of them. "Go on."

"You go on."

"You first!"

"No, you!"

Kyle turned suddenly and stared at them, and he
smiled. He worked to seem cool and distant. The boys
braked at once and stared at him, mouths hanging open.
"How are you doing, gentlemen?" Kyle used his best
Wanderer voice, smooth and very dry. "Can I do anything for you?"

One boy squeaked, "No, sir," and wheeled his bike
around, gravel spraying and his buddy saying, "Hey?"
after him. "Where are you going? Hey!" Then he was
leaving too. Both of them went down the block and
around the corner, pumping hard with their legs.

This neighborhood was mostly older homes, most of them diced into apartments. There were students like Billie, and there were hard-luck families. Kyle continued to the next street—an arterial with a little gas-and-eat shop on the corner—and he bought newspapers from the machines out front. Then he went inside and bought doughnuts and orange juice from the stout middle-aged woman behind the counter. This was his usual place for breakfast. The woman called him "sir" with a conspicuous tone, but otherwise she left him alone. Kyle slipped into a hard plastic booth and politely ignored the customers coming and going. He sipped the pulpy warm juice and all at once found himself thinking of Billie. Why the hell did he agree to take her to meet Jy? he asked himself. It was crazy. He was an idiot, a moron. He had pretended for so long that he'd forgotten what was possible and what wasn't . . . Jesus, he couldn't believe it!

Taking a healthy bite of a doughnut, he blinked and made himself read the newspapers. There were plenty of headlines about Geneva, as always. The Wanderers were still working to form a federation of nations—a modest, durable form of world government, in essence—but there was the endless resistance. North Korea and Albania and certain African hellholes were crying to be left alone, or they wanted special treasures because of their crushing poverty. Meanwhile the major powers, no longer major in the greater scheme of things, bitched about the whole concept. World unity was a daunting business, it seemed.

The diplomats among the Wanderers were patient but quite firm; it was obvious from what Kyle read and saw on television.

This earth was ripe for certain new technologies. That was the sober assessment of every Wanderer. They spoke about cheap fusion and new metals and ceramics and the makings of true long-distance spacecraft. The only stumbling block was the current political complexion. How could they give wonders to people divided into hostile camps, cooking plutonium and obeying no laws but their own?

Wanderers wanted nothing but for this earth to

thrive. Spaceships and closed ecologies would open the entire solar system for settlement, and they believed that such a future would be stable and vibrant. It had been for thousands of other human species. All that was needed was a modest change in the social order. There had to be a true world court, plus a practical and minimal unity of the races. The Wanderers weren't here to build a utopia. They confessed to being pragmatists, and they would settle for reason and an appreciation of the Wanderers' great mission.

Kyle nodded to himself.

The mission.

"We feel responsible," claimed one diplomat in Geneva. "We don't want to bring on wars and genocide. That is why we cling to our demands." Kyle read the quote and studied the diplomat's photograph. She resembled a Sasquatch dressed in gray trousers and a huge gray shirt. Long rust-color hair spilled across her face, and her massive breasts strained against the shirt. What showed of her mouth and eyes seemed quite determined. "Satisfy us of your good intentions," she had announced, "and we will give you the means to explore your galaxy. Once you are ready, we will have no other choice."

Kyle thought about the gifts promised.

He shut his eyes and recalled a television show he had seen some months ago. The Wanderers had bought blocks of time on every network, then they had shown off a variety of possible Marses. Mars, it seemed, could be rebuilt and made habitable. Kyle remembered a deep blue river rushing through a High Arctic canyon with strange long-legged sheep bounding up the lofty red cliffs. A second Mars, in contrast, was mostly ocean. Native ices and a transplanted moon of Saturn had been melted by an artificial sun, and its people lived in sprawling cities along the new shoreline. Then there was a third Mars choked with jungle, a hundred orbiting mirrors feeding the greenery, and elegant birds as large as airliners rode thermals born on the wide flanks of Olympica Mons.

The Wanderers knew how each Mars was accomplished.

However, they liked to say that this earth could take the new technologies and invent its own elegant vision. There was always good in the fresh and the unique.

The Wanderers were staggeringly rich with knowledge. Their oldest race, the Founders, were smashing atoms more than a million years ago. They were so smart, it was said, that they had never found an earth with any technical edge. Never. And certainly if they had picked up a trick here, a trick there . . . well, they would have learned how to benefit from other people's work and hard experience.

The Wanderers were a mixture of gods and wide-eyed students.

Most of them did nothing but travel about the countryside, talking to whomever interested them. They didn't threaten and couldn't be threatened, and typically they held their vast potentials politely out of sight.

Yet they hadn't kept all their treasures just for themselves.

When they first appeared, eager to prove their good intentions, they had shown scientists how to heal the ozone blanket, neatly and quickly. Then they had outlined half a hundred proven means for disposing of toxic wastes and nuclear poison. From other earths they brought new crops—wonder crops meant for rain forests and hard deserts and the open sea—and most famines would soon be finished. Plus the Wanderers helped every military power to update its security systems; accidental wars and stupid intrigues were made virtually impossible.

The Wanderers called these things "sweet gifts."

And in return, with quiet reasoned voices, they had asked for pieces of land for their portals, plus doses of local currency. Their diplomatic corps wrestled with the largest questions in Geneva—politics, like everything else, being something in which the Wanderers excelled—and the rest of them traveled, acting like undemanding and tirelessly curious tourists, always polite, always eager to pay their way. The current scuttlebutt was that they would remain a few more months before vanishing back into the Bright . . . most of them, at least

. . . millions journeying to the next earth . . . then the next . . . .

The Bright.

It was a highway, strange and ancient and vast.

Jy and her species, the Founders, had more than a million years of written history, yet they were nothing next to the Bright. It was at least as old as the million-plus earths it lashed together, and it was leading . . . well, nobody actually knew where it might lead. Or how it had been built, for that matter. Or by whom.

The Wanderers admitted to being as ignorant as everyone else. They were nearly cheerful when they made the confession.

Of course they had guesses and assumptions, but they were careful to call them such. Several times Kyle had explained the possibilities to Billie, and she had listened without sound, watching him with her tiny hands laced together and set on her lap and nothing else mattering. The Makers had built the Bright, he had said. The Makers were ultraadvanced entities, or gods. Or perhaps the true God, he threw in. And the Bright itself was built for the Makers to use, or for human beings. Or maybe for someone or something else entirely. Who could say? Nobody, Kyle maintained. Looking straight at the girl, he had claimed that nobody knew any answers and nobody could know, and that was that. At least until they found these Makers.

Kyle was chewing on his last doughnut, and he was thinking about the girl again.

A stew of emotions worked inside him, some intoxicating and some just painful. *I can still say no if I want. I'd make up some excuse and growl, and what could she say?* He blinked and breathed, becoming aware of someone talking . . . to him? "Sir? Excuse me?" He turned reflexively. A couple of men were standing at the counter. Painters, he realized. Big sun-browned men with heavy guts and paint-speckled white overalls, painters' caps tilted at bold angles and cigarettes leaking smoke. One asked Kyle, "How are you doing?" with enormous politeness. "Sir?"

"Quite fine," he replied. "And how are you gentle-men?"

They grinned and nodded.

"Are we treating you good?" the other man wondered.

"Oh, yes."

"Pestering you too much?"

"No."

The first man wondered, "So how's our little city seem?"

"Nice." Kyle gave them the Wanderer's smile. "I like it quite well."

"Good," they said in tandem. Then they paid for their coffee, wished him well, and left, plainly pleased with themselves.

Kyle returned to reading, concentrating on the local news. A huge color photograph graced the front of the local paper. A temporary stage had been erected at one end of the university stadium, and workers were busily assembling the exotic Wanderer equipment. Jy was scheduled to arrive tomorrow afternoon. The rallies had been on the calendar for many months, her movements organized more thoroughly than those of any president or potentate. Tickets were free and everyone was invited. Jy herself was pictured at the bottom of the page, no need for captions. She resembled a peculiar little ape staring out at Kyle—a spry lady with charms and presence and a vast intelligence. She was dressed in the standard gray, her bare black face smiling. A million years old, he kept reminding himself. Her dark eyes were rimmed with gold, and that swollen brain made the long, long forehead. Jy was this mission's soul; she was its closest approximation to a leader. It was Jy who had pushed her own species—the ancient Founders—into following the Bright. It was her conviction and unblinking gaze that kept all Wanderers pressing onwards, the centuries mounting and no end found.

Kyle put down the paper and sighed, shaking his head.

"What the hell do I do?" he said without sound.

He had promised Billie the impossible. It had been

a late night and his defenses had been down, and she had gotten him into this bind. How fucking stupid could he act? He couldn't believe it.

"What's going to happen?" he muttered.

"Pardon?" The doughnut woman was out from behind the counter, wiping tabletops. "What did you say, sir?"

"Nothing."

She broke into a strange oversized smile, "If you want more juice—"

"No," Kyle managed. "Thanks, no."

3

CONSIDER THE word *Wanderer* if you would. It is our common name, and it is terribly inappropriate. We cannot wander; we have no freedom of motion in any large sense. We follow the Bright exactly as it is laid out for us. No deviations are possible, and each earth must be taken as it comes.

We earned the name on a long-ago earth. As always, we were busily studying the native people and the wildlife and everything else novel about the place. There weren't so many of us then, but otherwise little has changed. We traveled here and there, from tribe to tribe, and the tribes saw us moving in our constant, apparently pointless fashion. And with their simple languages they named us the Wanderers because, so far as they could see, we had no direction whatsoever.

—*Jy's speeches*

His full name was Kyle Stevens Hastings, and he wasn't any sort of Wanderer. Not high-ranking. Not low-ranking. Not even a novice.

It was a ruse on his part.

It was his elaborate strange game.

Kyle's real home was just a few hundred miles east of Lincoln. He didn't come from any odd alternate earth back down the Bright. Until the Wanderers arrived some fifteen months ago, he had been a bland fellow with a sapless career and few friends and a scattered family whom he rarely saw. Kyle didn't have a happy life, but he didn't expect one either. He had security and his comfortable routines. He felt close to nobody, but any loneliness was ignorable. Wasn't it? He believed so. Besides, Kyle was smart enough to entertain himself. He existed day by day with few changes and no real aspirations. On those rare evenings when he considered what was to come, he imagined thirty-plus years of steady work and a quiet retirement and then an uncomplicated death.

Then the Wanderers arrived, no warnings given. They pushed one of their big crystal portals up the Bright—an enormous sphere suddenly floating in the Pacific Ocean—and through the portal came their egg-shaped flying ships. Within the hour the leading wave of diplomats were scattered across the earth, ten thousand voices bringing greetings from someone named Jy. Several million more Wanderers were ready to accompany Jy. Every television set was full of the news; the diplomats were speaking to political leaders, scientists, and common people. They were strange apparitions with their odd builds and odd faces, or not so odd, each one speaking perfect English or Russian or Swahili. They were fluent in whatever language was required. They told about the Bright and their grand mission, their explanations brief and clear and almost simple. Then they told of the opportunities they would give everyone. Opportunities, not intrusions. They were to remain here for only the briefest while. And they wished this earth nothing but the best.

Kyle remembered watching the news and feeling an excitement. A runaway sense of awe. He was smart enough to learn the bare bones of everything—the Bright, the mission, the Makers—yet comprehension didn't diminish the spectacle of the thing. It was too wondrous, too strange . . . it still could make his breath come up short and his body nearly shiver.

This earth was one of many similar earths. There might be an infinite number; nobody knew for certain.

Sitting at home, resting in his favorite chair, Kyle could practically feel the world around him changing . . . nothing able to resist this sudden whirlwind . . . .

The Bright was like a string woven through the ultimate universe. (That's how Kyle imagined it; he saw the clean geometry of a string.) The Bright itself seemed to be built from degenerate bits of matter and lumps of shadow matter, odd intricate plasmas and things entirely beyond human reach. All these elements were sewn into each earth's matrix: the core, the mantle, the crust. Nobody here had suspected the structure's existence. It was perfectly camouflaged. The Wanderers themselves thought the Bright had been constructed four and a half billion years ago, utilizing each earth as a bridge might use pillars to cross a wide, wide river. A million pillars stood in a line, carrying the bridge across the fluid vagaries of time-space.

For billions of years each earth had had the same history. The same weather and the same species arose, the same individual animals and trees and twirling motes of dust. Even identical electrons, ghostly and swift, had traveled the same graceful existences on the brink of Reality.

A couple of million years ago the earths had divided.

Nobody could point to a specific cause. The fossils didn't say, "This is what started things, here." The Wanderers liked to speak of tiny motions at the subatomic level and how those might lead to chaotic and profound macroscopic changes. Atoms in a single breeze might move in different directions, and those differences would mount over time. A storm would follow a variety of tracks, or perhaps not form in the first place. Weather systems would diverge. One earth might grow dry where its neighbors would flood, seeds and game herds responding in kind, and that would lead to subtle changes in natural selection and variable mutations and eventually novel adaptations.

Humans existed on most earths found to date.

They showed enormous variability in their looks and natures. A few had developed big brains and industry in the ancient past; a few had retained their primitive features, hunting game with sticks and their muscles; and the rest were in the middle somewhere, Kyle and his species included in that multitude.

One species had gotten a tremendous lead on the rest.

They were the Founders, a rigorously peaceful, truth-hungry folk, and they had discovered the Bright some million years ago. It was an accident which led to Jy's defining the mission. The Makers were waiting somewhere, and Mankind was to be united by this grand quest. Two equal-size groups of Founders had started to travel on the cosmic string, one in each direction; and after ten thousand centuries and recruits from each inhabited earth, they were leading two enormous bodies of highly trained, highly motivated, and highly diverse people.

Kyle had spent days and nights watching the strange people on his television. The Wanderers were hairy or hairless, giants or midgets; sometimes they were indistinguishable from the average Hank and Harriet on this world. He saw them fielding questions with charm and a gentle humor, their honesty easy to see. Wanderers looked so different from one another . . . yet they didn't. Not in certain ways, Kyle decided. He saw their changeless gray clothes and the ways they held themselves, and he studied their wise, perceptive eyes. Immortal eyes, he realized. This was how people seemed when they had lived five thousand years. Or five hundred thousand.

Every inhabited earth was represented somewhere in their numbers.

There were the Founders from Jy's home and the Cousins who came from the most primitive earths—one or two from each, wasn't it?—and the more populated and advanced earths sent dozens, maybe hundreds of people. They were entitled because they were richer, more complicated places.

Most of the Wanderers here were high-ranking. It

seemed to take time and flawless service to rise to the forefront of the mission.

All Wanderers loved talking about the Makers. Kyle felt a delicious tingle whenever he heard them, particularly when it was Jy who was talking. She would describe how one day all human beings would stand together, humanity showing its best face . . . and before them would be the Makers, every mystery answered and every cost worthwhile . . . .

He used to sit at home and wonder how it would feel to be among the Wanderers. How would it seem to belong with them? They were so determined and passionate, so strange with their immortality and their apparent wisdom. Kyle found himself starting to mimic them. At first it was almost accidental. He might quote them aloud, in their own voices. Or maybe he would glance at a mirror and try a Wanderer's expression. Then he began to tape interviews, and he propped tall mirrors by the television and watched himself using the same stances and the knowing voices, polishing his act, always asking himself just whom he might fool.

It was a delicious question.

Kyle hired a tailor to make the appropriate clothes, matching the fabric and even making the polished wooden buttons for the shirts and the sturdy trousers, and he managed a few cosmetic tricks with his homely face. He plucked his eyebrows and devised an odd haircut, then for several weekends he went to nearby towns and pretended to be an emissary from along the Bright. Just for fun. Just to see if he could manage it.

Kyle had a wonderful time.

He found himself drifting into his new identity, a weekend lark becoming a modest obsession and his own life suddenly pale and dull and entirely forgettable.

How could he have lived that way? he wondered.

All the wasted years seemed like a tragedy, and he felt lucky to have realized it before it was too late.

People treated him differently when he was a Wanderer. Which was natural, he supposed, but nonetheless illuminating. Kyle was noticed all at once. He was a prince among happy peasants. Of course there were a

few who didn't approve of Wanderers—the paranoid,
the religious worriers, and so on—but they didn't matter. Groundless fears and grudges simply added spice to
everything. Living on the road without a job, living on
his savings . . . it was a wonderful existence. Most people
perceived him as a godlike being. Kyle had the eyes and
the stance and the dry smooth knowing voice. After
weeks of travel, hitching rides and taking buses and
meeting hundreds of innocents . . . after everything he
reached a point where he felt like a Wanderer without
trying. Of course it was a ruse—only it didn't feel like
one anymore. Kyle got to where he was thinking as he
imagined Wanderers must think, considering the Bright
and the Makers and all the mysteries embodied within
them. He dreamed of reaching the Bright's end and of
everyone's holding hands, millions and millions of mismatched people standing in the presence of . . .

. . . what?

What indeed? thought the Wanderer inside him.
Indeed!

4

I'M OFTEN asked about immortality and how it
feels. Is it sweet or perhaps boring, and can I
describe it? Well, I like to respond first by saying that none of us is truly immortal and that
we do enjoy long lives, yes, and we are protected from many forms of abuse, yes, because
of our medicines and the hard-memories woven
into our minds. Hard-memories augment most
of our intellectual processes and they mirror
what is most essentially *us*, and they can survive
most tragedies. Yet the truth is that I have lost
friends, countless fine friends, over these millenia. The unthinkable accident always thinks
of a way to happen, in time, and not enough of
the hard-memory survives to allow for survival.
We might build a new body, yes, but there's

nothing to put inside the body. We are far from
immortal and we have precious few illusions.
Please believe me.

> —*Jy's speeches*

PEOPLE IN the middle of the most powerful
nation-state tend to be more reserved than their
fellow countrymen. Do not expect to attract
crowds while traveling through the region, particularly once they have grown accustomed to
seeing us in their midst. And you should expect
to have trouble measuring the moods of the
most agrarian citizens. These people carry their
emotions inside bottles mostly kept out of view.
Shake hands only if a hand is offered. Do not
make a show of returning favors; favors are
granted without any overt desire for reciprocity.
Compliment their land and their decency; by
nature they are rather insecure people. And
should all other conversation fail, try talking
about the weather. . . .

> —*Final scout report*

Kyle walked south towards the campus and downtown.
There was a viaduct over the railroad tracks, and the
stadium stood to his left. Semis and smaller trucks were
stacked up in the entranceways. Workmen scarcely noticed him. A woman wearing tight lavender slacks held
high a handmade sign, standing motionless beside the
street. "SATAN AND HER ANGELS ARE HERE!!!" Kyle read.
She gazed at him with fiery eyes, and he smiled weakly,
stepping over the snaking cables and trying to treat the
woman with the appropriate distance and reserve. He
was careful to show no trace of disrespect.

He wasn't in any danger. He kept telling himself
so.

True or not, people believed that each Wanderer
was protected by force fields and other trickery. Everyone had heard stories about muggers and zealots left
unconscious after some failed assault, no harm done to

them but for the embarrassment and the helplessness. Kyle couldn't count all the unsavory fellows who had shied away from him, worried by the simple reputation.

Now he allowed himself a thin smile and a backward glance at the woman, only she wasn't staring at him anymore. Her eyes were fixed on something else.

Kyle breathed and turned again.

Wanderers, true hard-memory Wanderers, were standing in the shade at the stadium's main entranceway, talking to workmen.

His heart began to hammer against his ribs.

There were two of them. A man, he saw, and a woman. The woman was a glossy coal color, brick-shape with a mass of silver-white hair tumbling from beneath her fluorescent hardhat. The man was tall, maybe Kyle's height, brown like leather and dark-haired and narrowly built. He had a handsome hairless face and strong fore-arms, the sleeves of his gray shirt rolled to his elbows. Both Wanderers seemed to belong there; they looked *right*. It was the man who happened to glance at Kyle, and Kyle felt his heart flutter and die, time in suspension. And then the Wanderer nodded at him. There was rec-ognition in the dark eyes, a hint of a smile, and with that he returned to his work, saying something to the work-men and gesturing at one of the big semis.

Nothing happened.

It was like some test, walking past here. And Kyle continued on his way, just like that, feeling empty and feather-light and very close to joyful. He had never been so close to a real Wanderer; he had intentionally avoided all direct contact with them. Yet he had fooled that man. Right? Of course he had done it. Kyle had to fight the urge to throw up one fist. Was that juvenile? But fooling that man was a good sign, wasn't it? Of course it was good. He started thinking how Wanderers were people, after all, and they would see what they expected to see. If he could act the role to the best of his ability . . . well, maybe it would work. It could be the biggest thrill of his life . . . Fooling all of them and actually meeting Jy herself. What a thought! Just imagine it!

Summer students were everywhere—young girls

with cultured tans; boyish men wearing polo shirts and cocky smiles; and foreign students, dark to varying degrees and mostly serious. Some students watched Kyle, and sometimes they nodded. Some muttered "Hello" in passing, nothing more. Either they recognized him from the other times he had come here, or they assumed he was part of Jy's entourage. A few Wanderers had arrived early, making ready and shaking hands and saying good, wise Wanderer things to everyone, paving the way for Jy.

Kyle remembered when he came to Lincoln. There was an all-night bus ride, and he had stepped onto the pavement with shaky legs and his overstuffed travel bag in both hands. It was midmorning, early and oddly cool for summer, and for some reason he had decided to linger. He had stowed his bag in a bus depot locker and found the campus. A tourist handout had recommended the natural history museum, and he knew Wanderers liked such diversions. So he found the big brick building and paid the flustered girl at the door, always polite, then he had roamed the long air-conditioned hallways and the towering rooms, mammoth skeletons and plesiosaur skeletons and slabs of crinoid-encrusted limestone lining the way.

He ended up in the basement, feeling alert despite the bus ride. There was a series of dioramas, large and elaborate—stuffed bison on plaster grasslands; glass-eyed deer standing behind paper oaks; a pair of battered whooping cranes rooted in a plastic marsh. A girl was sitting in front of the crane diorama, in the middle of a hard wooden bench. Kyle could remember everything. An astronomy text was beside her, closed and ignored. She was reading from a collection of Chekhov stories, and Kyle walked past once, looking at her pretty face and feeling some imprecise urge that made him stop and come around again. She was pretty, he thought, and maybe prettier than her looks. Did that make sense? "Miss?" he managed. She didn't seem to hear him. Her brown eyes were sliding back and forth, and her mouth was slightly open. "Miss?" asked Kyle. "Could I join you for a moment . . . miss?"

Her face lifted, and the eyes became huge.

"If you don't mind."

"Oh, no . . . *no*." She looked as if she might faint, shutting her book and straightening her back and doing nothing at all for a moment. Then she set Chekhov on the textbook and stroked her dress with both hands. "Let me just . . ." She bent forward and pulled a book bag from under the bench. Kyle watched. Weeks later he would remember her tropical red dress and the way its neckline dipped when she bent forward. For an instant, he gazed down at one of her little breasts with its river-mud nipple, tender and precious. Then she grunted once, then again, pushing the overstuffed book bag back out of sight. "There," she announced. She sat on the bench and stared at him, chewing on her lower lip while her hands wrestled in her lap.

Kyle sat down beside the girl, not close, and told her, "Thank you."

She made a low scared sound, imprecise and endearing.

He would always remember the delicious tingle running under his skin and the way he grinned, feeling self-assured, everything easy for him. "Did you hear about the whooping cranes?" he asked, and he pointed to the diorama. "How long have they been extinct here? Thirty years? Well," he said, "we're bringing some from another earth. Did you know?"

It was true; he had read it on the bus.

The girl said, "Really?" and hugged herself. She had smooth legs with a good shape, and she was kicking them.

"As gifts," he added. "Along with some other species." He listed a few examples—sea cows and woolly mammoths and desert pupfish—then admitted, "They're not quite identical to your cranes and whatever. Not genetically, not down deep. But they look and act the same, and if you're careful with them they should do just fine—"

"It's wonderful," she blurted.

He smiled and nodded.

"What you're doing," she told him. "I think it's . . . it's all so amazing, and special . . ."

"We want to be helpful," he stated.

"Oh, I know. I do." She nodded and hugged herself. "I'm always thinking about you—"

Kyle straightened.

"—and I'm so glad you came. To our earth," she told him.

Kyle said nothing.

The girl was obviously excited. She kept talking, thanking him for everything good done by the Wanderers and admitting she'd never been so close to one, not ever, and her legs kicked and her hands straightened her red dress, and she hoped she wasn't talking too much. It was a problem of hers. "Sometimes I get started, you see . . . when I'm nervous? And I can't stop. Oh, I can try. But the words just keep coming . . . ."

Kyle thought of a thunderous lie. "Do you know what?" he interrupted. "On my earth, way back down the Bright, do you know what? You would be one of our great beauties. That's how pretty you are."

"Me?" she gasped. She started to laugh and shake her head, startled and numbed and absolutely thrilled. "Are you sure? *Really?*"

"I'm sure you're a beauty here too," he offered.

"Fat chance!"

"No?" he teased. Then he touched her with his fingertips, stroking the soft thin fabric of her sleeve. "I think you're awfully lovely. I do." He was a Wanderer and confident, and if she laughed at him she simply didn't know any better. It didn't reflect on him.

But she didn't laugh, nor did she seem to breathe for a long moment.

There was some . . . *quality* to this girl. Other people were interested in Wanderers, but she was enraptured. Kyle watched the liquid-quick expressions on her pretty dark face that might have been a little bit Chinese, or something . . . and what? Was he in love? All at once it was like a blow from a big fist. Just asking the question made him a little bit crazy. He felt a longing and a fear, and with his voice cracking at the edges he asked, "What's your name?" and she told him. Billie Zacharia. A strange name, unique and somehow perfect, and he certainly loved her name. Then he heard her asking for his name, *sir*, and he uttered it. The phony one, convulated and intense, adding, "You can say Kyle. That's enough," and she did repeat *Kyle* several times, giving the single syllable an exotic taste. Then she happened to glance at her wristwatch, and he noticed. Did she have to go somewhere? Did she have a class?

"No, it's nothing," she squeaked.

He remembered the textbook. "You're in astronomy?"

"It's up . . . well, in the planetarium." She pointed towards the ceiling. "But I don't have to—I mean, I can just—well . . . ."

"Take me." Kyle felt alert and happy. His solution took both of them by surprise. "I'll be your guest."

"My guest?" She was dumbfounded.

"I'm here to learn," he replied. "Show me your class."

"Well . . . all right." She stood slowly, arms spread as if she was ready to lose her balance. Kyle knelt and lifted her book bag, offering to carry it. Then they went upstairs and into the back of the museum, arriving just as the big doors were being closed and the lights were coming down. Nobody seemed to notice Kyle. Darkness gave him a delicious anonymity. The professor, small and bland, stood armed with a tiny blood red laser beam he used for pointing out constellations and their slow wheeling motions. He called their home *The Earth*, as if there were only one in all of Reality, and when people spoke among themselves he coughed ominously into a fist.

Billie watched Kyle until he glanced her way, then she focused on the lecture. Or at least she pretended to focus.

Kyle sat and listened, always aware of the girl beside him.

After a little while she leaned toward him and wondered, "Do the skies change?"

"Excuse me?"

"From earth to earth . . . do the stars stay in the same places? I've always wondered."

People had asked him all sorts of questions. They wanted to know about his home and traveling on the Bright, and about Jy too. But nobody had ever asked if the stars held steady.

"Yes," he whispered. "They're just as they look up there." Which was true. Kyle had read it in the science magazines when he did his early research. "Stars don't care about the earth," he informed Billie. "People can turn out any odd way, and do anything, and the stars and the galaxy just keep spinning in the same patterns."

She nodded, and he felt her body. She was close without touching, and there was a damp, sweet-scented heat. Kyle had to shift his weight, and he reported, "It's comforting. Some things never change, like the constellations, and I like that."

She nodded.

The professor heard them, and he quit talking to cough and stare into the darkness for an angry moment.

Kyle watched Billie's face in the artificial starlight. She had a sweet dreamy smile. He felt the blood in his temples and the steady rubbery hammering of his heart, and he imagined it was just them sitting close, at night, some mossy glade surrounding them. The air-conditioning was the wind, moist and persistent, and the professor's steady old voice was a whooping crane muttering in its sleep. The crane was dreaming about fat frogs and cold snakes, no doubt, and then Kyle imagined pulling Billie's red dress over her head, and those small hands were touching him and he was smelling her and stroking her thick black hair. He knew exactly how that hair would feel, stiff and springy and warm beneath . . . Kyle breathed and made himself look at the false sky and the changeless stars, feeling what? What? A tangible guilt, the first he had felt in a long, long while. But he resisted the urge to confess anything. Why should he? Instead he breathed again and asked Billie where she lived. On campus? Nearby perhaps? She gave him a look and bit her lip, appearing startled. "If you don't mind telling me," he added. "Please?"

The professor made an angry noise, then continued.

"Because," said Kyle, "I might stay here a few days

and maybe you would show me what I should see. If
you'd like. Okay?"

"Oh, yes...."

"You're sure?"

Billie sighed with her entire body and nodded yes,
yes, yes... hands held close as if she didn't entirely trust
them.

5

ONE SECRET of ours is that we move fast, each
earth seeing us for a moment or two and en
masse, and then we are gone again, at least most
of us are gone, and nobody has the time to find
anything wrong with us. We hope.

Hopefully we leave feelings of acceptance
and admiration, and our largest hope is that we
are appreciated in the very long term. I mean
after a thousand golden centuries. We work to
be like lovers of your youth whose value only
soars with time, and when you reach maturity
and your hair turns as gray as mine, your life
wholly secure... then you think of us and nod
and give wistful little smiles....

—*Jy's speeches*

There was an open plaza with a roaring round fountain
at its center, and past the fountain was the student center—a monument to brick and glass and sheer utility.
Kyle crossed the plaza and entered through revolving
doors, feeling the chill air and blinking until his eyes
adapted to the dimmer light. People were buzzing
around him, then the buzz diminished. He saw faces
staring and heard the collective pause, then whispers,
and he went downstairs and entered the bookstore.

Janice was there. The roommate; the best friend.
Billie was stocking shelves in the back, and both girls
were laughing about something. Then they turned to-

gether and saw him approaching. "Hello, hello!" Billie squealed, and she grabbed him around the waist. "I told!" she reported. "Everyone. And they're excited and jealous, and I know they hate me! Just like I knew they'd be, and I can't wait!"

Janice smiled at both of them, making an amused sound.

"What shall I wear?" asked Billie. She turned quiet all at once. Circumspect. "Tell me what."

"Anything," said Kyle. "Don't worry about it."

Billie started to dance in place. She was gushing and glowing, throwing sparks and sputtering pinwheels. She was like some human-shaped conduit through which flowed everything about life. Nobody else had such emotions. All at once Kyle felt as though he himself were deadened inside. He was a dull automaton standing upright by accident and smiling from practice—which was true, wasn't it?—and he was completely unable to imagine how Billie must be feeling.

Janice was watching Kyle and staying quiet.

Her expression made him uneasy, for no clear reason. He turned away from both of them, and Billie said, "I've got to finish. Okay? Could you guys wait for me? A sec?"

"We'll be here," Janice assured her.

The roommate came up to him and grinned, and he couldn't help but notice her figure and face. How many times had he been close to Janice? But it was bad this morning. She looked particularly fine, and Kyle suffered from a delicious lust and the obligatory guilt. He found himself thinking Billie wasn't the world, was she? He wasn't bound to her for an eternity, was he? Of course not. He was going to eventually leave, and she would have to understand. How else could things end? he asked himself. This episode would run its course, there was no choice, and he would never come back here again.

Sometimes Kyle felt like packing his bag in the night and walking to the bus station, no warnings given. He had a bus pass that had cost him enough and summer was ending, he thought, and God she drove him crazy, Billie did. Always asking questions, almost as if she was

testing him. She would read some of the more popular
books, the ones drawn from Jy's speeches and her se-
lectively released chronicles, then she would ask about
the earths back down the Bright. They seemed wonderful, and it was too bad the Wanderers couldn't tell
everything about every earth. But she understood. She
realized Wanderers had experience in these matters and
she was a primitive soul and all, but she loved hearing
about strange cities and stranger people. She would listen to Kyle's bullshitting stories, and sometimes she
would catch . . . well, problems. Tiny minor inconsis-
tencies, she admitted. "You said such-and-such, and now
you're telling me it's such-and-such?" Not that she was
suspicious, of course. Billie wasn't. She just assumed she
was an idiot beside any Wanderer, Kyle included. Inside
Kyle's head were all those strange hard-memory circuits
that enlarged his intellect and preserved his soul through
the ages, and she was curious, that was all. She really,
really loved hearing him talk about any subject. She
loved to stroke his scalp with her little fingers, and sometimes he felt like some modest god. He felt just wonderful. Then other times his mood swung and he was
anxious, thinking about slipping away in the night, and
wasn't that just nuts? Enjoying himself one minute, then
in the next wanting to be gone . . . .

Janice was talking now, telling him about Billie's
enthusiasm and wasn't she precious? *Precious.* He heard
the word and blinked. "Before you," she told him, "that
girl never took herself seriously. Believe me. She'd date
these drips, always drips, and I couldn't convince her
any decent boy would want her." Janice shook her head,
her long light brown hair smooth and flowing across her
shoulders. "You've done her good."

"Have I?"

Janice asked, "Is she really going to shake Jy's
hand?"

"I don't know. We'll see."

"She will," she said with assurance.

They were walking through the classics section.
Kyle paused to pick up two thick novels, a Dickens and
a Dostoyevski. He knew them from his schooldays. He

examined them and planned to buy them, then he would pretend to read them this afternoon. Wanderers were famous as quick studies. They digested languages and cultures in no time, and since this was familiar ground he could skim and bullshit and leave the girl astounded. He had done it plenty of times before.

"It's exciting," said Janice. "Tomorrow night is it!"

"It will be fun," he promised.

"Have you ever met Jy?"

"Oh, yes."

"When?"

The question made him pause and think. Then he was talking, inventing an earth not too different from this earth. He mentioned cities and cars that burned alcohol, not gasoline, and he had met Jy in Africa. What Janice called Africa. The Glorious One had been about to hold a rally, and they hadn't spoken for very long—

"A busy gal."

"—but she was wonderful," Kyle said. "Jy is everything she seems to be on television." And now he remembered the story he had told Billie. He had invented a different earth some weeks ago, and he'd forgotten. What if they were comparing notes? he wondered. What then?

"I wish I could stay with you guys after the rally," said Janice. "I'd like shaking her hand too."

He felt one breast clip his elbow, and he struggled to keep his face still and his eyes fixed on the books. "She's such a flirt, that Janice," Billie had said. Janice was a flirt and man-hungry and too damned beautiful. "If you want to see what's lovely on this earth," Billie had warned him, "look at my roommate."

"I prefer you," Kyle had told her more than once.

"Really?"

"Absolutely." What else could he claim? "The best women have tiny breasts and your mouth and are quiet. Would you? Please?"

Kyle breathed now and glanced at Janice, and he offered a tempered smile. He couldn't help but notice all of her, and of course that was when Billie arrived. She came down the aisle, and Kyle turned and straightened his back and stood very still for a moment. He was squeezing his books and working with his face.

"And have you found what you want, sir?"

"Yes," he managed. "I have, miss."

"Well, and they're fine selections too. Sir." It was a game. Kyle-as-customer. She took the books from him and started toward the register, then she was skipping. A book was in each hand, and she lifted her arms out straight and did two turns and gave an effervescent little hoot.

"Billie?" said Janice. "I've got to motor. I'll see you at home tonight, girl."

"You have to go?" She pushed out her lower lip, little-girl fashion. "You're leaving *me*?"

"I am."

"Oh! Okay!" She giggled. "Bye, bye."

The roommate rolled her green eyes, telling Kyle, "*You* try to keep her happy for a while. Can you?"

"I'll try," he promised. "Good-bye, Janice."

Janice was smiling slyly. She had no right to tease him. Or was she chasing him? Or maybe this was a test of character, tempting him to protect her dear friend. *Can Kyle be trusted?*

Billie seemed oblivious to all of it. Janice was gone, and she totaled the purchase. "How long will it take?" she teased. "Ten minutes to read them?"

He laughed softly, saying nothing.

She put the books into a plastic sack, folding it and handing it to him with precision and ceremony. "I wish we could chat and chat, but I've got tons to do. Mountains. I can't."

"I understand."

"But I'll come visit tonight. Okay?"

He felt a reassuring desire, saying, "I hope you do." He would pack before the rally, he decided. He would do it tomorrow and have his bag ready, and he'd slip away after they tried to see Jy. It didn't matter what happened. He could write a note of explanation and sympathy—something about lingering too long in one place—and maybe he could give her some gift. How about all the books he had bought this summer? Billie would love them. He glanced at her while she walked him to the doorway, and she took one of his hands and squeezed with both of hers. Students watched them. He felt the press of eyes, and he said, "Have a good day," with an unnatural stiffness. What was he thinking? Maybe he resented this public place, or maybe it was his identity. Was it wearing on him? Then a Wanderer's smile surfaced of its own accord. She was staring at his face. Billie had this way of seeing everything as if she was the first. To her everything was new and meant for nobody else, and sometimes Kyle envied that intensity. Her hyperawarenenss. Only now he felt more resentment than anything. He had to make himself turn and leave, and Billie said, "Bye," and he nodded, mounting the stairs with weak legs and pushing through the big revolving doors.

The heat outside was sudden and nearly unbearable, and the students on the plaza watched him. They stared, almost none of them talking.

It was as if they knew who he was and who he wasn't.

No secrets seemed possible.

It was as if all this cleverness on Kyle's part was useless, and everything that happened was part of some enormous joke being played on him and nobody else.

COTTON

1

THE WALLS were simple native stone worn smooth by the steady slow passage of bodies, and the ceiling was the same stone braced and rebraced with columns and arches of alloyed metal. Panels of a thin brittle glass were fixed to the ceiling, and they glowed with a weak bluish light. The floor itself was hidden beneath the tightly packed bodies. We watched those bodies while our probe clung overhead, mimicking one of the few native insects. We saw blue-gray hair, thin and dull, and dull faces with eyes opened or closed or somewhere between. There was a sameness to all the features. The noses and cheekbones were interchangeable. We saw absolutely nothing of interest, at least with the first glance. Each body was dressed with a sketchy bit of cloth at the waist, and each appeared motionless. The closed eyes stayed closed, and the opened eyes were apparently indifferent to their surroundings. It was in such sharp contrast to the scenic sunlit places, to those wealthy, high-caste enclaves built on mountaintops. In those realms everyone—the rare everyone—would be in motion all the while, sprinting back and forth while chattering with their strange too-quick voices, and the platters of cooked meats and rich nuts would be picked bare in no time whatsoever....

The society is as truly bizarre as any we have ever encountered....

Our advice is to be quite careful at all times. We have never, never seen the likes of these people before....

—*Final scout report*

He was eating candy. He had bought several sacks of red string licorice in a store full of wonders, and he was discovering he liked them even more than he liked chocolates. Cotton was finishing a couple of strings now, and in the corner of an eye he noticed someone approaching. He turned and saw a Wanderer, and he quit chewing for an instant. He stared at the figure and decided it must be one of the Wanderers working for the entourage. But doing what? Cotton tried to relax, leaning back against the shade tree and feeling its bark cutting into his spine. He made himself relax, then he finished his chewing and swallowed, closing his mouth to a tiny pink slit and feeling his eyes start to burn.

Moliak wanted him ready.

"Flood yourself with calories," Moliak had told him. "Enjoy a feast. Just get your liver and muscles loaded and put down as much fat as you can in these next days. Eat whatever you need, but stay inconspicuous. And stay cool."

It was unsettling to hear Moliak using the local language, complete to its accents and rhythms, and it was even more unsettling for Cotton to understand every word. The appropriate knowledge had been spliced into both of their hard-memories; they knew English better than they knew their own tongues.

"Between bites," Moliak had suggested, "why don't you try to get comfortable with this place. It can only help you blend into the scenery. Agreed?"

"Agreed," Cotton muttered to himself now. Throughout the day he had been eating—doughnuts and candy, hamburgers and candy—and too many calories were fighting to be stored within him. The excess was starting to burn, and he couldn't help it. His metabolism was creeping higher; his surroundings were becoming syrupy-slow and sounds were sluggish and dreamy. It seemed as though he had seen the Wanderer minutes ago, yet the slap-slapping of the sandals hadn't brought him much closer. *Be careful*, Cotton told himself. *Give nothing away.* He made himself stay against the tree and wait, guessing the Wanderer would walk straight past him. He was nobody after all. He was just another piece of this landscape.

The Wanderer was relatively tall and wearing the changeless gray, and he walked along the cracked sidewalk with a yellow sack tucked under an arm and his big eyes focused on the ground.

Cotton belched and tasted the masticated red candy.

He remembered he was a small, thoroughly ordinary man of imprecise age. He had blond hair and fine features, and up close he showed some weathering. There were a couple of milky scars on his neck, and one ear had been partly removed. His skin was marred with a network of fine long wrinkles—the mark of someone who had radically changed his weight—and there was a weariness within him. It was something not to be cured with feasts and sleep, and it showed best in the dead cold faraway gaze of his eyes.

The Wanderer was passing him, giving him a slow brief glance.

Cotton nodded and said, "Sir," while keeping his voice normal.

The Wanderer replied, "Good day," and continued along the sidewalk, lost in his own thoughts. Cotton watched him. Then he pulled fresh sticks of licorice from the sack too fast and shoved them into his mouth.

It was a blurring motion, like a toad taking a fly.

He narrowed his eyes, chewing with tireless joy. If he ate enough now—this was a strange thought—he would never have to eat again. He could live on his reserves and lift his metabolism to its maximum, holding it at that rarefied level for as long as there was fuel. That was the kind of achievement Moliak expected from him, and Cotton was fully prepared to do anything to reach that ideal. The close approach of the Wanderer had pricked his sense of loyalty, making everything even more immediate; he was here as much for Moliak's sake as for any good cause; and somehow Cotton had to coax his weary flesh and his weary soul into giving what used to be his predictable best.

"One more time," Moliak would say with his new voice. "Just once, my friend. Can you do that for me?"

Cotton belched again, smelling licorice mixed with his own hot belly juices, and he was thinking about everything to come. There was the timetable and their goal, then came the final cleansing. "A glorious cleansing." Moliak had explained all of it. He never kept secrets from Cotton. Their plan left nothing to chance, and nobody would be able to stop them.

Cotton glanced down the street at the plodding Wanderer.

The creature was the living portrait of innocence, thought Cotton; and he tasted something that wasn't quite pity or hatred or anything else easily named.

Innocence.

He listened to the slap-slap of the lazy sandals, and after an age they were gone.

2

THERE IS only one strict dietary taboo for the Termites—one food which no sane citizen will eat—and considering its abundance, that is a rather remarkable trait....

—Final scout report

Cotton was the closest English translation of his Termite name, and Moliak had allowed him to keep it, for convenience's sake.

His home was called Termite Mound by the Wanderers. Their scouts had seen the masses of people, the rigid caste system, and the common foods . . . and they had thought of the insects. No other earth had so many people, and treated woods fed the lower castes. It was one enormous termite colony. Of course the Wanderers had meant no malice with that name. They never considered its inhabitants to be merely bugs. No, Cotton knew about the Wanderers. They were not malicious. Their demons embraced different evils. Larger ones, he knew. Their demons were much worse than simple name-calling, and more subtle.

The caste system on Termite Mound was ancient.

Their crowding began tens of thousands of years ago, and each turn of science and engineering had enhanced the social structure. Termites were small people; Cotton was half again larger than the norm. They had variable metabolisms made more variable with genetic tailoring, and more efficient. They drank little water and made little waste. Each caste had its own distinctive appearance and manners, and none ever doubted its station. The highest castes could afford quality foods day after day, and they lived at enormous speeds. Their bodies were blazingly hot and their minds quick, and they died of old age after eighteen or twenty years. By contrast, the lowest of the low-born lived for centuries. It was a modest leveler. The low castes lived in deep tunnels woven through the crust, in the damp heat, standing shoulder to shoulder like statues. They felt dead to the touch, cold and damp from condensation, and only with patience could the faster observer watch them slide their feet forward, one and then the other, or hear the faint slow voices, or catch the miniscule rise and fall of their chests.

Cotton belonged to one of the middle castes.

It was perhaps the strangest existence on a unique earth, or so Moliak claimed. Cotton's enclave had variable wealth. The luckless ones lived like the extremely poor. Those with industry and talents could manage periods where they were indistinguishable from the high castes—mostly during holidays and private celebrations when there were feasts, each family doing its best to find honest meats and rare candies—and life for them came at variable speeds, sometimes even changing day by day.

The Wanderers preferred to hire the middle castes. They had tough, dangerous work to be done, and they paid each volunteer a substantial wage. When Cotton was young and luckless, living an apparent day for every week that passed, he had seen the Wanderers as his only possible escape. He had gone to the gray-clad strangers and pledged himself to their work, claiming nothing scared him and look at him, he was a big Termite, and strong. He had been trained and employed for a very long while—he was gone from his homeland for years— and somehow he had managed to return alive and rather intact, not quite wealthy for his troubles but certainly ready to be comfortably warm-blooded for the rest of his days.

He had been home several months, and one day he was sitting outside watching the busy local thoroughfare, watching Termites of his build and complexion while trying not to think about anything at all. He wanted his mind empty. He would have liked to nap. Yet just as he began to relax, without warning, a Wanderer appeared. It was a little Wanderer not much taller than Cotton, and something about the man seemed familiar.

"Hello," said the Wanderer.

The voice meant nothing to him, however.

"Cotton?"

The Wanderer had vivid blue-black skin, absolutely hairless, and a thin-featured face that nodded and said, "Cotton," again. He was using the standard Founder language. "How are you, friend?"

"Friend?" Cotton felt puzzled, then tasted anger. "How do we know each other?"

"Don't you remember me?"

He gazed at the dark face, saying nothing.

"I am quite glad to see you, my friend."

Cotton had been eating enough to keep warm, yet

trying to maintain some semblance of discipline. He looked at the eyes and noticed an intensity, a sharpness, and he couldn't shake the sensation that he knew the eyes.

"What name do I use?" he wondered.

The Wanderer didn't seem to hear him. He shut the eyes and fiddled with a wooden button high on his shirt, then he turned and looked at the crush of warm pedestrians sliding past them, watching them briefly, and those cooler ones bunched in the middle of the thoroughfare, his head nodding and the unfamiliar voice asking, "Are you keeping busy, Cotton?"

"No," he replied.

"Good." A broad smile emerged. "I imagine you must be trying to recover your old self. Are you?"

Cotton said nothing.

"Only you don't sleep well because of the nightmares, do you?" The Wanderer said, "The nightmares are waking you and you shiver afterwards and I would think nothing seems entirely right while you're awake either. You left your enclave and now you have come home, one of the few, and sometimes you wonder if this really is the place you left because it doesn't taste as it should taste, does it? Does it?"

"Stop!" snapped Cotton.

The stranger smiled and asked, "Do you hate us?"

"Hate who?"

"Wanderers."

Cotton said, "Maybe." It was an honest answer. Cotton wasn't sure about the flavor in his mouth. There was hatred but also a strange, almost desperate sense of devotion because for so long he had done so much for these miraculous demon-riddled strangers—

"You don't hate *me*, do you?"

Cotton said nothing.

The blue-black face was laughing with a bitterness showing. "Oh but I do know you and I know exactly what you are thinking."

"No," Cotton snarled.

"I do." He shook his head, saying, "You feel sick of everything as it stands because you are smart and you've certainly seen plenty, you were innocent once but no more, and more than once I've heard you exclaim just what you would do if given the chance."

Cotton held his breath.

"What would you do, Cotton, if you were given the chance?"

Nobody else could understand this conversation. The Founder language was ancient and convoluted, used by almost no one in this realm.

"You told me your plan, my friend."

He felt a slight cold tingle.

"The first time . . . let me recall." He touched his temple and seemed to concentrate. "We had lost three comrades that day when nobody should have died, all due to the negligence of others, and afterwards you were drinking liquor for the first and only time. The poison was playing games with your metabolism and both of us were sitting in one of those little bunkers they don't put deep because they rely on their littleness to save them and you were drunk and sitting across from me no further than the distance between us now—"

"Moliak?"

"Yes?"

"Are you?" asked Cotton. "*You are Moliak*—?"

"None other."

"No!"

The Wanderer winked with a certain style and a tilt of the head, and Cotton was certain. It was exactly the kind of wink Moliak would use, and now he recognized those eyes.

"Did you ever believe you would see me again, my friend?"

"No, my friend."

They embraced, Moliak feeling a little cool to the touch because Cotton was excited, his sugars burning faster by the moment.

"But why are you here?" Cotton wondered. "That disguise—"

Moliak said, "A complicated tale. Everyone else thinks me dead now, dead and lost, and this body is something I pulled from the genetic banks and grew myself, for myself—"

"Explain!"

"Not here." The smile had vanished. "Perhaps later. First I need to hear if you meant what you said that time, and the other times too. Did you?"

Cotton started to nod. He always meant everything he said, drunk or not.

"Oh, that is lovely," said his friend with deep seriousness.

"Now come inside," Cotton prodded, gesturing at the narrow two-story building that was his home. "We can have privacy and perhaps a little feast as well—"

"First," said Moliak, "will you agree to help me by standing with me, will you, and follow my every order?"

"Of course!"

"Good. I knew you would say it that way," and the strange face nodded. One hand scratched the hairless scalp, and he claimed, "Because we are going to do this thing soon."

Cotton nearly laughed.

This had to be some remarkable joke. Wasn't it?

"I mean what I tell you," replied Moliak. "Don't you believe me?"

"How can I?"

"The unspeakable, yes." He gazed out at the streams of people and nodded to himself. It was a clear day for Termite Mound, warm as always and quite still, and the high blue sky was speckled with the orbiting farms and the power stations beyond number. Cotton looked up at the sky too and shivered, and Moliak said, "I am going to do it, my friend, and you are the only one who knows."

3

HE ISN'T my best candidate by most measures. Cotton has spent too much time at the highest metabolism, aging himself prematurely, and I have to consider his weathered nerves. (Not to

mention my own.) Yet Cotton has certain in-
tangibles including a proven devotion to me,
and he has talents. With his experience and
boldness mixed with a desire to see everything
made right, to see our wrongs cleansed, I have
no choice but to approach him first and make
him prove himself to me.

I have decided.

—*Moliak's private journal*

The tall Wanderer had gone, and now a pair of children
happened past. They were riding bicycles and laughing,
and when they saw Cotton beside the tree they braked,
saying, "Mister! Hey, mister!"

Cotton turned towards them, careful to move
slowly.

"Did you see him?" asked one boy.

"We thought we saw him coming this way," said his
friend.

"Who?" asked Cotton.

"The Wanderer guy," they reported. "Where is
he?"

"Oh, him!" Cotton smiled and pulled the last bag
of licorice from his pocket, opening it and saying, "Would
you like some?"

The boys wanted the red candy, and they didn't.
Their mouths came open and their backs straightened,
then they walked their bicycles forwards and took one
stick each, handling the sticks with the tips of their fingers. Their first bites were small and tentative. Then
they gulped the licorice down and grinned, Cotton saying, "The Wanderer turned at the corner down there,"
while they finished eating. "Any more?"

Sure. They didn't hesitate this time.

"It's funny," said Cotton. "I wouldn't think a big
important Wanderer would come here. You know?"

"Oh, he lives here," said one boy.

"Yeah!" said the other.

He wasn't part of the entourage, in other words.
Cotton realized as much all at once.

"Up in an old house," said the first boy.

"Not far away," said his pal. "We could show you where."

Cotton shook his head. No thanks. He said, "Here," and gave them the rest of the bag, then he retreated a step.

"He won't be here much longer," said the first boy. He pulled his mouth into a button and tried to seem wise.

"Oh, no? Why not?" asked Cotton.

"Because he'll go away. All the Wanderers are going away."

Cotton said, "Are they?"

The boys shook their heads, saying, "Sure, mister. Don't you know?"

"Go where?"

"Where Wanderers go."

"Where's that?"

They looked at him as if he was an idiot, then told him, "You know. Where the Makers live."

"Yeah?"

"Yeah!"

"And where's that?"

One boy moaned and said, "Nobody knows *that*."

Cotton laughed, shaking his head and leaning back against the shade tree, feeling the reliable gnawing of the bark.

"Want any, mister?"

They were offering him the licorice.

"Take some."

He pulled out a string and said, "Thanks," and held it in his too-warm hand, the candy turning moist and then gooey and then starting to run.

QUENCÉ

1

THE PORTAL was constructed at the mid-Pacific facility, not far from the place where the Wanderers came to our earth. All of its materials were taken from the seafloor and the surrounding seawater, and a little more than five weeks was required to complete it. Afterward a standard Wanderer flier carried the new portal to its prepared site, and it was activated early this morning.

The hill itself is northwest of Lincoln. It was called "a reliable geographic landmark" by the Wanderer in charge of the project, Miss Kruk'kee'kee. It has a foundation of Dakota sandstone, she explained, and similar hills exit on every other earth. The positioning of the portal was an exacting process. It had to be aligned with the hidden elements of the Bright and with every other portal fixed to the similar hilltops, hundreds of thousands of portals in all.

"This is not a major facility," Miss

Kruk'kee'kee confessed, "but it's vital in connecting your earth with all others. In that respect it is the same as the largest, most heavily used facilities."

Miss Kruk'kee'kee promised that visitors are and would remain welcome, but of course nobody can be allowed inside the portal.

"This is for your safety," she told reporters, "as well as for our own."

—Newswire account

"I'll tell you something," said the man sitting across from Quencé. "I haven't felt this way since my folks bundled me up and took me out to meet Santa for the first time."

There was a pause.

Quencé felt the pause more than he heard it. He was the tall lean Wanderer seen by Kyle that morning—the hard-working representative of the entourage—and now he lifted his head and watched everyone. What was happening? Some of these people looked offended; others were afraid he and Wysh would be angered. He read them through their faces and their postures, and perhaps this was a small issue. Yet small issues were Quencé's main concern tonight. They were here to help set the tone for tomorrow's visit, and he wanted no misunderstandings whatsoever.

Santa?

Cultural files in his hard-memory produced a figure named Santa Claus. He was a harmless gentleman, fat and short and elderly with a snowy beard and an apparent problem with blood pressure. Magical ungulates pulled his sleigh down from the Arctic every winter, on the eve of the major Christian holiday, and he brought gifts to young girls and boys.

So what is our situation? thought Quencé. *What are these people thinking?*

A child's myth might seem demeaning when applied to Jy. Or was it the image of a magical figure dispensing toys to the good cherubs? Was there a tinge of satire? Quencé looked straight across the table and wondered.

The man, Mr. Phillips, was a local business leader—successful and well regarded and rather forgettable. Quencé studied the man's quiet pale blue eyes and his pleasant, one-dimensional smile. Mr. Phillips was middle-aged, balding, and graying, and he seemed wholly incapable of satire. That was Quencé's snap judgment. He imagined the man as a child, three or four years old, standing between bland parents while waiting to meet Santa Claus in some local department store. Cultural files supplied the generic scene. Young Mr. Phillips had a round grinning face, there was a trace of snot under his nose, and his whole body was jittery with excitement. That's what the man had meant, Quencé realized. It took him a couple seconds, then he nodded and asked, "You mean the thrill of it, don't you? Is that what you mean?"

"Absolutely!"

Faces turned towards Mr. Phillips, then back at Quencé.

"I didn't sleep well last night," the man confessed. "I keep trying to count the hours till I meet Jy."

Tensions evaporated. A few people nodded in agreement—they knew the affliction—and others giggled nervously. Quencé gazed down the long table, finding Wysh, and he saw she hadn't sensed any of this business. She was working her way through the guest list, making certain that an appropriate cross section were invited into Jy's own ship. They wanted a mixture of the important and the ordinary as well as the poor. Quencé looked at Wysh's dark face and the bright silvery hair and the studious unimaginative eyes, and maybe she felt him staring. She blinked and looked up at him, saying, "Everything seems in order. Agreed?"

They were in an otherwise empty restaurant inside the city's best hotel, everyone sitting about a mishmash of little tables pushed together into a wobbly line. They had been here since dinner—huge steaks and steaming baked potatoes supplied by the Chamber of Commerce—but now there was only one waitress bringing the occasional drink, coming past every few minutes to see if anyone needed anything, anything at all.

Nuance wasn't Wysh's specialty.

She was concrete and utterly competent. Sometimes she could be relentlessly competent, and the two of them made a reasonable team. Nuance was one of Quencé's favorite things. Lists and figures and other humdrums bored him. It was the grayness behind the hard facts that caught his attentions. Smiling up at him, Jy liked to boast, "You are my master of the little touch, Quencé, and that's why I need you." He certainly liked hearing those words, particularly when he knew they were true.

Quencé was famous as one of Jy's favorites.

The entire entourage, Wysh included, grudgingly accepted the fact. What could they do about it?

No, Quencé wasn't the best Wanderer among them. He didn't have the customary fire for the mission, and he never lost himself in the Bright's endless mysteries. *Why not?* he oftentimes wondered. Managing people and human situations were his main talents. He had an undeniable instinct for complicated, slippery circumstances. Some biological fluke, subtle and scarcely understood, made it possible for him to hold and interpret extra doses of hard-memory, and when those traits were added to his native skills Quencé ended up perfectly suited for certain essential jobs.

Here he was in his natural environment—sitting in a dimly lit restaurant—busily polishing people's moods.

"Oh, Mr. Phillips? Sir?" Wysh was speaking with a tight, officious voice. "You have down . . . let me see, a nephew? As your guest?"

"Yes," said the man. "Is there a problem?"

Quencé glanced at his own hard copy, saying, "We just need to know something about him, for our records," and he smiled without rancor. He made a show of his smile, then asked, "Is he your own nephew?"

"My oldest sister's oldest boy, yes."

"His name?"

Mr. Phillips told the name, then explained, "He came into town the other day, you see, and I just thought—"

"No, no. That's fine," Quencé promised. Mr. Phillips was a bachelor without any nearby family, and he was entitled to his guest. "Your nephew is most welcome. I hope he enjoys himself."

"He will," the man responded, smiling gratefully.

There was a long gentle pause. Even Wysh seemed pacified. Quencé found Mr. Phillips's file in hard-memory and did a cursory check for irregularities. His life and business interests were without blemish. There were no hints of insanity, no taints of hidden furies. Bringing some nephew at the last instant was a minor issue, and Quencé decided to let it pass.

Every earth had its potential dangers.

Yet Quencé could do only so much. There were security systems that would keep Jy safe. There were invisible scanners and triple-strength shields, automated and airtight, and scramblers to destroy most weapons. Assassins mattered as embarrassments and because they were dangerous to the ordinary people, and that was the pragmatic truth. This earth's entire arsenal and all of its furies would not be adequate to do Jy any physical harm. Quencé was simply trying to avoid any ugliness brought on by some fanatic.

The meeting had moved to the timetable for one last check. The rallies would be held at two-hour inter-vals, crowds entering and leaving the big stadium and the city itself controlling the crush of bodies. Then Jy's entourage would fly to the hilltop and stop at the newly minted portal—a suitable symbol with parking and ad-equate open space.

These people were proud of their portal. He could see as much with a simple glance.

The portal was still unused. A single Wanderer, a novice, kept guard over it—a ceremonial position since every portal was shrouded with its own antiweapon sys-tems. That little portal was an overflow route, and even then it was intended for cargo. The Wanderers them-selves would move through more comfortable and spa-cious chains of portals, even in times of dire need.

"Imagine," said one woman. "We're connected to the most important . . . what? Highway? The most im-portant highway ever built?"

People were nodding and grinning, and Quencé made a mental note to himself. A generation or two from today, on some suitably symbolic date, Wanderers should make a goodwill stopover. By then Jy would be a memory among the elders and the portal would have become a peculiar piece of the landscape, and two or three modest-ranking Wanderers could come for an evening's festivities, in the guise of seeing how life was progressing here. Why not? thought Quencé. *Good.*

Wysh began to stand, finished with the timetable, and with a conscious smile she declared their meeting closed.

Others stood as well and stretched, laughing and making exhausted sounds. "It's been good working with you," said Mr. Phillips. He offered his hand to Quencé, reaching across the table, and Quencé took it and squeezed. "Perhaps we'll see each other tomorrow night," the man ventured. "After the rallies?"

"It's very likely," Quencé responded. "And I hope so."

There was something transparent about the man's face. Quencé hadn't noticed until just now. Its flesh seemed to be made from pink-tinted glass, and it invited scrutiny. Beyond it was no rancor or despair or anything remotely forbidding.

Others were eager to shake Quencé's hand.

He gave each of them their moment, repeating names and never letting his own smile waver. Someone asked how long he and Wysh were staying. Until the day after tomorrow, he replied. There was to be a huge string of rallies in Chicago, and they had to stay at work. Then they went to Detroit, Washington, D.C., and New York City. Plus there were a couple of dozen smaller events in scattered little cities, and maybe afterwards Jy would smile and tell Quencé, "You have done a masterful job, and I thank you. I knew you would not let me down." Quencé imagined the moment, and he could almost feel the warm glow percolating through him as Jy gave him a dry light touch. It came very close to being real, and he breathed and gave a little shudder.

"Are you leaving?" asked Wysh. "For your room?"

"No," he said. "I have a few jobs to do first." Everyone else had gone. He waved her off, saying, "Get to
sleep and I'll see you early." They had a ceremonial
breakfast with some of the local religious leaders, and
Quencé was scheduled to speak. "All right?"

She looked at him for a moment, her black face still.
Then she nodded and left him, nothing said and nothing
needing to be said.

Quencé sat at the empty table, thinking to himself.

It was almost tomorrow, local time.

In thirty-some hours he would blank his hard-memory of this place and these people. Their faces and names
and professions and biographies would evaporate into a
simple whiteness. Maybe a few of them would linger in
his soft neurons, though he doubted it. By the time
Quencé was on the next earth, coping with its oddities
and nuances, everyone would be entirely forgotten. It
was a sad fact. Leaving anyone and anyplace had this
way of making him feel sorry.

It was Quencé's lot.

He was forever leaving.

2

THE INCIDENT began after my rally, with the
villagers coming to me and announcing there
would be entertainment with our meal, if I
wanted, and I said, "Yes, that would be lovely,"
so maybe it was partly my fault. I had just
learned the local dialect, and I may have been
told more than I managed to hear. Regardless,
I was given a huge bowl of stew, fatty and overly
salted, and while everyone ate the village
square was prepared, two massive stakes driven
into the ground and chains attached to them.
The other ends of the chains were then lashed
to a pair of enormous collared bears.

These are very durable people, and I have
to keep reminding myself of that salient fact.

Hard lives have given them suitable genes, and they are dulled to their pain and to the pain of others. They tolerate awful diseases without a whimper and survive horrific accidents and bouts of hard famine, and theirs is the kind of toughness that possibly retards their development. They almost never stop to wonder if some task could be done more easily or more gently. They are intelligent people by any measure and we have reason for hope . . . yet in that one quality, their stubbornness, they may be too remarkable for their own good.

I sat with my stew and watched while my hosts made the collared bears fight one another, the entertainment brutal and illuminating. The bear masters were plainly disappointed by the level of carnage, and I watched the whips crack and heard the hard curses from everywhere and finally I could take no more. In my rally I had claimed a certain moral ground. The Wanderer's mission meant peace, and peace implied certain colors of decency. But instead of becoming upset in public, I merely gave a subtle signal and watched both the mangled bears and their masters put into a deep, deep sleep, no warnings given. One of my security people did the deed with a neural probe. The villagers were astounded and silent, scarcely breathing while my entourage and myself finished our stew and then rose, thanking our hosts for the meal and their hospitality and then walking off between the mangled creatures, bears and masters both.

—*Jy's chronicles*
(Quencé's earth)

The Wanderers came to Quencé's earth when he was a young man, scarcely sixteen years old. They found a landscape populated by simple farmers and fishermen, their lives unadorned and steady and oftentimes hard. There were few true nations and few meaningful roads, and suddenly strangers were everywhere, walking through the forests or riding magical ships in the sky, making treaties with every cluster of villages and every calloused patch of humankind.

Low-ranking Wanderers came through Quencé's tiny village, and he made a point of speaking to them. They learned the dialect overnight, and all of them did their best to explain the portals and the Bright and their great mission. They seemed wonderful to Quencé, full of strange living powers, and they were talking to him. Him! Their attentions seemed like the greatest wonder of all.

The Wanderers promised to bring gradual, measured changes to this earth—new ways to farm; new ways to travel; sweet new ways to think. It would be done through a small council of Wanderers left behind to oversee each stage. No, the visitors admitted, Quencé wouldn't see much new in his own lifetime. There were dangers in letting people, any people, advance too fast. Unimaginable horrors could be born, they claimed. And besides, they didn't want to disturb those things unique and irreplaceable on this earth, whatever those things might be.

Quencé considered the hard landscape, and particularly his own ugly slice of rock and tired soil. His father and grandfathers had died as old men at not much more than twice his age, and now he could see that that didn't have to happen. There was a golden future. Someday everything would improve, lives would grow easy, and that made him ache inside. That was the one time he found himself almost angry with the Wanderers.

He loved best their stories about Jy.

Jy was touring this earth; she toured every earth. Her entourage—a strange collection of the oldest and best humans—were accompanying her wherever people were halfway abundant, helping her give rallies for the curious crowds.

She was a great and wise person; every Wanderer said she was a saint.

Quencé was more than simply curious. How could any person start such an incredible undertaking? he wondered. And how could she keep all these bizarre people united all the time?

He wanted to meet Jy for himself. He wanted to see her queer monkey-fur body and her strange heavy-brained monkey face. Sometimes Quencé could think of little else, working his lousy ground with worn tools and big blistered hands. If he could just speak to Jy, he felt, and touch her strange, ancient body. She was the greatest spirit among these spirits, and he kept imagining how her magic would transform him. It would surely turn his life around.

Jy never came to his village; it was too small to bother. But there was a rich village on the coast and Jy was going there. It would be soon, claimed one Wanderer, and Quencé collected provisions in a blur and told his family good-bye and started out of the mountains. He had never gone so far from home. It was a tough walk, the pack digging into his shoulders and the path curling through the mountains full of bears and rock slides and ghostly bandits; yet he arrived without incident, exhausted but elated. The seaside village was an enormous place, nearly a thousand families living behind a rambling wooden stockade; and Quencé dashed about the muddy streets, asking, "Where is she? Where is she? Is she coming soon?"

Nobody knew his dialect, or they didn't want to speak to any backwoods bumpkin.

"Where's Jy?" he persisted. "I want to see Jy!"

"Do you?" someone finally responded. "Is that so?" He was laughing in Quencé's face, telling him, "She flew away days ago, farmer. Where were you? Shitting in your fields, were you?"

Gone? Truly? Quencé felt his life drain away in an instant.

"Go home, farmer," he was told. "Your goats need your love."

He ignored the insults and the graphic gestures, stumbling away without another word. It took days for him to regain any semblance of composure. Return home defeated? He couldn't stand the thought. More than ever he wished he could see Jy and speak with her. Only how could he catch her? Unless he could sprout wings . . . how?

Quencé hiked along the rocky coastline, then he turned inland, and he scrambled up a small mountain to where one of the famous, miraculous portals had been set. It was strange to behold, bigger than any house and clearer than the finest glass. Its entranceway was closed tight, and he knew it was protected by spells. There was a Wanderer there, too. She was a tall woman, even taller than Quencé, and she saw him standing with his face pressed against the crystal and climbed the rocky slope to gaze at him with strange colorless eyes.

"What may I do for you, sir?" she asked in a common dialect. "Let me help you." She smiled as all of them smiled, with trust and a certain steady coolness. "No, you cannot go inside. I am sorry. But if you can tell me what you want—"

"To join," he announced.

"Join?"

"I want to become a Wanderer."

Her smile brightened. Her mouth was missing every other tooth—a cosmetic brutality left from her past life—and she informed him, "It is not an easy course, sir." There was a hint of something. Amusement? Or disdain? Quencé bristled and held his breath, waiting. She told him, "You will have to undergo tests and training, I'm afraid. It will take many years, perhaps all of your natural life, and only then will we know if you are suited to a Wanderer's existence."

"Whatever," he snapped. "I'll do anything you want."

Again there was the smile. "And even at that point, I have to warn you, you'll be at the beginning. There will be simple jobs on whichever earth needs you. You'll have unromantic work in maintenance and transportation, or you might guard the portals." She gestured at the simple stone hut partway down the slope. It was her home, small and mostly hidden from view. "Young Wanderers," she told him, "do whatever is deemed best. They have no voice of their own."

"I still want to join," Quencé persisted. "I'm going

to be a Wanderer." He had to meet Jy and see the Bright and maybe find something better than this earth. He wanted a place where people didn't wear out and die in the midst of life. "I wanted to join," he lied, "from the first time I heard about you and your mission."

"Sir," she told him, "I myself am a lowly novice."

Her confession was followed by a frown.

"I would make a good Wanderer," he promised. "Wait and see!"

She shrugged as if it wasn't her concern and what did she care? "Do you know how long I have been a novice? Can you guess?" She paused before telling him, "More than forty-three thousand years. Sir."

Quencé nodded and felt a little weak in the knees.

"Do you honestly want to give away your life? In hopes of this sort of existence?" She looked at the mountainside with its stunted trees and bits of dirty snow, plus the endless rocks. "Are you ready to stand guard on wastelands like this one and wait, talking to natives and talking to yourself?" She grumbled, then said, "The high-ranking Wanderers will stream past you, while you are in one place. You'll have but only the faintest hope of ever being called into their realm."

Quencé knew his response.

Her bitterness made him certain what to say.

"I want to join," he repeated. He thought of his home and felt nothing but a cold hollowness inside. Then with a stubbornness prophetic by sheer chance, he told the novice, "It won't take me as long as it's taken you. It won't."

"No?"

"And stop smiling," he warned. "Keep looking at me that way, and you'll be missing more teeth. I mean it!"

3

EACH EARTH has exactly one thousand portals set at regular intervals across its surface, and we do not know how any of them operate. Does that sound strange? But it shouldn't, I think. Consider yourselves and your own high technology. Think of fission reactors that produce heat and hot water from the decay of heavy atoms, and you don't know why a given atom decays or when it will happen and your best experts have only a guesswork model of the nucleus and they know they are fundamentally ignorant too.

We do not know how our portals operate and we may never know, though we persist in our research and are forever making new guesses. In the meantime we try to remain pragmatic in the best sense of the word. We know that certain intricate machinery, employed in a precise fashion, will cause the material within the portal to leave this earth and enter the Bright, and with sufficient energy we can move people and equipment a huge distance along the Bright. Is this the way the Makers employed their handiwork? We do not know. Is there some easier means? Perhaps, but we have never found the tricks. And perhaps—here is a potent speculation—perhaps between the earths that we know there are more earths, millions more, and maybe the Bright's vastness will someday be magnified a trillionfold.

Is it possible?

Who can say?

I confess that I am baffled and quite the fool, and I stand before you feeling very much lost.

—Jy's speeches

Quencé quit working on his morning speech, and he sat back in his hard chair and kicked off his sandals, breathing deeply and feeling spent. The restaurant was nearly dark and absolutely silent, and he thought he must be alone, locked away and forgotten. Then there was motion and he spied the waitress sitting across the room, perched on a barstool and smoking. She was a blond girl not much more than twenty years old, he realized. She was wearing a short black dress tailored to resemble a maid's costume. She would tilt her head whenever she took a pull on her cigarette, then she blew the smoke high in the dark air, with an artful touch. She didn't seem to notice Quencé, but someone had brought him a fresh bottle of French spring water. He sipped and started to relax, winding down, using a string of internal commands to turn off most of his hard-memory.

The girl mashed out her cigarette, stood, and approached him.

She seemed pretty, then her prettiness left her. She had sharp overdone features accented by the bad lighting. She asked, "Can I get you anything?" Quencé saw the smile and a tough self-assuredness. "Maybe something stronger?"

"No, miss," he allowed. "This is perfect."

She looked straight at his eyes. Her nose was too long and her mouth too large for Quencé's tastes, but she had a snug dress and an obvious body and a certain carefree way of carrying herself. "Care to sit with me?" he asked. "For a minute, perhaps?"

"Why not?" She shrugged and grinned, taking the chair beside him.

Quencé was in a mood, a jittery, end-of-the-day mood, and he smiled until her smile brightened, something sly and knowing about her face. Then he introduced himself. She said her name, Sally something, and they shook hands with a certain mocking formality. When Sally retrieved her hand she pulled her fingertips along his palm and fingers, slowly, saying to him, "You know what? Some people are certain that touching one of you, just once, is enough to change them. That you're so old and so smart—have you heard this?—that your wisdom bubbles into us. Remaking us." She grinned, lighting a fresh cigarette. "You ever hear that?"

"Maybe once."

She blew the artful smoke to the ceiling lights, and

she shook her head. "So what do you think of our little earth?"

"Excuse me?"

"Is it special? Ordinary? What is it?"

"Every earth is special," he responded. "And yours is the same size as every other one."

She gave him a suspicious, sideways glance. "Are you a diplomat or something?"

"But it is true." He laughed and shrugged, turning his palms skywards. "I have seen a few earths, believe me, and all are different. Their genetics vary, and their languages vary. All the details are unique." He paused a moment, then added, "Even the ones that do the same things—going into space, for instance—they never manage it the same way twice. What happens to you and yours is one of a kind."

"I suppose," she allowed.

He thought of a hundred examples, but he kept quiet.

"Okay," she said. "But are we trouble?"

"Trouble?"

"Tough to handle?" She shrugged and puffed. "Are you taking special precautions with us? Are we dangerous?"

He understood. She wanted her earth to be a problem for the Wanderers. She had a romantic affection for outlaws, it seemed. Quencé made an affirmative gesture, saying, "You have the nuclear hell-raisers, of course. And your history is violent at all levels. So yes, we try to be careful. We don't want you hurting us, and we certainly didn't come here to start any apocalypse."

Sally seemed pleased with herself. She nodded and took a drag, then said, "I've heard where you've had troubles with some earths. Back down the Bright?"

"What have you heard?"

"Like they blew up on you?" She was curious, not passionate. She wasn't pressing him or enjoying this too much. "I've heard some noise about it. That's all."

"We have made mistakes. Maybe you haven't noticed, but we are human." He shrugged, remembering the worst of those mistakes as things that happened before he joined the mission. They were tens of thousands of years old. "We can't give details, but we don't hide the truth either."

She nodded.

"We changed some halfway advanced earths too fast," he admitted. "They were poor and harsh, but they had potential. We hoped we could skip some of the ugly periods—"

"But you couldn't."

He said, "It eats at us even today."

"Good," she replied.

Quencé thought about his own earth. It had seemed wrong at the time, the Wanderers moving so cautiously. Yet now, knowing what *might* go wrong, he was thankful for the sluggish measured pace of change. His distant relatives were basically comfortable today. Science was established, industry was beginning, and the populations were small enough that the earth itself wasn't being mangled by the process.

"I do resent that one word," Quencé mentioned.

"What word?"

"'Handle.'"

"What handle?"

"What we do to you, in your mind." He shook his head, then said, "We really do very little 'handling.' We don't treat people like putty."

She watched him, seemingly amused. "Yeah? You think?" She showed her polished teeth and said, "You folks are smooth. So smooth. Don't get pissed, I'm not bitching. I'm all for what you're doing here. But the way you orchestrate these rallies and the way you keep yourselves on the news every night, always smiling, always doing good . . . well, it's pretty damned impressive. To me, at least."

Quencé sipped his water and said, "I'm glad."

"I heard this other story, a different story," she continued. "A friend of a friend told it to me." She gave him a hard look, then said, "When you first arrived, all of you? I heard you took a bunch of big players down the Bright. Politicians and that sort of thing. You made them honorary Wanderers for a day and spent a bunch of energy to show them one special place—"

"We can't give people tours on the Bright," he interrupted. "Energywise—"

"I know, sure. It costs too much and even *you* have limits, I know." She sighed and said, "Anyway, *my* story goes that you took these important natives on a field trip. In secret. There's this earth where people got the Bomb and in a giant way, and you showed them what can happen if people don't think before they shoot. You let all the nuclear-equipped presidents and dictators go walking in the rubble, wearing some fancy stuff to keep them alive—"

"You heard this story?"

"Are you denying it?"

"I am a diplomat," he allowed. "How would a diplomat answer?"

"'No comment.'"

"No comment."

She was laughing. She said, "Good," and seemed satisfied.

Neither of them spoke for a little while.

Quencé drained the bottle, and she crushed her cigarette. Then she was staring at him, her large mouth devilish and her eyes satisfied. Quencé asked, "What are you thinking, Sally?"

"I'm wondering." She paused, then asked, "Where are you from? On your home earth, I mean."

"From?"

"You look kind of Arab to me. Your skin, your face. Too tall, but otherwise that's how you look."

"I was born," Quencé confessed, "on the northern island of what you call Japan. Is that what you mean?"

"You're a Jap." She shrugged and giggled, telling him, " Each earth is different, I know. I can't generalize. People were the same when we were monkeys, something like that . . . and now we're like two kinds of sparrows, you and me. We look the same and fly the same and sound the same to anyone who doesn't know better. Only we aren't the same." She took a breath and shook her head, the smooth blond hair catching the light. "You know what, Quencé? People say something else about you Wanderers."

"Do they?"

"That you're all so deep and so mysterious, and nobody can really know what you're thinking—"

"I have heard that said."

"Maybe once?" She was amused. She sat back in her chair and pulled a foot from its shoe, and Quencé felt the pressure against his leg, the long toes curling.

"Honey," Sally announced, "you know what?"

"What?"

"For being old and mysterious and all that crap, let me tell you, I'm finding it awful easy to read your mind."

4

IT WAS once so easy. For our first half million years we found empty earths and nearly empty earths with the majority of the human beings living as hunter-gatherers, and there is a certain spoiling reliability about hunter-gatherers. They can vary in their size and strength and their tendencies to violence and the artistry of their tools, but they have similar outlooks and similar limitations and honestly, we became rather complacent after five hundred thousand years of the same challenge, as you can well imagine.

Then we came to a certain earth, quite a different earth, whose people hadn't just evolved to a higher intelligence nor invented wonders like agriculture and steel fabrication. No, its people had built cities on the moon and Mars and put robots into orbits around distant stars. We—the Founders and the Cousins— had to meet an enormous challenge in the form of sophisticated souls like yourselves, and I will admit something here. It was a blessing, a dash

of icy water to the face. *Here is the future*, we
realized. *At least for many earths . . .*

And would we have guessed this future if
we had been left to ourselves, sketching the
directions for humankind?

I think not.

I honestly think not.

—Jy's speeches

Quencé had vague and rather confused memories of his
years spent guarding portals—a dull and thankless task
that would have killed his desire in time—yet he remembered with perfect clarity the day when a full-
fledged Wanderer, a modest-ranking one, came to save
him. Batteries of tests had shown Quencé's special talents. It seemed this ex-farmer had some innate feeling
for complicated circumstances, and the Wanderer reported, "We have an important job for you. You should
feel honored."

He was terrified, in truth. They traveled up the
Bright in a slow fashion, conserving energies. They slid
past almost every other Wanderer, Jy included, and
reached a new earth through a tiny temporary portal.
Suddenly Quencé was part of the mission's vanguard.
"You have the makings of a scout," he was told. It was
a vital job, and dangerous, and several thousand Wanderers and novices did nothing else. They surveyed the
approaching earths and made recommendations. What
technologies would stabilize them? Which ones would
do harm? How could the governments be placated? What
about the people themselves? And how could Wanderers
keep their portals safe into the future? *What would work?*

Quencé had always carried within him an image of
the ideal Wanderer. Working as a scout, then as a team
leader, he strove to make himself fit that perfect self.
Those were tough, splendid centuries with most of the
earths advanced to some level of industry and raw power.
There were endless challenges to guess moods and defuse shooting wars and curb ancient hatreds. One earth
was particularly 'tough' with its high populations and long

wars that had made whole regions uninhabitable, runaway viruses and persistent toxins poisoning the soil and water. It was Quencé who devised the complex scheme to diffuse the fighting and start the cleansing process. He used political marriages and inventive media campaigns, and he was the one who invented the tours of dead earths. He took the hardened leaders to the worst places, and he made fun of those men and women. He charged them with incompetence, and worse; he challenged them to improve; and later, when everything turned out for the best, Quencé was told that he was wanted by the entourage. He had to leave at once.

He assumed he was in trouble. He had handled the natives harshly, he realized, and he would have to defend himself now. The Wanderers in the entourage prided themselves on treating natives with a uniform respect. But what was he supposed to do? He had insulted some near-sighted fools and saved an earth and he felt himself bristling at what was to come.

Founders and primitive Cousins surrounded Quencé. He stood his ground, asking, "What is this about? Can you tell me?"

"She wishes to meet with you," he heard. "Now."

"She?"

"Absolutely." There were nods and sober gazes. "She is granting you an audience, youngster."

The Glorious One herself?

Quencé was shocked and thrilled and unsure of himself. For centuries he had wished to meet Jy, and now he was ushered into her room while her ship drifted above a gardenlike landscape. This was a peaceful, easy earth and she was on a holiday. "Hello, Quencé." She greeted him as if they were old, old friends. They spent the entire afternoon together, drinking aromatic teas and nobody daring to interrupt. Hardships were suddenly forgotten. Quencé was glad for every sacrifice he had made. Jy possessed an indescribable presence, a holiness perhaps and certainly a cutting wisdom. She was the ultimate Wanderer—the best of humanity, in other words—and that was when Quencé realized he would never excel at this life. He could never achieve Jy's high standards. He listened to her speaking about the Makers and the Bright, her yellow-rimmed eyes full of fire, and he felt inadequate. He was practically indifferent. He couldn't begin to encompass a sliver of the mystery, and a chill formed deep inside him.

"What is it, Quencé?"

He stared into his steaming tea, barely hearing the voice.

"What are you thinking, so glum and all?"

He was here because of his skills, not because of his outlook. He had no illusions. A true Wanderer would see his destiny tied to the Bright. Quencé just saw his work, interesting and intense but nonetheless work. Stubbornness and pride had carried him this far, and he felt weak in the Glorious One's presence. He was transparent and completely unworthy.

"I wanted to meet you," Jy explained. She seemed to have forgotten her questions. "I wanted to make a request." The long apish head nodded and the patient gaze focused on him. "Would you consider leaving your current post to join me as a full-ranking member of my entourage?" She paused, amused by his surprise. "This is no command and you can do as you wish, either way, but I could use your skills." A smile emerged, her teeth thick and worn. "You seem shaken. Are you?"

It was all Quencé could manage to remain conscious, sitting upright and breathing with care.

"If you feel uncertain," she said, "delay. Take your time and consider your own mind, my friend, and please don't feel pressured."

Yet he heard himself speaking, giving his answer with a dry, steady voice. "Yes," he managed. "I would like to be part of things . . . here." Despite his being unworthy, he was thinking. He was certain of his failings and fully expected Jy to see them, then she would rescind her offer. Yet she did nothing of the kind, and Quencé became confused—a rare thing for him. He responded to his confusion by working even harder, eager for Jy's little encouragements and her gracious praises, feeling her goodness and strength washing over him while an inner voice, ceaseless and secure, told him that twenty million years wouldn't be long enough to bring him to perfection, or anywhere close.

The dreams began later.

They didn't come often or regularly and he never told anyone about them. Many Wanderers had vivid dreams. It had something to do with the hard-memory spilling data into his soft neurons, and of course he was under stress with work and his feelings of inadequacy. Sometimes his mind got too full, too focused, and he was dreaming of vivid landscapes shot with colors and textures and strange clinging smells. Quencé would find himself visiting a perfect earth, beautiful and comfortable and populated with perfect people. The details would vary. There were golden castles on the hilltops; or cities sculpted from diamonds and plasmas; or simple stone cottages done with a wondrous artistry. Technologies were more appropriate than advanced. Always, always Quencé would walk along the avenues, admiring the strong and effortlessly happy people around him; and somewhere he would bump shoulders with a woman . . . a great beauty who made him tremble . . . who made him weak . . . .

He and the woman would converse for a little while, walking together and ending at some private apartment or house where they would make love. Time after time they would enjoy one another, Quencé virile and the woman insatiable and in the midst of everything the dream would dissolve. Quencé would wake with a start, drenched in sweat and semen, and he would pant and lie still, feeling helpless. Then for months and years he would remember everything, with a shocking clarity and without effort. He couldn't stop himself from seeing and feeling what wasn't any more real than a storm of electrons, scalding and bright, raging inside his tired old head.

The only detail lost to him was his lover's face.

He couldn't summon the color of her eyes or the curl of her nose or any other trace of her self.

It was a sign. Quencé didn't feel he was superstitious; he had left that part of himself on his home earth. No, he believed, he was pragmatic. These dreams were just the hardest evidence of his doubts and his weaknesses, of his not belonging here. It was idiocy to chase phantoms up a cosmic highway . . . pure idiocy! That was what he truly believed.

5

IT BECOMES harder, all the time harder, because we cannot move any faster and meanwhile the peoples and earths ahead of us are advancing, learning new tricks and making new troubles for themselves, human inventiveness trying its damndest to frustrate us. I hate myself for thinking in such terms, but I cannot stop wondering what happens in a million years. What happens when this mishmash of species evolves into stranger forms still? How do we make sense of them and reason with them, and can we adapt in turn?

Then I think, of course we will adapt. We have always adapted.

What other choice do we have?

—*Jy's private journal*

Someone was knocking on the door, steadily and firmly. Quencé listened to the sound for a long while, or for a moment. He wasn't sure about time. Then the knocking ceased, and he sat up in bed and heard nothing but the slow wet breathing of the girl. Climbing from his bed, he found his trousers and dressed before opening the room's heavy institutional door. Wysh said, "We have the breakfast," in the Founder language. She was staring at his bare chest, then his face.

"I know. I was awake," he lied. He had learned English so well that Founder felt like a second tongue. "Give me a moment."

Wysh started to lean forwards ever so slightly, and she sniffed. She possessed a potent sense of smell—an oddity among primates, and irritating—and Quencé watched her quick and thorough probing sniff. Then she blinked, asking, "Who is she?"

Quencé said, "Who?" and waited.

Wysh said nothing. Her thin mouth was set and her expression was quite serious.

"I will be out in a minute," he promised.

"She likes tobacco," said Wysh. Then she gave a wistful smile, and she added, "Her period is beginning."

"I'll wake her and tell her the good news," Quencé responded. Ages ago—was this possible?—he and Wysh had been lovers themselves. They were bad lovers and it had ended quickly, and he could recall none of the details. "Is there anything else?"

"You will hurry?" asked Wysh.

"Go wait in the lobby. I am already there."

Ignoring Wysh's eyes, Quencé shut the door with a heavy *thunk*. The girl was dead asleep. He sat on the edge of the huge hard bed, watching her while he put on a clean shirt. The sheets were pulled over her waist, and he could see her breasts hanging sideways against her chest, nipples fat and salty. They were too big for infants, he was thinking. They were nipples built for sex. Then he sat there feeling nothing whatsoever. There wasn't any lust within him, or affection, or even something as concrete as disinterest.

Quencé remembered his latest vivid dream.

It seemed minutes old, the lover crouched on her perfect hands and knees and Quencé behind her, working in a tireless dream fashion. The woman cried, "Yes," once, then again, and then from somewhere deep inside, with force, and Quencé had felt himself waking all at once. He had clung to her smooth hips, trying not to be swept away and of course losing his fight in the end.

It had happened eleven years ago.

It was four earths ago.

Without his hard-memory engaged, he couldn't recall the continent where he had had the dream or any other simple fact. All there was was the lover saying, "Yes," and her long muscled back and the flowing hair and no face. Only her voice and the fine feel of her skin were real.

Quencé shook his head.

Sally Something shifted her weight, burying her chest and face into the small hard hotel pillows.

He rose, finding his sandals. Someday, he reasoned, he would happen upon his perfect earth and his ideal lover and then he would approach Jy, telling her, "I am sorry, I can't continue. I wish you well and everyone well, and I hope for your forgiveness. But this is where I have to step off the Bright. I'm sorry—"

It sometimes happened to other Wanderers.

They lost their love for the mission—who knew why?—and they ended their days wherever they had resigned. Those were the rules. With their resignation they gave up every advantage of being a Wanderer. There were no more medical wonders, no maintenance for their precious hard-memories. They were subject to the laws and customs of ordinary citizens, and they could never rejoin again.

Most of those who resigned were younger, low-ranking or novices; but sometimes it happened to the highest of the high. Nobody was immune simply because of his or her station.

Eventually Quencé would realize he had pretended too long.

He didn't belong here. His energies would run dry . . . it was inevitable . . . .

Entering the bathroom to relieve himself, he looked at his face in the wide mirror. Sally Something was muttering in her sleep, softly. Quencé said, "Jy," without any sound. "I am so sorry." He paused, then he said, "I can go no farther, and I wish you all the luck possible." Then he blinked and shut off the bathroom light and left the hotel room as quietly as he could.

JY

1

ONE OF my earliest memories is of the day I
decided to leave home. I was large for my age,
three or four years old, and I suppose rather
bold. I slipped out of our village and struck out
across a hundred-crop field, pressing between
the ranks of tailored grasses and the fruit-laden
shrubs and the little nut trees and the vegetable
meats. I came to a knoll in the middle of the
field, and with my hands and feet I managed to
climb to its crest and stand straight, looking back
at the ancient white buildings of the village.
They seemed small and painfully remote and I
felt as though I had gone some tremendous distance, more than I had planned, and I made a
heartfelt vow to myself to never, never go so far
from home again.

—Jy's chronicles

It was Jy's idea to alter their course and their rigorous
schedule and set down in a certain Kansas town of her

own choosing. She came from her private chamber and told her assistants, in English, "We will stop for a few minutes to make an impression." She waited a moment, then announced, "I want to stop," and smiled, pointing at the projected map floating against one rounded wall. "Please?"

It was the name of the place that had caught her attention.

White Cloud.

The closest assistants blinked and stared at Jy, calculating the troubles this would bring and steeling themselves against their doubts. They couldn't afford to doubt her; it did no good. Many of them had been with her in some capacity since the earliest times. "And if you know someone for a few thousand centuries," Jy liked to joke, "you start to understand her mind."

There was no point in debating. Jy's mind was set and everyone else would have to make do.

There were Founders like herself—long-armed; heavy-brained—and there were Cousins, and there was a mixture of younger species too. Jy saw heads starting to nod, some turning to make the preparations, and she told them, "Thank you," while starting for her chamber again. As always, her wishes were being carried out.

Motion meant effort. Jy gripped handholds and toeholds, climbing along a curling tunnel, and she thought of White Cloud to distract herself from her taxed muscles. How many communities had she visited with that name? Thousands? Probably tens of thousands. She entered her small chamber and triggered the floor, a reclining chair growing in a few seconds. It fit her perfectly. She leaned back and looked out through the shielded windows while her hard-memory linked with the ship's library, dozens of examples of White Clouds being disgorged. She could see mountain villages and seaports and rude hamlets scarcely worth any name, plus at least two great metropolises. She had glimpses of stone streets and concrete streets and every sort of building, everywhere a multitude of strange faces. Every continent was represented. There were even a couple White Clouds set on the cold southern continent, one sturdy and buried beneath the flowing ice and the other community part of some warmer, partly flooded earth.

It felt good to sit. Jy's muscles were begging to be refurbished, or perhaps she would have a new body produced. Wouldn't that be lovely? Her tired eyes were aching even when they were shut. She was a frail creature, and the frailty was a nagging but important feature. Where most Wanderers kept themselves rigorously fit and youthful, Jy managed to avoid the temptations of untempered medicine. Most earths had the implicit expectation that wise old women should at least appear to be old, their bones brittle and their muscles soft and something charmingly unstable about their walk. In youth Jy would be strong, even for a Founder woman. It seemed a shame that stiffness and glossy gray fur held benefits. Most people felt reflexive emotions when faced with an elder, and it was sad that Jy needed every dose of their respect in order to help the mission.

She sat motionless, looking forwards.

The countryside was green with trees and greener crops—each field dedicated to a single species—and she noticed the richness of the land and the imposed geometry of the square fields and the straight white roads and all the while she was planning simultaneously for White Cloud and twenty other tasks too.

She was feeble in appearance and strong of mind.

Jy sat in her seat as her ship moved, slowly and stately, and she let the bulk of her mind skip backwards, recalling places and people and some of those things she had said to both.

2

HAPPENSTANCE MAKES each species of human being.

With the Founders it began as a peculiar ecological twist whereby my ancestors became gardeners before they became truly intelligent—like certain species of ants who harvest

the fungi that grow on clipped bits of leaves—
and in those ancient times they would tend their
simple crops and live in set locations and their
first tools were for cultivation and irrigation.
They were not hunters; they were shepherds of
life. The early Founders ate meat only when
there was carrion and war was not a winning
prospect, any innate sense of violence would
have strained a tight-knit village, and besides,
they were incompetent with killing tools. We
Founders are still passive by nature. Carefully
tended ground and familiar homes and a very
low birthrate . . . these are part of the Founder
heritage. This is where happenstance has put
us. We were civilized before we were smart,
and when we became smart it was a string of
lucky mutations that made us very, very smart
indeed.

—*Jy's chronicles*

Every person on every earth seemed to ask the same
question.

"How did this whirlwind begin, Jy? What happened?"

No answer was exact or even honest, and Jy knew
better than to tell the whole story. Instead she had a
practiced tale not too far from the truth. Audiences heard
how she was one of ten scouts exploring an empty earth
some years after the Bright was discovered, and she was
working alone when her skimmer lost power and crashed
and burned. She barely managed to save herself. She
found herself without water or food and with no way to
call for help. Her ribs were cracked, and she was bruised
everywhere else. The empty earth surrounded her, and
nobody was aware of her pain.

She told audiences about standing on a table-flat,
drought-stricken plain with the sun blazing an arm's
length overhead.

In those times, she said, the Bright was something
freshly discovered and its use was expensive, all its po-

tentials unrealized, and she was very likely the most *alone* person in existence.

Jy picked a random direction and started to walk. Sometimes she would suck juices from the vegetation, and come night she slept wherever she found shelter. She remembered a shallow ditch and a dried animal wallow before her luck changed. One afternoon she came upon a stack of weathered gray stones full of shade, and beside the stones were half a dozen ripe melons growing on tough green vines. Jy broke the melons against the stones and ate, then found a comfortable nook and lined it with grass and curled up and drifted to sleep with the stones surrounding her, protecting her and bleeding a delicious slow heat.

Here something happened that she never admitted to any audience, or even to her closest associates.

She woke in the morning and heard a voice. It was a clear and quite persistent voice, absolutely senseless, and Jy opened her eyes and looked skywards. Standing on the topmost stone was a stranger. Jy was staring at a young Founder woman, her black face smiling and her long arms hanging at her side.

Jy was startled, naturally.

She tried to call to the mumbling stranger, but her sore ribs cut her voice short. Suddenly she was sweating, her fur drenched and her body starting to tremble. A fever had begun. She told people later about waking with a fever and vague delusions, and in both the true story and the public story Jy shut her eyes and breathed, forcing herself to stay still while her body seemed to float in space with blackness all around and nothing to be heard.

It was an hallucination, she would tell herself. The stranger must have come from Jy's suffering and her potent fears.

Again she opened her eyes. She was alone and desperately thirsty, easing herself from between the stones and down onto the baked ground. The woman had vanished. Jy walked around the stack and found nobody, then she picked a likely direction and hoped against hope to find water. Or at least some more melons, please?

She walked through the morning with the dead brown grasses stretching on into the brilliant haze, the heat tremendous and the sky incapable of holding any clouds, and if there wasn't one stroke of luck before dusk she was quite sure that her body would die.

Jy told audiences about her state of mind during that walk. She had come an enormous distance to die, it seemed. She had traveled up the Bright and at no small cost, and why? Where was the purpose? Scavengers would find her corpse and pick apart her brain, exposing her primitive hard-memory, and nobody would find her in time. The hard-memory would be scattered in buzzard dung and between grains of sand, and what a sorry stupid ugly waste!

As if for the first time, she began to think about the Bright.

It was an immeasurable artifact, clearly beyond human comprehension. People were like field mice who had found a mag-lift highway in their realm. What could mice make of fluxes and superconductors? All they perceived was a natural pathway leading in two directions. In the human case, however, the pathway was expensive to reach and to utilize. Sending just one person to the next earth required the fire of an entire fusion reactor. Launching colonies to the far side of the galaxy would prove to be cheaper than putting colonies on the alternate earths, and regardless, the Founders didn't require any new lands. Of course some scouting missions had a certain practicality. Research and sheer caution meant they should understand their surroundings. But how far would the scouts move? What was a reasonable cost? And what about the strange and quite primitive people living on some of these earths? All of them seemed like simple-minded hunters. They were nothing like the Founders. Wouldn't it be best just to leave them alone? Let them have their own homelands and forget them? That was the common verdict . . . the voice of careful reason . . . .

"I have seen the arguments from all sides," Jy would confess to her audiences. "I was making my death march, and there were times when I was in the skeptics' camp and couldn't imagine any reason to use the Bright. Then there were moments when I looked past my own circumstances, past my pain and certain death, and felt an insane curiosity. I wished I could move at will along the Bright. I wished I could visit hundreds of earths and find splendid ones as sweet as or sweeter than my own . . . if such a thing were possible."

She told of pushing through the furnacelike heat, the sun high above and her body near collapse and her mind busily arguing with itself. Part of her was furious at her misfortune. She was going to die in every sense, and the situation stunk. Yet some other muddled part of her wanted a purpose, some cause, and she found herself hunting for a logical thread to make her agony matter and her death gain some modest stature.

At one point she stopped and happened to notice a line of elegant tall trees standing on the grass. What were trees doing there? she wondered. Was there water? And maybe some big cat waiting for a kill? It didn't matter. Jy stumbled ahead with one arm pressed against her sore side and her breath short and her strong young body trembling once again. She helped herself walk with her free arm, leaning forwards, but the trees refused to come closer. Her feet were sore and bleeding from a hundred cuts, and she bowed her head and kept moving because she had no other choice. Then all at once she felt the cool dappled shade on her back and her neck, and her tired eyes lifted and looked past the straight black trunks of the trees. There was water. It was a wind-stroked patch of the foulest seepage ever to grace a landscape, and she was running. Jy felt the warm mud on the shoreline and stumbled forwards and the water itself was nearly hot, silty and stinking and glorious. She drank her fill and then more and then retreated into the shade again where she sobbed and felt wondrous. When had she ever felt so fine? And after a while, from sheer exhaustion, she dipped her head and fell asleep.

At least that was how she told the story a million years later.

She slept and had a dream and everything became clear to her. She had a momentary insight, an inspiration, and that was how she answered the question: "How did the whirlwind begin?"

Yet she was lying. How could she tell people that she never dreamed, and when she woke she saw the Founder woman from the stones sitting near her, her back against a tree trunk and her voice steady and her face smiling like before? How could she admit such an unlikely thing?

This time Jy understood the woman's words.

The event was incredible and thoroughly ordinary in the same instant. Jy listened to the woman and knew it was another hallucination, and she promised herself never to tell another soul what happened here.

"This is what you will do, Jy."

Do? What does she mean? What am I to do?

"Are you listening to me? Jy?"

"I hear you," she muttered.

"Good." The hallucination was eerie because it seemed completely real. There were no shrouds of fuzzy light or anything else out of the ordinary. "The Bright leads," the woman reported. "It leads and you will follow it, you and your people will, because it is your destiny, because you and yours have no other future—"

"But why?" Jy interrupted.

"Find those who made the Bright," said the woman, "and knit together the people as you move—"

"Find who?"

"—and be strong," the hallucination concluded. "Always stay true to your nature, and persist."

"Who are you?" Jy asked. She made herself crawl forward, both legs cramping and a prickly plant cutting into a knee. She dipped her head for an instant and moaned and then the hallucination was gone when she looked again. There was nothing but the tree and a perfect memory of everything said.

"It is your destiny . . . ."

By evening the other scouts came to find Jy. Sensors had spotted the signature of a single human body, ill but alive, and the skimmers descended on the waterhole. "It was a joyful ending to my way of thinking," she would tell people, "and then the mission began. At first there was one Wanderer and then an entire species, devoted and peaceful and united, and then we grew to include representatives of a billion billion souls, like a host of field mice picking and sniffing their way along the strange path."

She paused a moment, then said, "Make no mistake, we are mice. We are farsighted and sometimes brave, but we are mice nonetheless." She would pause again and smile as that hallucination had smiled at her. "No," she declared, "we don't know any answers and we don't know how and where we might find them, but isn't that true of everything worthwhile? Any great mission has to be greater than human reach, and the key is faith in one's goals. One must have faith in the striving that leads toward the gray boundaries of the answer. There must be faith that in this enormous tangle of Reality something larger and finer than mice lives and waits."

Then she gave a long pause, letting her audience digest at least a portion of her words.

Then she told them: "Without such a quest, what does it matter? What does anything matter? Where can one find the sober linchpin called 'purpose' if one won't try the impossible?"

3

WE CALLED our species the Founders long before we found the Bright. The name comes from a tale of Creation in which the ancient gods held a contest among themselves. They went for a walk on the newly made earth, each collecting one specimen of the newly made animals, and the god to return with the most remarkable beast would become the leader of all the gods for all time and in all ways.

One very minor god called Reason hunted and hunted, but she was so small and weak that she could catch nothing whatsoever, not even after days of constant effort. She finally sat and cried to herself, and a human being happened along. The human was moved by compassion and approached her and asked what was wrong, what could she do to help the poor god? "Come with me," the little god responded. "Would you please come with me?" And the human being, kind and charitable, agreed and took the god by her hand and made the the journey to the summit of the snow-capped volcano where every god dwelled.

The other gods saw the human, and they knew at once that she was a rare and unusual beast and that Reason was the victor. She was now their only leader.

"But how did you catch the human?" asked her friends. "Humans are quite rare and wily and we had no luck with them."

"It was simple," Reason allowed. "I stayed in one place and let her come find me."

Thus the name—*Founder*.

—*Jy's speeches*

How DOES it feel to be a million years old and have a core of hard-memory that has persisted for so long? Well, honestly it feels very much like being ten years old forever. That is the secret. The engineering and the medical technologies enhance whatever I have always been, not diminishing or detracting, and that is the elegant key.....

—*Jy's speeches*

A voice said, "May I enter?" and Jy turned, knowing the voice but wanting to look at the face. She was curious about moods and motives.

He was a Cousin named Xen, a powerfully built little man with thin black fur and a bony head. He approached Jy and smiled with his hands empty and his gray-clad body slightly stooped in respect. Like all Cousins, Xen's natural brain was rather small and simple.

Hard-memory and synthetic neurons had made him into a competent associate, hundreds of thousands of years ago, and an artificial larynx allowed him normal speech. Every Cousin had had the same treatment. How else could the simpler people be included? The Founders had picked each Cousin for his or her personality and character, granting them a staggering intelligence. As a result they had a fierce commitment. They were grateful for their opportunities; and in one motion, in a most fundamental way, they had been completely and permanently severed from their homelands. In some ways, it was said, the Cousins were the ideal Wanderers.

"Enter," she told him.

"Thank you, Jy."

Xen's people had continued to evolve at their own pace. Wanderer guards lived beside each old portal on his earth, but the interactions were rare and mostly without consequences. Yet in perhaps another few thousand years, Jy knew, those people would be leaving their stone age. They had become a delicate willowy-tall people—nothing at all like Xen—and Xen would have to make the long journey to meet them and introduce himself. They were his own descendants, and it would be left to him to help ease them into their future.

That was a tradition for the Cousins.

Jy wouldn't miss Xen. He was rather a pest at times, always concerned about following the precise rules that Jy herself had devised and never seeing past those same rules. He was a pest because he oftentimes came here to complain about this infraction or that failure. Xen had long since stopped surprising Jy in even the smallest ways, and when he left the entourage Jy would be free to promote new blood. She would find new spirit and fresh ways of thinking, and nobody would have their feelings hurt with a demotion. Even someone like Xen deserved that measure of respect, she believed; and with that thought she asked, "What is it, my friend?"

"We are close to White Cloud," Xen told her. "It won't be long."

"Thank you."

He said nothing for a brief moment.

"Is there more?" she inquired, sensing there was.

"Two items." He paused before saying, "We have just received the latest reports from the Other Side, and it seems like a good deal of material. Several thousand volumes."

The Other Side meant the other Wanderers moving in the opposite direction on the Bright. Distance and the limitations of travel had separated the two groups long ago. There wasn't anything like radio or laser communication on the Bright, and all data had to be moved in some physical form, preferably in small packages moving at some modest speed. Of course should either group find the Makers, there were means for a few special people to make quick trips back across the million earths. Otherwise the Wanderers had to make due with the occasional multivolume gift full of written accounts and holos showing what those on the Other Side had seen and learned in the recent past.

Jy would have to make the time to read a synopsis.

Was there any important news in the reports? she wondered. Then she realized Xen wouldn't be the one to tell her if that were the case. One of the Founders would have come instead.

"There is another matter," Xen muttered.

She watched him. His face was plainly nervous, and she was amused by his groping for courage. He was obvious and silly. He began the traditional wringing of hands and that neurotic slip of a smile, then his too-smooth voice was saying, "I have news about someone, an associate, and I thought you would want to hear—"

"News?"

"Quencé."

Jy blinked and waited.

"Wysh is concerned about him. She has filed a report about his . . . interludes . . . with certain women."

Jy swallowed and gave a nod, nothing more.

Xen's expression became grave. Lust was always a serious concern in his mind. His species had had a rather remarkable sense of monogamy, and his voice became pointed as he said, "There have been quite a few incidents on this earth. One, two, three—"

"Xen?"

He paused, lifting his eyes but otherwise holding himself motionless.

"Is there a point to your telling me about Quencé?"

He clicked his tongue against the floor of his mouth, then he confessed, "I was unsure whether to bring these matters to your attention or not. You told me that if he became a nuisance—"

"Is he a nuisance?" she pressed.

He fidgeted before saying, "Wysh believes so." Each word was measured and dead. "Otherwise I don't believe she would make reports."

It was probably true, thought Jy.

"I will speak with him," she said. "If you think I should."

"Yes." Xen nodded. There was a brief flash in his eyes, a certain glee betrayed, and Jy had to ask:

"Has he broken any rules of conduct?" Sexual acts in and of themselves were not improper.

"Not overtly, no."

"Has he made babies, or dissolved unions between two or more people, or broken any cultural taboos?"

"There is the spirit in the failures," argued Xen. "They have a pattern that never changes."

Jy waited.

Xen saw her gaze and shut his mouth.

"I promise to speak to Quencé," she told him. "Is that enough?"

"I only want what helps us, Jy."

It was a typical nonanswer.

"May we drop this issue?" asked Jy.

"Yes, ma'am."

"And about the other matter? Bring me the synopsis of the reports, at your convenience." She made a vague gesture.

Xen straightened his back for the first time. Convention required a slight bow here, but he resisted out of anger. Xen knew that she granted Quencé too much latitude and that he had been promoted too quickly, skills

or no skills—who in the entourage thought otherwise?—
and now Jy was trying to ignore Quencé's problems. She
could admit that much to herself. She couldn't push
Quencé too hard, and no, she was not handling these
circumstances with fairness and an eye on the holy rules.

This wasn't a serious matter, she decided. It would
be different if Quencé had no sense of discretion while
being led about by his glands.

Did Xen and the others feel jealous of Quencé?

It wasn't too unlikely to picture them as secretly
jealous, she felt.

Yet some portion of Jy had to agree with Xen. She
felt a bitter pit in her gut when she thought of her young
associate bedding women as he traveled on the Bright.
It had been almost forever since she took a lover for
herself, lovers being distractions and worse. They were
luxuries the Glorious One could never afford, and being
her lover would give someone too much status within
this tiny community.

Jy decided to select a moment and a place and scare
Quencé with a few chosen words and a withering look.
She would startle him, perhaps even injure him in some
fashion. She wanted him to appreciate what a chance she
had taken by bringing him here. She was trying to find
new blood to move ever higher into the ranks, eager to
surround herself with the best and the freshest, and all
the while, the earths grew stranger and stranger.

4

WE ARE rare and remarkable for many reasons.
It is not just because we Founders evolved intelligence through a string of blessed mutations,
and not just because we are odd primates with
our females dominating both physically and socially, and certainly not just because we have
no strong instinctive heart for violence. It is the
combination of these rarities that makes us remarkable. More than once I have paused and

wondered to myself, inside my most secret self,
if maybe we are *too* rare and *too* remarkable
and our species arose because of forces other
than luck . . .

—Jy's private journal

Convincing the Founders to follow the Bright was an
epic onto itself. Jy had to persuade an entire world of
living people—stubborn and cautious and perhaps
afraid—and she had to persuade the dead as well. The
Archives were the stored hard-memories of former generations. Because life was precious and experience was
precious, they were kept inside special stone buildings
painted red to signify their importance. According to
Founder law, each Archive had the same voting powers
as anyone still alive; and without their support there
could be no great change in policy or purpose. The
Founders required unanimity for anything of the scale
Jy would propose—thousands of generations saying in
one voice that they would give their unconditional blessing.

The Archives became Jy's greatest champions.

She knew hard-memory was not an easy afterlife.
They were bodiless organisms who could distract themselves with simulated landscapes and complicated games
and nothing else. They were retained for their knowledge, but the truth was that it was a rare day when any
living person came into the red buildings to ask advice.
The Archives were opinionated and thoroughly bored
entities, and their dissatisfaction was tailor-made for Jy.

"Help me!" she pleaded. "I have a plan for a journey
unlike any other and I know how to carry it out, but I
need everyone's commitment. Let me convince you and
you can help me convince the others, particularly your
stubborn children and grandchildren." She waited a moment, then said, "You represent an enormous wisdom,"
and she bowed to the glass eyes that gazed down at her
from the high shelves. There were thousands of buildings
like this particular red building, and all the Archives were
listening to her obvious play for their pride. "I am quite

sure you will make the difference," she told them. "Will you please listen to me?"

There was a pause, long and unnerving.

Jy was standing inside the sunny entranceway; the old red building stood at the center of her village. Custom dictated that she come here and appear before her own ancestors while making her requests. She breathed and fought the trembling of her limbs and after a moment noticed the faint musty stink of tired air. Her ancestors surrounded her. They were small ceramic constructions, none larger than a pebble, and they were hidden within sealed boxes still nearly empty. Hundreds of generations could be born and die in this one village, and the Archives wouldn't need any new wings to the building or even any new boxes. There was so much room and so much time to fill it all . . .

"Of course we will listen to you." Jy heard countless voices speaking as one, and she shivered for a long moment. "You think this much of us," they told her, "to come here first; do you think we wouldn't listen? Go on and tell your plan, Jy. Please begin!"

She explained the basics of her idea. At first her voice was stilted and slow, but then the passion of her mission took hold and she was rushing too fast and starting to stumble—

"And what would we do?" asked a single voice. Later Jy would learn it was one of her own great-grandmothers who tried to make her stop and think, giving her the chance to collect her wits. "If we agree and the living agree, then what will be the Archives' role?"

"Something essential," Jy purred. "You will remain on this earth and oversee the work that must be done. We will need power, vast amounts of reliable power, if we are going to move people and equipment in both directions." She gave a few technical details to prove her competence, then she asked, "Is this coherent? Do you understand me?"

"Of course we understand," said the united voices.

Jy thought to bow very low in a sign of respect.

"Naturally we need time and more information,"

they warned, "but it seems quite promising at first glance."

Jy bit her hand with excitement.

"We will be important in this mission of yours?" they inquired.

"Vital," she responded. "Absolutely vital."

There was a pause and a strange rumbling sound, some great debate beginning within the Archives' ranks. Already Jy had her supporters as well as her foes, and it would be several years before every Archive was ready to vote for the mission and the quest for the Makers. But the process was begun, and eventually she was holding her first rallies, telling small crowds that this would be a pilgrimage, vast and glorious, that all other human adventure would be dwarfed by its scale. The robot probes they had sent to the stars and the galactic core were simple diversions in comparison. Their galaxy was beautiful and strange, but there was no other intelligence besides the human beings on the other earths, and the great Makers themselves. If the Founders wanted companionship, she argued, they had to strike out along the Bright. They had no other choice but to remain here and do nothing new forever—

"What if these Makers are hostile?" cried some people. "We will expose ourselves to them! Is this a smart thing to do?"

"And what about other dangers?" asked different skeptics. "There could be terrors that we cannot even imagine, and you want us to go hunting for them?"

Jy countered with a grin and hard words.

"We do take precautions," she explained, "because we are not fools." She had already devised safety systems, a score of them, and she challenged her audiences to invent their own. She wanted ideas! She screamed for ideas! Then she paused and shook her head and asked, "What do *you* want as our legacy? What else could we do as a species that could compare to the mission? We have found this astounding thing, we have a multitude of living earths under our toes . . . and do we ignore them? Is that what you would have us do?"

"How long will this mission take us?" they cried.

Jy had no clue. "A long while," she confessed. She waited a dramatic moment before saying, "Perhaps it will take thousands of years, or tens of thousands." She never imagined *a million years* as a possible reply. "We will acquire converts as we move among our Cousins, and the Archives will grant us more power and range." Again she used her smile. "We will give our bodies a durability for the sake of continuity. We are not colonists or invaders. We will be examples of our species, all of the species, and it will take us as long as it takes us. I can promise nothing else."

Jy won her battles, in the end.

By then she was even grayer than she looked today, and she was weaker. She had felt joyous and redeemed but very tired. The Founders picked a few tens of thousands of themselves to become pilgrims. Laws were changed and ethics were revised, and each pilgrim was given a fresh new body while the rest prepared to stay behind. They would live out their lives in the honorable fashion, and when their bodies failed they would join the Archives and help design the machines and robots and the changing earth.

It was a million years ago . . . and who would have guessed?

Jy couldn't imagine that span, although she had lived it. She had been present at the official start. She remembered the day with its music and the cheers and the great crystal portal with a rope of flowers being held across its entranceway. She could see herself lifting an arm, her right arm, and there was a sudden hush. She was untying the flower rope and smiling at the young Founders who held it, each of them picked specially for the moment, and her hands trembled and the flowers dropped and the crowd screamed in one joyous voice, dancing now, and Jy stepped into the portal and wept with her palms to her eyes and tears down her face, hoping it was joy that made her weep . . . only she wasn't certain. It was a wondrous day and an incredible moment and for an eerie while Jy was terrified, absolutely terrified, that this was a mistake and she was a fool and now she was starting something that would end horribly to-morrow or the next day or maybe the next . . . .

5

THERE WAS a time when I was completely in charge of every facet of the mission, but that time has passed as the scale of everything has swollen. Now I play only a glancing role in the day-to-day duties. I rule my entourage, in a fashion, and I read the reports that time allows me. I offer opinions to associates ten thousand times more expert than myself, and those experts treat me with that steady respect I hope I deserve. Then they conscientiously act in the best interest of the mission.

Some days I feel like a precious novelty, charming and ancient and well-intentioned, but a novelty nonetheless. . . .

—*Jy's chronicles*

White Cloud was much as Jy had imagined it.

The town clung to the margins of the muddy river, and for a moment she was remembering some of the hundreds of thousands of names for that river. Jy was stepping down the stairs from her ship's underbelly, feeling the skin-crackling pulses of its engines. Her ship was hovering above the concrete highway and the other entourage ships were scattered about the area, each one the color and texture of bone, egg-shaped, no two exactly the same. Some of her people came from the other ships and surrounded her, supplying escorts as she walked up from the highway to the brief central street with forested bluffs on both sides and the river behind her. The local residents gathered, eyes wide and their voices rather nervous, whispering, "There she goes," and then, "That's Jy, that one there. See her?"

She had a clear idea of whom she wanted to find.

She was hunting for a certain unmistakable face among the little crowd.

Her entourage had to look incredible to the residents of White Cloud. Here was a collection of strange upright monkeys and heavy-skulled dwarfs mixed with an assortment of younger races. Jy could appreciate the spooked expressions and the whispers. This was perfect! she thought. Then she found the face she wanted. It belonged to a man of some size and obvious disgust, a bitter and plainly ignorant man who hadn't liked the Wanderers from their first appearance. He was standing among the others, glaring at these abominations. He was disgusted, looking ill with anger and rather pale and sweaty. At any moment he might explode.

Jy herself was in no danger, yet she felt a palpable tension when she forced herself toward the angry man, legs aching and her brittle joints cracking and her softest voice asking, "Why do you hate me, sir? What have I done to you?"

The man was shocked.

His feelings were probably common knowledge in White Cloud. He probably had his corner in the bar or the barbershop and grumbled at length about the Wanderers, those treacherous invaders. But to have Jy herself come here and find him as she did . . . .well, it made him tremble. He shook his head. He had to put his feet farther apart like someone trying to keep his balance.

She repeated her question. "Why do you hate me?"

The other Wanderers spread into a fan-shaped mass behind her, and they waited. They had seen Jy attempt this trick many times.

The man growled and found his voice somewhere in his gut, telling her, "It's our earth! Ours!" He shook his head and halfway smiled, regaining a measure of his composure. This was his chance to tell his feelings to someone who mattered, and he damn well would. "You come here uninvited," he snarled, "you and your . . . your people, and you change everything! You can't leave anything alone, and that's what I hate." He snorted. "Bastards!"

Neighbors and his scarce friends were shying away.

Jy said, "We are not invaders," while letting the tone of her voice carry her message. She showed sympathy fused with sincerity, plus a measure of passion and an undeniable love. "We are simply passing through your earth, and briefly, and we won't disturb you any more than we must. I promise."

The man snorted again.

"You can't believe me?" she asked.

"I want you gone!"

Jy was ready for him. "You want?" she said. "Who wants? Just who are you, sir?" She glanced at the nervous faces around him, and she smiled in a large way. "Believe me," she told the angry man, "since the instant we arrived on *your* earth we have worked to leave again and leave you and yours happier, richer, safer, and equipped to meet your own destiny——"

"You're devils spouting devil talk!"

She waited a moment before asking, "Why are we devils, sir?"

"Because you talk *evolution* when anyone with Christian sense knows there's no such creature. We're all God's plan, and you can't tell me otherwise."

He was a religious fundamentalist, she realized, filled with considerable bile. Again she waited a moment, then asked, "What have we done that is devilish, sir? I want you to show me one specific thing." She didn't wait for a response. "I mean what I say, sir. You have had months to watch us and you have heard people talk about us, and tell me why you are confusing us with devils. Say what you wish. Perhaps I can fix the wrongs. I am quite eager to hear."

The man muttered something beneath his breath.

"Has a Wanderer come to you and told you, 'This is what you will think and believe from this day onward'?" Jy said, "Have we injured you in some financial way? Have we hurt any of your family or friends? Tell me. I want to hear everything." She sighed and brightened her smile, showing no malice. "Where have *I* gone wrong, sir?"

"Devil talk——"

"I can't hear you!"

Now his face became red and the eyes watered and the man's hard words stuck in his throat. Nobody else made a sound. White Cloud held its collective breath.

"We speak as we believe," Jy confessed. "Would you prefer us to do otherwise, sir? Should we suppress what we think and what we feel, lying to you and to everyone just to look better in your eyes?"

The man wheezed.

"Sir?" said Jy.

He shook his head, furious beyond words.

"Yes, sir?"

The man couldn't tolerate the tension any longer. He turned abruptly and marched down the street and around the first corner, one hand on his head as if he were keeping the vessels of his brain from exploding. All at once the community started to apologize for having him. Jy could see the apologies on their faces. This was what she had come to find, a bitter person beyond her reach and a chance to seem both tough and honest in front of sober people—only, had she seemed too tough? There were probably many more fundamentalists in this crowd. Wanderers must be a strange challenge to their literal faith. But no, she observed, people seemed to appreciate her honesty. Jy glanced at them and gave a sorrowful smile. She regretted the scene as much as anyone. Then she launched into a little speech about staying true to your beliefs and honoring the beliefs of others and she hoped she was no devil in their eyes— was she?—and she gave a little shrug and a grin.

Most of the audience seemed enchanted.

Then Jy eased into another speech about the Bright and the far Makers and how she would tell the Makers about this fine community set beside the strong brown river. She meant her words. She had done this work for so long, yet she rarely felt her energies ebbing or tasted anything wrong in her mouth. Suddenly Jy was pleased with everything. It was amazing how little rancor the Wanderers had left behind them. Their success was one of her great prides. A part of Jy watched herself talking to this small crowd until everyone was smiling, nodding to themselves and giggling and finally applauding. Then she was leaving again. She was walking to her ship and children were at her heels, and she said, "Good-bye and thank you," while waving a spidery hand. "The best of luck to all of you and thanks! Thank you for your patience and your time and good day! Good day!"

MOLIAK

1

MY NIGHTMARE begins with me entering the unFound's bunker in disguise, appearing to belong to this particular tribe, and the guards greet me and send me deeper until I am miles beneath the surface. I walk past chambers where the tribe synthesizes its foods and clean water, past the machine shops and the warehouses and the extensive armories. Then I enter the living quarters, the heart of the unFound, and they hug me and kiss me and I like their attentions. It is a horrible sensation. I feel a potent sense of belonging to this place, and then I happen to find my reflection in one of the polished composite walls, and I am not even in disguise. All I wear is my own body, and look at me! Look! I can't believe what I see! Look . . . !
                                    —*Moliak's private journal*

All at once Moliak forgot what was going to happen.
     He was standing at the front door, watching the

curling street and the identical watered green lawns and the cars both parked and moving, and he suddenly was aware of losing something important, sensing it and pausing and for a sliver of an instant searching within himself for this thing he could not name. How remarkable! he thought. Events were culminating today, in a matter of hours, and all of his effort and planning and the risks and the sheer nervous tensions were too much, making Moliak lose his place and his purpose.

He was surrounded by Mr. Phillips's home—*this* he remembered—and he was sipping some of the man's good whiskey from a knobby glass. Moliak took a long sip and breathed and cleared his mind, wondering why he was here. And after a moment he remembered. He was amazed he could forget any of it, for any time, and he gave a little shiver while swallowing, and he shook his head and allowed himself a momentary grin.

This was an enormous undertaking, and immediate, and that was why he had forgotten what would happen.

Moliak's harried brain couldn't cope and it had shut down, leaving him in a sudden darkness.

It was a human enough response, he judged—he couldn't let it happen again—and with that he took another sip and turned away from the door, walking into the big clean kitchen. Cotton was downstairs trying to rest. Moliak could hear the squawk of the television and Cotton muttering to himself and sometimes there was a faint vibration that was nothing. It was the water heater or the air-conditioning or a truck rumbling through the quiet neighborhood. Moliak started to think about the plan, every facet of it giving him doubts. He didn't dare to list all the details that might go sour on them. It was lucky he had decided on Cotton, he told himself, trying to accent the positive. More and more Cotton was proving he was still loyal and smart—an ideal soldier and his most trusted friend—and Moliak could scarcely imagine carrying out any of this without his linchpin beside him.

Moliak strolled through the upstairs portion of the house. There were a spacious dining room and living room, three bedrooms, and the main bath. There was a reassuring order to everything, and everything was clean enough to look new. By the standards of his earth, Mr. Phillips had led a successful life. His success showed in the furniture and the hanging artwork, in authentic antiques set in discrete places. The man had loved this home, and his mind still glowed with his affections. Moliak felt the emotions, and if needed, he could use them.

Mr. Phillips had been a good choice.

He was supplying the ideal camouflage—trusted and harmless. That was why Moliak had acquired him.

This was also the ideal location, he told himself. There was a small portal nearby and a brief visit that had been scheduled long ago. It helped Moliak's mood to consider what was working for the best. He was thinking about this place and Mr. Phillips and Cotton too, and suddenly it seemed as if some higher authority were overseeing Moliak's work, steering him in the proper directions—

—an illusion, of course.

He knew it was an illusion and not particularly original, and probably a dangerous way to think. Divine guidance led to complacency and worse. It was another human trait to impress order on your circumstances, and Moliak shrugged it off and grinned for a moment. Sometimes he wondered if he had retained his humanness, his essential self. He focused on his little failings as evidence that the damned unFound had not stolen his entire soul . . . and that seemed like very good news for a moment or two.

Everything *seemed* to be progressing well.

The local Wanderers were oblivious to them. Moliak knew their security systems better than they knew them, and his constant checks proved nobody was alarmed.

Why should anyone worry?

They had this innocent earth happy and excited. The news from Geneva, just this morning, said an accord between all nations was coming in a day or two or three and then there would be a final signing by all world leaders in attendance, and the innocent smiling sweet Wanderers would make everything into a grand ceremony.

Innocent was a curse in Moliak's realm.

People fought to the death because one had called another "innocent" with the wrong tone.

Moliak shut his eyes and breathed deeply, thinking about everything and nothing and then hearing applause coming from downstairs. It was on the television and very much out of place. He returned to the kitchen in an attempt to follow Mr. Phillips's routines, rinsing the liquor from the glass and setting the glass upside down on the dishwasher's upper rack, just so, and then he lifted the phone's receiver and punched the private number for work. Mr. Phillips's secretary answered on the second ring, and he asked about her day. What had happened at the plant and was any of it important? He spoke exactly as Mr. Phillips would have spoken, word for word. He even allowed himself small errors in judgement because the soft neurons in his head were a little bit drunk and careless.

Nothing should be abnormal.

Habit made Moliak want to play this role so even suspicious eyes would see nothing amiss.

"I'll come in tomorrow," he remarked. "Probably late."

"Now you have a good time tonight, sir. Promise me." The secretary was named Doris, and she had been with Mr. Phillips for nearly fifteen years. "Promise me?"

"Yes, Doris."

"And bring your nephew to work sometime. We'd love to meet him."

"I will." Here was another point in Mr. Phillips's favor—he had a vague family not seen in years. "I sure will."

"And shake Jy's hand for me, will you? And tell her she's one great broad?" There was a rasping laugh at the other end of the line. "Will you do that?"

"'One great broad.' I will."

"No, you won't, and I'll see you late tomorrow. If then." Moliak heard the *click* after a moment, and he felt Mr. Phillips's mind trying to think about his secretary. He was trying to recall her face and her steady mothering and he felt a nagging sadness—he knew pieces of what would happen soon—and Moliak heard

himself mutter, "Stop that," under his breath. "Stop!"
He found the mirrored toaster and lifted it to his face,
and he tried to make certain that the face and particularly
the eyes still held their blandness. He suddenly was
terrified that the conquered mind could be a threat to
him somehow. *Everything can betray,* he reminded himself, *and given enough time, everything will.*

2

> I MOVED him cold because it was the safest
> means. Cotton dropped his metabolism to
> where even the lowest castes would complain,
> and I packed him inside whatever was conve-
> nient and shielded him with all the best tricks
> and only once did someone discover him. A
> novice found him by chance, tucked inside ma-
> chinery, and I had no other option.
>
> Cotton never learned about the novice.
>
> He was too cold to perceive anything, not
> even motions, and I did what was best and kept
> the murder my secret because I know him. I
> know Cotton would accept what happened if I
> told him to accept it, but nonetheless feel in
> some miniscule way to blame....
>
>   —*Moliak's private journal*

Moliak had lived inside a variety of Wanderer bodies in
these last years, striving to make plans and always appear
entirely normal. His hard-memory was unusual, subtle
and woven into each mind and practically invisible to
probes and sensors. Autodocs made the transfers, and
every previous host was left to die. There were security
considerations involved. Cotton knew the considerations
and accepted the murder of each Wanderer, though his
innate sense of pecking orders meant he would always
grieve. Every Wanderer was worthy of Cotton's respect.
He had to take comfort in the image of the two of them

cleansing what was the greater wrong, and Moliak respected him for his grief. There were even moments when he felt guilty for not grieving too. Maybe he was envious. Certainly once or twice he had felt angry at his suffering companion.

The body-hopping tricks were extremely advanced. Jy and her people wouldn't understand them or suspect anything like them could exist.

Both men had started traveling toward this earth years ago. Moliak had read the initial scouting reports and shown them to Cotton, and Cotton had said, "A fat sweet earth, and almost empty."

"By your standards," Moliak had reminded him.

The small man had nodded and smiled, saying, "Fat and sweet and empty," with the wrinkles showing on his face.

Now Cotton was in a much more glum mood, watching a noisy television program with its contrived cheeriness washing over him. Moliak had just come downstairs. He paused and looked at the flickering screen, the program's host handsome by local norms and well-dressed and absolutely thrilled to be handing the keys to a car to one of the contestants.

Cotton and Moliak could talk as they wished in the basement. Baffles and electronic tricks kept away any prying eyes.

"What are you thinking, my friend?" asked Moliak.

"Not very much." Cotton was eating hard candy and licorice. Since yesterday he had laid down a thick mass of Termite fat, and the fat showed in his rounded face and through his thickening hands. "Uncle," said Cotton, and he offered a quick weak smile. "How are you?"

"I am well." Moliak sat beside him and they held hands. It was a friendly gesture between Termites—the ritualistic sharing of heat—and Moliak studied Cotton's posture and the heavy chin and the way he stared at the ridiculous program with something approximating interest.

"Do you know what we say about television?" he asked.

Cotton said, "What?"

"'Television is the window to its earth.'"

Cotton squinted without moving his face, without breaking his apparent concentration.

"Television opens every culture to us, and for free."

"Reasonable," Cotton allowed.

There was more excitement. A thickly built middle-aged woman started jumping in place and screaming. She seemed to have won a giant freezer filled with frosty chops and steaks and roasts.

Cotton was laughing without pleasure.

"How do you feel?" asked Moliak.

Cotton took several quick breaths.

"Are you keeping a rein on your heat?"

"Mostly."

Moliak nodded. "Will you be ready?"

"Yes."

They let go of each other's hands and Cotton was eating again. He pulled a box from under the sofa. Inside were oatmeal sandwiches filled with a whitish coconut and palm-oil mush, and he stacked them on his lap and began to eat them. Moliak leaned forwards. There was a large book on the coffee table and he pulled it into his lap with both hands. It was a collection of quotes from Jy's speeches and her chronicles—an ornate hardcover bestseller—and a stiff cardboard bookmark stuck out of one end.

Moliak withdrew the bookmark.

Cotton said, "Don't."

"Why not?"

"You lost my place."

They tried smiling and shook their heads while saying nothing. Then Moliak flipped through the book several times, going too fast to see anything but the blurring pages. He could smell a faint crisp chemical odor, then he smelled only paper and ink. Then he replaced the bookmark and wondered, "Are you reading it?"

Cotton seemed to shake his head. "No."

"Maybe you should in case someone asks a question." Moliak looked at the back cover—a large and artful photograph of Jy filled his lap, the gold edging of her eyes catching some unseen light—and all at once he was close to tears. The emotions came to him suddenly and changed his mood, and he breathed and put the book on the table and stacked magazines on top of it while giving a little moan.

This is insane, he told himself.

What happens when you finally see her?

Cotton watched him.

You shit-filled innocent!

Again they held hands, and Cotton's grip was warm and only a little too strong. "Do you know what keeps happening to me?" Cotton mentioned. "I can't seem to stop it—"

"What?"

"I looked around and it feels as though I am coming from a dream. I see what is around me and I don't know where I am or what I'm doing here . . . Isn't that remarkable?"

Moliak said nothing.

The well-dressed host on the television was waving out at them, wishing them good tidings.

The original free gift, thought Moliak. *The giving of good luck* . . . .

Cotton took Moliak's hand in both of his hands and squeezed firmly and made a soft low sound.

There had to be words to be said now, thought Moliak.

He was sure there was something smart and proper . . . only he couldn't find any words. He tried and then he quit, then he leaned backwards and shut his eyes.

BILLIE

1

WE STRIVE for a variety of people who want to
serve as Wanderers, all of whom adore the very
idea of the Makers.

—*Jy's speeches*

She made her decision that afternoon, during the lull
after the first rally began. She was stocking shelves,
kneeling on the hard tiled floor while thinking her usual
tangled thoughts—about beautiful wise perfect Jy, of
course; and Kyle, of course; plus Janice and her latest
noise. Janice was inside Billie's head, telling her that it
was silly to date a Wanderer and expect anything but
fun. She said a Wanderer would leave, he had to leave,
because Kyle wasn't going to give up everything for
a piece of ass. That was the truth, promised Janice,
and Billie had better not entertain foolish hopes
here. "Be careful," warned Janice. "Will you please be
careful?"

Billie shook her head, trying to clear it.

There were so many problems and so many things

begging to be done, and she felt as if her life were packed too tight. She felt like one of those bits of degenerate matter that the Makers had strewn throughout the earth—the ones Kyle had explained to stupid her, that helped the Bright work—and now she couldn't think of anything else. She was remembering how anything compressed could reach a point where it bent time-space in the right ways, where it was smaller than small, and that's what was happening to her life now. That's exactly how it felt.

These last weeks had been squeezing down hard on her. She had kept it from Kyle, naturally. He wouldn't want to hear about her stupid silly problems. Would he? She was concerned about the two of them and where they were going. She had been thinking about going to meet Jy for a long while, somehow never feeling sure enough to just ask Kyle if they could. But of course they could go. Right? She certainly felt happy, at least sometimes. And in love? Maybe. It felt like love when she was with Kyle and everything was going fine. But those times were happening less, which worried her something awful, because if she couldn't love a man as splendid as Kyle, she wondered, who could she ever love? And that kind of thinking made the pressures worse and worse, threatening to crash her into a spot of that heavy nothing. She could feel the collapse beginning.

Billie couldn't just talk to Kyle. It was Janice who had to hear everything, and it was Janice who told Billie not to think so much. She was always thinking too much. It did no good, argued her roommate, so quit doing it. That's how simple things were.

"Just have fun," Janice would say. "I mean it. I think he's a pretty odd bucket, but you enjoy him more than you don't and that's fine. Just keep remembering that he's got bigger things in life than you, girl, and don't fool yourself."

"I'm trying not to," Billie would begin.

"So don't," said Janice. "Just don't."

Everyday, maybe a hundred times everyday, Billie would see how inadequate she was for Kyle. She was stupid and slow, not worth any of his time whatsoever. How could she be? She tried imagining the impossible, exotic places he had seen. He was thousands of years old! He was so old he had never told her how old, and she felt like the most ignorant little girl when they were together. What could Kyle ever see in her?

"It's because you're adorable." That was Janice's guess. "And that you remind him of his girlfriends back home."

Maybe so, thought Billie. Maybe.

"And because he's a male," Janice added with emphasis. "And you keep treating him like men like. You act as if he's some kind of god."

Wasn't he? she wondered. What in the world else could he be?

Billie was busy shelving some of the new books about the Wanderers and Jy; and all at once she was thinking back to their first date and how Kyle had been such a gentleman, perfectly mannered and charming with his stories about people and earths she couldn't even picture. They had walked downtown for pizza and then gone to a movie. She'd carried the Chekhov book she was reading then because maybe he would leave her alone sometime and she wouldn't have anything to do. She always took a book wherever she went, and Kyle had understood. At least he seemed to. She remembered how they got to the movie late and they sat alone in the roped-off balcony, Kyle saying nobody would mind. And sure enough, the usher who found them saw what Kyle was and said to stay. As long as they wanted, he said. And did they want him to bring up any popcorn or anything? On the house?

Billie had such fun. The movie was funny and stupid, but Kyle seemed to enjoy it. That was Kyle. Then they went for a long slow curling walk through campus, and when it started raining they sat alone beneath a raised sidewalk and Kyle kissed her. Billie hadn't expected it, and she was glad to be surprised. Otherwise she would have been a quaking mess, worried and guarded and too ready. He was a good kisser—that was her first thought. Then Kyle pressed close and put a long thumb on her sternum, pushing but not hard, and she tasted the damp tip of his tongue pressing against her tongue. The thumb snuck closer to a breast, then it stopped. Later, when Billie admitted that much to Janice, Janice said, "He sounds like a schoolboy. Doesn't he? Afraid to try and afraid not to try. Go figure."

Billie had never admitted the rest of it. But Janice probably figured it on her own, knowing her roommate as she did. Probably at a glance.

They had gone to Kyle's new apartment after the rain. Billie was torn in a thousand directions, wondering what to do and what to say and praying everything would turn out all right. She knew how she *should* act, being a good and decent girl with upstanding parents and all. But she was with Kyle in his living room, and they were necking again. They were sprawled out on the musty floor, and she couldn't help herself. She kept thinking about what Kyle was and where he had traveled, and whenever he spoke she seemed to hear the centuries talking. Was that corny, or what? The centuries and all that wisdom, and Kyle removed her blouse and then the rest of her clothes, and his own, and Billie looked at his ropy penis, circumcised, and she heard herself repeating something she had heard. Every Wanderer was sterilized when they became a Wanderer, right? Because Jy said it wouldn't be proper or smart to make babies on strange earths. Was that true? And Kyle—she recalled this clearly—Kyle seemed to hesitate for a long moment. He leaned backwards with one hand touching himself, holding himself, and his eyes were distant and odd. He was such a strange-looking man. What was wrong? What was he thinking? Then he cleared his throat with effort, he cleared it twice, and he told Billie, "That's true," with a whisper.

She watched him, and she waited.

All her confusion had evaporated. She wanted to let him do anything he wanted, it didn't matter what they did. But then Kyle was talking, saying, "It's not so simple," with his voice tight and small. "On my earth . . . we have a tradition . . . ." He stood over Billie with a thin clear stream of fluid hanging in the air. "Just a minute."

He wiped himself and vanished into the bedroom. She heard a drawer open and close, then he emerged with a single sealed condom—an ordinary brand, lubricated and textured—and he told her, "We once had diseases on my earth, and we have customs . . . not that I have anything wrong. I don't. I've got little medical robots inside me and long-lasting medicines that kill anything wrong . . . you see?"

"A custom," she echoed.

"Exactly."

She muttered, "That's fine," and watched him unwrap the condom and position it, kneeling on the matted carpet with his odd face suddenly handsome to her. He seemed handsome and caring and timid; he seemed perishable in some curious way. Then he came over her and said, "Is this . . . am I?" and she said, "Almost," while positioning herself. Then she said, "*There*," and relaxed, giving a long slow bright moan with her arms reaching around Kyle's back and touching each other while she pulled him closer, pulling him down . . . .

Billie shivered and gave a little smile.

She stood. Every shelved book was in its place, at last, and she heard people coming through the store. There were more people than the girls in the front could handle. Billie went to help. Little groups of smiling adults wanted books about Wanderers. They had come here from everywhere to watch a rally, and what did she recommend? What told the most? Billie remembered the titles Kyle liked the best. There were books about Jy and her long-ago earth, about Founders and the Archives, and of course there were collections of Jy's speeches and selections from her famous huge chronicles. One customer wanted a list of the nearby earths, plus their descriptions . . . was there any such bird? No, there wasn't. The Wanderers tried keeping those details to a minimum, she explained, and for an instant she considered retelling some of Kyle's own stories to satisfy everyone. What would they think? She could say she was dating a Wanderer and would meet Jy tonight, and just imagining their faces made her smile and almost laugh to herself.

The customers started falling off again. Billie got busy with more shelving, and she started trying to picture tonight. Kyle would take her to the rally and then to Jy, and it seemed too incredible. It never felt real. So she quit thinking about that and returned to the decision she had made earlier today. It was her big brave decision. Billie was going to talk to Kyle, whenever it felt right. She had something important and serious to ask, and she would say it in one breath.

"Do you think I'd make a good Wanderer, Kyle?"

She knew how he would respond. She pictured them in bed, and Kyle waiting a moment before asking her, "Why do you want to be a Wanderer? Is there a reason?"

"There's nothing better to be," she would tell him. "Is there?"

He would say, "I don't think so," or something similar.

"I think it would be splendid," she would admit. Only what kind of answer was that? It sounded incredibly shallow, didn't it? "What do you think, Kyle? Would I help the mission? Would Jy be proud of me?"

Kyle would keep still and silent, his face unreadable. She knew just how he would look. Then he would clear his throat, and he would say, "No. No, Billie, I don't think you would make much of a Wanderer," and that would be that. He would have to answer honestly, and that was all Billie wanted. She had to hear the verdict, just once.

"No," said Kyle's voice, "you couldn't join us. It's too demanding and you would waste your life in the end."

That was all she wanted, really. She had to ask and hear that there wasn't any reason to try.

She would know the truth and accept it.

She'd make herself accept it.

And from then on, she decided, she could go on with her life and know that whatever happened was for the best.

She would know for sure.

2

MY ANCESTRAL village had a proud unbroken history reaching backward for nine hundred centuries, and it was rather famous as home to some great scientists and thinkers. My people helped discover that the earth revolves about the sun and that hydrogen burns with ease, making light and helium, and we helped formulate the first world government in human history—the essence of what is the Wanderers today. And one of us, an ancient and grand philosopher at the very beginning of the Founder society, helped to codify that school of thought whereby our species cared for our earth as we cared for our flesh. Everything was in moderation and no village asked for more than its fair portion. People acted like the organs and tissues and cells of the competent body; no cause was loftier than the search for the unimpeachable good . . . .

—*Jy's speeches*

Billie came out into the heat of the day. She could hear the distant, tireless buzz of thousands of people in the stadium, and she walked with a quick step, her book bag tugging on one shoulder. She kept glancing at her watch. She was supposed to be home by now. Janice was probably wondering why she was late and muttering to herself, "That girl. It's just like that girl."

She crossed the filled parking lots and climbed onto the graveled railroad beds, crossing the polished steel tracks and then going down again. The stadium lay to the south. It was capped with a thin blackish tent meant to keep out the sunshine and any rains. The Wanderers had brought the tent. Kyle had tried explaining how it worked to keep the air inside cool and clean, but Billie had never quite understood his explanations. She was always a little bit too dim, it seemed.

Janice waited in the kitchen, tapping one foot.

"First scrub up," she commanded. "Then we'll make you into the most delectable primate anywhere on the Bright."

Billie took a steamy bath.

Afterward Janice took a fast shower and came into Billie's bedroom dripping, and she saw the clean red dress hanging on the closet door.

"Too slutty," she warned.

"I was wearing it when I met Kyle."

"That explains a few things." Instead, Janice picked cool slacks and a frilly feminine blouse the color of ivory, then she added her own jewelry to the package. Janice had collected all sorts of jewelry over the years, from suitors and lecherous uncles and such. There was a gold necklace and a gold bracelet and then earrings that looked like fishing lures. Then came the bitch-business of makeup. Was this enough makeup? Janice promised it was. Don't worry. Then she was dressing herself, and Billie tried to help her pick and choose. Janice started teasing her about her ignorance of fashion, and that meant Billie could tease Janice about her string of well-built, smooth-brained manly males. It was good-natured teasing and quite fun, and they ended up giggling in the kitchen. Should they eat anything? Oh no, thought Billie, she was too nervous to eat. It was already night outside, and where were their men? A quarterback was going to take Janice to the rally, and it somehow bothered Billie that she had Kyle and Kyle was the better man. This wasn't the natural order of things, was it? She started toying with the borrowed bracelet and sighing, then someone was knocking on the door. *Dunt, dunt, dunt.*

It was Kyle's knock, regular as a metronome. Janice said, "Yours," and Billie opened the door to find both dates waiting. Kyle was standing beside the quarterback—a third-stringer on a so-so team—and both men were smiling shyly while white moths fluttered around the porch light and their heads.

She felt herself weaken and heard herself say, "Come in. Please?"

There was still time to sit and do nothing. They joined Janice at the kitchen table, and Kyle said, "We met on the stairs. We arrived at the same time," and he looked at Billie's watch. He held her wrist and looked, and didn't seem to notice the jewelry or anything else about her appearance. Why should he notice? she asked herself. Then she was suddenly quite hungry, and she rose and pulled a sack of chocolate chip cookies from a high cupboard.

Everyone took cookies.

Kyle didn't eat, however. Two or three times he put a cookie to his mouth and almost took a bite, then set it down on the tabletop and stared at the delicate brown stains on his fingertips.

He was acting odd, even for Kyle.

Janice noticed and gave Billie a glance while shrugging her shoulders. Oh, well. What can you do? *Men!*

Billie kept eating; she was suddenly famished.

The quarterback tried to talk to Kyle, forcing aside his own shyness. "So you're a Wanderer, huh?" He said, "Huh! Isn't that something?"

Janice said it was time to leave.

Kyle shrugged and said, "Do you play football?"

Everyone was up and filing out the door. They went onto the porch with its fierce soft moths everywhere, then they went down the creaking stairs. Janice's man was asking, "Where you come from, do they have a game like football? Anything like it at all?"

Kyle shook his head. "Not really," he muttered.

"Do you know the game? Have you ever seen it played?"

"No."

The quarterback burst into a breathless explanation of the rules and the basic schemes, talking about taking territory and holding it. Then he told stories out of his own nonlustrous career. He described hard runs up the middle and long passes just out of reach. They had crossed the railroad tracks and reached a parking lot, rows upon rows of cars stretching in all directions, and he said, "Hey, I've got it!" and began to pry a red Styrofoam football from the top of a car antenna.

"What are you doing?" snapped Janice.

"Kyle?" the quarterback said. "Go on out." He had a boyish voice and a confident pose. "Go running that way and let me loft it to you!"

Billie was embarrassed, but she kept quiet.

"Will you stop?" asked Janice.

But then Kyle was running forwards, his motions jerky and short and his sandals slapping beneath him.

"Here it comes!"

The quarterback shoved the little football into the air, and it fluttered and fell short by quite a distance. Yet Kyle kept running past the parked cars with his face forwards and his graceless long legs moving faster. Billie watched him reach the end of the row—"Hey, Kyle! You went too far, buddy!"—and for an instant she believed he was going to keep running. He seemed to find more speed for a moment, then he sputtered and stopped and looked down at the pavement. He was waiting for them. He put a hand on a fender and didn't move.

"You've got to look over your shoulder, buddy!"

"Leave him alone," said Janice.

"Is everything okay?" Billie asked Kyle. She got up against him. "Is it?" Something was wrong. She knew it with a glance.

Kyle shook his head, saying nothing.

She grasped his hand and found it drenched with perspiration.

"You run funny," the quarterback declared.

Kyle lifted his eyes. "Do I?"

"I thought Wanderers would run prettier than that." He seemed genuinely relieved, saying, "You stink," in a friendly manner.

Kyle shrugged and produced a dreamy smile.

"Let's get motoring," said Janice.

"Can we?" asked Billie.

Then they heard the crowd in the distance, all at once, and the clapping and cheering rose until the air around them seemed to quiver.

3

TODAY A cute imp of a boy came to me and asked if I was married. He was lovely. His scalp and neck and broad back were covered with masses of golden hair and his bright turquoise eyes were plainly hopeful, and I smiled at him and informed him, "I am thoroughly married to my mission."

"Not to a man, huh?" he exclaimed. His expression seemed disgusted, and he shook his head and sneered at me. At me! "So what do you do for fun?" he wanted to know. He was such a crude imp. "What do you do when you want—you know—"

"I hold rallies," I exclaimed.

"Rallies?" he asked.

"They are my lovers," I maintained. "They are my passion, dear boy."

—*Jy's speeches*

The rally preceding theirs had started late and gone long. The four of them had to wait outside, standing behind barriers, watching the smiling crowd file out and away. Then Janice told Billie to say, "Hi," to Jy for her. The quarterback's tickets put them with the rest of the team, over on the other side of the stadium. She gave Billie the car keys. "Take care, roommate. Bye, Kyle. Have fun!"

The atmosphere inside resembled that of a rock concert. Or did it? It was certainly a well-mannered rock concert. Kyle's tickets took them close to the stage, and Billie sat and thought it was more like a religious event than any concert. Then she was thinking it wasn't that,

DOWN THE BRIGHT WAY

either. There were too many kinds of people here, too many sorts of clothes, and wasn't it lovely? Everyone was quiet and orderly while being excited too.

People were noticing Kyle.

Billie was halfway accustomed to glances and outright stares and the way people would whisper and smile. Yet there were so many people doing it, she had to work to ignore them. She looked overhead at the weightless lights drifting against the black roof. Those were Wanderer lights, yellowy-white like miniature suns, and they made everything feel pleasant and warm and somehow close. There was an intimacy here, and she gave a large sigh and looked for other Wanderers scattered through the crowd.

"Do you know her?" Billie asked. "Do you know him?"

She did her own pointing now.

Kyle said, "No," every time. There were millions of Wanderers, he had to remind her, and he didn't know any of *them*. "Sorry."

People quit filing into the stadium, and the lights diminished to embers. Billie had seen a thousand rallies on television, in full or in part, and certain elements were set in stone. Yet this wasn't television, she reminded herself. This was reality, large and bright and sweet. A blue-green image of the earth formed overhead, and Billie gave a start because it seemed ready to crash down on them. It was a real earth with the clouds showing depth and the brilliant Antarctic icecap producing a tangible chill. A voice was saying, "This is our earth. Everyone's," and she felt the voice echoing against her bones—a deep sexless voice sounding familiar and exotic in the same instant.

Everything was explained as if for the first time.

Billie heard about the Wanderers and the Bright, and she watched while she listened to every word.

The floating earth divided and divided again. It resembled an egg transforming itself into a blastulalike mass of little earths, and the booming voice spoke of Reality coming in many forms, perhaps endless forms. The words were simple and direct. There were moments when she very nearly understood all of it—when her tiny brain could almost comprehend this tangled endless Reality—and she grasped Kyle's hand and squeezed until he returned her squeeze. Then they were bathed in a radiant white light and could see nothing else. This was the Bright, she knew. This had to be the Bright, and she squinted and oohed and began to shiver.

Kyle made a sound under his breath.

Billie leaned to him and gushed, "It's wonderful! Isn't it?"

This Bright was an illusion. Projection devices created the illusion, but to her it was still strange and wondrous. "We are following a highway beyond human comprehension," said the voice, "and we are pledged to a great quest." She felt the power of the words. She was sweating, the air becoming close and stale. The voice told of following the Makers along the Bright and touching every earth along the way. Then the Bright dissolved into blackness. There was silence for a moment. Then the voice cried, *"We will find them and everything will be made clear!"*

Billie giggled and sighed and felt splendid.

Lights appeared above the stage, clustered together, and a lone bent-backed figure stood on the yellow planks of new wood. It had to be Jy. She was dressed in gray, her chest thick and flat and her long arms ending with long elegant hands. Her swollen head twisted from side to side. Then a soft, almost feathery voice lifted over the crowd. Jy was speaking to Billie and no one else.

"We are the humble servants of our mission," said Jy. "At least I hope we are humble," and something honest showed through her words. Billie heard a musical laugh, then Jy continued. "For all the knowledge we have gathered and all that we might learn in some future day, we are truly an ignorant lot. I mean this." She paused, then told Billie, "What a person knows is much like what she owns. The more she puts into her coffers, the more easily she can see her considerable limitations."

The echoing voice receded into the distance.

Billie felt Kyle's hand squeezing until her hand ached.

Then Jy said, "We try to ask little of each earth we visit," and Billie noticed nothing else. "We require tiny parcels of land for our portals and a certain freedom of motion, and in exchange we give what helps people the most and for the longest time."

She spoke about making this earth better. She wanted it greener and sweeter with every major problem solved, she assured them. It was the same message Billie had heard a hundred thousand times, all of it, and it was wonderful nonetheless. So fine!

There came applause. Billie clapped and felt lucky to be alive now and see this happening. She glanced at Kyle and very nearly asked her question. *"Would I make a good Wanderer?"* It lay coiled inside her mouth . . . and she couldn't. This wasn't the time. There was too much noise and too much bustle, and she bit her lower lip and looked forward again.

Jy spoke about people. There were many different species of people, but what were their similarities? Were there any traits common to all of them? She paused for a moment, then she said, "Most are like you in one respect." Was she smiling? "They evolved while they moved through endless wilderness, blessed with innate urges to explore and exploit." A blue-green globe appeared overhead. It was some sister world with the continents oddly shaped and the icecaps missing. The vegetable greenness of the land was too pronounced, Billie thought. Then Jy was saying, "You will thrive when you can return to that wilderness again," and she realized what she was seeing.

"Where is that?" she asked. She didn't remember this alien world from any televised rally. "Kyle?"

He didn't seem to hear her.

She said, "It's pretty. Do you know where it is?"

"Listen," he warned. "Just listen."

Jy paused before saying, "This is a gentle world circling a quiet nearby sun." She paused again. "It is ideal for colonies and your dear brethren from other earths have given it names like Paradise and Eden." The green world vanished, replaced by a string of new worlds from around the galaxy. There was an icy world with a narrow emerald waist; there were twin ocean worlds dotted with islands and spinning about a common center; there was a giant world blanketed with clouds and habitable only on its mountaintops; there were perhaps a dozen earthlike worlds just minted and waiting for life to bloom in their quiet new seas. Jy showed them perhaps fifty worlds, more than Billie could put to memory, then she concluded by saying, "These places are yours. You can do with them as you wish, and of course I hope you use wisdom and love. And will you please promise to be careful with them? Yes? Say yes."

The crowd cried, "Yes!" in disorder, a few hands showing over the masses of heads. "Yes . . . yes!"

"Wonderful," said Jy. "Thank you!" The last alien world dissolved into the Bright again. The glare fell over them, and Billie squinted. Jy was saying, "You have a wonderful city and you have been most charitable hosts and all of us thank you."

Applause began somewhere behind them, from above, and it swelled until it filled the stadium. "Thank you!" said Jy one last time, and she was gone. The illusionary Bright flooded the stage and crowd until nothing else seemed to exist, nothing to see but a strange fog seeping light; and for an instant Billie felt as if she were floating in the damp air. She felt she was out of her seat and rising, then Kyle grasped her hand and tugged, ending the spell.

4

How LONG will we persist?

I have to admit that I do not know. As far as I am concerned we will be doing what we do for another billion years, not one day less, and with that frame of mind I have to answer by saying, "Forever."

Forever.

—*Jy's speeches*

They walked north from the stadium, going home to get Janice's car. Once again Billie considered asking her question, and again she thought it was the wrong time. People were everywhere, but few were talking. The mood was introspective, contemplative. They crossed the railroad tracks on the old viaduct with its rusted steel girders and its sidewalk built from splintering railroad ties, and Billie looked at her watch and realized it was already eleven o'clock. It was a warm night with the nearly full moon hanging to the east and the rails below shining with a silverish gleam.

Janice's car was a little thing, all noise and oily fumes.

Billie started the car on her third attempt. Its brakes were iffy, and one cockeyed headlight shut off the street lamps as they worked their way along the crowded streets, people walking everywhere in little groups and oftentimes holding hands.

They slipped out of town on a side street.

Kyle leaned against his door and watched the moon-lit countryside. Which way? Billie wondered. She went straight at an intersection and drove across a grassy plain with shallow ponds on both sides, then the road crossed the main highway and rose past crops and the airport and went into the high hills. This was the park. Some-where nearby was the new portal. She followed the traffic to a newly made road, and she wished they had been here before. They used to talk about coming to see the portal and watch its Wanderer guard . . . only things had gotten in the way. *Oh, well.* They topped a little rise and saw Wanderer ships floating against the western sky, and there were a couple of graveled parking lots choked with cars. A police officer waved them back. Billie cranked the wheel and got around and went back up the access road. She parked on the soft shoulder with every-one else, and that was fine. She didn't mind walking. It even seemed appropriate. She told Kyle, "We should have to walk to meet Jy. Shouldn't we?" and he halfway nodded and shrugged.

There was a breeze coming over the ridge, and it

blew through her light clothes. She felt cool and fine, but mostly she was nervous. She wanted to hurry and couldn't help but get ahead of Kyle. She didn't even notice he wasn't beside her anymore. Then a police officer, a big man, put the flashlight beam in her face and asked if she belonged here. "Are you invited, miss?"

Billie swallowed and straightened. Where was Kyle?

"Otherwise," said the policeman, "you can't use the park. Not for tonight. I'm sorry."

She turned and saw Kyle and took his arm, saying, "I'm with him. Him!"

The beam drifted sideways and found the strange face.

"She . . . is my guest," Kyle muttered.

The beam dropped. "Sorry, sir. Go on." The voice was cold but proper. "They'll pass you through."

Kyle whispered, "Thank you, sir," and made a tired sound.

They walked together. State troopers and the police gave them looks, but nobody stopped them. They pressed through a little crowd gathered along a fence, then they were on the matted grass and Billie couldn't believe her good fortune. She found Kyle's hand and squeezed, feeling a cold greasy sweat. Wanderers were everywhere. Many of them were Founders with their small, thickly built bodies and huge heads and huge brains . . . look at them! Floating lights drifted overhead, illuminating the ground and the house-size ships, and Kyle took her on a strange course. He didn't seem to have any direction in mind. Where was Jy's ship? Which one was it? She turned and turned, then Kyle was talking. "Over there," he muttered. "There . . . see it?" That must be the ship, she realized. It was the egg she remembered from photographs, with a staircase below and the big crystal portal beyond it. People stood in line waiting to go into the ship. Jy must be inside, she realized. Why else would there be a long line? She was walking fast, and Kyle wasn't keeping up. She felt halfway angry because of his delays, and she slowed herself. What was he doing? Then she saw a tall Wanderer, dark and maybe twice as handsome as Janice's quarterback, who was standing at the end of the line, greeting each visitor. Ahead of Billie was a balding man and a little man, both of them wearing suits and ties, and the tall Wanderer said, "It's good to see you again, Mr. Phillips," and took the bald man's hand.

Kyle had quit walking. His legs were rooted in place, and Billie took one of his hands and squeezed. "What's the matter?" she asked. "Is something the matter?"

"I'm just . . . it's Jy," he whispered.

Kyle was worse than she was, she realized. It was almost funny to see him so nervous. They started walking again, and she was nearly calm all at once. She stood behind the little man who was with the balding man, and the little man looked nervous too. He was pudgy and holding a large book under his arm. She recognized the book; it was one of their biggest sellers. Oh, goodness! She should have brought something for Jy to autograph. How could she forget? The little man turned towards Billie for a moment, his face round and buttery, then he looked away and took a couple of deep breaths while hugging the book close to his chest.

Someone said something about a nephew.

The handsome Wanderer said, "Hello," to the little man and then gave Billie a wink. Or did he? She wasn't sure.

Kyle coughed and said, "Excuse me?"

The Wanderer turned to Kyle and waited for a moment, then he said, "Yes, friend?"

"I have someone . . . who wants to meet Jy . . ."

Billie couldn't read the Wanderer's face. He reminded her of Kyle.

"If it's all right," said Kyle. "Is it?"

"Is it?" The Wanderer grinned.

"It's the custom," Kyle responded.

Nobody spoke.

Then the Wanderer said, "It is perfectly fine," and bowed to Billie while he smiled.

The balding man broke in. "You should thank Quencé for letting *you* come tonight," he said. He was talking to his companion. "He's the gentleman who gave the okay."

"Thank you," said a quick voice. "Thank you very much."

"You're welcome," Quencé replied. More people were arriving, and the line was moving forwards. "I hope all of you enjoy your visit," he told them, then he strolled past them to greet the others. He called to everyone by name, every name sounding like a friend's.

The line continued forwards.

Billie felt her skin starting to tingle, and she looked at Kyle. His face was even paler than was normal, but he was smiling. He couldn't have smiled any more. "I never thought I'd be here," she confessed. "You know? I never believed this would come true." And with that she spun in a circle, then another, so happy that she felt like dancing and she couldn't stop herself. She went around on the matted grass with her arms lifted, then she quit. Kyle and everyone were watching her. *No more*, she thought, and she stood in one place and sighed with her entire body while hugging herself.

Be normal, girl, she told herself.

Be dull.

BOOK TWO

•

THE BRIGHT

COTTON

1

EVERY DAY without exception one of the cult's followers would try to assassinate me. In every other respect it was a lovely earth, relatively free of war and the worst aspects of poverty and environmental decay. Yet the cult—The Children of Favor—was widespread and convinced an antimessiah was coming. They believed I was she. Thus they sent their followers by the dozen, night and day, arming them with every weapon at their disposal. I saw knives and bombs and crude missiles and bare fists. The fists got closest, but none of them actually touched me. Every last would-be assassin was captured and restrained by my security people, then released to the native authorities.

We rarely try to supplant local laws when the natives are involved. We learned long ago to honor our hosts' sense of law and propriety. Yet I found myself unsettled by my time on that earth. I was never in danger in any real sense, yet the parade of anger and violence had its effects. I reached a point where I hated to appear in public and feared giving rallies, and worst of all were my constant feelings of guilt and empathy when I saw my assailants led away in chains. Many were bound for prison, and more than a few were making the proud self-assured march to the gallows...

—Jy's private journal

The stairs were smooth and white, resembling cool strips of freshly quarried stone. The Wanderers had brewed the stairs with their magic. Atoms flowed within a tame plasma, becoming the substances and shapes desired. All of the surroundings were planned, Cotton told himself. There were stairs and railings that looked like wood, dark and lustrous, and the interior above them was whiter than stone and soothing and warm. Even the air itself had an intent, smelling like fresh-cut flowers. Cotton's mouth was watering, nearly filled with saliva, and he was thinking how Jy possessed a remarkable home. *This is Jy's,* he heard himself thinking. *I am this close to Jy. Now relax... relax...*

The people ahead of them climbed the stairs in distinct groups, some groups talking and the others giving the talkers disapproving looks.

Cotton glanced at Moliak, then he studied the guards standing at the top of the stairs. There were two of them, huge and apparently twins, their meaty arms laced with veins and their purpose mostly ornamental. They meant nothing whatsoever to Cotton.

Relax, he told himself. *Will you please relax?*

It was the Wanderer behind him who kept him concerned. It was the same Wanderer he had seen walking yesterday, and the coincidence made him suspect more than a coincidence. Cotton had to concentrate and remind himself that he was Mr. Phillips's relative and guest and he belonged here. He had ample identification, and his biological oddities were camouflaged with Moliak's tricks. Besides, he thought, he was completely unarmed. Sensors were probably scanning him for the hundredth time—he knew the Wanderers' methods frontwards and backwards—and everything would seem nominal. It had to be nominal, otherwise there would have been an alarm and the big guards would have come at them and the stairs and railings would have turned to fluids and engulfed Moliak and himself, trapping and disarming them in a form of plasma sap.

Cotton felt his body temperature edging higher.

He couldn't help himself. Nervousness made it happen. A Wanderer was breathing the same air as he . . . what lousy luck! Nothing like this was foreseen, and Cotton was expected to stay normal regardless.

He took a long slow careful breath and glanced at Moliak.

The four of them were mounting the stairs together. A little male Founder had asked them to be a group. Cotton climbed the stairs one at a time, and he kept telling himself nothing was wrong. He took more breaths, too many breaths, and he started to stroke the edges of the big book. Sensors could examine him a million times and they would see nothing. Jy and her people were primitives in comparison to Moliak's abilities. He knew it. He felt a hard knot of certainty under his breastbone, then he glanced at Moliak once again.

Moliak was making himself smile.

He gave Cotton an almost imperceptible nod, then turned and started talking to the girl behind them. "It looks like we'll go in together," he commented. "To meet her."

She said, "Jy," and squeezed the tall Wanderer's arm. "We're almost there!"

Her Wanderer whispered, "Yes, we are."

He was a quiet one, or he was preoccupied.

Moliak told the girl, "You look excited," and he tried to laugh.

"Oh, but I am!" she replied. "I am!"

"I am too!" said Moliak. "I've been waiting forever to see Jy. Or it seems like forever, at least."

"It does," she said.

"How about you, Cotton?"

Cotton blinked and forced himself to grin. "I'm thrilled," he told his friend. He was wondering what would happen if the Wanderer recognized him. What would he say? Then he told himself it wasn't possible. He had changed too much in too short a time, the weight filling his face and his various scars obscured with a plastic flesh. Besides, he realized, the Wanderer had barely looked at him yesterday. He had seemed distracted about something . . . *Just stay calm, you innocent* . . . .

When they reached the top of the stairs and the ornamental guards, Quencé passed them. He said, "Soon," to everyone who was waiting, then he was down the hallway and out of sight.

"Is he important?" asked the dark-haired girl. "Kyle?"

The Wanderer said, "Yes," with a weak voice. Cotton quit breathing and turned, feeling his metabolism shooting upwards and the seconds creeping past and his body begging for oxygen even after he breathed again, pulling in the air and absorbing everything before exhaling. He stared at the Wanderer's blue eyes, tired and nearly dead, and those eyes saw nothing. Cotton knew it in an instant. All at once he felt more confident, not relaxed but not ready to explode either.

This could be easy.

Moliak had claimed it would be easier than any other project they had faced together. It was a simple and foolproof plan, he had maintained, and nobody would suspect any of it.

They continued along the hallway for a little while, and Moliak stood on his toes and said, "There she is," with a little gasp.

Cotton looked between the bodies, giving the Glorious One a cursory glance. "It is," he allowed. "I see her."

Quencé was standing inside Jy's large room, smiling brightly and watching everything.

Cotton squeezed the large book with both hands. *Be ready*.

"Are you going to get Jy's autograph?" asked the girl. "Sir?"

"I hope so," Cotton told her, and he nodded.

She said, "That'll be nice," and leaned against her Wanderer. The Wanderer put an arm around her because that was what she wanted, and he dropped his face and stared at the floor.

Cotton was ready.

He flooded his lungs with a series of enormous breaths, hiding them as best as he could; and the sweet fats inside him began to ignite; and the flowery scents in the air made his guts think of food, their contractions making one huge wet endless roar.

2

Jy LACKS technical wonders like our weapons and our capacity to deceive, yet we have many more advantages at our disposal. Cotton and I know how to carry out an operation of this kind. Jy and her unblooded people would not know how to begin or that simplicity is vital or that nothing succeeds like boldness, and perhaps our greatest advantage is that we can think in terms that Jy has never considered. She and her millions have their innocence and apparent good fortune, and they will not have the vaguest clue of what is happening or what will come....
—*Moliak's private journal*

Jy was sitting on a modest chair on top of a raised platform in the center of an otherwise unadorned room. People in suits and fancy dresses were gathered before her, talking with syrupy voices. Cotton's runaway metabolism pressed their words flat and made them linger. Everyone wanted to shake Jy's hand. They were desperate to somehow touch her. Someone produced a cheap pen and a slip of paper, and the pen leaked blue ink that splattered on the floor. Jy laughed. Then everyone was laughing, and the ink was absorbed into the floor, and Quencé brought another pen. "There," said Jy with a flourish of her hand. "And thank you for coming to see me. Thank you."

Scanning the room, Cotton counted the Wanderers.

A pair of Founders stood beside the far doorway. A Cousin was to Cotton's left, and Quencé now stepped to his right, behind the platform, joining a stocky tar black woman he called by name: "Wysh."

Cotton glanced over his shoulder.

Moliak was gazing at Jy and nothing else. He was showing too much with his face, his moist eyes awestruck and his mouth pulled into a sorrowful curl.

The group ahead of them was finished.

The Founders escorted those people through the far doorway, and it was their moment. Cotton saw Quencé smile and beckon them forwards. "Oh, my," said the girl. "How do I look? Kyle?"

"Fine," said the Wanderer, then he coughed once.

Cotton's temperature was climbing higher every moment, energies flooding through him. He was fighting himself to walk slowly and naturally, crossing the smooth white floor with the book in both hands. Moliak was beside him and the Wanderer was practically walking in his footsteps, breathing his stale air and probably feeling his heat too. Cotton was a furnace running hard, producing a sweatless heat, and he kept remembering what Moliak had promised him. The sensors would be hunting for weapons and aggressive moves, and there were no weapons to see. All he carried was his book, and the tiny electronic baffles sewn into his clothes would mask his racing heart and the scalding blood . . . .

Quencé climbed up on the platform beside Jy, smiling and smiling. He started to introduce Mr. Phillips, then Cotton, and Cotton started to shift the book as if finding a free hand to shake Jy's hand. Then he let the book drop. He watched it fall in slow motion, opening as it fell. He shouted, "Shit," and the book spread like a fan and hit the floor upside down with pages crunching and a new smell rising in the air. It was a chemical stink, sudden and expected.

Cotton got down on one knee, saying, "Of all the shit," with a despairing voice.

Everyone was watching him.

He felt stares and glanced upwards, seeing Jy and Quencé, and he told them, "I guess I'm nervous," with a forced laugh.

There were nods and understanding smiles.

Cotton's body felt weightless now. Another minute and he would approach his absolute maximum, but already he was quicker and stronger than anyone. He took countless little breaths and pulled the oxygen from each one, grasping the book with both hands and lifting it while thinking about the trillion-plus nanorobots burrowing into the floor. They had been embedded in the ordinary paper, full of latent energy and a clear image of their tasks. Now they were manipulating the atoms within the ship itself, reproducing themselves and reassembling everything in their way. This was the perfect environment for them. Jy's ship was designed to change its form and function, its substance enormously plastic, and the robots were borrowing that ability for a little while. Cotton stood and worked to uncrimp the pages, and he gave Moliak a quick glance. "I'm clumsy tonight," he confessed.

Everyone seemed sympathetic.

Then the floor rolled to one side and the other.

Quencé noticed the motion, squinting and looking at his own feet.

Jy said, "Mr. Phillips?" with a certain poise. "It is a pleasure to meet you and your nephew."

Moliak offered his hand, and Cotton watched the face torn with emotions. They seemed to shake hands for an age, then Jy asked, "I am sorry to have flustered you. Is there anything I can do?"

She was speaking to Cotton.

Cotton decided to have some fun. He grasped the long spidery hand with one of his hands, and the floor rolled again. It was a sharper motion this time. Cotton smiled while he watched Jy's eyes grow huge with surprise. She could feel his heat and the hard grip, and suddenly an alarm was sounding in the distance. It was a soft keening, the ship feeling the disease within itself, at last, its flesh dying and its energies vanishing and its senses going suddenly blind.

The alarm weakened and stopped a moment later.

Infected controls caused the doorways to seal. The nanorobots were everywhere and in complete command. Cotton saw nothing but wall surrounding them, the room isolated, and he released Jy's hand and watched her staring at him. Her expression was astonished and alert but not scared. Then Quencé stepped in front of Jy and tried to grab Cotton, wanting to wrestle him to the floor.

Cotton used one hand and gave Quencé a slight shove.

The big Wanderer tumbled backwards, landing with a grunt and sliding off the platform. He looked dumbfounded and suddenly angry, and the dark Wanderer woman, Wysh, stepped towards him, asking, "What—what is it?"

There was a motion behind Cotton. He turned and shoved Kyle to the floor, and the girl said, "Huh?"

Moliak was kneeling. He seemed to have no left hand; his wrist ended with the white floor. He was concentrating, his mouth small and his eyes narrowed, then all at once he started to smile.

Cotton knelt too.

He felt the floor yielding to his hand. The nanorobots recognized his flesh and engulfed it, and there was warmth and a sharp tingling sensation racing up his arm, making him ache and flinch for an instant.

His body hurt for a long moment.

Moliak rose and said, "You have no protection. Your shields are gone. Now please be still." It was Mr. Phillips's voice, only some of Moliak's could now be heard. There was an edge to the voice and a power. Cotton saw the apparent glove on his partner's hand, the color and texture of a well-cleaned mirror. He made a fist with the glove. "Keep very still," he repeated, "and do whatever we tell you to do."

Quencé made a tentative motion.

A blue bolt jumped from the mirrored fist, throwing sparks as it streaked up into the ceiling. There was a thunderous *crack* and more hot sparks raining down, and Quencé retreated one step. He blinked and glanced at Jy. Then he was watching Moliak while holding his hands high and close, as if he did not quite trust them.

"I am dangerous," Moliak declared with a quiet, intense voice.

Cotton pulled his own left hand from the floor. He flexed the glove several times, making certain that it was operating and all the essential connections had been made by their miniscule servants.

Little droplets of golden light seeped from between his fingers, falling and then evaporating before they reached the floor.

Then Cotton remembered when Moliak told him the plan. They had been alone inside Cotton's home on Termite Mound, and the hairless blue-black Moliak had said, "Do you know what we will be at that moment? Do you know what we will have achieved once we take possession of Jy?"

"No," Cotton had said. "What will we be?"

"The two of us will comprise the precise center of humankind, Cotton. We will be the undisputed heart of humanity—"

—which they were.

He looked at Moliak, and Moliak regarded him for a moment. Then they nodded to each other, and everything was worthwhile. An enormous journey and endless risks dissolved into a feeling of shared success. They were underway at long last.

3

IN MY dream Jy knew what we wanted and saw through our disguises, and she rose while telling me, "I wondered when you would come for me," and it was easy. "Shall we leave?" she inquired. We walked from her ship without incident, and she asked if there was any way she could help me. She was eager to help. I told

her, "Listen to me." She said, "But I know what
you want and why and you cannot tell me anything that will surprise me." Then I growled at
Jy, telling her, "Just please listen to me, old
woman! Will you please be quiet and listen?"
She asked, "Why?" And I said, "For my own
sake just hear what I have to tell you!"
                                    —*Moliak's private journal*

The doors remained sealed. Nobody outside would know
how to get past the doors, much less help Jy. Cotton
turned and counted their hostages. There were five Wanderers and the native girl, and they regarded him with
a mixture of shock and horror and a desperate curiosity.

Cotton felt his glove tingling. The nerves in his
hands were interfaced directly into the glove, and he
could feel through it and move his hand normally. His
every motion was rapid and graceful. He turned and
turned again, letting everyone see his speed, then he
took a light step to one side and pivoted while aiming
the fighting glove at each round-mouthed face. *Look at
me*, he was saying with his body. *Look at this marvelous
creature standing in front of you!*

Jy spoke first.

"What do you want from us?" she asked, her voice
tense and rather forced. "Who are you?"

Moliak ignored her, saying, "We are going outside
in a group and I want everyone to act obedient."

Nobody spoke.

Moliak opened his fighting glove and glanced at his
reflection in the palm. Then he told Cotton, "Claim
three."

Cotton picked Quencé first. He had never expected
that a Wanderer would try to wrestle him; Wanderer
instincts were supposed to be intellectual and passive
and he didn't want the man out of his reach. Cotton told
Quencé, "Turn," and then he helped him spin and
grasped him by the thick waistband of his trousers. He
held him with the fighting glove, and he let the glove
glow hot at the knuckles. He kissed the flesh with the

knuckles, and Quencé jerked and straightened his back
and began to sweat while the pain sliced into him. Then
Cotton cooled the glove and said, "You," meaning Kyle
and the girl. He told them to stand on both sides of
Quencé. They moved as if the room were filled with
some transparent syrup, and Cotton was impatient. He
struggled just to talk slowly enough to be understood.
He told them to put their hands into the glove while he
still gripped the gray trousers, then he gave them a shake
and a squeeze before saying, "Surprise me and everyone
is fire and gas, and dead."

The girl sobbed and shrank.

Kyle was staring at the floor in front of him, saying
nothing.

Moliak said, "Now," and Cotton saw Jy in the middle
and Moliak's gloved hand planted on the back of her
head. Mismatched hands were in his grip—the Cousin's
and the tar-black woman's—and Jy looked weak. She
seemed small and fragile because in a million years of
constant travel this had never happened to her. The
Wanderers surrounding her didn't even have contingen-
cies for such an event. Reality had become so slow now
that it felt like a series of clear images blending seam-
lessly into one another, and Cotton breathed like a spar-
row, fast and deep, and he pushed his hostages to the
vanished doorway while telling Quencé to touch it. "Put
a finger on it anywhere," he commanded.

Quencé did what he was told.

The doorway flowed up into the wall, and half a
dozen Founders were waiting in the hallway. They took
a collective step forwards before Quencé shouted, "No!"
His big voice seemed to push them aside. "You have to
get out of our way!"

They hesitated for a moment, straining to see Jy.

Jy called to them, saying, "Go outside and wait for
us," with a slow voice pressed calm.

"Who is with you?" asked one Founder. "Wysh?
Xen?"

A second Founder asked, "What is happening,
Xen?"

"I don't know," muttered the Cousin. "This is . . . strange."

"*Get out of my way!*" screamed Cotton.

The Founders retreated in disorder. Cotton's hostages began walking along the hallway with the lights weakening and then flickering, then they stepped down the stone stairs one at a time. They were clumsy at first, concentrating on their motions and improving to where they moved together. They reached the prairie with Jy's ship above and behind them and something rumbling deep within it. A crowd watched them. The natives were gone, probably ushered away with the first alarm; only Wanderers stared at them. Cotton took a long nourishing breath of fresh air, and he smelled the hostages sweating. He heard Moliak behind him. He was telling his hostages to turn around, then Moliak put his back against Cotton's back, his flesh seemingly icy cold.

Keep alert, Cotton warned himself, as if he needed warnings now.

They moved sideways toward the portal. The Cousin, Xen, took a breath and moaned. Quencé started to turn, jerking his head, and Cotton said, "No," in time. He made Quencé stop whatever he wanted to do and suppress his instincts, saving everyone, and they continued shuffling through the long grass with the portal nearby and a few Wanderers between them and it.

"The portal won't work for you," said Quencé.

Cotton ignored him.

"Mr. Phillips?" Quencé persisted. "We have failsafe systems and safety mechanisms—"

"I know you do," Moliak interrupted. "I know every one of them."

Nobody spoke.

With whispers and meaningful glances the Wanderers decided to block their way to the portal. They made a passive wall of bodies, and Cotton saw their resolve. He barked, "Out of our way!" and Moliak said, "Now!" with nothing of Mr. Phillips's voice left in it. He screamed, "I will butcher all of you!" with conviction and fire. Then when nothing happened it was Jy who was sensible. She said:

"Please move for us, please," with a begging voice.

The Wanderers started to drift aside.

Cotton saw the portal with its entranceway sealed, outer and inner doors both, and Moliak reached with his bare hand and touched the proper pad, both doors pulling open with a tingling sensation and a soft crackling sound. "Master?" said a thick voice. "Jy?"

Who was there?

A figure was standing before them, blocking the inner door.

Cotton saw a vast, ape-shaped Wanderer with massive long arms holding up its bulk and enormous face. This was the portal's guard. He must have slipped inside with the first alarm, sensing his duty. He was huge and obviously powerful, with a heavy face wet from crying. "I tried to hold the seals," he said, "only they refused to lock for me. Jy—?"

"It is all right," Jy croaked.

"Then I tried clipping free . . . ."

He had attempted to sabotage the portal, separating it from the Bright itself. Moliak had anticipated that too.

"I couldn't," the guard confessed.

"It is all right," Jy repeated. She sounded sober and steady, yet she looked painfully frail. "You did everything possible."

Moliak said, "Back out of my way."

The big face looked at him and then Jy, steadily leaking tears. There was moonlight in his face, and the Wanderer's lights, and Cotton saw the massive jaw clench. He had a grazer's heavy jaw and teeth—it was a very odd human—and he heard the voice saying, "No, I will not let you," with a sudden courage. "No, I will not."

Cotton moved.

Instinct told him the guard had made up his mind, and their timetable might be in jeopardy. Cotton released his grip with his gloved hand and lifted the glove and aimed between the bodies, using a kinetic blast to push the guard off his feet. He was tumbling and screaming, then Cotton used a blue plasma bolt and there was a larger scream cut short. The dying guard writhed on the floor with the blue fire crawling up his legs and body. Cotton wished he would die. Suddenly his training and practice as a soldier dissolved, leaving him as a Termite with an innate respect for all Wanderers—for any species or caste better than himself—and he was weak and sick, despising Moliak for an instant, not able to make himself move or even breathe . . . .

There was the sudden luscious odor of cooking meat and blood, then came the harsher stink of ashes. The guard was dead; his hard-memory was a puddle of ceramics on the portal floor.

The girl said, "Oh."

Nobody else spoke.

Then it was Moliak who made them move again. He pushed and pulled and forced them inside, then he released his hostages and began to work. The girl was crying. Jy was crying too. Everyone else seemed numbed, standing with their backs bent and their legs bowed and their hands closing into useless fists.

Cotton approached the corpse.

What else could I have done? he wondered.

Moliak had the poise to shut the entranceway, both doors. Then he locked them with new codes and came to Cotton and put the bare hand on his shoulder, giving him a long stare before saying, "You did what was best. Believe me."

The floor was absorbing the ashes and the ruined ceramics.

"Are you with me?" asked Moliak. "Can I trust you?"

Cotton breathed and nodded, saying, "We need to move," and he returned the stare until Moliak was convinced and finally turned away.

KYLE

1

IT IS named for what we see when we travel upon it: the brilliant white light extending well beyond the visible range, in both directions, with the microwaves and radio waves and the hard radiations having that same characteristic whiteness . . . the Bright, partly constructed from the screaming unblinking chaos that is the entire spectrum . . . .

—*Jy's speeches*

Suddenly he would be thinking about nothing—his mind floating in ink; his senses working on pure empty instinct; his body moving as told, no more—and that was fine. He was doing fine. Seconds would pass, or maybe an entire uninterrupted minute. Then the spell would be finished and Kyle would suffer a moment of panic. His heart would buck, his breathing would double, and some black voice between his ears would ask, *"Where is this?"* while his eyes shot left and right, up and down.

Inside a portal . . . damn, they were standing inside an authentic portal. Billie and Jy and the rest of them!

The people outdoors were staring in at them. They were Wanderers with their noses pressed against the crystal and their hands beside their eyes, cupped against the light, and they had dark old sorrowful faces. They were Founders and Cousins and a few others. Kyle could feel their stares and their shared grief. Why didn't they come help? he wondered. Why did they just stand and watch? Why couldn't they do something . . . try something . . . this was their precious Jy, weren't they going to do something?

The balding man, Mr. Phillips, was touching lights and buttons on top of a narrow rectangular box. A control panel? His gloved hand was working beside his normal hand, and he seemed intense and certain in whatever he was doing now. Kyle looked towards the other one, the one who couldn't be any ordinary human . . . small and round and incredibly fast, his head pivoting and his lungs working like bellows, his eyes missing nothing and that impossible heat radiating out of him.

Kyle remembered feeling the heat when they walked together, not sure of its source. What kind of human was he? Or was he? Maybe Jy knew. Kyle looked at Jy, then at Quencé, and both seemed to be confused and possibly as scared as he.

That made everything worse. Twenty times worse, at least.

Kyle clamped his eyes shut and tried to summon that convenient forgetfulness, only it wasn't there now. He thought he had it for an instant, but no, it was like groping in the dark for an oily bead. He lost the feeling and sighed aloud, frustrated and cold, then he opened his eyes again.

Someone was standing beside him.

"Kyle?" Who was talking? He turned and saw Billie. She was with him and holding his hand, and only now did Kyle become aware of her grip. She said, "Kyle?" again.

"What?" he managed.

She squeezed and waited for an explanation. Her face was open and alert, ready for any thread of logic.

"I don't know," he said. He gazed down at the girl, and she surprised him. He expected her to dissolve into anguish, folding and collapsing and certainly crying. Yet instead she started to nod. He didn't know what was happening; she could accept his ignorance. She chewed on her lower lip and sighed and looked at their captors, then she gazed back up at Kyle. He watched her eyes lifting, fixing on him, and he said, "I don't know what they want," with his voice losing its force at the end.

"We'll be all right," she whimpered.

What did she say?

Both of her hands squeezed his hand, and she said, "Everything will turn out fine," with an astonishing conviction.

Kyle didn't believe it. He resented her sudden courage, real or not. Then he resented her presence. Kyle began to feel a strange collection of runaway emotions. He breathed and looked at the hard white floor, wishing the girl was elsewhere. He wanted her gone and safe because he felt a vicious raw guilt for bringing her tonight. They were going to die, probably soon and in some awful fashion—the Wanderer guard was still screaming inside his head—and this was his fault. His lies brought them here, and she was sharing his punishment. What a shitty mess!

He wiped his damp face with his free hand.

His thinking skipped sideways, without warning, and he was seeing everything from a different vantage point. He remembered Billie lying with him—normal life suddenly delicious and remote—and she asked if they could come meet Jy. He heard her voice and felt the sheets and tried to change the past with his own will. He imagined himself saying, "No. No, we can't," only he couldn't make it feel real. He'd never had any choice, and she had known it. She had used him, manipulated him and won. He felt himself becoming irrational. There was an anger, a fine scalding anger, and Kyle felt himself starting to slip free of his guilt . . . .

They had been standing here, waiting for weeks.

For years.

Kyle looked at the other hostages—the blacker-than-black woman named Wysh; and Jy with Quencé; and the ugly small-brained Cousin someone had called Xen—and almost as an afterthought Kyle remembered he was a Wanderer too. He belonged to them.

Now he shivered.

Billie dropped his hand and asked, "Where's *he* from? What earth?"

She meant the little one who had murdered the Wanderer. Cotton? Mr. Phillips's nephew? Kyle looked at him, thinking back to walking home the other day and the little man he had seen eating licorice by the road . . . that face! He was wolfing down the candy then and thinner in the face, with a bad ear . . . wasn't that he? It had to be the same person, there couldn't be two!

"Kyle?"

Quencé volunteered an answer. He told Billie, "He might be a machine or tailored genetically, or maybe both things." Quencé gave a shrug and said, "We don't know just what he is . . . miss."

The murderer made a sharp sound, then said, "Be quiet, stop," with his swift voice.

"Is your name Cotton?" asked Quencé. He glanced at the shiny glove, then said, "What do I call you?"

"Cotton," he claimed, "and be quiet now quiet *quiet* . . . ."

Quencé nearly spoke regardless, but then a sound blossomed around them. It was music wrapped snug around a soft voice. The language was strange, but the voice was familiar. Kyle remembered the sexless narrator from the rally, and it seemed to be using a peculiar language known to the Wanderers. He watched Quencé straighten his back and narrow eyes, and Jy flinched as if she were in pain.

"What's happening?" asked Billie. She tugged on his arm like some demanding child, but it was Quencé who answered again.

"We are going to leave."

Leave?

The Cousin said, "We have been given permission

to enter the Bright," with a flat voice, colorless and nearly breathless. His bony face dropped and his arms folded tight around his chest.

Mr. Phillips started to talk.

"Everyone needs to sit and remain still," he said with a distracted tone. "There will be a quick journey before we make our first stop, and I think you should make yourselves comfortable."

There was an odd sensation. The floor beneath Kyle's feet softened and bubbled, forming a padded circle large enough for his butt and legs. He found himself kneeling gratefully. Everything was work now, but standing was a worse burden than sitting.

Our first stop.

The words implied there would be other stops, maybe many of them, and that meant time taken and life prolonged. He felt the padding give beneath him, shaping itself to fit his own curves, and his skin began to tickle while a powerful humming sound rose from within the floor.

Billie felt it too. She was beside him—everyone was rather closely packed—and her mouth was to her knees and her arms were wrapped around her shins. She was clinging to herself and waiting.

Jy was talking with what seemed to be that odd language.

Quencé answered with a whisper. Was it the Founder language?

"We're really going into the Bright?" gasped Billie.

Kyle risked a nod.

"They must have stolen our access codes," said Quencé, his tone steady and gray. "What you're seeing is . . . is remarkable, miss."

Cotton watched them talking and made no sound. He seemed rather more at ease now. Mr. Phillips walked past Cotton, removing his jacket and his tie and unbuttoning his shirt partway, a sweaty white undershirt showing against a remarkably hairy chest.

"Jy?" he said. "Look at what they are doing, my friend."

He meant the Wanderers outside.

"Do you see their faces?"

Kyle glanced at Jy. She wasn't speaking or even breathing, and her eyes never blinked.

"They seem furious," said Mr. Phillips. Or whoever he was. "Can you see the fury boiling out of them, my friend?" He walked straight to the crystal wall and stopped, then made a mocking gesture. The gray-clad bodies pressed close and banged on the crystal with open palms and fists and sometimes their skulls. They couldn't be heard. Not even a whisper of sound could pass through the massive crystal and be heard over the humming sounds. "Look at the anger and fear making them ill!"

Jy seemed to give a half nod.

"It is a mob," he declared.

Nobody spoke. They watched the angry bodies for a long moment, then Jy rose and took a step forward. She said something in that other language, not loud, and Mr. Phillips seemed to understand her. He nodded knowingly and turned, admitting, "You are right," in English. "You do know me. I'll admit that much for now."

"But who—?" Jy started to ask.

"Quiet, my friend." His face was working to be hard and calm, the portrait of someone in control. Everyone could see him struggling with his face. He stepped away from the wall and walked past them, Cotton watching everything, and then he was standing at the controls and touching one glowing pad—

—and the outside world dissolved into a cool radiant light.

Kyle gasped.

He looked skyward and squinted, remembering the fake Bright at the rally. This one was different, more vivid and more complex. Streaks and flowing arcs raced past them, and he felt a sudden motion but no sense of acceleration, no change of weight . . . and they were riding along a passageway greater than any other, Kyle stuffing his fist into his mouth and fighting himself to keep from screaming.

2

EVERYTHING INSIDE every portal moves as a unit. The passengers and cargo and the floor and the buried machinery are together, as is the innermost portion of the crystal wall; and meanwhile the portals on the other earths—the ones through which everything travels—are emptied in preparation. All of their contents are compressed and folded within a matter of moments. Even the atmosphere is stored in this fashion. Then this small volume of material is set into a chamber beneath the portal itself. Nothing remains within the sphere but for an inviting vacuum through which people can travel in comfort.

—A Wanderer's introduction

Kyle grew accustomed to the humming of the machinery; it was the least remarkable element in the madness around him.

They were somewhere between portals, between earths, and gaining momentum. Nobody was talking. A new earth appeared around them and then vanished into the Bright, then it was another earth and Kyle watched with his heart racing. He was very much afraid, yet he still had to marvel. He sat motionless and gazed outward like a little boy with all these strange places streaking past him.

The lay of the land around the portals didn't change.

They were sitting at the same precise point on the same durable sandstone hilltop, the time night and the moon inches from full. Kyle knew what to expect—he had read the books and watched the best programs—yet all of it was an enormous shock. Peoples and weather changed with every earth, often dramatically, while the geologies held relatively steady. He knew this country-side, and that itself was unsettling. "You've been here," he muttered under his breath. He had the distinct impression that he wasn't moving at all and this was always the same earth and everything was being rebuilt around him, over and over again.

The weather was entirely unpredictable. The first earth had storms to the south, bolts of lightning coursing over the sky. They sat there for perhaps half a minute, then the humming machinery found the strength to push them into the Bright again. Kyle watched radiant coils moving within the whiteness, pulsing and wavering . . . were they real? Or were his eyes and mind inventing them? It occurred to him they might be illusions like the tick-tock of clocks, a blandness made interesting inside the bored mind, and he blinked to clear his senses—

—and the next earth surrounded him, cloudless and moonlit. Kyle blinked again. Were those farm fields below? They had to be fields. He saw huge squares laid on the landscape, the nearest square reaching up the hillside and stopping just short of the portal. There was a tall, shaggy crop. Corn? It resembled corn packed stalk to stalk. Kyle found himself leaning forwards and squinting and then the Bright came again. It didn't linger long this time. Then they were on a dark, dark earth with a slow rain falling, the portal's outer shell dripping wet and prairie on all sides. He watched the heavy-seeded heads of the tall grasses as they lapped against the crystal, then there was motion above the grass. For an instant he was watching a human shape. A figure was standing in the rain . . . or was it another illusion? Kyle could swear he was seeing an arm lift, greeting him, and it occurred to him that the portal itself was playing with the light. Accenting it now, shading it at other times. How else could he see out there? A Wanderer guard? Was it? Only then they were past and the Bright was shining in from all sides, no land to be seen, no air, no weather or life or anything beside the Bright and this one tiny bubble in which they rode.

Kyle felt enormously tired.

Sometimes he could barely pay attention to the new

earths. He would give a quick and furtive glance, and maybe he noticed crops or the changeless silvery moon. But he didn't bother with even a second glance, feeling cold and tired within.

Then an earth would startle him, jolting his senses, making him gaze out at it wide-eyed.

There was one earth with a massive city set against the eastern horizon, broad skyscrapers reaching miles high and countless twists of flying light moving around the skyscrapers like swallows. The city must be along the river, he thought. A few high puffy clouds were pushing between skyscrapers, lending height and depth to the scene. The city stretched for a hundred miles north and south, maybe more, each structure cut into thousands of floors and each floor glowing with a cool blue-white light . . . everyone home, it seemed.

Then came an earth that was more water than land. Was this a reservoir? Or had someone raised the ocean and brought it inland? Kyle gazed down the hill at a huge expanse of calm water dotted with houseboats and barges and anchored platforms, few lights burning, the floating community deep asleep. Wholly unaware.

Kyle wiped his face with both hands.

There were several earths he barely noticed, maybe half a dozen of them: dark and ordinary with a few distant camp fires and porch lights showing but no other trace of people. He began to grow accustomed to the blandness. Then suddenly they were set inside a city with buildings standing within a few feet of the portal. These were homes, he realized. He was looking at massive, ageless homes built from native sandstone and brick. Yet the inhabitants, by contrast, were sticklike people. They seemed unsubstantial, almost cartoonish. Knots of them stood on the stone-paved street that ran along the hill's crest. Familiar yellow lights drifted overhead like huge fireflies. Were they the same as Wanderer lights? He couldn't tell. He blinked and stared at the closest people, noticing thin faces and big teardrop eyes and the way they never walked, not really, even the oldest ones breaking into an easy long-legged run when they saw people inside the portal, now coming at them . . . and then there was the Bright again, encompassing and spectacular.

The earths themselves felt like abnormalities.

They were flaws in the Bright, he was telling himself. It was the Bright that was the constant, rigid and absolutely reliable.

Kyle tipped his head and gazed upwards, tired eyes damp and aching. He wanted to be home again. He could see his apartment and the musty bed, and the desire rushed into him and made him shut his eyes and shake his head sorrowfully.

There was a sound near him, soft and quick. He breathed and opened his eyes and glanced at Billie. She was staring out at some new earth—Kyle didn't bother looking, not this time—and she said, "I wonder where we're going?" with precision. She spoke softly but clearly, then she turned and looked at him.

He didn't want to hear her voice; he was sick of her voice.

"Kyle?"

Her face was concerned but sober, illuminated by the moon and then the Bright, then the moon again. A sickness worked on his guts. He felt a tight cramping sensation, and he shook his head and turned forwards, dimly aware of sod buildings and grass and his eyes squinting and his face actually hurting because he was working so hard to keep it under control. He had to keep a hold on his reserves and his identity.

"Kyle?"

"I don't know where . . . where they're taking us."

"I don't think anyone knows," she responded.

He took a breath and held it, and for some reason he found himself remembering Janice's quarterback boyfriend. Kyle was thinking how the fellow had explained football to him, speaking with passion, and how he had made Kyle jealous. It had been a strange moment. The quarterback would never, never consider pretending to be a Wanderer or anything else false. He was not that sort of person. And then he'd sent Kyle out for the pass, and for an instant Kyle had planned to run out of sight. All at once he was sick of his charade and wanted to be normal. If he had just kept running—was he nuts?—he would be normal now. He would have transformed himself into an ordinary citizen with one action. Normalcy had acquired a sudden golden sheen, and he felt himself craving it.

"Why do they hate Jy?" Billie said softly. "I don't understand."

He shook his head and pulled his knees to his mouth, tasting the salty fabric of his trousers.

"Why are they doing this?" she asked.

Perhaps Quencé heard the question, or perhaps it was coincidence. He turned to Mr. Phillips and said, "You have done some extraordinary things, sir."

Mr. Phillips said nothing.

"You circumvented our security systems and used our portals to suit your own needs, and I don't think we've ever seen such a trick." He asked the others, "Does anyone remember anyone who hijacked a portal?"

Mr. Phillips was standing at the controls, arms relaxed and his bland face betraying nothing. He had a thin smile almost too thin to be seen, and he didn't speak.

"You admitted knowing Jy," Quencé continued. He had a strong, reasoned voice. "Why not admit to a few more details and humor us?"

Their captor gave no reaction. He glanced down as if to check some gauge, and Kyle studied him for the first time. He saw how the remnants of Mr. Phillips's hair had been combed backwards with a hand, and he stared at the gloved hand and the ordinary hand, then he looked at the man's eyes. The eyes seemed pale and very wrong. Ignore those eyes, Kyle decided, and Mr. Phillips would look like someone who drove buses. That's how ordinary he appeared. He was like one of those eternally middle-aged bus drivers who would sit at the steering wheel without speaking, hour after hour, using a minimum of motions and never appearing to breathe and the pavement rolling out before them and nothing else to life.

"A bold beginning," Quencé allowed, "but I'm sure you know you have lost your surprise now. Our people are sending warnings down after us, sending them ahead, and they will start chasing you too. They'll chase us. They aren't going to let you escape, believe me."

The bland face lifted and smiled with a certain force.

"Your communications are in shambles." Mr. Phillips spoke while touching controls, the pale eyes watching his own hands. "I know your timetables and tricks and believe me, I am not just lucky. I know exactly what I am doing." He seemed ready to laugh all at once. His smile grew, and he said, "Nothing has left that earth. I gave your central control system half a billion instructions, all prearranged, and it's going to take time to send even a warning down after us."

The eyes were like chips of hard glass, cold and inert.

Kyle had to look away.

He wiped his face and realized they weren't moving fast anymore. Or was it his imagination? No, he looked outside again and decided they were obviously slowing down.

The Bright lingered for a long while, then they appeared inside a forest of pine trees. There was a furious rain and flashes of lightning, and he could see the trees were of the same size, straight and aligned in perfect rows. Man-planted? They had to be. He watched the nodding branches until the Bright came again, and they stayed within it for an even longer while. He sat sucking on his knees, his mind suddenly empty. And when they came out . . . what? Was this real? Kyle could see a city to the south and east—a flat city with straight streets and familiar lights, one red traffic light aligned so it was visible from miles away—and he was thinking this had to be Lincoln and they were back again. The traffic light turned a sweet green. Look! Some wondrous fluke had delivered them home again, and he felt his heart pound faster while he started to grin.

Or was it Lincoln?

No, no. It couldn't be their earth, could it? They hadn't doubled back, and besides, where were the Wanderers? They should be in the foreground, and the prairie should be matted flat. Where were the floating ships? And the airport? It wouldn't be much of a coincidence, he realized, for two similar cities to be built on the same ground. It probably happened all the time. Damn!

Kyle leaned forwards, feeling such an ache in his chest.

Again came the Bright.

Then there was an empty earth with the hillside eroded and bedrock showing to the east and knots of weeds scattered across the hard ground.

The Bright.

A cold earth. He could see rotting drifts of snow nearby, in August, and he wondered if there were some ice age and how it could have started. Suddenly he felt like a tourist full of questions, and he had to stop himself from asking about the snow. He held his mouth closed and breathed through his nostrils once, then again.

The Bright.

Then it was a weird earth lit blue and populated with cloudlike cities. He saw the cities against the sky, wreathed in real clouds, and a gray-clad guard was standing beside the entranceway to the portal. She was a woman with a tattooed skull. She didn't realize what was happening. She saw them and waved automatically, smiling with her face washed in the blue glow, and Kyle looked higher. The moon was too high and too large. It was a crescent, gemstone blue and brilliant. He realized he was seeing an ocean wrapped inside a thick atmosphere, milky clouds here and there. The dynamics of its orbit had been changed by someone's work. What kinds of people could do such a thing? Then Billie said, "Oh," and sat taller.

Kyle said, "It's something," and nearly smiled. He surprised himself by nodding and halfway grinning, saying, "It is lovely, isn't it?"

Jy spoke all at once.

She seemed to be asking a question with that senseless language. Kyle glanced over his shoulder. Mr. Phillips was wearing a knowing expression. "Use English," he warned. "My mouth is built for English!" He must have understood Jy. It was Kyle's gut feeling, but of course that meant nothing. Learning Founder was probably easy for someone who could kidnap Jy and use the portals . . . that person could digest any language, at any time. Yet Kyle kept wondering if Mr. Phillips was a Wanderer too.

He shook his head and watched their captor while he fiddled with more controls, not saying one word. His hands were deft and the face was quite intense now, the eyes like big bright marbles stuck into that doughy flesh . . . .

Something was about to happen.

Everyone sensed it. Kyle looked at the other captives, particularly at Billie, then he stared at his own bare toes. The Bright was all around them, but he refused to look at it.

Mr. Phillips said, *"There,"* with force.

They were out of the Bright again, and that sense of motion had ceased. Yet Kyle would not look anywhere but at his toes, and they curled and uncurled and then slowly curled again.

3

I GIVE AT least one rally on each earth, even the uninhabited earths. It is something I have to do for myself; it is a habit and a tradition and a point of no small pride.

—*Jy's speeches*

THERE HAD been a war, a terrible long hard nuclear contest, and nothing larger than bacteria had survived. Besides the poisoned rubble nothing remained of civilization but for the weapons themselves. The weapons were my audience—sleek and black tritium-fired machines along with hard-eyed battle computers—and I stood inside one of their deep bunkers and spoke at length, giving my obligatory rally. Of course our scouts had made the bunker safe, and of course none in my audience could cheer or squeal or in any way respond, and of course

my noise and gestures accomplished nothing in
the end, which is what I expected, and which
in its own way was perfect, the lesson of the day
meant for me and no one else.

—*Jy's private journal*

It was the strangest Earth of all.

When Kyle finally looked he didn't recognize any
of the landscape. The portal's high hill was not beneath
them and Lincoln's riparian basin was choked with
masses of dark glass. He turned his head until his neck
ached. They were somewhere high in the air, and it
looked as if titans had used jackhammers to remake the
land, something planned and nothing finished. There
was a sharp new ridge to the east, and he followed the
ridge with his eyes. It lay to the north and west and
vanished to the south, and he thought: *Crater.* He imagined a comet falling to its death, the continent laid to
waste. He remembered the moon and found it out of
position, almost straight overhead, its familiar face erased
by a bright white dust. The moon was fresh and simple,
and it occurred to Kyle that what happened here was
connected to there and maybe elsewhere too. A rain of
comets? What?

Mr. Phillips said, "Now," and Cotton walked towards the entranceway, his strides short and blurringly
quick.

Nothing seemed to live outside. Kyle could see no
lights or vegetation, and he noticed that the portal's wall
was triple thick, implying poisons and other hazards.
Radiations? Bombs? But what sort of warhead could ex-
cavate tens of square miles of countryside? He could
imagine the physics in a slippery way but not the anger
involved. The anger was beyond him.

Cotton was past the inner door, standing inside a
cramped chamber half filled with a tall upright box. It
was a locker of some kind. The little man opened it and
removed pieces of a heavy suit and helmet. Kyle thought
of an armored spacesuit, watching each piece change size
to fit Cotton's proportions, always shrinking, and after a

few blurring seconds he was dressed and moving again, the outer door opening for him.

"Where are we?" asked Billie.

It was a supremely reasonable question. Kyle cleared his throat and said, "It's the same place as always." He couldn't think of anything better. "It's another earth . . . a changed one . . . violently changed."

Cotton was standing on a platform fastened to the portal's waist.

"Was it a war?" Billie wanted to know.

"An enormous war," Quencé answered with a colorless tone. He looked towards her and nodded, saying, "A remarkable war did this, made this, and it wasn't finished until after we arrived. The people who started it became extinct centuries ago, but their weapons kept fighting and building new weapons and we had to put those weapons to sleep . . . ."

Billie sighed.

Kyle looked outside. The platform and Cotton had vanished.

"We keep the weapons asleep," Quencé explained. He glanced at their captor with his eyes steady and inquisitive, and he didn't seem to be speaking to anyone in particular. "The bombs are a useful source of energy," he was saying, "and we keep them because we'll someday want to heal this earth in some suitable way. Once the background radiations drop far enough, we will find volunteers to come and oversee the work—"

"A decent gesture," said Mr. Phillips.

Quencé nodded.

Jy said, "We have an obligation to the earths."

Mr. Phillips moved his gloved hand with a flourish, touching controls, then he said, "An obligation to the earths?" with an amused but bitter look on his face. "I'm glad to hear it."

"But we're using it as it stands now," Quencé explained. He made a large gesture and glanced at Billie. "We bring world leaders here and use the ruins and bunkers as classrooms. Certain people need to see the fate they're tempting. Do you understand, miss? We try to give them an inoculation of rationality."

"A reasonable purpose," said Mr. Phillips.

Jy stirred.

Billie sighed again.

Quencé stared at a patch of the floor, thinking aloud. "We don't use guards here because the radiation makes long stays hazardous, and there would be little purpose anyway. This world is dead and remains dead." The voice was gaining momentum. He squinted and said, "Everything dangerous is sleeping within security systems, entirely out of reach. But of course those systems are the same as the systems protecting the portals from intruders, and someone with enough cleverness might be able to circumvent and warp and transform . . . making mischief."

Mr. Phillips watched Quencé.

Kyle saw motion in the corner of an eye, and he jerked his head and saw Cotton rising into view, legs apart and riding the same platform. An enormous bundle floated behind Cotton, silverish armor protecting its contents, and he was tied to the bundle with a cord. He towed it into the portal, the thick outer door opening and closing for him. Then he was undressing. He pulled off his armor and the bundle's thicker armor, exposing a package of tough gray fabric, plain and resembling luggage. It remained floating, and Cotton got behind it and pushed it through the inner door. He was breathing faster than a sprinter, his body shaking and his spent voice saying, "Done," between the gulps.

"Good," Mr. Phillips responded.

There was a sudden hum of machinery beneath them. The Bright returned an instant later, and Kyle braced for the next earth's appearance.

Yet they remained in the Bright.

"I want to show you something," Mr. Phillips told Jy. "I can dip back into the dead earth for microsecond intervals and link with one of your old scout satellites." The Bright diminished ever so slightly. "Watch," said Mr. Phillips. A projection appeared overhead. It was like the earths floating at the rally, coherent light making a sphere of oceans and continents and clouds—only this earth seemed dull and miscolored. The clouds were gray or rusty brown, and the icecaps had vanished. The bombardments must have melted them, or greenhouse gases had boiled off the blasted crust.

Their captor said, "Watch," to Jy.

Jy made no sound, no motion, her big eyes fixed on the globe.

There was a single bloom of scalding white light. It came from the nightside—South America?—and a moment later there were more explosions racing outwards. The sleeping death-machines seemed to be awake, smelling a fight and finding their arms intact. Were they shooting each other? he wondered. Or the portals? What if they were obliterating the portals?

"What's happening?" asked Billie.

Kyle spoke reflexively. "He wants to cut the Bright in two," he said too loudly. The Cousin, Xen, turned to him with a panicked expression, and Kyle added, "At least I think so."

"Can he?" Billie shook her head. "How can he?"

"We made it easy for him," said Quencé with a cold assurance. "We left the tools lying about with nobody watching, and all it would take is time and patience and a certain talent—"

"The Bright won't be cut in two," Jy interrupted. "The Makers . . . they built it too well for that to happen."

"True." Quencé nodded, pulling a dark hand across his face and sucking air through his teeth. "The Bright's machinery will survive without so much as a bruise. But the portals are going to be destroyed or knocked out of alignment, and it might take days, or longer, to stop the fighting and move a working portal into position." He shook his head and regarded Mr. Phillips. "I guess we should applaud. You've accomplished something remarkable . . . ."

His voice lost its purchase and heart.

Quencé was sweating through the gray of his uniform, and his expression was pained.

Jy made a soft quavering sound.

The image overhead trembled and dissolved. Now only the Bright was visible, for an instant. Then there was a new landscape: the familiar hillside dropping to a quiet lake, smooth water shining under the traditional moon. It was a startling place, too tranquil to seem real. Kyle shivered and shook his head and felt his heart slamming against his chest and aching guts. *What now?*

Jy rose to her feet and turned, asking their captor, "Where are you taking us, sir?"

Mr. Phillips stared at her face, saying nothing. Some slippery emotion made his jaw clench and his nostrils flare, but he refused to answer, his stance telling them he wasn't going to offer any explanations now.

They were in the Bright again.

Then they were on an earth with great rings built from tumbling moons, brilliant and numberless, and Kyle stared up at the arching rings while Jy said, "I think you want me. These others don't matter to you, do they? Why not just leave them somewhere?"

Kyle felt a warm rising hope. He looked down the hillside and found a cluster of buildings lit from within, and he tried imagining himself walking down there to pound on a friendly door—

"If you are any sort of person," said Jy, "have compassion—"

"No," Mr. Phillips replied.

Kyle made himself turn and watch their captor shake his head, arms crossed on his chest.

I don't belong here, he realized.

All at once he was imagining himself standing too. He would clear his throat and say, "I was lying. I'm not a real Wanderer. You've made a mistake by taking me . . . ."

This involved Wanderers and not him. It was a family matter, and it seemed supremely unfair that *he* should be swept up by their troubles. He and Billie both. He glanced at Billie and readied himself. He'd admit anything at this point. He turned to Mr. Phillips while trying to find the strength—

—and he saw the strange hard eyes glaring at Jy.

"Compassion?" Mr. Phillips said.

Jy made no sound. The gold fringes of her own eyes shone with the Bright, and her mouth was set and certain.

"Compassion," Mr. Phillips repeated.

Quencé reached for Jy, saying, "Please sit," and lightly touched her on the back. "He wants to keep all of us, Jy."

"Sit," said the Cousin.

"Yes, please," said the black woman.

Mr. Phillips seemed to mutter, "Compassion," once again. His face darkened as he shook it slowly. Then he made a wet snorting noise, and Kyle was glad he had made no confession. He wouldn't tell the truth; the secret belonged to him. It was some sort of victory, his identity beyond the reach of this brutish creature . . . and the thought made Kyle start to smile, on the sly.

QUENCÉ

1

JUST AS no gene has a single effect, no policy of ours has a lone intent. For instance, there are a multitude of reasons why we will not talk about the other earths, giving you textbook explanations of each of them. We pick what you should hear—what seems informal really is carefully considered—and there are a tangle of reasons why.

Partly it is because we came here to see *you*, not to serve as tour guides and talk about things past. *You* are who matter to us. And it is because we want you to remain original and unique. We want your innocence, in a sense. And we have had some hard experiences of our own—too much said and too many people left wishing they could live on another earth—and we don't want you dissatisfied. If you sit and dream about prettier and richer and more just earths, what have we accomplished? Your time is wasted, as is ours, and this is why we try to keep relatively mute on the subject.

There is another reason too.

Perhaps this is the central reason.

We have visited approximately one million earths, and that is a crushing number. Yet it is abstract. Nobody can envision such a number or handle it, and that is a blessing. If I began to tell you about each one of the half million earths I have seen myself, you would be astounded and then numbed. We wouldn't reach a thousand earths and you would sense your precious homeland was nothing. A hundred thousand earths described, and each of you would feel like an atom fused to a single grain of sand. And then if I tried to explain everything that had happened on each of the earths since I left—if I would have the time and voice to read the histories of the migrations and great accomplishments and the disappointments and tragedies—how would you feel in the end? How could you look at each other and consider your own histories to matter?

I know, I sound like some overcautious parent. I know.

Consider me guilty and hate me if you wish. Please think whatever you wish, and often, and with all the emotion you can find. I do not mind.

—*Jy's speeches*

He might have seen them for what they were, which meant he should have seen through them and stopped them before they had reached Jy's ship. Quencé couldn't quit thinking about Mr. Phillips and his supposed nephew joining the orderly line and his standing beside them for several precious seconds. Memory had its way of making details obvious. He could see Mr. Phillips's persistent friendliness and Cotton's vague wrongness while feeling a certain palpable tension being emitted by both men. At the time Quencé had mistaken tension for simple nervousness. And what about earlier? he thought. He remembered Mr. Phillips in the restaurant and the way the man had deftly managed to seem thoroughly ordinary, even forgettable. He had invited a hard look to defuse any possible suspicions, ensuring Quencé's support through subtle acts and words and a few well-timed silences.

Quencé took a deep wet breath.

He felt his hand come to his forehead, and he sagged against it. He was helpless. He hadn't felt so helpless since he was a novice, or maybe not since childhood. Yet even then he couldn't recall any time when he could do so little in the face of trouble.

Quencé pulled the hand across his eyes and nose and tightly clamped mouth, and he shook his head in despair.

Cotton watched him for an instant. Was he smiling? It was hard to tell what was on that strange quick face.

Where was Cotton's home? Quencé concentrated, juggling some of the possibilities. He assumed Cotton was human, not alien or mechanized or anything even stranger, yet no earth seemed to ring true. He skimmed through his hard-memory, glancing at tens of thousands of earths, and none of them possessed such people. If he could somehow get access to a library, he was thinking, and have a few minutes to concentrate . . .

It was a silly wish. He knew he wasn't being reasonable.

Yet it felt good to focus and work with what little he had available to him.

Plowing the rocks to make the weeds grow fast.

It had been a saying in Quencé's home village, an often-heard phrase used for awful circumstances, and it seemed appropriate here. Yet he kept telling himself there were clues lying about and perhaps flaws in their captors' plans. Something somehow would give them an advantage, however slight, and it was up to him to find that advantage and act accordingly.

What do I know? he asked himself.

Quencé prepared an empty file within his hard-memory and placed inside it each quantum of information. He compiled everything he knew about Mr. Phillips and Cotton and everything he had seen, then he added the implications and a few gray-edged conclusions that already had occurred to him.

Glancing sideways, he found Jy. She was sitting on the padded floor with her short legs crossed in a stiff, old-woman fashion, both hands on the floor as if to steady herself. He kept watching her, and after a long moment she lifted her eyes and gave him a sluggish nod.

"He understands Founder," Quencé began, whispering.

"I had the same impression," she answered, her words slow and quite precise.

"Perhaps he does know you."

She closed her mouth, acting as if she wouldn't want it true. She seemed almost offended.

"Perhaps he was a novice—"

She shook her head. "Knowing what he knows?"

It wasn't a serious suggestion. Quencé was trying to manage this with grace and tact. He glanced at Mr. Phillips—whoever he was—and saw that he was concentrating, punching in codes and new commands. Quencé wondered how a novice might gain access to the right facilities. It felt too incredible, he decided. Even most true Wanderers would know perhaps a tenth of what they needed to get this far, and they would have bungled it early and been caught.

"Yet he has to be a Wanderer," said Jy.

Quencé nodded. "He is or he was." Was he someone who gave up the mission out of bitterness? And if so, where in Reality did he find a creature like Cotton?

"Was," Jy allowed, "and he wants revenge for something, I think."

Quencé waited, considering all possibilities.

Jy exhaled and seemed to grow smaller. Then she lifted one long dark hand, examining the blunted nails of her fingers as if they held answers. How was she tolerating the pressures? She had lived forever with security and established routines, he thought, and here she was tossed into a trap without warning. What was

Jy feeling? She seemed to be strong enough, but Quencé wanted a sign that the strength was more than a veneer.

The other Wanderers looked exhausted. The one who had brought the girl—Kyle—was the worst. His expression was weak and scared, practically devastated, and that was worrisome. They had to stay united, thought Quencé. Coming apart would help nothing.

He glanced at Mr. Phillips. How did he manage the disguise? Unless he had arrived before the first scouts, there had to have been a real Mr. Phillips. What did he do? He might have cloned the body or managed a string of cosmetic surgeries on a similar body, or perhaps he had changed the real Mr. Phillips in some fashion. There was a list of possibilities, and he filed each one away for later.

"He was high-ranking," muttered Jy.

Mr. Phillips regarded them with his face eerily composed, almost serene.

"I am sure he was high-ranking," she repeated.

Quencé took a breath and exhaled and said, "Perhaps a Cousin," without confidence. "Perhaps his augmented brain failed somehow, leaving him insane and incapable of judgment."

Jy said, "A disturbed Cousin," with her voice diminishing to nothing.

Quencé glanced at Xen. Could he hear them? Did he have any opinions? Xen's mouth opened and his bright thick pink tongue moved along his teeth. *Have augmented brains ever gone sour?* Quencé asked himself. He toyed with the technical aspects, earnestly wishing some scenario that would answer every question neatly and without fuss. It would be an endurable story. Insanity? It would leave nobody to blame, no villain or evil; it would mean a series of mistakes that could be corrected; it would be infinitely better than a sane enemy who was intimate with them and who knew their every weakness.

Jy made a low sound.

Quencé turned again. Their captor was starting to walk with his head tilted forwards and his mouth smiling in a dead fashion and his arms hanging at his sides.

"Who are you?" asked Jy.

Cotton was laughing at everyone.

Quencé gazed across the portal and found the little man. The face and voice were hypnotically swift. Cotton was sitting on the big field pack he had retrieved from the dead earth. How did it feel to be he? Quencé wondered. What was happening inside his skull?

"Who are you?" Jy persisted. "When were you with the mission, and what did you do for us?"

"What did I do for you?" responded their captor.

Jy quit speaking.

Quencé felt himself straightening, listening with the whole of his body. He could miss nothing that was said or done.

"I do know you," said the man. "Would you like to learn how?"

Jy gave a tiny, almost imperceptible nod.

"Then I will tell everyone," he announced with force. The earths were rushing around them and the Bright was between the earths. Nobody was watching and nobody was moving and the only thing was this man with the forgettable face and the hard eyes and that steady, knowing voice. He said, "Now—"

—and Quencé felt himself falling, nothing beneath him and nothing above and his hands instinctively lashing at the empty air as he fell faster, spinning and twisting for what seemed like forever.

2

IN MY dream I was the first to reach the end of the Bright, though I had no idea why it happened to me or how. I do remember feeling unworthy of the honor for no clear reason, perhaps even a little angry to have had the honor given to me. The Bright ended inside a large room with a colored dome above and colored tiles under my bare feet, and sitting at the opposite end of the room was a Maker. I knew it was a Maker in that instinctive way common to dreams, and of course I walked towards the figure at once. The Maker was sitting behind the most unremarkable desk, waiting for me! I reached the center of the room trembling with excitement; then an instant later I remembered why I was not worthy to be there. The realization struck me like a physical blow. My legs collapsed and my body fell on the tiles, and I wasn't inside the room anymore. I was in some different place that was cold and dark and quite small, and as I lay there with my limbs too heavy to move, I saw figures built of smoke and soot advancing on me, grinning at me, coming from everywhere . . . .

—Moliak's private journal

Quencé became aware of a voice and then a figure standing before him, and at some point he realized it was his mother speaking to him, saying, "You are too young, absolutely too young, to attend any rally and particularly a rally where Jy speaks to fools." Quencé found himself bristling, the waves of disorientation beginning to fade. "You know our feelings about the idiotic mission of hers," she told Quencé. *Our* meant his father too. "We find nothing to merit any journey along the Bright, for any purpose. If there are Makers then it is their possession and we would be trespassing." The language was from Quencé's home village, yet at the same time it was distinctly different. The word *trespassing* held connotations implying an enormous crime, something basal and universally scorned. "And if the Makers are extinct," concluded his mother, "then where is the slightest good reason for making even a fraction of the sacrifice Jy asks of us? Why should we destroy our earth for her ludicrous cause?"

Quencé stared at his mother.

She was a large woman who had grown comfortably fat in these last years—how did he know this?—and she leaned forward on her long arms while telling her son her earnest feelings. She was a Founder woman, and suddenly Quencé felt his wrong-shaped body, and the odd round-edged architecture of their house made him nervous, and some small sober part of him knew precisely what was happening. What he saw and heard and felt now was an illusion. Mr. Phillips, who was not Mr. Phillips, had injected him and perhaps the others into this perfectly rendered simulation of some old event. Advanced earths had invented such technologies many times, using these same devices as a means of education and entertainment. Quencé's own soft neurons were being manipulated into believing he was standing inside a young Founder's skin and mind, and he was experiencing some small part of another person's youth.

What is your real name? he wondered.

"Quencé," said the Founder woman. "Are you listening to me?"

He heard himself say, "Yes," too loudly. Apparently the real name was a secret. Quencé shook his head and told her, "I am listening," and he waited, glancing at his blunt fingernails.

"You know how I feel," said the woman, "and now I expect you to stay home through the day and study. Can I trust you?"

With a careful voice he said, "You can trust me." Then he turned and entered his room, shutting the door and walking to the largest window and climbing outside without fanfare, and he continued walking. His home was beneath the Mountains of Mountains on the Founders' earth, and the village was set on the rich broad floodplain. He watched the sun above and the village robots working among the crops and he tried to keep out of their sight, believing in his boyish fashion that they might notice him and report him to his parents. The young Founder imagined they were loyal to his parents because his hard-hearted mother shared the robots' mechanical certainty about everything. "The stupid woman," he grumbled aloud, and he beat the ground with a long stick. "The stupid, stupid, stupid, stupid woman!"

People from every village in the region attended the

rally. Entire villages arrived en masse, but Quencé sensed that only a few faces were from his home. He avoided those faces as he filed into the ancient stone amphitheater, a one-time holy place built by human labor and elephants and intended to honor an assortment of ancient gods. Quencé looked up at the weathered statues over the entranceway, his eyes fixing on one huge woman who smiled at him and reached towards him with one hand. She was Compassion, he seemed to know. Compassion was one of the greatest gods among them, and her smile was meant for him alone.

The rally itself was wondrous and remarkable, and Quencé found himself committing every word and gesture of Jy's into his hard-memory. He was young, just entering puberty, yet he sensed that the rest of his life was being formed around him while he sat and listened. He had never seen Jy in person. He was motionless, absorbing the words and imagining the Makers for himself. He pictured himself in their midst and Jy stood just ahead of him and their journey, the mission, was finished after an enormous span of time and countless challenges and untold sacrifices.

Jy was an old gray woman at the rally. She was even more feeble than the Jy one million years in the future, many decades spent holding rallies and making converts from skeptics. The rumor then was that soon she would have to die and join the Archives because her flesh was reaching its legal end. Jy would have to do the honorable deed and make room for the young, like Quencé, and she would be set on a shelf and likely be forgotten. The forgetting process would be gradual but irreversible, her mission left to her followers and their chances at the very best poor.

Perhaps such possibilities were haunting Jy. Time was precious, yet there remained hard knots of skepticism in the world. Quencé's homeland was a famous bastion of inertia, indifferent to all changes in what was deemed the proper lives for Founders. She had come here to meet her worst skeptics and win their good will. Yet sometimes during the long rally, under the raw sun, Jy began to lose her energies and her voice and her age became painfully apparent. She was a very old woman quite suddenly, and Quencé felt a dull ache in his false self and in his real self too. He found himself rather scared for Jy.

Then she quit talking altogether. She was telling about the Makers and how they represented the triumph of intelligence and compassion. Only a vast intelligence could have constructed something as miraculous as the Bright, she argued, and surely that intelligence must have left the Bright for humans to use. It was wonderfully suited to the mission she proposed—energy limiting the numbers to be moved; peace and prosperity required on every earth left behind—and then Jy shut her eyes and seemed to shake her head. She had quit speaking. She sagged with exhaustion, and everyone in the audience could see she was drowning. Quencé wasn't sitting as close as he would have liked, but he saw everything and grew sick inside for a brief horrible instant.

This happened to Mr. Phillips, he reminded himself. *It is nothing more, or less, than a vivid memory.*

Yet while the real Quencé reassured himself, the false Quencé decided to act. He rose to his feet and began to applaud in the Founder fashion. He slapped his belly with both hands. He began to shout praises that everyone could hear, and every other supporter in the amphitheater stood and applauded too. They were following Quencé's example. They granted the Glorious One a reprieve in which she could collect her wits and milk the strength from her tired muscles before beginning again, and it worked.

Disaster had been averted at the last possible instant.

It was a glorious moment. Jy found the strength and self-assurance to continue, launching into one of her finest speeches. The real Quencé could only watch and marvel. How many rallies had he seen where Jy had done wonders? Yet never, never did her fire and will and wit and charm do as much. Quencé watched the crowd's sullen mood shift in stages. Jy told them about the beginnings of the mission for her, how she had nearly died on the empty earth and about the startling inspiration to have come from the moment, then she described the Makers with a mixture of certainty and electric vagueness that brought everyone to their feet, hands slapping bellies and the excitement intoxicating and adults asking one another, "*Who* would be better to start this mission than we?" They nodded and applauded louder, bruising themselves. "Some species will do it someday," they reasoned, "and why not the Founders? *Why not us?*"

Suddenly the crowd and amphitheater began to evaporate.

Quencé knew what was happening when he heard the girl cry out, "Kyle?" and he felt the floor beneath him, blinking fast to bring back his sight. "Kyle?" she asked. "It was . . . a dream?"

"Yes," muttered her companion. "A dream . . . sort of . . . sure . . . ."

Mr. Phillips stood watching them. His bland face was flushed and sour; the hard eyes had a sudden fire pointed towards Jy.

"Did it happen?" asked Jy. "As you showed us?"

"Exactly," said their captor. *The one-time Founder*, thought Quencé with a sick sensation. "I built the illusion from my hard-memories, and I tried to stay faithful."

"Who are you?" she asked again.

The man gave a tiny shrug with his shoulders.

"I remember the rally," Jy admitted, "and the applause, and it did end well, I think . . . ."

"It ended perfectly," he responded.

"Yes?"

"It could have destroyed the mission—a bad rally at an unfortunate time—but instead you earned enormous public goodwill and pressed forward and won everything you desired in the end. Those who couldn't support you at least agreed to step aside and keep out of your way."

"Yes," said Jy. "I remember that."

Their captor stepped forward and reached with his gloved hand, and he stroked Jy's short ragged hair. He was touching the crown of her head, Quencé bracing himself, yet the motion and pressure were affectionate.

Quencé didn't dare move; he didn't trust himself to even flinch.

"Who are you?" asked Jy.

"If you remember the rally," he promised, "you remember me."

Jy glanced at Quencé.

"You remember me."

"I . . . I cannot."

Everyone watched the gloved hand caressing her scalp, mirrored fingers about the ears and then her forehead and then descending down along the back of Jy's neck and finally lifting an instant before the man began to step backwards, his confident voice saying, "Yes, Jy, yes you do . . . ."

3

THOSE WHO understand physics tell me that the Bright is not a straight line. True, we never feel its bends and twists while moving upon it, but our perceptions are not real evidence. Nobody can judge what is real when they are on the Bright. My experts claim that its structure is drawn into virtual knots in places, the knots existing in a variety of hyperdimensions, and the reason is a mystery. Is the Bright avoiding invisible obstacles? Are there other Brights in its midst? Or perhaps—this is a remarkable thought, I warn you—perhaps the Makers perceive what we cannot and they constructed the loops and bends and tight curls to make their journeys more interesting, not unlike carnival rides . . . .

—*Jy's speeches*

They had been gaining velocity since they had left the dead earth. Quencé watched the landscapes blinking past them, every feature blurring and his eyes aching and his mind reeling. This mysterious Founder had used the emergency codes—the codes intended for the day the Makers were discovered—and now every other concern of the portals was secondary. More and more of the system's energies were being absorbed here, used to move the eight of them, and the velocities were rising even higher as the portal's heart hummed sharply and steadily with a pitch well above any Quencé had ever heard in the past.

"I apologize to you, miss," said Mr. Phillips. Quencé still thought of him as Mr. Phillips. "I'm sure you were surprised by my tricks. One moment you were here and in mortal danger, the next moment you were an adolescent Founder, a male, somewhere very strange and long ago dead."

The girl whispered, "It was . . . was strange," and she dipped her head with her mouth pressed into a thin straight line.

Kyle sat beside her and stared into the floor, saying nothing.

"I want everyone to learn the history of certain . . . well, certain conditions," said Mr. Phillips. "When I realized what I wanted to do and how to do it—how I had to do it—I promised myself that those who came with me would have the opportunity to see what I have seen through my own eyes. I want nobody to be ignorant in the end."

People glanced at each other and waited.

"What is your name, miss?"

"Billie," she said softly. "Zacharia."

"I was very close to your age when I joined the Wanderers, Billie." He nodded with satisfaction, then he said, "It was my calling and it soon became my entire life, and I suspect I never truly existed until I was part of the mission. Can you imagine how that must feel? If I had been born outside that particular age, perhaps only fifty years earlier, I might have always felt an emptiness that I couldn't explain or cure or even ignore. Can you imagine?"

She seemed to nod.

Mr. Phillips said nothing for a long moment, his bare hand sweeping his hair flat against his damp scalp.

The moon was a flickering presence overhead, and Quencé tried to make sense of the images he could see. There were green moons and strip-mined moons and moons clothed in glass or left alone, and sometimes the moon was out of position or occasionally completely removed. They were already a long distance down the Bright. They had passed Quencé's homeland and thousands of others, and he shuddered and blinked and happened to look up into a series of raw changeless moons that stared back down at him with those distorted dead eyes.

"Billie," said their captor, "I am going to reach inside everyone's head once again. I'm warning you—"

She whimpered.

He said, "Now—"

It happened more easily this time. Quencé felt the layers of strange flesh and the stranger soul come over him and draw up against him, remaking him. He found himself looking at a crescent moon high on a hard blue sky, and there were shouts and he looked ahead and recognized the place and the time with absolute certainty. It was the Day of Beginnings. Quencé was standing on the short sharp brown tropical grass at the geographical point where Jy, marooned on another earth, had had her inspiration for the mission. There was to be a ceremony beside the portal in a little while. He could see the portal shining in the sun and he felt a wave of youthful enthusiasm, wishing the ceremony could begin now—and then he was watching the Founders themselves. There were several thousand of them. They constituted the entire population of the entity not yet called *Wanderers*. This was holy ground and a holy day, he told himself, yet the scene was remarkably informal. The mission that would swell, becoming relentless and sophisticated, seemed remarkably small and even ordinary at its outset. Quencé had seen holos of the Day of Beginnings, but standing here and looking at the scene with what felt to be his own eyes . . . it was more than a little bit deflating to him. Here was no grand mission shaping the destinies of countless earths. He was witnessing a gathering of like-minded eccentrics who had no idea what they were attempting to do and absolutely no appreciation for the scale of the coming events.

A familiar voice spoke to Quencé, saying, "Walk with me and listen, will you? I need to tell you several things, my friend."

He turned and found Jy smiling at him. Her hand grasped his shoulder and squeezed with a startling force. She was recently rejuvenated, her fur quite black and glossy and every large white tooth in her mouth newly grown, and when they were alone Quencé heard himself asking, "What can I do for you, my friend?"

"The selections are made," Jy announced.

Quencé understood what she meant. Or rather, the Founder he had become understood her, and suddenly he felt ill at ease. Computers had randomly selected which of them would travel with which group upon the Bright. The results were supposed to remain secret until the ceremony itself, when Quencé would help hold the flower-rope that Jy would break. Yet for some reason she had taken him aside, explaining, "We will work for the same purpose, my friend, but in different directions. It is decided."

Quencé felt heartsick and then angry. He had always been one of Jy's favorite students and certainly one of the most loyal members of their mission, and he was startled by how much it hurt to know he might never see Jy again.

"I had hoped we could work together," he muttered. His Founder voice was brittle and slow. He noticed they were again using Quencé's native language, as if in this illusionary state nothing else was quite so comfortable and easy. He said, "I wanted to serve you," and he shivered.

"We will meet again," Jy said hopefully. "Perhaps you will find the Makers for us, and I will come to you and meet them too."

Quencé stopped walking.

Jy took his hand and said, "Listen to a secret," and she smiled with all the life in her. "This is our secret.

Do you know what I believe? I believe that of everyone here today you might be the best of us, that you have the patience and the vision. Sometimes you make me envious, my dear friend, because you do seem better suited to this mission than I."

"I do?"

Jy took a step and stopped again. She said, "I was tempted to cheat and place you in my own group, but then I realized I needed you with the others. We needed you. Perhaps you can help lead them while I help lead my group as well as possible. Selfishness aside, perhaps this is for the best."

It was for the best, Quencé was thinking. He wept and tried to see what she meant.

Jy was staring at him.

"I understand," he groaned.

She made a noise. She seemed to whimper and grow cold all at once, then she said, "I know you," with the softest voice.

Jy was both Jys, Quencé realized. She was the youthful Jy on the Day of Beginnings, excited by her successes, and she was his Jy, the ancient one, riding inside the portal with a madman holding them captive.

"I do know you," she sputtered.

He couldn't speak any longer.

She said, "Moliak," and reached for him with both arms, and now she was weeping too.

Who was Moliak? he wondered. Mr. Phillips—?

"Why do you do these things, Moliak?"

Quencé kept silent.

"What does this mean? What do you want?" Jy had become gray again, taking a faltering step forwards while saying, "Talk to me and tell me why you have done this harm!"

Someone said, "Not now."

"No?"

The savanna evaporated. Once again they were inside the portal, and their captor was watching them and half smiling. *His name is Moliak*, thought Quencé. *Moliak*. He was standing beside the controls with his expression amused and then serious. The captives stood in a

closely packed group, and Jy walked towards him and
screamed, "Moliak!" with her arms rising over her head.
"What do you want, my friend?"

"First, my friend," he explained, "I need to do some
work." Then he lifted his gloved hand and a white bolt
jumped at her, striking her chest, and the blow lifted
her and slammed her backwards and Quencé jumped
too late. Jy twisted past him and landed on the floor, the
air stinking of ozone and her eyes shut tight.

Quencé shrieked.

He cried out and knelt and touched her closer arm,
feeling the loose meat and the bone and nothing else.

There was no motion and no breath.

Then he fell away, hands across his eyes and his
mouth making a slow keening noise, the other Wanderers coming around him and asking, "Is she dead? Is she?
Is she? Quencé? *Is she?*"

4

EVERYTHING HAS gone wrong, extraordinarily
wrong.

—*Moliak's private journal*

Cotton grabbed Quencé by the shoulder and pulled him
away from Jy.

She died, he was thinking. *Did he kill her hard-
memory too?*

Instinctively Quencé braced himself for the misery
and guilt certain to come, but they were worse than he
had imagined. The ache struck him and made him insane,
and Cotton kept pulling on his arm with a small hand
stronger than any hand should be. He could feel the heat
from Cotton's body, dry and steady, and Quencé let his
insanity take control of him. He spun and swung hard,
finding air, and Cotton was behind him again and driving
him to the floor. "No no no no no no," said Cotton's too-
quick voice. Quencé felt a foot strike him in the side.

He grunted and moaned and rolled, the floor becoming padded wherever he lay, and Cotton told him, "No no no not again no . . ."

"Is she dead?" Quencé grunted.

"She is unconscious," said Moliak. "Believe me, I want her alive and healthy as long as possible."

Quencé shut his eyes and felt a watery motion. He kept his eyes shut for a moment, an age . . . then Wysh was touching him. "Does it hurt?" she asked. She put pressure on his ribs, and no, nothing hurt badly. He was the tough spawn of hardened people, he reminded himself. A kick from a horse was worse than this love peck. Jy was alive and Quencé felt relief and a senseless hope. Wysh looked down at him, white teeth showing and her smile not working, and he was oddly pleased that she would try to smile. It was as if there had never been hard feelings between them.

"Would you like to sit up?" she asked.

He sat up on his first attempt. "Where is she?"

"There," said Xen. The Cousin stood with both hands in his trouser pockets, his breathless voice saying, "They are doing something to her."

"What?" asked Quencé.

Wysh offered her hand, and he rose to his feet.

Cotton was sitting at the far side of the portal, his back to them and his head turning every few moments with a blurring motion, scanning everything. Beside him was the field pack he had pulled from the dead earth. Packets of food and large water jugs were scattered on the floor, and Xen said, "They removed . . . an autodoc, I think it was."

"Yes," said Wysh. She shook her head, eyes dampened. "It looks like a standard autodoc."

Nobody spoke.

Then the girl asked, "What are they doing?"

Her Wanderer said, "We don't know, Billie," with a tight soft voice.

Cotton glanced back at them and frowned. His chest was like a pump working fast, and Quencé wondered how he managed to remain intact. His bones and tendons had to be reinforced, and he had yet to eat anything.

The man was like some human-shaped shrew, a metabolic firestorm raging inside him—

"She moved," said Billie. "I saw Jy move. Did you, Kyle?"

Quencé watched Moliak huddled beside the autodoc, and suddenly a familiar hand lifted into view, opened, and dropped again.

"I see her," said Kyle.

Quencé's senses were beginning to clear. The feeling of helplessness made him weak inside, but at least Jy was alive. *At least I'm alive*, he thought. Cotton had given him a warning when he could have kicked him to blood and meat, and that was positive too. Was he reluctant to kill? Or perhaps Moliak wanted them as well as Jy. Perhaps whatever he had planned required some or all of them.

The autodoc was deploying its many surgical limbs, and Quencé heard it clattering as it made ready.

He turned and glanced at the portal's controls. They were most certainly locked, but if he could see their settings, perhaps he could guess their final destination . . . .

Quencé took a couple tentative steps.

"Stop!" shouted Cotton.

Quencé turned and saw the man standing on his toes, his gloved hand moving with one finger pointing and a shimmering ball of golden light forming on its tip. How did they make those gloves? How did they control them? He had never seen weapons like them, yet apparently they had built them inside Jy's own ship.

Quencé retreated at once.

Wysh told him, "We don't want confrontations."

The golden light was reabsorbed into the glove.

"Please," said Wysh. She sounded angry with him and frustrated, her old habits returning. "We've got to do what they want now."

"I know," he managed.

Xen said, "Yes," and nodded. "We have to control ourselves."

Quencé could see the autodoc's arms in motion and the prostate shape of the Glorious One restrained by more arms. Moliak was overseeing the autodoc. He sat hunched forwards while concentrating on the patient's head, watching the rapid cutting.

Quencé looked at the people around them. They were an exhausted collection, everyone broken and past sadness. One after another they would look outside the portal where the earths passed them as countless glimmers. It was still nighttime but approaching morning, and he looked towards the west and the dropping moons. Most of the skies seemed clear, and the moons seemed to hold their familiar ashen color for a long while. Quencé could see nothing else. The landscapes bled into one another, and he couldn't be sure what he was seeing now. He felt tired and sore all at once, and he sat on the floor and breathed and began to think of everything until the facts and hunches were totally unmanageable.

He began to drift into a trance.

He was marshaling all his concentration, wanting to find some sense in this craziness, relaxing and shutting his eyes and scarcely hearing Wysh as she sniffed at the air.

Xen asked, "What do you smell?"

"Blood," said Wysh, "and Jy's hard-memory too."

"Why would he want her hard-memory?" asked Xen, mystified more than angry. "How could he use it?"

"I don't know," Wysh replied.

"Oh, goodness," said Billie. "Oh, goodness."

Then Kyle said, "It doesn't make sense to any of us." His voice was soft and slow, full of authority.

BILLIE

1

SOMEDAY WE will be done with the mission, and I shall face the prospects of finding some new existence and purpose. I would like to believe that the Makers and humanity could use me as a conduit between them, although I'm not certain I would be good at the task. Perhaps all Wanderers could help serve in that role. Yet perhaps it won't be possible, not for us and not for me alone, and after the mission each of us will return to our home earth and finish our natural lives with poise and a measure of character. Sometimes I imagine myself living upon the Founders' earth once again, and I wither and die and my hard-memory soul is set beside the souls of my family, my long time finished and my rest well deserved....

—*Jy's speeches*

She watched the sun rising between snatches of the Bright, her eyes unable to focus on anything but the sun.

Suns, she reminded herself. She kept forgetting there were as many suns as there were earths. *Why can't I remember?* Kyle muttered something about their speed within these portals and the energy required to move them, his voice colorless and slow. It was as if he was forgetting why they were here. "If we were moving at the normal pace," he told Billie, "we could appreciate the earths." He smiled weakly as if trying to cheer her. They were sitting close and eating some of the dried meats and fruits that Cotton had brought them. Kyle said, "Most of the time you have a minute or more on every earth, and you can look outside and see the most miraculous things."

She managed to say, "I suppose so."

Then Kyle's expression changed. He glanced at Cotton and Moliak, his face darkening and his mouth pressed shut as if he were suddenly aware of their circumstance.

Jy and the other Wanderers were sitting nearby. They were certain something had been taken from Jy's hard-memory, and the others were testing her facilities as best they could. Billie watched and tried to listen. Jy was upright and alert—a remarkable thing in itself—and there was a bare patch on the top of her head, seemingly shaved, some liver-colored cream applied to the wound in a thin line.

Moliak had helped walk Jy back to them not long ago.

Moliak is his name.

Billie could never forget his name or anything else she had seen or heard or felt during that forced dream. The experience had been startling and then terrifying, and it continued to unsettle her. It was as if someone had sewn a complicated novel into her brain, and every so often she would find new details that she hadn't noticed with her first reading. Suddenly she would smell hundreds of Founders sweating in the sunshine, their odor sharp and reassuring, or maybe she would sense her arms were too long and too strong. Once she thought about the ordinary frame house where she had grown up, on the most ordinary street in the universe, yet it was as if she were a Founder thinking about its home.

Homes were holy. The ground beneath any home was beyond cost. She could feel an aching loss—her parents had sold it after she left for college, for something more convenient—and she wondered if every Founder felt this way today. Did they still hunger for the villages where they were born? Or had they devised some way to adapt and forget, thinking only of the mission?

Jy was telling her little audience she was tired. "Let me rest, and then you can ask more questions. We can hunt for what's missing when I can keep my head up again, please?"

They made her comfortable and gave her room.

A moment later the Glorious One was curled up in a fetal position, eyes closed and her breathing regular, and Quencé took her pulse with a light touch. "She *seems* strong," he announced. "Moliak could have purged her of age-induced radicals, or maybe scrubbed her blood—"

"Why would he bother?" interrupted Wysh.

Nobody spoke.

Wysh shook her head in disgust, saying, "You're the clever one among us, Quencé. What do you think Moliak will do with each of us?"

"Quiet," he replied. "I don't know. Be quiet."

Billie took Kyle's hand and sighed.

"You don't know?" Wysh persisted. Her voice was tense, edging into anger. "You must have some clever guesses about what they want. Don't you? Tell us your guesses and charm us like you do your women—"

"Enough," snapped Xen.

"—and make us think you're in complete control. Would you, Quencé? Try to sound confident and smart as you always do."

Quencé kept silent, staring hard at Wysh.

Moliak and Cotton sat in the distance watching them and talking to one another. Moliak was holding some type of elaborate tool in his bare hand, a coin-shaped object in his glove, and both men nodded. Cotton's face went up and down as fast as a paint shaker, and both men seemed to smile in a sober fashion.

Billie felt exhausted all at once. She let go of Kyle and told him, "I want to rest too."

Kyle was colorless and weak, particularly in the face. Rivers of blood were in his big eyes, and his feathery soft voice said, "Rest," while he glanced at his associates.

"Maybe you could sleep," she wondered.

He didn't seem to hear, yet a moment later he was on his back on the softening floor and his tired eyes were closed. She lay beside him and tried relaxing, which didn't work, then she forgot to try and drifted into a deep sleep full of strange dreams. First she was a Founder boy playing in a hundred-crop field, whatever that was. Then she was herself, traveling from earth to earth, and she stopped on one earth where the people had roofed in the sky and vast metallic spiders crawled upon the high ceiling while weaving vast golden webs meant to catch who-knew-what. She walked inside a little building and found herself back home, in the ordinary frame house, and Moliak's parents were sitting with her parents at a bridge table. They were drinking coffee and sharing stories about their children, laughing loudly every so often. Billie watched them from the next room. She saw her father challenge Moliak's father to arm wrestle, and while the two men grunted and strained the mothers laughed, talking about what fools men were and look at them and who was winning now?

Billie came awake with a start. It was nearly noon, the high suns flickering in skies mostly clear. Kyle was sleeping while the other Wanderers talked among themselves. Jy was awake and responding to questions, Quencé asking most of them. They spoke in English and other languages too, and it sounded as though they still had no idea what had been stolen.

Billie had to pee.

She looked at Moliak. He and Cotton were dressed in gray now, the gloves still on their left hands. She rose and walked to the toilet that had magically been made around dawn. It was simple and exposed, but there was no other choice. Billie managed to pull down her slacks and panties and relax until she could hear the tinkling stream striking inside the bowl. All at once she was imagining herself with Janice; they were sitting at their kitchen table, and Billie related her story of peeing in front of strangers. "Not you, girl! I know you," said Janice, howling with laughter. "You're teasing me, aren't you? You wouldn't. Couldn't. You're making this silly story up!"

She missed Janice and everyone else horribly.

The toilet wiped her, and she stood and dressed and returned to the Wanderers, feeling out of place and scared and suddenly starting to cry. She surprised herself by dissolving into tears, and the Wanderers watched her with compassion or curiosity or nothing but their eyes. Kyle was awake now; he averted his face and stiffened. She couldn't stop crying, collapsing onto the floor and weeping hard with her little hands on her face, and Moliak of all people came to her and said, "None of this is in any fashion fair, miss." His voice was trying to be soothing. "This is sad and cruel and believe me when I tell you I wish there were some other way."

She looked up at the man. He was holding the coin-shaped object in his gloved hand; it was clear as glass but for one speck of something in the middle. His face was neither evil nor insane, she realized. He was merely intense, and somehow she sensed that he did indeed grieve for her, in a sense.

Billie dipped her head and clung to herself.

"Yet you are appropriate," said Moliak, "because your earth should be represented here, and chance has decided on you."

What could she say?

She let her mouth fall open, but no response seemed right.

Then Moliak turned to Jy and asked, "Do you recognize what I have?" and he held the transparent coin high in the air. The suns shone through it, sparkling fragments of light flying everywhere. "No, my friend? Well, I have to explain. I want everyone to understand the story." He paused for an instant, then he slipped the

coin into one of his gray pockets and smiled, saying,
"Consider this to be a rally and the six of you have come
to me, innocent and curious, and we begin—
        "—now."

2

> WHAT COTTON dislikes most is the audience,
> yet I tell him and tell him that the audience is
> half the reason I need to do this thing.
>   —*Moliak's private journal*

From the beginning of the mission, almost from its first
day of inception, the Founders were concerned about
what would happen if they found someone or something
that proved to be dangerous. What if they made enemies
who infiltrated their portals? All their hard, well-meant
work would lead to horrors for countless people, and that
would be a tragedy and a burden and they didn't want
to have to bear it.

(Billie experienced the story as if she were being
dipped into it, as if its plot and characters were some
thick clinging liquid bubbling in a vat and she was swallowed completely. She wasn't anyone but Billie in this
story, and that meant she was nothing but a miniscule
point drifting in the massive dark currents. Presumably
everyone experienced it in the same way.)

Two groups of Founders moved outward from their
beginning place, and one of many precautions was to
separate Jy's portals from Moliak's portals. They were
identical systems out of alignment with one another, like
railroads of unequal gauge, and the Founders' earth
served as a filter and a barrier as well as the homeland
for the strange ageless Archives now left completely in
charge.

It was even more of a barrier today.

The Founders' earth saw no regular traffic besides
the occasional communications. Should some danger

ever arise, the Archives would neatly and nonviolently cut even the possibility of traffic. The Founders, being cautious and reasonable people, had reasoned that perhaps someday it would be best to save half the mission from contamination or worse. Then their old homeland would serve as a passive fortress; no evil could ride the portals as it wished; and any horrors would be barricaded at one place, at least.

Jy traveled in one direction upon the Bright, Moliak in the other direction, and in not very many centuries they were completely separated. The Glorious One held a tighter control on her half—Moliak was merely one of several gifted leaders—but otherwise it was the same to bé a Founder or a Cousin with either group. The high-ranking Wanderers were as far from the center as possible, always advancing. Both groups made the same basic decisions independently. Sheer blind chance gave Moliak's group more uninhabited earths, and as a result he and they moved faster and with greater ease; fewer strangers needed to be understood before portals could be fabricated and aligned. The mission rushed forwards.

Moliak had taken a secret pride in their speed and efficiency and in their good fortune.

Yet eventually chance, being chance, balanced all circumstances and slowed Moliak with tangled problems and stubborn peoples. New earths were thick with technological species and species on the brink, and errors in judgement were still wreaking havoc today. An example formed before Billie's eyes. She saw Moliak still wearing his Founder body, standing beside a wide and slow and thoroughly murdered river. An empty city stood on the far shore. The air and muds stank of poisons and lazy decay. She was standing beside Moliak, she realized. She was wearing her own body and gray clothes, and Moliak was telling her, "We are guilty," with his voice cracking and dying. He slumped down onto the poisoned muds and began to cry, hands pressing the muds into his fur, screaming, *We killed them!* Billie felt his guilt and scalding anger as if it were her own. Now she was part of the mission, an associate of Moliak's, and she was as much to blame as he was. She felt she should join him in the mud. It would be a suitable beginning of her penitence, she told herself, but then as she started to kneel the scene dissolved into a complex mishmash of images and sensations and concrete data points.

A few hundred earths were maimed or even killed through blunders made by the mission. Perhaps every last one of them would have suffered the same fates; it was halfway comforting to hope so, at least. Certainly Jy and Moliak and the other millions of devoted followers took comfort in the measurable good they accomplished in most places. Innocent people might suffer, yes, but Wanderers did learn from their failures and they made improvements, mastering the complexities of aggressive and advanced and enormously volatile earths until they made miracles every day.

Sometimes Moliak would speak at the rallies, no great Jy to rely on.

Billie found herself sitting in an audience, surrounded by strange heavyset people with squarish heads, and she watched Moliak prance about the stage using charm and wit and sheer logic to turn their moods. Moliak extruded a sense of peace and purpose coupled with fierce good intentions, and even stubborn souls like these found themselves drifting into Wanderer thoughts and dreams, if only for a little while.

Warfare was defused on tens of thousands of earths.

Humankind was being joined together and then scattered among the endless stars, and wasn't it lovely?

Billie felt honored to belong to such an undertaking.

Perhaps she felt as Moliak had felt in those times: People were sweet children meant to be coddled and instructed and finally weaned; people were and would always remain simple and transparent and potent; and in the final summation, thought Billie, people were no less malleable than the soft clays from which they were born.

The Wanderers could always shape people according to need.

With sufficient talent, Billie sensed, there were no boundaries to what could be accomplished and what could be rightfully dreamed.

3

NOTHING IS so sweet
as the husk of an enemy
hung dry
putrified
and sucked to bone and skin.

—*UnFound ballad*

There was a tendency among Wanderers, all Wanderers, to try to anticipate the coming earths.

Billie sensed this fact without knowing how it could matter.

Suddenly she pictured herself looking backward and drawing conclusions from the earths just passed. Everything felt real. "I see such-and-such an earth," she muttered aloud, and she found herself sitting inside a ship much like Jy's own ship. Moliak was sitting close to her. His Founder face grinned, and he asked, "Is that what you see?" Then he laughed aloud, saying, "You are wrong, my friend. The next earth will be such-and-such. I have an intuition about such matters, my dear friend, and you are mistaken."

There was absolutely no means to predict, of course.

Intellectually Billie understood the obstacles: the chaos and sheer weirdness, each earth divided and existing unaffected by its neighbors and altered in more ways than any thinking entity could hope to number. To spend time and neurons on the simplest guess was a waste, and every Wanderer realized it was only a foolish game.

Yet Moliak had been succeeding in his latest predictions.

Billie thought about his successes as she sat across from him. They were now passing through a tangle of interesting, challenging earths. One was named Termite Mound unofficially because of its population and its caste system and because its greatest multitudes ate cellulose. The part of Billie not sitting in the ship—the real Billie— knew enough in an instant to recognize Cotton's homeland. He was a Termite. She could almost see the bodies pressing shoulder to shoulder, a world covered with human flesh, and her real self took a deep breath and shivered.

Moliak had predicted the Mound.

"It will be crowded," he had said, "and socially strange, and we will need to stay alert if we aren't to damage their social order too much. We may not agree with their status quo, but unless we have an easy substitute we should work very carefully."

He had predicted the Mound and overseen its successful incorporation into Jy's mission, and he had been the first to admit only luck had made him correct.

And there were other successes too.

He guessed that one earth would be exceedingly rare, and indeed, it was one of the rarest types: Two distinct human species had evolved on separate hemispheres, each ready to destroy the other as soon as practical. The Wanderers had arrived at the proverbial last heartbeat, and they managed to effect a truce and then set about changing cultures through argument and charm, example and lavish bribes. In the end the species were knitted together—they complimented one another wonderfully, in truth—and every Wanderer had felt an enormous satisfaction in having helped with the impossible.

Then Moliak predicted a series of more typical earths, and he continued to be right. There were earths much like Billie's, loud and desperately poor in some quarters and oftentimes dangerous to themselves. There were also earths that had been dragged back into more primitive states because of famine and war; their people were grateful for any help, and they looked on Wanderers as angels brought for their salvation. And one particular earth, said Moliak, would be advanced but nonetheless in some kind of trouble. (He was intentionally vague with every guess, and he smiled while telling them, trying not to take these mystical predictions seriously.) And again he was correct. His long streak was intact. Scouts returned from the next earth and described people at peace with themselves, wealthy and united. Yet at the same time they were waging an endless war with an enemy from deep space.

It was an unusual circumstance. Man-made robots, it seemed, had mutated while replicating. They had been sent into the Oort Cloud to mine comets and bring home the rarest hydrocarbons; but now they were returning in the hundreds of thousands, and they were violent. They attacked human ships and peaceful robots. They were bug-smart and prolific, tough and swift. Of course the Wanderers decided to help their brethren. The robots weren't life, after all. They were vermin. To exterminate the vermin, Moliak and his people designed machines that channeled the sun's energies into withering beams. Every enemy body was cooked with a minimal effort, and if more would ever come racing out of the Cloud. . . . well, finishing them would be nothing. It would mean nothing. Vermin were vermin, and even the peaceful Wanderers wouldn't hesitate to destroy what was so painfully wrong.

Billie felt a sudden chill.

A round room formed around her. They were on board the Wanderer ship again, and she was sitting opposite Moliak while he grinned and asked, "Would you like to hear my next prediction?" His fur was gray like Jy's and his smile was equally gentle. "Shall I tell you, my friend?"

No scouts had been sent forwards; every Wanderer had been needed to build the sun-weapons.

"Friend?" he persisted.

Billie found herself nodding, and she said, "Tell me."

"My guess is a pretty earth," he told her. The smile grew. "I think it will be a sweet fine earth, one of the very best, and we won't have to do anything but enjoy its countless delights."

Yet Billie found herself shivering. She was having a premonition of her own, vague and black at its core and bitterly cold, and she held herself while trying to understand what was happening.

"Of course I can only guess," said Moliak, and his smile brightened.

She tried to nod and speak.

"Don't you think we deserve something easy now?" he asked. "What do you think, my friend? What do you think?"

MOLIAK

1

THIS PLACE is sick with green. Water and air have no flavor. Throughout the day the Heart of God burns naked in the sky, and everything is weak. The flesh here is hopelessly weak, by every measure . . . .

The ugliness is appalling . . . .

We will have to work to make this place habitable. It will take time and considerable fire . . . .

— *UnFound communication*

They had sent probes first, as always. Moliak remembered everything they had done—each step and each misstep—and at the same time he experienced the story along with his audience. All of them were characters in the illusion while Moliak was Moliak, and Cotton was the only one spared. He stood somewhere nearby, clearheaded and hyperalert, watching the rest of them mutter to themselves and turn their heads at nothing, sometimes rising and then sitting again and sometimes doing nothing for a very long while, eyes wide and glassy and strange.

The Wanderers had sent probes through small temporary portals, and some probes returned intact.

Moliak was sitting inside his private chamber, inside his personal ship, watching the images as if for the first time. He saw darkness and then a sudden flash of pink light betraying a distant horizon, rugged and barren. The entire countryside was barren. The local time was noon, yet there was no sun. He saw brighter flashes of light, and from the flashes came cobalt blue objects, swift and weightless. A string of thunderbolts shook the portal and probe. One of the cobalt objects dove close and became huge, jerking to a stop a hair's breadth away, and it glared at the probe for an instant before it extended one insectlike arm that cut into the portal without any apparent effort whatsoever.

Moliak had been wrong.

This was no sweet Earth. The probes that did return brought samples of poisoned air and ocean. Greenhouse gases kept the climate oppressively hot despite the darkness. It seemed to be a war-ravaged place where the machines kept fighting among themselves, humans extinct and dusts kicked into the sky. Some difficult work was left for the scouts who volunteered to make the journey and produce an earth that was reasonably safe.

Each scout was talented and experienced and unquestionably brave. They wore armored suits with motorized limbs and electronic camouflage, and they were armed with various shields and scramblers to kill machinery at a distance. A dozen scouts formed the lead party. Moliak himself had wished them luck and watched them vanish. After a day's wait the eroded shell of their portal was brought back. A dozen more scouts volunteered to replace them, adjusting the equipment and picking a different site to examine, and they too vanished. Then a great many others stood and said, "Let us go!" out of a sense of commitment to the mission and to their missing associates. A handful were chosen and coached, their equipment modified in a thousand ways, and afterwards one of them managed to return, in a sense.

When their portal was retrieved, a single twist of hard-memory was found on the floor. It belonged to one of the scouts; nothing of the personality had survived, only memories. Some force or entity or happenstance had placed the charred bit of ceramic in the portal, and at once Moliak and the others coaxed it awake and tried to learn what had happened.

The illusion gave Moliak, and everyone, the scout's perspective. All at once he was running hard across the pulverized ground. Everyone was the scout. The other scouts were dead. Moliak felt his heart racing and an awful fear that made him tremble, and he climbed a low ridge while trying to make it to the portal and safety.

Distant explosions threw up harsh shadows.

Moliak felt the ground shift beneath him, and suddenly he was sliding down the slope and something shouted behind him. He turned in time to see half a dozen human shapes emerging out of the darkness. Each of them was thick and plainly strong. They wore sketchy armor plates, their chests and groins and skulls marginally protected, plus each wore a single glove made of some mirrored substance. *What are they?* he wondered. Then he found his balance and began running again. But they caught him easily and surrounded him and tripped him an instant later, bolts of sputtering light ruining his armor's motors and fusing his joints and leaving him on his back, completely helpless.

Moliak had experienced this illusion hundreds of times, perhaps thousands, yet the immediacy and horror were as awful as the first time.

The gloves were glowing with a dull red light.

Fingers melted into the best Wanderer armor, and Moliak was peeled like some crustacean found beached by curious children.

How can these people live?

They had to be machines. Common sense and common science told him nobody could survive more than a few minutes exposed to this toxic world, thus they had to be robots mimicking their dead inventors. Yet they grinned like humans and possessed human voices, and one of them had been injured recently and was bleeding something resembling the best red blood, impossible or not.

Moliak himself was perishing.

Nerve toxins seeped into him, and radiations crashed through him, and his captors knelt and began to use their strange gloves on him, doses of heat and light damaging his flesh at the perfect speed needed to keep him both alive and conscious while wrapped in utter misery.

The illusion of pain rose to a modest point, then there was the dreamlike idea of a seering pain causing him to scream.

"No, no!"

His surroundings began to turn pasty and diffuse, the edges beginning to evaporate.

He squinted and saw faces hovering over him.

"*NO!*"

They smiled in unison, enormously amused, white teeth and smooth clear skin implying vigorous good health. They existed within this carnage. This was their native environment, their homeland and their paradise. They began removing their bits of armor, becoming nude, and some were men and some were manly-built women, and they joked and laughed happily and pushed each other like children playing. Then one woman claimed Moliak as her own, climbing onto him even as his fragile life began to retreat into hard-memory. He could feel himself dying everywhere else, yet she had him as a prize and a lover, straddling his poisoned dead flesh with her friends cheering and Moliak trying to imagine what she intended—

"*—NO!*"

He shut his eyes and held them closed a long while.

Then he opened them and saw Jy staring at him, her face glistening with tears, and the rest of his audience sat stunned and silent.

Moliak gathered himself. His pulpy body was dripping sweat and his hands shook and his knees shook, and he explained. "We inserted several dozen teams of scouts and perhaps twenty thousand probes and almost none returned in any form," he said, his voice rising. "For ten years we struggled to learn all we could learn about those people." He paused, then said, "They were people. They were not robots or any other vermin," and he wiped his face with his sleeve.

Jy said nothing.

She had no heart for these concerns; she was sad and weak and suddenly quite old.

It was Quencé with the presence to ask, "Did you try to make contact with them?" He had been a scout at one time, Moliak recalled, and he seemed skeptical of his associate's abilities. "You should have found a city and a political center, or perhaps some scientists, and you could have talked to them—"

"Assuming such creatures existed," Moliak cautioned.

Nobody spoke.

He watched them, then he quoted Jy. "'Always move in the most perfect peace you can imagine.'" He took an uneasy step towards the Glorious One. "We quit sending scouts for a long while, we allowed only probes, and meanwhile we weighed the data and exchanged opinions and built sophisticated computer models to explain that incredible place. It was an earth in need, misery upon misery, yet it seemed entirely stable and even joyous. We wrung ourselves dry trying to find some gentle caring plan to solve the problems and make you happy with us too."

Jy opened her mouth. She said nothing.

"There was no gentle way," Moliak promised.

Jy whimpered, asking, "Did you compromise yourselves?"

He had expected the question. He produced a thin smile, nodding and saying, "We did not then, no."

He waited for a moment.

Then he said, "We are clever people, Jy, and of course we did not compromise ourselves or the mission or your own ideals. There was no need to compromise any of it."

He made his face turn bitter.

"I will show you," he said. "Now!"

2

THE BRIGHT Heart of God burns the perfect
fire. The fiercest fire. The cleansing fire that
belongs to all true [human beings]. It is the fire
that shapes and shapes again. It is all that is
noble and pure and right.
  We breathe that fire upon death.
  We are that fire upon death.
  And for always, on and on....
                    —*UnFound religious tract*

THE UNFOUND are the Makers.
                    —*Graffiti inside portal*

Moliak's Wanderers had recently passed through a string
of warring earths—pools of experience and instinct from
which they could draw help—thus the Wanderers themselves didn't have to become soldiers. Nor did they make
the soldiers into any form of Wanderer. There were distinctions. Perhaps they seemed like artificial distinctions
today, but then there was a sense of distance and discretion to the undertaking. The Wanderers were too
clever to taint themselves. They merely allowed volunteers to enter the hell-earth and do whatever they
wished. They never built the weapons used; they merely
showed their allies some tricks of physics and biology,
leaving them alone to borrow and build whatever they
wished. Yes, the Wanderers supplied materials and facilities and sometimes advice, but there was a certain
ambiguity nonetheless. There was a gap, distinct and
visible, between Jy's followers and the ugliness.
  It was not an easy decision for the Wanderers.
  The debates raged for years, different groups voting
for different solutions or nonsolutions. The Cousins were
the ones who first thought to involve the other earths,
and Moliak had fought them for a long while. He re-

nounced any violence towards their enemies. He remained a pure Wanderer while scouts died horrible deaths and the mission remained in stasis; he respected the wishes of Jy—or what he imagined her wishes to be—and argued with the Cousins and the swelling numbers of Founders who felt they had no choice whatsoever. He argued, in truth, out of habit.

"Yet what is *the mission*?" he asked himself one day.

He was sitting alone in his chamber looking across a tropical blue sea, feeling drained and frustrated, and some vague switch deep inside him was beginning to flip.

It occurred to him—not for the first time—that there were two missions.

One mission was the search for the Makers, and the other was the peaceful knitting together of the human species. Jy had seen these halves as the equal parts of one great cause, but in the beginning she knew no one else but the compliant Cousins. She had never imagined any hell-earth. There were junctures, Moliak could see, when the knitting mattered less than the search. Sometimes a choice had to be made, and it wasn't a difficult choice in these circumstances. Their enemy was human only in substance, after all. It was actually a monster without pity or empathy or charity, indistinguishable from the vermin they had had to kill on other earths, in other circumstances.

Nothing could matter as much now as finding the Makers.

The realization made Moliak gasp and sit back in his chair and shiver for a long while.

"*We have to continue,*" he said aloud. "*We have to find the Makers!*"

He had made his decision. He was the highest-ranking Founder to come to that decision, and with his vote others decided to change their votes and allow their allies to begin cleansing the hell-earth.

It was simple to find volunteers. Tens of thousands of young people and adventurers believed fighting somewhere on the magical Bright would prove infinitely more rewarding than riding inside a starship towards some merely remarkable alien world. They wanted the novelty and the wages promised to them by the Wanderers—a modest fortune to those with the luck and skill to survive—and they were eager to prove themselves in an arena more demanding than any other.

The first soldiers brought home bits of the enemy's flesh, then whole limbs and organs and entire corpses.

The Wanderers purchased these items and anything else useful, and they learned how the enemy thrived in the corrosive environment. The enemy was an organism advanced beyond all estimates, it seemed. Radiations and most toxins were irritants or they were nothing. The enemy's flesh and blood was impregnated with nanorobots, sophisticated and sleepless, and the robots moved within them and repaired every fractured cell membrane and replaced every twist of lost DNA. The Wanderers had no matching tricks; they couldn't understand how billions and trillions of the virus-size wonders could be organized in the first place, then controlled through every phase of their existence.

It was disheartening to realize their own backwardness.

The enemy was advanced beyond them in one technology and perhaps in others too, and the Wanderers shook their heads and wondered what new surprises awaited them on that hell-earth.

There were no cities and no political centers and no scientists within the enemy's ranks. It was an ultratribal species, violent and intelligent; and it was thoroughly adapted to total warfare, each tribe possessing the fighting gloves and nuclear warheads and armored tanks that chewed tunnels down into the sprawling underground bunkers.

The hell-earth's biosphere was unique and utterly simple. There was the enemy, plus certain hardy microbes used for food, plus an assortment of wild robots with allegiance to nothing. Every prairie and forest and elephant and insect had gone extinct on every part of the globe.

Even with the portals and every resource, it took the Wanderers' allies several years to win beachheads.

And all the while the attacks against them were ceaseless, launched from every side, even from above. The blackened sky was ripe with homeless tribes hunting for weaknesses. The moon was honeycombed with bunkers. Mars was warmed by the carbon dioxide driven from its crust, and Venus was cooled by the mountains of dust in its upper atmosphere. (It was a bizarre kind of terraforming, thought Moliak in passing.) Mercury was nothing but a vast mining camp where tribes landed long enough to pull up a share of iron and nickel. The gas giants were milked for their hydrogen to fuel the tough and efficient enemy reactors. And there were asteroids and comets and millions of flying bunkers moving about the sun in every conceivable orbit.

The Wanderers decided they needed to know more about the enemy.

A prisoner was sought, a bounty was offered, and eventually one team captured a young enemy and brought him home alive.

Moliak felt a new illusion coalescing around him. He found himself standing inside the central chamber of his own ship, and before him was a naked man screaming and weeping and finally breaking one of his own arms as he jerked against his bonds.

Moliak's audience stood beside him as a slump-shouldered, sorrowful figure with a ghostly undefined face.

Moliak spoke. The prisoner had been taught the Founder language with implants into his own odd hard-memory, and he listened while Moliak promised him that they wanted nothing more than a few little patches of ruined ground. Was such an agreement possible? If he were granted those safe havens, said Moliak, their allies would stop fighting. A truce could be established. And perhaps there could be other incentives, he allowed, smiling in his most charming way.

Nothing happened for a long moment.

"Just tell me," Moliak prompted, "can I deal with your tribe? Will your people give me anything at all?"

The prisoner smiled up at him, then bit off the end of his own tongue and spat the dead pink mess past

Moliak. It struck his audience in their collective face, and he heard six distinct voices cry out in surprise and pain.

Humankind had two prospects according to Wanderer experience. There were two distinct and reliable courses for any developing earth. Sometimes a human species would vanquish itself with its own weapons and violence. Other times the species adapted to its nature and spread over huge distances, achieving some form of lasting peace.

There were two choices, thought Moliak, and only one was reasonable. People were not utter fools.

Yet the hell-earth had followed neither course. Its species of human animal had gotten fusion power and hard-memory and the worst forms of total warfare, yet it had never succumbed. It had merely adapted its behaviors and science to where the battlefield was home. Technologies were tough and adaptable and always small-scale. The tribes themselves were mobile units, no territory permanent and nobody essential. Life was a short and furious concern and always glorious, and only your tribe lived forever.

Despite the ruined tongue, the prisoner began speaking in a steady rhythmic voice. It was part song, part poem, and each person in the audience heard the language that fit their mind best. It was an epic work about the Heart of God—the enemy's name for the sun— and about the beauty of death and rot and endless violence. No other existence made any sense to the prisoner. Everything that didn't think likewise was weak and practically useless to him. His mouth filled with blood, bright red bubbles rising, and his garbled voice persisted for an age before he managed to suffocate himself, or perhaps simply will himself into death.

They were being called the unFound by certain Wanderers.

UnFound was an ancient word never used in Jy's time. It referred to certain Founders in the primitive past who were outcasts, banished for horrific high crimes.

Yet the word meant more than outcast to any Founder. The unFound had minds that couldn't be imagined.

They existed past all human feeling and human law.

In the midst of the fighting and chaos, some forgotten Founder had given the enemy the name unFound, and ever since, without fail, they had worn it with sterling conviction.

3

THE NATIVES have tailored themselves into buttery seallike creatures living in every sea and along the inland waterways. They are pleasant and gregarious and sing with startling strong voices. They wish us well in our travels . . . .

HUMANS HAVE stopped living on this earth. Their homes are in orbit and within the moon, and they come here only to worship what they call The Grand Cradle; and when they do return it is as holo projections and synthetic sensations so that they appreciate their beginnings without having to taint the winds or water . . . .

HUMANS BECAME extinct here in the remote past, as did most higher primates, raccoons having splintered into many species, some rather large and surprisingly intelligent . . . .

A SAD dead empty earth . . . .

. . . AN EARTH flooded with cometary waters . . . only the highest of the Mountains of Mountains show above its smooth blue face . . . .

—*Scout reports (fictional)*

The unFound could never see reason nor imagine any allegiance to anyone not of their tribe, thus no choice remained for the Wanderers.

A conference was called with every high-ranking

Wanderer in attendance, and Moliak addressed them. He stood on a stage at one end of an enormous stadium built specifically for this day, and he told his sober audience that there were various options available to them, and that all were flawed. The most reasonable choice, terrible as it seemed, was to quickly enlarge the war and win it and exterminate the unFound with all the efficiency they could manage.

"The unFound," he declared, "are vermin in every sense but heritage. They live in a horrifying state that will eventually make them extinct—*how can they endure forever as they are?*—and if they pass into extinction tomorrow instead of ten thousand years from now, won't it be a blessing? If we can put an end to their suffering and to the abomination they represent, then we can again continue on our mission." He paused for a long moment, gathering himself. "Remember," he cried out, "there are perhaps millions of earths ahead of us which will need our touch and our love, and there are the Makers too. What we must do now is put aside our better natures just long enough to do what is best. We must succeed and continue our mission. *Think of this as a test of our resolve.* Then afterwards we will be free again and moving again and normalcy will return."

Votes were taken and tabulated among the Wanderers.

Moliak's logic won every count, and immediate changes were made in the war. Forces were revamped and enlarged. Recruits were found on Termite Mound— they were wonderful soldiers once trained and fed, and they were abundant—and then the Wanderers themselves entered the ranks. The allies would fight better, it was decided, if they saw they weren't alone. The Wanderers had to make the most essential commitment; they now were willing to be burned to nothing and die. Even the habitually peaceful souls such as the Founders, people with no history of weapons or anger, managed to make the transformation. After all, Moliak mused, they were clever enough to find ways. They decided to manipulate their hormones and glands and their hard-memories, becoming excellent warriors. Moliak himself had decided he owed it to his convictions and the mission, and he rebuilt himself until he was a fine soldier and an even finer butcher.

The Wanderers devised new and more powerful weapons, and more.

They found the means to refashion their hard-memories, making them with invisible materials, then they planted their hard-memories into the unFound prisoners. They took control of those bodies and slunk back over the lines, entering the deep bunkers and spreading chaos. Moliak did such work. There were ways to undermine the unFounds' social orders, tribe by tribe, and as the tribes collapsed, one after another, more of the hell-earth was conquered.

In the end they won the entire prize. Moliak opened his eyes and saw it floating before him, a dirty battered lifeless globe, but the rest of the solar system was inhabited by millions of tribes spread through billions of cubic miles. There was no hope to fight all of them and win quickly; nor could the Wanderers find any means to fortify the hell-earth and make it last. Something had to be done, it was reasoned. What was done was to limit for several months all travel along Moliak's portion of the Bright while the energy reserves were stored within superconducting reservoirs on nearby earths. Meanwhile a silvery tower was constructed on the hell-earth's equator, rising above the atmosphere with its flattened tip glowing with a cold colorless light. The tower resembled the prow on certain starships—a structure that built force fields meant to ward off radiations and light-speed impacts. Here it was a millionfold larger and vastly more powerful than any previous design.

Moliak stared at the tower from his high vantage point.

He felt the chill of anticipation as his view shifted, the sun and hell-earth coming into alignment and the sun's glare making him blink for a few painful moments.

He had imagined this moment and this circumstance countless times in these last years. His innocent audience was floating in the same illusion, helpless and progressively less innocent by the moment. What were they thinking? He imagined conflicting emotions coupled with a certain horrible curiosity. *What next?* he could almost hear them thinking. *What next? What next?* He was particularly interested in Jy's confusion and anger and deep frustrations. He had sculpted the entire illusion for her benefit and education. It was designed to make the greatest impact in the smallest possible time, and even Moliak, knowing everything, found a part of himself feeling anxious about what was to happen next.

Suddenly he and the rest were moving backward faster than light. The mighty sun became a pinprick, nothing more, and the vacuum was colder than could be believed.

Then the pinprick exploded.

The Wanderers had used plasmas and neutrino buckshot and gamma-ray lasers to attack the sun itself, causing a series of flares building into a seering soundless blast. Mercury evaporated. Venus and the moon and Mars were melted and then torn apart as the shock waves swept over them. Every asteroid and unFound bunker was obliterated. The gas giants lost their moons and their atmospheres, and the unFound were eradicated throughout the solar system. Only the hell-earth survived. Its starship prow protected it just long enough, Moliak knew, and then the diluted shock wave swept over him and his numbed audience and everyone felt its amazing heat percolating down into their bones.

The new sun was smaller and ruddier and cool to the eye.

They had halfway destroyed the sun to cleanse the solar system. In the end, Moliak reflected, the Wanderers had simply lifted the scale of destruction higher than the unFound had ever managed, and they had won as a result, standing as lords over a great volume of vacuum and one drab dead world.

They were left free of the scourge and free to continue their mission, chasing the Makers along the beautiful and innocent earths. It had been a strange moment of elation for Moliak. He remembered the emotions as he experienced them once again. He was thrilled to have the nightmare finished and sorry to have had it at all, and he was eager to begin to work for the old ideals with a renewed energy, wanting to make amends for the wicked things he had done.

Someday, in some hard-to-predict fashion, he knew Jy would learn what had happened here. Moliak's people had done a wondrous job of hiding the truth—inventing earths and sending false reports to Jy while making distant eyes believe everything was normal—but this was too large a secret to keep hidden forever or to ever even partly forget. Jy would learn. She would hear something that seemed odd, an investigation would begin, then she would come here and look at Moliak and ask, "What did you do and why did you do it, my friend? I want to hear all of it."

He could imagine her ancient face glaring at him.

"I am waiting, Moliak!"

He had fought the unFound in a variety of ways for many years, yet at that instant when it seemed as though the war was won, the unFound beaten in every sense, Moliak had found himself more afraid of Jy and Jy's own wrath than he had ever feared the unFound.

It was a strange thing to realize.

At that time, for half an instant, Moliak had laughed aloud and shaken his head, amused by the trembling of his hands and glad the day might not arrive for another ten million years, or longer.

1

EVERY SO often my hard-memory becomes too full and I need to forget. I have to pick and choose from what I wish to keep and what I will transfer to the Wanderer libraries and what, if anything, is pointless enough to be thrown into a trashcan and left behind.

Being long-lived has its hazards.

I can learn too much of any one thing, for instance. I can retain too many painful memories of earths where we failed and where people suffered from their own ignorance and cruelty, and that makes me bitter and hardened and absolutely useless to the mission. Yet the other extreme is as awful. If I clung to the sweetest memories and the greenest earths, bliss building upon bliss, what would happen to me?

I would become a dreamy idiot, I know it.

If I did not choose with the greatest care, I would turn into a simpleminded doll with a

permanent toothy smile painted between her
ugly wooden ears....

—Jy's speeches

The greatest surprise, in retrospect, was how little surprise she felt when she learned about the hell-earth and the unFound and the Wanderers' violent responses. Jy could envision horrors as bad as the unFound, perhaps worse, yet she and the Wanderers around her had never faced such challenges. It was as if Moliak's bad fortune served to balance her own good fortune, and a selfish sliver of herself felt glad it had been his burden and not hers. She was free to feel tangled emotions directed at Moliak and the others; she was removed and superior and uncorrupted.

The illusion brought the maimed red sun closer again, and the unFound earth appeared beside it.

Perhaps it was all some elaborate lie, she thought. What if it were? But what would be the reason to create such a story? No, she told herself, it was true. Moliak was giving her the truth as far as he could see it. For a few moments Jy tried to convince herself that the abductions and these last hours were Moliak's method of telling the story. Could it be? Yet why not simply come and tell her what happened if he wished to confess? Why not throw himself at her feet and plead for forgiveness? Why did they have to murder one Wanderer and threaten others, plus that young girl, if all he desired was to educate his long-ago teacher?

Jy was diving towards the battered earth, gaining velocity without any sense of acceleration; and at the instant of impact she found herself standing inside a little portal with the Bright surrounding her, bathing her with its perfect light. She was moving past the unFound earth, she sensed. She was a scout traveling onward, hoping for a quiet, easy earth where she and the other Wanderers could rest and recover their senses. She felt a strong pang of excitement as the Bright began to evaporate, her hands pressing against the crystal and her mouth beginning to smile.

She found herself on the next earth . . .

. . . and she recognized the landscape in an instant. She saw darkness in what should be daylight and dust in the air and flashes of colored light followed by thunder and quakes, some clear-thinking part of herself knowing exactly what had happened. The earth was nearly identical to the one she had left behind. Its craters were in different configurations, and perhaps the solar system was rebuilt in different ways; but the half dozen figures that emerged from the smoke and dust were mirrors of the unFound. They wore nothing but patches of armor and the shiny fighting gloves, and they gazed into the portal while smiling. Jy stared out at them. She couldn't move or think or even feel fear. Then they lifted their gloves, and spinning balls of light cut through the crystal dome, and Jy, and she jerked and screamed as she felt her body splitting in half. . . .

She was elsewhere, alive and drifting within a warm blackness.

Perhaps it had been a simple coincidence, she thought. It could be a remarkable mirror of the hell-earth, and meaningless.

Moliak had made the same guess. What if the earths were similar but unrelated? Could two species of humans evolve to become the unFound? He had ordered new prisoners to be taken and interrogated. Their languages and cultures were studied in depth. Their genetics were mapped, then laid beside the maps of the extinct unFound. Differences were measured and counted; there were very few important distinctions. It became apparent in no time that the unFound were closely related to one another, and the mangled fossil records from both earths showed that neither earth was the original homeland for the species. They had supplanted other human beings in the recent past, and they must have originated from somewhere else up along the Bright.

The war began again; more prisoners were taken.

How could such creatures find the Bright and build portals? Jy wondered. It seemed too unlikely to believe.

Yet certain tribes had long histories and ancient myths, she learned, and sometimes prisoners would sing epics about their glorious pasts. They had been rich and strong and living "on the far side of God's Heart," and because of their wealth they were able to look hard at the Heart and learn. Some unFound weapons were extraordinarily delicate and sensitive; it wasn't too unlikely to imagine them tinkering with their weapons and sensing the Bright as a consequence. Perhaps the Bright had been discovered and portals had been reinvented countless times. Perhaps the wealthiest tribes had been able to find the energies needed to inject themselves into the new green earths, then they bred and expanded outwards like a contagium, eventually splitting into warring tribes while driving every native species into extinction.

Jy was stunned, tired and painfully sad.

She could believe in the unFound, but it was almost impossible to imagine them using *her* Bright. Her Founder's sense of property made it her Bright, her own rightful possession, and she felt anguish at this sudden horrid turn of events.

Moliak's nightmare was very much her own now.

How much worse would it become? she wondered. What other terrors would she have to face?

Again the Wanderers fought the unFound. Again Moliak became a soldier, and Jy found herself serving with him. They were riding inside a small Wanderer ship downed early in the new war, and the unFound had them trapped. They were back to back inside the central chamber and the unFound boiled in from two directions, and Jy's fighting glove cut and burned and left the air thick with awful smells and strange furious screams. She was a soldier. She felt a soldier's instincts and runaway fears. Her fighting glove weakened and sputtered. She screamed, "Now!" and Moliak knelt with her while both slipped their bare hands into the receptive floor and continued to fire, fending off a quick assault. New gloves formed around their hands and they rose together with a desperate grace and aimed and cut apart the last unFound warriors, wide faces and wide hairless bodies evaporating, and the chamber walls started to melt and flow. The air was poisoned and wounds were sprinkled across Jy's body and now that body was dying, her soul beginning its rapid retreat into the hard-memory to wait and pray that she and Moliak would be found by friends and soon.

Moliak had died in that manner on the second hell-earth; it was a traumatic experience, scarring for the bravest person, and Jy could half sense how it must have felt for him.

That second hell-earth was won and its solar system was cleansed with the nova of the sun. Then there was a third hell-earth and a fourth and a fifth, each of them similar and none quick or easy. The Wanderers and Moliak could become only so good at eradicating the unFound, and there were the inevitable costs to be tallied. Jy could see some of the dead Wanderers paraded before her; she felt she knew each of them, and indeed, there were dead Founders whose hard-memories were lost and whose names welled up at her from her own remote past.

A dozen hell-earths had been conquered to date.

Another twenty or twenty thousand of them might lie between the Wanderers and the ends of the unFound domain. There was no knowing the truth. Any guess was the same value as any other, and all guesses were absolutely worthless.

Why do you keep fighting? Jy wondered.

Moliak had anticipated her question, and he answered it in the next instant, explanations exploding as if under pressure.

They had continued the fight because no other course seemed reasonable. Perhaps the unFound had invaded only a handful of earths, or perhaps they were destroying themselves in most places. Both were hopeful possibilities. There might be long stretches of devastated earths left dead and the unFound homeland in the midst of them. If the Wanderers could reach the homeland, it was thought, they could study it and make their first intelligent guesses about what remained for them.

Yet after a dozen hell-earths there was little reason to hope.

A new logic had taken hold of the high-ranking Wanderers. Each of the earths had had its own species of human beings. Bone fragments and the occasional ornament testified to peaceful times and gentle cultures. Jy imagined the horror those people must have felt when the unFound burst from their portals without warnings, butchering and burning with delight; and she saw what the unFound meant to her and every other Wanderer. The unFound were the vigorous opposites of herself. Moliak and his associates had continued fighting them, earth by earth, because they were heinous criminals and powerful and if the Wanderers did not stop them, who would? The question posed itself inside Jy's tired and anxious mind:

Who else could pay the costs and destroy them?

She felt a cold bar of steel being rammed down her backbone, and she stiffened and gasped and wanted to cry out.

The costs included the dead, of course, and the maimed. There was the energy required and the materials required and the distortions of the nearby earths. Termite Mound and the others were being kept in a permanent state of war. How was it changing their social structures and norms? But then Jy realized what was being changed more than anything. It was the nature of the Wanderers that was different. It was the way they thought and why they would act and their dreams and their goals and how they responded to challenges. She could feel Moliak's presence, his ceaseless anger and paranoia and the cold calculations, and he was nothing like the kind caring Founder boy she had known. He was like no Wanderer she had ever met, and suddenly she feared him so badly that she could neither breathe nor think for a long moment.

Moliak had remained a soldier on every hell-earth. He couldn't guess how many of the unFound he had killed, and he couldn't stop cursing each one that escaped him.

"I am damned," he told her. "I let myself be damned decades ago, and do you know why, my friend?"

Jy said nothing.

"Each cause," he professed, "requires you to make some sacrifice. To begin the mission we had to destroy the Founders' earth, and to become a Wanderer I had to sacrifice my way of life, and to fight the unFound I had to give away my innocence and my careless decencies and whatever else made me an effective Wanderer."

Shadows swirled around Jy; she couldn't speak aloud.

"There was a filthy job," she heard, "and I believed we could succeed."

The shadows closed upon her and grasped her throat and squeezed for a very long moment, then they released her again.

"I was wrong," Moliak said with a soft and sober and very cold voice. "I was very much mistaken, I want to tell you."

Jy braced herself and waited.

"Success is an impossibility, I realized at last," he cried, "and now the one thing left for us is to find the very best way to fail."

Jy said nothing.

"Do you hear me, my friend?"

She had heard every word and the blackness between each one.

"Jy?" said Moliak. "Jy?" he said. "Do you see what I mean, my dear friend? Jy?"

2

I ADMIRE them because they are utterly loyal to one another and utterly vicious to those they do not know, and every distinction is clear and easy for them. They never pretend kindness. They are strong and enduring, and they do their best work under pressure. Intellectually they are more pragmatic than artistic, though they have a surprising flair for all arts. Beauty is apparent to them every day of their lives. (I have no beauty in my life anymore.) They live fully and go to death gladly. The Heart of God is the sun. Their earth is God's Good Testicle. They fear nothing. They know enough. They thrive where I would succumb.

A lot of us have begun to admire the unFound.

I see it more every day.

—*Moliak's private journal*

Jy is one of the unFound too....

—*Graffiti inside portal*

Damnations are not simple.

What Moliak had seen as his duty, other Wanderers had begun to regret and deny and finally try to leave behind. They didn't want to serve as soldiers any longer, and of course they had well-considered reasons. They pointed to their casualties and calculated that another hundred hell-earths would decimate the highest ranks of Wanderers. The Cousins and Founders would be sketches of their former selves, and if there were another thousand hell-earths nobody would be left alive who could remember Jy or the Day of Beginnings or any other foundation of the mission. Novices and the incompetent would have to be promoted, and the heart of Jy's grand cause would be eroded to nothing. Where was the good in such tragedies? they argued. How could the Wanderers ever return to any semblance of their former selves? Thus more and more of the oldest Wanderers left combat, and most of those remaining were quick to stay inside the safest bunkers in the quietest sectors, their immortality intact.

Moliak had fought the changes, in words and deeds; and Jy felt a sudden tiny warmth towards the man, recognizing his sense of honor amongst the unforgivable violence. Every Wanderer had to fight, she reasoned, or there would be problems. Novices and Termites and the rest would eventually feel bitterness toward the distant leaders. As the fighting dragged on, tireless and hopeless, the bitterness would have to worsen. There would be fewer volunteers demanding more payment, and what could the Wanderers do in response? If there were too few soldiers to fight the unFound, what would be their options?

Moliak had seen one possibility. Another Founder showed him the plans with a certain eerie pride. Termite Mound constituted an enormous reservoir of manpower. What if some of the cold low castes could be moved to the conquered hell-earths? What if those earths could be terraformed—mirrors throwing the weakened sunlight down on them and the radiations scrubbed away and soils built from the rubble—and what if the castes could eat at will and feel gratitude? The Wanderers could begin to sculpt them into a new society. The Founder speaking to Moliak almost smiled, saying, "We will teach them how to fight and how to raise their children to be fighters, and for this they will get entire worlds and endless feasts and warmth like they have never imagined."

It was possible, Moliak realized. He examined the broad outlines of the plan and realized it had no apparent flaws.

"They will fight the unFound for us," said the ancient one. "They will have to fight them because the unFound are going to be their neighbors. They won't have any choice. And of course each earth they conquer can be theirs. They can use them as they as they wish."

Moliak nodded, took a breath and held it.

"Look at our projections," said the Founder. "Their metabolisms will give them an advantage, as you well know, and we can build them into a pure warrior society. They can be our equivalent of the unFound. Eventually they can take the entire war for themselves, and you and I won't ever again have to fight. What do you think of such a future, Moliak? Moliak? Why are you wearing that frown, my friend? What are you thinking?"

Moliak had told Cotton about the plan. Cotton was one of his best soldiers, loyal in that instinctive way all

Termites were loyal to people of higher status, and he told Cotton, "I have never seen a more cynical, workable scheme. I'm certain something like it is going to be used." It had been a bad day for both men. There had been an ambush and three companions had died, no hard-memories to save, and now both men were sitting inside a little bunker with the ground trembling around them. They were drinking from a bottle of colorless tasteless liquor, Cotton already quite drunk, and Moliak told him, "We are going to perform surgery on your world—"

"There are larger crimes," Cotton blurted.

"—but what we are going to make . . . it is horrible, my friend. Do you understand? Wanderer skills and Wanderer experience are going to build a culture with no purpose but the killing of unFounds. But what happens when we get past the unFound? What do we do with your brethren in that event? Do you understand? Suppose we win but create an even worse race in the process?"

Cotton said nothing, but the horror showed on his reddened face.

Moliak took a burning drink, then said, "I have always been willing to pay for my crimes, my damnation—"

"I know," Cotton muttered. "You can't be faulted."

"What would be better," Moliak claimed, "would be to fight and die for ourselves and allow the novices, the eager young untainted novices, to replace us after the war and continue the mission."

Jy watched the conversation as if it were a hyperclear dream, and she thought: *That might be the least awful solution.*

"Argue with them," said Cotton. "Use your charm and your power and make your associates see it as you see it."

"My associates have made up their minds."

Cotton was a very thin man on that day. His bony hands held the bottle by its neck, and he drank before saying, "Then do something else," with a quick slurring voice.

"Do what?" asked Moliak.

"I don't know. Perhaps you can find some way to stop everything," he allowed. "You can turn off the portals, finish the war and the mission, and be done with it."

Jy felt a sudden ache in her belly.

Moliak said, "What if someone could stop everything?"

"If there were a way," said the drunken man. He took a huge last gulp and handed back the bottle, belching once, then he said, "We can do it together, my friend. You invent the plan and I will help you carry it out, and nobody on the Bright will ever again have to worry about goddamn Wanderers coming to them . . . trying to help them . . . fucking up everything in the process."

"Maybe," said Moliak.

Jy, outside the illusion, felt the sharper ache of her wounded head, and she lifted a hand and touched the dried clotting foams.

"Perhaps we can," said Moliak. "There might be one way."

3

SOMETIMES I dream that I am hunting for Jy while she hunts for me, and we meet in the middle and stare at each other for a moment, then each says to the other, "I know what you want," with the same tired and determined old voice.

　　　　　　　　—*Moliak's private journal*

Jy blinked and found herself in the present again, sitting on the softened portal floor with the earths streaking past and her companions surrounding her, some of them crying and others appearing stunned by everything they had absorbed. They had experienced the same story; they had felt Moliak's black presence; they understood some of what was happening to them. Yet only Jy could stand and say, "I know what you intend, Moliak. I know why you came to find me and what you stole from my head, and I know where we are going, and I know exactly what you intend to do when we arrive."

She felt the sudden soft touch of Quencé. With his eyes he seemed to ask how she felt.

She was miserable, but it didn't matter.

What mattered was Moliak, and she stared at that stolen face of his and shook her own head, saying, "You took the trigger from me," with an anguished voice. "You needed me for the trigger."

Quencé asked, "What is the trigger?"

Nobody spoke.

Moliak shut his eyes and smiled and opened his eyes again. "There is an ancient contingency plan. Only a very few Founders ever learned of it. I knew, and Jy knew because she designed the contingency, and perhaps another couple dozen of us were aware."

"What trigger?" Quencé repeated.

"The portal system depends on vast energies emitted by a single source," said Moliak, "and if that source were missing the system would be useless. All its intricate machinery would die, and the portals would be novelties, nothing more, slowly corroding under the suns."

"What does he mean?" asked Quencé.

People were stirring, looking about and whispering to one another.

Jy's nightmare was complete. *I can wake now.* She brought both hands to the crest of her head and grasped handfuls of hair, tugging until the scalding pain made her moan aloud. *I want to come awake now.*

Moliak asked her, "When did you last think of the trigger?"

She couldn't recall.

"But why think of something so awful, so heinous, when everything goes so well for you?" His voice held a distinct bitterness. "Am I right, Jy?"

She turned to Quencé.

"Part of the trigger was inside me," she explained, "and a few chosen Founders carried the matching part."

"Moliak?" asked Quencé.

"He was a favorite student," she allowed.

"But what does the trigger do?"

"Let me show you," said Moliak, and the portal dome darkened an instant later. In the gloom overhead floated a holo image of the Founders' earth, a featureless black sphere of indeterminate size. People gazed up at the sphere while Moliak said, "The trigger was intended for the very worst events. Should there come a time when there was no other answer, a code within Jy's hard-memory would be merged with another code and the trigger would be formed and ready to be used to start a series of runaway nuclear fires—"

Quencé grasped Jy by the shoulder, trying to lend comfort and strength. She wanted neither. She wanted to feel the crush of events and succumb to them. Her destruction held an intoxicating promise that she could taste, sweet and coy.

"—and then the greatest example of human ingenuity would detonate," said Moliak. "The Founders' earth is going to be destroyed. We are going there to destroy it, and ourselves. Even the enduring work of the Makers will be obliterated, in theory, and the Bright will be permanently severed into two pieces!"

The explosion was sudden and soundless, the black sphere dissolving into gas and plasmas and expanding outwards at the velocity of light—

—and someone was screaming, the voice piercing—

Stop the screaming! Stop it now!

Then Quencé clamped his hand across Jy's open mouth, the wave front of holo light washing over them, and nobody was screaming. Nobody made any sound whatsoever. Jy felt her eyes watering, tears rolling onto Quencé's hand . . . . The awful glare cut into her . . . yet she kept her eyes opened in the feeble hope she would be stricken blind.

BOOK THREE

•

THE FOUNDERS' EARTH

KYLE

1

THE ARCHIVE who met me at the portal rode inside a ceramic box set inside a robot's ceramic head. The head possessed enormous glass eyes and a temporary mouth, and through the mouth the Archive asked, "What is your first impression of our world?"

"It seems austere," I responded, perhaps too hastily. I was gazing out at the absolutely flat countryside and the remote horizon, and I said, "At least to me it seems a little that way—"

But the Archive agreed. "Yes." The head lifted and the eyes fixed on some far point. "Austere is almost the best word," I heard. "In some ways, this must be the perfect place for the dead . . . ."

—*Courier's private journal*

Nobody moved.

What could anyone do? thought Kyle.

Everything was hopeless. Moliak was taking them to the Founders' earth to destroy it and destroy them too, it seemed, and they were doomed. They were going to die.

Kyle felt an enormous weariness. He lay on his back, the floor soft beneath him, and Billie gave him her brave face. Then Kyle managed a deep breath and tried to soften like the floor, working to relax, his eyes closing and a sudden deep sleep coming over him. The relentless stress had exhausted him. He slept, and he dreamed. Then he was awake again and alert, and he sat upright as if startled, wondering what was happening. What woke him? He saw Moliak at the controls, as always, and Cotton was watching him and everyone else too. Time had passed. Cotton's gray clothes hung limp on his shriveling body, and one fast hand, the bare one, combed his thin blond hair once, then again. Nobody had moved while Kyle slept, it seemed. No one was speaking now. The dream had wakened him. What was the dream? He could remember being a Wanderer and a soldier, and it was like one of the illusions Moliak had put inside his mind . . . only it wasn't. The battleground was an ordinary street flanked with unremarkable houses, and the enemies were young boys riding bicycles. They came towards Kyle, and he felt the glove on his one hand. He thought of firing at the boys but couldn't make himself, and he remembered their aiming gloves and firing even as they pedaled, and the blows had lifted Kyle and torn him into ugly red scraps—

—and he shivered to himself, grabbed himself, and waited.

The other prisoners sat around him. But for the rising and falling of their chests, they might have been so many statues carved from softened wax.

Billie tried another brave smile.

He wished she would stop trying to cheer him. Everything about Billie was making him sick. Didn't she notice how he felt? he wondered. She had to notice something, he couldn't hide his thoughts *that* well. What was she thinking? Was she as scared as he? Then he stopped himself, remembering that he didn't care about

her anymore. He shook his head and breathed and carefully turned away.

The portal's dome was transparent again.

It was late afternoon—he must have been asleep for
several hours—and the lowering suns were flashing past
at an astonishing rate and with a variable strength. There
were clear skies and hazes over the suns, and broken
clouds and churning black thunderstorms. It was like
flipping fast through a book of brightly colored landscapes, brief white pages between each picture and
everything past before it could be seen. Kyle had vague
impressions of weather and the landscapes. Great masses
of vivid green stretched towards the west, and other
times there were gray earths and gold earths and earths
dressed in bright city colors. He could see the sudden
silhouettes of buildings now and again. They must be
well into the Cousins' realm, he decided. When Jy came
through here eons ago people were scarce and simple
and looked like Xen, and now some of them or most of
them had evolved into their own style of intelligence and
their own cultures. How did the Wanderers keep in
touch with them? What had he read in the various books?
Then he realized that it didn't matter. This kind of travel,
this vast unity, was going to be finished soon. Nobody
else would travel through these portals. Moliak would
see to it.

Kyle looked at the other prisoners. There was an
indifference to their faces, a sense of deep resignation.
Jy couldn't have seemed older or weaker, her dark face
shot full of a new grayness, as if some kind of corrupting
illness were working its way from within. Quencé was
watching Jy too. Once, for just a moment, he touched
her on the forearm and halfway stroked her fur while
shaking his head. What was he thinking? A Wanderer
could hold a hundred thoughts in his mind at the same
instant. Did Quencé have some idea of how to get free?
If so, thought Kyle, he was hiding his optimism. The
handsome cut of his face and his strong build made him
seem like the kind of man never to look beaten. Yet he
did. With his eyes he seemed to tell Jy, "I am sorry, but
there is nothing I can do . . . nothing."

The suns were dipping close to the horizons.

Xen said, "I feel hungry," with a whining voice. "Can we eat something?"

Moliak gave a slight nod.

Cotton skipped to the pack and returned with food and bottles of water. As he approached Xen—as Xen reached with one hand—Cotton dropped everything and somehow circled the Cousin. He was suddenly behind him, making no sound, and Xen jerked and turned while dropping, arms raised and his heavy face startled.

Cotton laughed and returned to his old position.

It was a game and a warning, his showing everyone his speed and eerie grace.

People began to eat, though no one seemed hungry. Quencé took shares for himself and Jy. Billie brought dried meat and fruit and pushed the larger portion to Kyle. A large bottle of sweetened water was passed to everyone, and Kyle ate and drank in a mechanical fashion.

Moliak snacked, but Cotton took nothing.

The abstinence worried Kyle.

He could remember the little man beside the tree, stuffing himself with candy, and he remembered him being thirty pounds heavier just a day ago. Yet Cotton didn't see the point in eating now. He watched them with the faintest of longings, his feet changing positions and his head turning and his eyes trying to see everything at once. The only part of him that kept still was that shiny gloved hand.

The hand was always in a fist, Kyle noticed.

Always.

2

"WE SLEEP for a thousand years," said the Archive, "then we wake and work for ten years along with those who have the same schedule. The ones who are awake manage the robots that maintain the enormous reactor and the robots that bring new fuel and the robots that mine the hydrogen from a variety of sources. Most of the hydrogen belonged to the gas giants. Other duties include the security systems and escorting couriers like yourself—"

"Thank you," I responded.

"You are most welcome." The Archive waited for a moment before continuing. "We also make reports that are sent in both directions on the Bright, to both leaderships, describing our work to them. Then after our tenure we are granted another thousand-year sleep."

"While awake," I inquired, "do you do anything but work?"

"Nothing else is so interesting," he informed me. "We have enough rest. When we are awake we have no other purpose."

"When asleep," I asked, "do you dream?"

He said, "No."

"You don't have dreams?"

There was a pause.

"I didn't mean sleep," he told me. "I am sorry. I didn't use the best word."

—*Courier's private journal*

They began to slow around dusk.

Kyle half expected Billie to turn to him and ask how many earths they had seen. How many lay between theirs and the Founders' earth? He knew the exact number; he had read it many times. It was five hundred-and-some odd thousand, only he was having trouble concentrating. Kyle felt stupid and slow, and he started to massage his temples, trying to knead his brain back into condition.

Billie didn't ask her question, regardless.

She sat beside him and chewed her food, and sometimes she watched Jy with her big sad eyes.

"God," Kyle muttered under his breath. "I'm sorry...."

She didn't hear him.

If they hadn't gone to see Jy, he was thinking, this mess would have meant nothing to them. It would have been Jy's problem and the Wanderers' problem, and he didn't give a goddamn whether Moliak got his way or not. Kyle decided he didn't care so long as he could go home in the end, and Billie too, and maybe that wasn't noble of him. So what the fuck? He didn't care. *Fuck everything!*

Kyle dipped his head and felt a sudden sweet anger.

He imagined himself with a gun. It was a small black machine gun, lightweight and vicious, and he saw everything with striking clarity. The gun had a cool feel and sprayed explosive bullets that cut through meat and bone. Two minced corpses were left dead on the floor, blood was everywhere, and he emptied the long clip and threw the gun down and . . . and nothing. He couldn't decide what would happen next, and the daydream evaporated. He shut his eyes and opened them again, and suns were starting to kiss the green horizons.

They were lingering on each earth.

Kyle could see antelopes or something resembling antelopes, hundreds of them, eating their way across the backside of the hill. The prairie was cropped short and well watered. A single herdsman trailed the antelopes. He was extraordinarily tall, maybe eight feet or more. He had long legs and long arms and a peculiar splotchy brown-and-black skin that made him oddly attractive. He happened to glance sideways with a face as narrow as a knife blade, and he was startled. Someone was inside the portal. Perhaps in his entire life he had never seen anyone in the portal, and he put his hands into the air and took a weak step backwards—

—and the Bright appeared again, changeless and reliable and almost dull.

The next earths seemed to be empty of people. There were oceans of grass and various skies. Then came a sudden city that stood in the way of the sun, towers of curling glass shot full of colors, brilliant golds and flowing crimsons and electric blues, and he sensed the beauty of the place while feeling an enormous detachment. He waited for the Bright, and nothing happened.

They seemed to have stopped. Only this couldn't be their destination, Kyle knew. The people around him were stirring, whispering something, and he heard only the tone of their voices. Where was this? What was this?

The floor seemed to shiver and buck.

The Bright came slowly this time, melting the curling towers and the sky and coming through the close green ground like milk seeping through a sponge, the whiteness expanding and joining and the Bright complete again.

"What's happening?" asked Billie. She looked at Kyle and nearly grabbed his hand, then she stopped herself.

Quencé said, "We're very close."

"Very close," Kyle echoed.

The other Wanderers had lifted their faces, becoming more alert.

The Bright swirled around them. Its whiteness became a thin creamy gray, and the shuddering increased. "We have to move in several dimensions at once," Quencé was saying. He looked at Billie and said, "The next earth's geometry is rather . . . different," and he turned to Kyle. "Isn't it, my friend?"

Who did he mean? thought Kyle.

"It will take a little while longer."

Kyle said, "Yes," and stared into Quencé's eyes. The man was gazing at him, and for no reason. What was he thinking? It was impossible to know.

Kyle shut his eyes, and the portal grew still and silent.

Nobody was talking.

Kyle held his breath, refusing to open his eyes. He waited with his legs tucked up against his body and his mouth tasting foul. He needed a toothbrush, he decided, and a scalding shower. He imagined a big soft bed in a big clean room. He kept thinking of anemic comforts, then he heard a voice.

It was Cotton.

"Up, up," said Cotton. "Up, up."

Cotton streaked past him and clipped him with one foot, and for a moment the air felt distinctly warmer.

Kyle opened his eyes as he stood.

Wherever they were, he realized, it was nighttime.

He was gazing out at a featureless landscape running on and on. It felt vast and perhaps endless, but there was nothing in the way of landmarks. There were familiar stars overhead and the ground around them looked like polished metal, like something made in his grandmother's time, and it was like no place he had ever imagined.

This was no earth, he told himself. Not at all.

3

WE WERE riding inside one of the mag-cars intended for the rare traveler, and I remarked about the enormity of the place and the achievements it represented. Had the Makers used similar means to skip along the Bright? I asked. They could have used many earths as we used this one. . . .

"Possibly," said the Archive.

I looked at his ceramic face.

"But my own guess is that we are doing everything wrong," he told me. "You and I are primitives who have found a fusion reactor, and somehow we learned to build hot fires inside the reaction vessel. We use wood and coal and tinder and sparks, and we sit about the blaze while cooking fresh meats, telling each other that we are extraordinarily clever. We found this wonder, after all, and comprehended it so easily . . . ."

—*Courier's private journal*

The portal surrounding them seemed unremarkable. Its entranceway opened, both doors emitting a sharp hissing noise, and they were walking outside in single file with the air rushing past them. Kyle thought of airplanes decompressing and related horrors. Billie was ahead of him,

Quencé behind, and he felt his own feet starting to lock in place. He couldn't help himself. He stopped and froze, then Quencé's hand touched him on the back. The tall Wanderer whispered, "You are fine," with a comforting precision. "The atmosphere is lean, but it's ample."

Kyle took a tentative breath, then another.

They went outside. Kyle felt a furnacelike heat and a dryness, and the ground was tabletop flat and smooth and metallic. Kyle glanced at the sky. He spotted the reliable Dippers and Polaris. Then Moliak yelled at them from behind, saying, "Hurry! Straight on!"

Cotton was in the lead. He was towing the pack as if it were so much painted air. What was inside the pack? Kyle looked back over his shoulder and saw the portal illuminated by starlight. He saw empty bottles and food wrappers and some of the tools Moliak must have used. But that spidery machine, the autodoc, was gone. Cotton had taken the autodoc for some reason. With its trash and its familiarity the portal looked like an old campsite, and they were leaving it. They were striking across this bizarre landscape, and Kyle felt uprooted and vulnerable and particularly strange.

He began to cry.

Tears crawled down his face. He didn't sob or make any other noise. Everyone was walking alone, and the loudest sound was the slap-slapping of the sandals against the metal ground.

Something lay far ahead.

It looked like a blister of glass or crystal. What was it? He kept telling himself this was an earth, just another earth, and it had been swollen to many times its normal size. The Founders and their Archives had rebuilt this earth to serve them; he had read about it and Moliak had caused him to live pieces of the story too. What was that object? It was set only partway to the horizon, yet it took them more than an hour of steady walking before it had a form and an apparent function.

A man-high rail ran razor-straight on the ground. The crystal blister straddled the rail, and it seemed to be waiting for them. Cotton started to trot forwards. There was an urgency to his stride, an excitement, and

he extended his gloved hand as if he were half blind.
The glove seeped a silverish light, and Cotton watched
the glove now. He kept moving it from side to side.

The thin swift voice called back to them.

"Clear!"

Moliak said, "Hurry," but nobody was willing. It
was as if his prisoners had decided this was enough, they
were going to stop obeying. Wysh turned to look at
Quencé and Kyle, then she shortened her own stride.
Again Moliak said, "Hurry," and a bolt of sputtering blue
light sliced across the ground beside them. Kyle felt the
heat, then the voice. "We don't need most of you,"
warned Moliak. "I can choose someone. I can be remarkably unkind."

Their pace increased.

Kyle started to jog and breathe hard. He felt enormously heavy—was the gravity stronger here?—yet he
made the blister without incident. Cotton had opened a
doorway, waiting with his head pivoting and his eyes
sweeping the landscape. Was something wrong? Was
there any reason to hope something would go wrong?
The image of dead people set on high shelves came into
Kyle's head. Those had to be the Archives; they lived in
this realm. He had read about them and Moliak had
implied them in his dreamlike illusions, and suddenly
Kyle hoped against hope that they would discover what
was happening and save everyone.

The crystal blister was the size of a small house.
Seats sprouted from its floor, each one perfectly fitting
one of them. They were immediately in motion. Moliak
sat before a bank of controls, and Kyle felt the quick
acceleration and heard the whine of the thin air flowing
past them. It was like the steady strong takeoff surge of
an airliner, only it never quit. The huge landscape raced
past them, and the blister itself changed shape, drawing
itself into a longer, more streamlined configuration. Kyle
blinked and trembled and looked forwards. He could see
the rail glowing with a faint ruddy color, and the air
around them began to sing.

He didn't care where they were going.

He was cargo, utterly inert and beyond opinions

and fear. There was an ease to being cargo. He felt as though he were packed in Styrofoam beads, warm and secure.

After a while he could hear other cargo talking.

It was Quencé's voice. He sounded steady and amazingly sober, and maybe he had been talking for a while or maybe he had just begun. There was no telling. ". . . because there wasn't enough room for orbiting solar collectors and fusion reactors to be set on a normal earth's surface," he was saying. He was looking at Billie. Had she asked a question? Whom did she ask? "The Founders," said Quencé, "devised a new means to produce power. They decided to reshape the planet itself, creating a single enormous reactor vessel, and they left the Archives here to construct the facilities. The earth's core was the beginning. Its pressure and its heat were helpful, and the Archives used fuel from the oceans and then the outer solar system. They injected hydrogen into the rebuilt core, like gasoline into an automobile engine. Do you understand?"

She gave one of her weak nods. Kyle recognized the expression; and no, she didn't understand. She didn't feel at all confident.

But Quencé kept talking. "Stored beneath us," he claimed, "are several dozen earth-masses of hydrogen. They are compressed and ready for burning, and vast robot tankers bring new hydrogen all the time. That's what causes the earth to expand, like a balloon expands, and the deep mantle is welling up to the surface. Some of the metallic core is doing the same thing." Quencé glanced at Kyle for no reason, then he stared at Billie again. "The portals have to be moved frequently. The crust is constantly shifting them out of alignment." He used his hands in the air, explaining, "As long as they remain at the same relative positions on the globe, they operate without flaws. The Makers' machinery is everywhere, and it doesn't seem to mind being twisted and stretched this way . . . ."

She gave half a nod.

"There are no continents or oceans anymore," said Quencé. "They were obliterated a long time ago."

Jy made a soft sound, and she shifted in her seat.

"The atmosphere," said Quencé, "comes from oxygen liberated by the expansion and certain chemical tricks."

"We destroyed our earth," Jy stated. She turned to Billie and said with a plaintive voice, "It was a beautiful world, our homeland, and we gladly sacrificed it for the mission."

Billie didn't want their attention. She laced her hands together and dropped her eyes.

"My species made its choice, and it made the choice unanimously." Jy pointed a defiant finger towards the sky. "What other human species could have such unity? Is there one?"

"No," said Quencé.

Wysh and Xen said, "No," together.

Kyle said nothing, forgetting who he was.

Then Jy turned forward again. "I don't know you!" she said with sudden life and fury. "Moliak was a good person, strong and decent. He couldn't do anything monstrous."

Their captor shook his head, saying, "Haven't you been paying attention, old woman? Everyone is a monster—"

"No!"

"Yes!" he screamed.

Jy pulled at her gray fur, saying, "You are not he. You couldn't be he! I know Moliak, and you are somebody else. No! No, no, no!"

4

IN THE fullness of time the Founders' earth will be stretched thin, and we will have to mine silicates and metals from the nearby worlds. We will bring them as we bring hydrogen today. Research, I understand, predicts that we can dilute the Makers' machinery about a thousandfold without diminishing its capacities.

"Imagine such an earth," I said to my companion.

The Archive said, "Yes," with a trace of pride in the voice.

"But what about the fuel? Won't we have used the gas giants by then?"

"We have plans to cool the sun," he told me, "bringing it to a more manageable temperature. Then huge robot craft will skim off its outer layers one at a time, collecting them and purifying them, leaving nothing but the helium-rich core—"

"We are going to digest the sun?" I sputtered.

"Eventually." The Archive waited for a moment, then he informed me, "We have outlines for even larger projects. If the Makers' machinery can be diluted a thousandfold, perhaps it can be diluted a millionfold—"

"Yes?"

"—and we will start dismantling the nearby suns as well."

I trembled at the prospect.

"It would not be a very difficult project," said the ancient voice, "provided we can engineer self-replicating and self-correcting robots in modest numbers. And if we can dilute even farther, we estimate, we could acquire a significant fraction of our galaxy's mass in the next billion years, all of it serving the mission . . . ."
                    —*Courier's private journal*

The single rail continued to run straight across the vast landscape, and the blister quit accelerating and changing its shape. For a little while nothing happened. Then they started to slow all at once, people turning their seats around and Kyle feeling the familiar hand pressing against his chest. He tried to relax. He looked sideways as they crossed a wide red river of molten goo. Was it a rift? What was it? Quencé seemed to hear his mind, saying, "That is core material being thrust upwards. It's being driven by the reactor's heat and masses of new hydrogen."

Billie was staring at the red river, and she wasn't.

Quencé seemed to glance at Kyle for an instant. He felt the eyes but didn't quite catch them. "We are riding on the crust of a man-made star," said Quencé, and he smiled. "Every Wanderer would like to come here, and almost none of us have had the chance."

He sounded ridiculously calm, thought Kyle.

It was almost as if he were flirting with Billie. What was the point? It had no point. He wanted Quencé to leave Billie alone.

The rift was behind them, a faint blood-colored glow in the west, and they continued to slow. Kyle reminded himself that he was cargo. There was no point in thinking any other way. He had no cares and his fate was sealed and he would die when this man-made star exploded. He felt sorry for Billie, and the blame was all his own. He came to that conclusion, yet it didn't matter how he felt. His feelings made no difference, he understood, and there was no point in dwelling on them.

He was past exhaustion now.

Kyle existed in some new realm where flesh was immune to all weakness. He felt weightless and calm and strangely wise.

Flecks of color showed to the south.

Were those Archives? Were they robots? They might be a thousand miles away, he realized, and they meant nothing. He accepted the hard fact with a nod and a thin weak smile.

The blister was slowing to a stop, nothing around them but miles of frozen metal and rock. This was the dead heart of the earth turned inside out. He heard the doorways open with a hiss and smelled the dry metallic air, and Moliak told them to stand and follow Cotton. He said that Cotton knew the way.

Where were they going?

But Kyle didn't need to know. He was a package, free of all will.

Cotton streaked ahead of them, using his glove as

before. He was hunting for traps and sensors, and Moliak was behind them. He was impatient but suffering, Mr. Phillips's body drenched in sweat, and the body refused to move as quickly as he wanted. His frustrations were obvious. "Keep walking!" he shouted. "Fast!" The sweating face was sour and tense and maybe a touch doubtful. Could he be doubtful? It was as if he were realizing how far they had come, nobody trying to stop them, and he couldn't believe his luck. He was worried because everything seemed too perfect.

"Faster!" Quencé told him. He had come up beside Kyle, and he whispered, "Walk faster," to no one else. "There. That's fine. We aren't racing."

Cotton was an animated speck ahead of them, and Moliak was falling behind. Quencé and Kyle were leading the captives, and where was Billie? Suddenly he missed her shadowing him.

"I asked her to stay behind," said Quencé, anticipating the question. "I told her that I needed to speak to you, Wanderer to Wanderer."

Kyle saw a quick sideways glance and said nothing.

"Now slow the pace," said Quencé. "This is a good enough lead, I hope."

Kyle waited.

Quencé stared at him. Starlight showed the intensity of his stare and the clenching of his jaw.

A moment passed.

He said, "Kyle."

"What?"

With a clear, quiet voice the Wanderer informed him, "I know what you're not, Kyle. I know."

He nearly stopped walking.

Quencé grasped his arm and pulled.

"Easy," said Quencé. "Stay calm."

Kyle said, "But I am," with a fragile voice.

"Quiet," the Wanderer told him. "It just occurred to me, and I don't think anybody else suspects."

Kyle bit his lower lip and made himself keep quiet.

"It's all right," he heard. "People pretend now and again. Don't worry. Pretending... is understandable. Don't worry."

Kyle kept his eyes forward.

Quencé waited a moment, then he said, "Whatever happens to us, whatever Moliak wants us to do, I want you to keep pretending. You cannot let up."

Kyle couldn't believe it.

"Are you listening?"

He tried to nod. He tried to say, "Yes."

A large hand touched his arm for an instant, squeezing and then letting him go again. "You have to be strong," Quencé warned. "You can't flinch and you aren't going to quit." He was smiling all at once. He offered a soft, encouraging smile. "I think Moliak is going to need one of us. He has to choose one of us—a Wanderer—and I think it will be you."

"Yes?"

"Because you seem to be the weakest one. He will take you."

Kyle tried to say, "I understand."

"That's what we want," said Quencé. "It's the best possible thing for us."

How could that be?

"Kyle," said Quencé, "you have made it this far already. So what's a little farther? It's almost nothing, my friend. We're almost there."

QUENCÉ

1

THE WANDERERS don't know where the hell they are going.

—*Graffiti inside portal*

For a long while he had been seeing perfect plans, every element in its place and every variable measured and marked. He had been concentrating on these schemes for hours, with no breaks and few distractions; and with the bulk of his hard-memory lashing at the problem, some new perfect plan would emerge every few minutes. He would see some combination of actions and inactions that would set them free.

Only whenever Quencé would give the plans a hard honest look, turning them over in his hands, not one of them seemed remotely sensible. They were nothing but dreamy fluff. His cleverness was generating them in some misspent urge to make him happy, and there wasn't any stopping the process. It was a flood of wishful thinking that would continue until Moliak ignited the world beneath them.

The last hours inside the portal were miserable. If only he could alert someone, he believed. If he could somehow find an alarm . . .

And in the midst of everything, for no clear reason, Quencé would find himself watching Kyle for several seconds at a time.

Why? he would wonder. Why bother?

Kyle was an unremarkable Wanderer and apparently an unremarkable person too. He was quiet and stiff, acting cold to the girl he had brought and cold to everyone else too. Yet Quencé would gaze at the man, noticing tiny things. He noticed the way Kyle would shiver, for instance, or the way he would look about with a sorrowful expression, a stew of emotions showing behind those big pale eyes.

What was his earth? Quencé wondered.

What did it matter?

All the while Quencé's brain churned and sputtered, making no progress with their dilemma. Then they arrived at the Founders' earth, the portal vibrating. He was aware of what was happening. They were twisting their way to the proper place, curling through normal dimensions and the Bright's dimensions. He had never been here, but he knew the mythical stories and the basics of the science, and he wasn't concerned. Even the lowest novice had imagined such a moment.

Again he had glanced toward Kyle.

The eyes were huge, he saw. His hands clung to each other, knuckles showing white through the pale skin, and he was trembling as if he were dipped in ice-water.

What was the man thinking? Quencé asked himself.

When they arrived at their destination Kyle gave their surroundings a long look, one lip quavering and the eyes starting to moisten. Then the portal opened to the outside and their air flowed past them, Kyle suddenly startled, and Quencé understood. It was a simple, obvious truth. He had kept staring at the young man as he had—*because*, he thought, *you aren't even a novice. Are you?*

Kyle was a native pretending to be a Wanderer.

Maybe it was a game, or maybe it was more. What were the odds? It wasn't all that remarkable in itself, he realized. How many pretenders were scattered across the new earth? Probably thousands. Quencé dug into his hard-memory, finding estimates. Thousands wouldn't be unusual; every earth had its own pretenders. The Wanderers looked upon them as a form of flattery and a show of acceptance. The best pretenders actually lost track of their own identities while playing the role. They would emulate the Wanderers, perhaps wishing they could join, and somewhere they forgot where the truth stopped. The best of them lost their own pasts, imagination giving them lives that seemed so much richer.

Neurotic, socially constricted people were the best pretenders.

Kyle?

He had a talent. Only when they left the portal did he seem entirely out of his element. Quencé offered him encouragement, thinking it wouldn't serve to have Moliak or Cotton see the truth. It was amazing that Kyle hadn't confessed yet. Did he believe his identity gave him protection? Or was he eager to maintain appearances in front of the girl?

Quencé focused on Kyle, and he contemplated the circumstances.

Nobody else suspected. There were too many distractions now, too many pressures. Besides, thought Quencé, the man was very good. He had the motions and the clothes, creating a polished, almost unconscious portrait of a Wanderer. All he required, it seemed, was a measure of confidence.

They walked to the mag-car and traveled east, Quencé thinking all the time. What did Kyle mean to them? Anything? He reclaimed some of his better plans and tried incorporating them with the revelation. Countless searches of hard-memory had given him huge mounds of data, most of it useless. Quencé asked himself: *What will Moliak need to obliterate this world?* He recalled certain technical reports—ancient but probably still valid—and they described the security measures used in the early Founder times. He could see energy barriers and alarms and unsophisticated designs needing no maintenance. Only registered Wanderers were allowed to pass into security zones, otherwise the Archives would be alerted. Being a Wanderer meant having a proper hard-memory inside a proper body . . . and Moliak would have to have the right camouflage. Quencé thought about the autodoc inside the field pack. Perhaps this explained why Moliak had taken the extra hostages. *We are candidates.* He was going to have to change bodies with a Wanderer, incorporating Jy's portion of the trigger with his own portion, and only then could he initiate the ancient systems that would destroy everything the Wanderers had done.

Moliak needs one of us!

Quencé knew it. The Archives were supposed to be conservative entities and wouldn't change the security systems, particularly with devices never used. Moliak probably was watching them now, judging who would be best. Which captive would provide the easiest host for him?

More details welled up inside Quencé.

He had to make Kyle more self-assured, he decided. That was why he turned to Billie and lectured about the Founders' earth, wanting Kyle to listen and learn and feel more at ease. Then Jy argued with Moliak, and it was good to hear the life returning to her. A million years of life and purpose were threatened; she had been stunned by Moliak's incredible story; but now the reliable fire was returning, Jy telling their captor that he couldn't be Moliak because she knew Moliak would never be capable of doing such a heinous thing. . . .

Quencé had quit breathing when he heard Jy.

All at once his head became empty. He had no more plans and no thoughts whatsoever. It was as if he contained a sudden vacuum, cold and black and delicious; and he glanced at Kyle once again, for an instant.

No plan emerged.

It was nothing so rigid as a plan.

But there was an inspiration, inarticulate and urgent, and it made him approach Kyle with his first opportunity. He went to the uprooted man and warned

him to keep pretending. Regardless what happened, and
for everyone's sake . . . he could not stop!

Everything depended on him! ·

2

WHAT WERE our scientists doing when they
found the Bright?

Actually they were trying to produce the
perfect clock, and by the greatest good fortune
they had positioned their prototype in perfect
relation to the Bright's elements, and there was
a power surge because of a string of blunders.
The clock's intricate workings vanished. This
led, of course, to questions and more experi-
ments in the centuries before I was born, and
the incredible truth was realized.

A remarkable set of accidents made the
portals possible.

But before you make too much of the accidents, I think you should realize that coincidence is the lifeblood of every event. Without
a string of incredible, almost impossible accidents—the dances of genes; the blurring ran-
domness of each atom—you would not exist
today. Not one of you would sit before me. And
I, strange old Jy, would be nothing but a possibility never born, or ever imagined . . . .

—*Jy's speeches*

Cotton stopped and waited for them at a place without
significance. It was different from the rest of the ground
only because it was glass, not metal—ground that had
been melted at least once, perhaps a thousand times—
and Cotton seemed anxious. He was even more alert
than usual, if that were possible. The thin atmosphere
gave a little gust, then nothing. The stars overhead were
barely turning. This earth barely turned. As its mass had

increased and its equator had expanded, its rotation had slowed in order to conserve angular momentum.

The universe,·in its wisdom, gave nothing away.

Cotton was breathing fast, but he didn't appear spent. He did look quite lean now. Quencé wondered how time must feel for Cotton. In his quick mind this journey must must have taken many days, and he had never slept or eaten or even grown cool.

How much longer before he succumbed to exhaustion?

Quencé made estimates. With hard-memory he guessed calories and the metabolic parameters and the amounts of fat left to be burned, then added fatigue into the mixture. Cotton was existing several times faster than they. He was a wondrous soldier and the perfect sentry, but what were the costs? And what were the opportunities offered?

Wysh and Xen arrived, accompanying Jy.

Whatever Quencé did, it had to be immediate and spontaneous.

What if Moliak chose someone other than Kyle? he wondered. What if the worst happened and it was Quencé taken for hosting?

No, it wouldn't be he.

He could only guess how the technology worked—entering another body; plugging into the existing hard-memory—but it couldn't be an effortless process. It was too involved. Moliak's hard-memory needed to integrate with foreign circuits, and he had to suppress another person's will . . . and Quencé had shown a fiery temper more than once.

And it wouldn't be Jy, either. Jy was his mentor and his audience, and Moliak seemed to take an inordinate interest in her opinions and silences. Besides, she would act like Quencé. She would probably put up a long angry fight.

It was Xen or Wysh or Kyle, he reasoned.

But Xen was a Cousin. He was full of added systems and subsystems meant to give him intelligence, and they would slow the transfer or perhaps make it impossible.

Wysh or Kyle?

Everything equal, thought Quencé, and it was a one-in-two chance. There was something appropriate in those odds, wasn't there? He thought so. From now on he was taking a leap into a void, kicking and screaming all the way down, and one-in-two probably were the best odds he would find.

Taking a deep nourishing breath, Quencé felt stronger and slightly more relaxed. Moliak had just arrived. With Mr. Phillips's hand he pushed the sweat from around Mr. Phillips's eyes, and he looked spent. He knelt like a man on the brink of collapse and paused. Then he uncovered a set of controls hidden with a close-fitted lid and paused before starting to punch buttons.

It was an old design, Quencé realized, yet each button looked new.

There was noise and motion, and a buried chamber emerged from the glassy black ground. There was a hiss of gases and the sudden stink of rancid lubricants, and Quencé saw the chamber opening. It had a massive doorway pulling apart in the middle, and the interior was filled with a faint light the color of new straw.

It was some type of elevator.

They were ordered inside, and the doorway shut with a mechanical ratcheting noise. Then they were descending, Quencé gripping his own wrist and counting heartbeats to estimate time and their velocity, and he studied the simple controls set Founder-high at the doorway.

Moliak kept panting, leaning against the round wall.

Nobody looked alert anymore. Even Cotton seemed ready to sit and sleep. His face was covered with long wrinkles and his mouth was slack and the quick eyes were shot full of a vivid blood.

Quencé breathed and looked at Moliak.

He stared without blinking, then he started to smile.

Finally Moliak noticed him and returned the stare, asking, "What do you want?" He sounded angry and ill-tempered. "What are you thinking? Why don't you tell what you want?"

3

THE CLOSER I come to *her* and the more I see
the earths where *she* herself has walked, the
more I realize how much the woman means to
me. After everything and all of the years, Jy
remains at the center. That is the way it feels,
and I cannot help but adore her, in a fashion.
                                    —*Moliak's private journal*

"I was thinking about you," said Quencé. He used a
careful tone to tell Moliak, "I was wondering . . . about
you. . . ."

"What?" the man persisted. "What do you wonder?"

"Never mind."

Moliak pursed his lips and considered dropping the
subject.

Quencé made his stare more intense, and he
laughed aloud. His laughter sounded real, a genuine
amusement, slightly bitter and rather superior, and Moliak shook his head and shrieked, "Tell me or stop! I'm
in no mood for games!"

"I was just wondering to myself . . . are you real?"

"Real?" Moliak repeated the word, his voice flat and
disinterested.

Quencé glanced at Cotton. Cotton was on the other
side of him, his narrow chest rising and falling, and perhaps he was listening. He had shut his eyes, and perhaps
he was asleep on his feet. Quencé coughed sharply and
told Moliak, "You might not be real."

"I see."

"I keep remembering Jy's saying that she didn't
know you, that you aren't the eager young student she
cherished—"

"Because awful things have happened," he replied,
"and I'm not the same creature. How could anyone remain the same?"

"You don't understand." Quencé tried to treat Moliak like a slow little boy, giving his voice a certain distance and disappointment. "You aren't paying attention, or you're pretending to be dense."

"What I am is confused," Moliak reported. He shrugged his shoulders and said, "Just tell it simply."

"Moliak is dead."

"Dead?"

"Or he exists in captivity," Quencé allowed. "The unFound captured him and replaced him. You are his replacement. I realized the obvious just a moment ago."

Moliak frowned as if he were let down.

Quencé turned to Jy. "He *could* be an unFound. He was planted among the Wanderers as a spy, and now he wants the mission destroyed in the simplest, most effective way possible."

Moliak was offended by what he heard.

Quencé didn't glance at Cotton; but he felt a tremor, a spark of interest. Or was it his imagination?

"Moliak was captured during a battle," he continued. "An unFound tribe with resources found his hard-memory and disassembled him, then reconstituted a new Moliak and used him for camouflage." He gave a big lazy shrug, telling Jy, "We can invade the unFound's ranks. He told us we have spies. Why not reverse the process? The unFound are smart and inventive. Why shouldn't they adapt? They put someone among the Founders to cripple them. I'm sure such a plan would occur to the enemy, and there would be ways . . . ."

Nobody spoke.

Quencé grinned and shook his head. He kept his eyes fixed on Jy, her face perplexed and curious. He thought he saw a faint show of comprehension, then she was shaking her head too.

"I can see the possibility," she allowed.

Quencé persisted. "The unFound spy slips into Moliak's role. We can't know when it happens, but *when* doesn't matter. What matters is that he finds an undercurrent of dissatisfaction, and perhaps he feeds the dissatisfaction. Then he reaches out to an ally, someone entirely loyal to Moliak, and since he knows everything Moliak knew, everything leads naturally to here. He knows about the trigger and the Founders' earth, and he invents a plan that culminates with an outrageous act of vandalism—"

"Enough!" barked Moliak.

Quencé paused. He gave their captor a hard level gaze, shook his head and turned towards Cotton.

Moliak sensed his error.

He made a sudden flustered sound, then said, "That is a stupid idea. I have never heard anything so ridiculous."

Cotton seemed to nod and grin.

Was Cotton absorbing any of this noise? What was he thinking now?

"Preposterous," Moliak grunted.

But Quencé decided to press while hoping for the best. "Think of it in these terms," he said to the doorway. "An unFound spy destroys this place, by any means, and that splits the Bright in two. It also cripples the Wanderers' war effort. Since the spy's tribe is wealthy and alert, it's in a position to capitalize. It knows there is a string of empty and battered earths back down the Bright, and the resistance from the Wanderers will be disorganized at best."

There were a couple of affirmative sounds from the audience.

Jy whispered, "Yes, yes."

"And past the battered earths are fat ones." It was the perfect word, he felt. *Fat*. "The unFound would have learned about Termite Mound and the other half million earths leading to here. Perhaps they never suspected there were so many earths for the taking. Imagine what they could accomplish if they were to rebuild an earth like Termite Mound, making it into a power station like the one here—"

"An unFound tribe would fragment first," said Moliak. "They always split when they become too large and too wealthy."

Quencé looked at Cotton.

"Perhaps," he remarked. "Perhaps."

"But what does it matter?" asked Wysh. She groaned and said, "He is Moliak or he is an unFound spy. Either way we have the same result. What is the difference?"

Quencé kept his mouth closed, offering nothing.

Wait, said his instincts. *Watch them and bide your time*.

Moliak glanced at Cotton, obviously measuring his companion's mood. What was Cotton's mood? He seemed flat, even bland. They might have been discussing inconsequential issues, his face showing nothing. There wasn't even a spark of curiosity now.

Quencé pressed him.

"Have you ever lost track of Moliak?" he said. "Cotton? Did he ever vanish for a particularly long time?"

Moliak wheeled and nearly told him to stop. His face was ruddy and sweating hard again, but he managed to shut his mouth and hold it shut. He dared not intrude; he couldn't afford to be too upset by this noise.

Cotton made a soft long sound.

"It would have happened recently," Quencé ventured. "Could it have happened on the newest unFound earth? Do you know?"

The small man's face responded for a moment.

Quencé couldn't see any emotions. There was just a definite and sudden sobriety, Cotton's alertness being lifted another notch—

"Cotton?" snapped Moliak. He had also seen the change, and he seemed astounded. "Don't even entertain his garbage!"

"I was home," said Cotton's rushing voice, "after my service, and he came to see me—"

"Moliak?" said Jy.

Quencé simply watched.

Cotton's face became puzzled. His mouth and eyes moved so fast that it was impossible to follow his emotions. Was he angry? At whom or at what was he angry? The circumstances had him spooked, guessed Quencé. His own doubts had him spooked. And now Cotton turned to Moliak as if to look at him for the first time, as if to test every past judgment with some ultimate stare. The quick eyes fixed on the fiery blue eyes, and neither man spoke.

Finally Moliak wailed, *"You know me!"*

Cotton held his breath for a few seconds. Then he said, "You *are* Moliak," with a measure of certainty.

"Of course I am!" He wiped the sweat from his face. "Could you imagine the unFound capturing me and doing . . . doing those unlikely things to me?"

Cotton said, "No."

"It would never happen. Never!" He shook his head and claimed, "I would obliterate myself before I became anyone's slave!"

"Like the unFound do?" asked Jy.

Quencé very nearly smiled. Nobody moved or made the slightest sound while the elevator softly jostled from side to side, dropping fast, and now he began to hear the faint but swelling hum of machinery beneath them. He listened to the sound, and he felt it through his toes.

"No," said Cotton, "I don't believe it."

He had made his decision, right or not, and nothing would sway him. He sounded unwilling to change his mind.

Quencé kept silent.

He needed to relax and gather himself.

The others looked at one another and tried measuring each other's sense of things. Moliak was relieved to have the challenge countered. Jy seemed to have let the possibilities slide past her, and there was no knowing her real mind. Billie looked small and forlorn; Wysh and Xen were simply exhausted. And Kyle, the pretender, stood beside Billie with his back straightened and his mouth pressed into a thin line.

The young man was trying to be everything at once. He was a Wanderer and brave, and he was doing his best. That was one twist of good news, thought Quencé. At least one of them was trying to live up to expectations at the end.

The elevator was slowing its descent.

Quencé felt his weight and the tension bundled in his legs and back, and he breathed and found himself starting to laugh.

Chances were that they were doomed. This entire earth was a sleeping bomb, and Moliak would set it off in a very little while. Most likely nothing Quencé did would make any difference. *So be it.* Yet in the midst of everything, all of a sudden, he was learning something that he hadn't suspected about himself.

His frantic efforts to find some way, some scheme, to save them and the mission—he had squeezed himself like the proverbial sponge and found untapped reservoirs within his memory and his will.

Quencé wasn't concerned only with their lives. It was the mission itself that begged for help. He was part of the great adventure, for better or not; and for an instant he considered shaking Moliak's bare hand, without warning, telling him, "Thank you, thank you." Moliak had come an enormous distance to capture him and bring him here, and now everything was apparent. Quencé had been a moron for too long. He had to laugh. He didn't let the laughter bloom on his face, but it was there nonetheless, twirling through him like an electric bolt with nowhere to escape.

BILLIE

1

THE HOMELAND was green and sick when the [unFound] were young, but then the Heart of God came to touch the homeland, and everyone, spreading its strength and its great wisdom while it cured the sickness....
—*UnFound religious tract*

The elevator gave a shudder when it stopped falling, and she shuddered too. Both men watched each other—Moliak and Cotton—then they looked away. It was as if they had exchanged some miniscule signal, a coded half-blink or something, and together they decided to forget what had been said. Or bury it. They were eager to move on.

The shiny door opened with a hiss and that distinct smell—what was the ugly smell?—and they were bathed in a golden light. Cotton flinched, lifting his gloved hand as if to ward off some blow; and Billie took a reflexive step backwards and caught a heel with Kyle's toe, nearly falling.

Get a hold on yourself, girl!

It was Janice's voice. For these last terrible hours Janice had talked to her, steadily, almost brazenly, telling Billie that things weren't hopeless and be tough and if she got the chance, kick ass. Don't hesitate. *Boot their butts over their heads, the bastards!*

She was thankful, so thankful, for that voice.

No doubt about it, she would have crumbled otherwise. Janice was the perfect companion, brash and quick-tempered and entirely sure of herself.

Bastards!

Billie managed a ragged breath and started forwards with the rest of them. They entered a hallway with high arches overhead and a cool white floor. It resembled the hallway inside Jy's own ship, only there was a sense of age and disuse to the place. It wasn't dirty or decaying, no. Every surface was free of corrosion, everything glossy as if new. Yet the air itself held a stuffiness, a laziness, and there was a lingering and faintly metallic taste that made her cough once, then again.

Nobody was talking.

Moliak was leading them down the hallway, Cotton remaining in the rear. She glanced over a shoulder and saw him towing the floating pack, protecting them from no one. This place couldn't have felt more empty.

Kyle was alongside Billie. She turned and saw him giving her a quick vague smile. It was an odd expression. There was something hopeful about it, his face showing a brittle tension and his eyes weepy and his lips pulling flush against his teeth.

What does he want?

The imaginary voice had a venomous tone. Billie felt like arguing with Janice, as incredible as that seemed. Kyle was trying his best, she would reason. Yes, he seemed distant, but he was scared like all of them. He was scared for Jy, and for the mission—

Not you?

Her too. Of course he was concerned, she told herself. Just now he was acting concerned and supportive, thinking to smile at her—

He's an asshole!

She didn't drift into the argument. There wasn't the

time or energy left inside her. Janice was grousing, not Billie. She could never, never think about Kyle in such terms, nor could she blame him for anything that had gone wrong. How could she blame him?

You're too nice, girl!

Maybe so. So what? she thought.

Then Kyle made a sound and tried to bolster his smile, and he was the one to grasp for a hand. His flesh felt cold and damp, even inside his palm, but he squeezed with determination. Kyle had changed, and Janice had nothing to say. There was something different about his mood and his stance . . . what was different? She couldn't decide.

Something was going to happen, she thought.

What?

Be ready, cautioned Janice.

I am.

For anything!

I am.

2

THE HEART of God came to teach the [unFound] what mattered and what was insignificant, and who mattered and who were the enemies . . . everyone not of The Tribe were the enemies . . . and how many proper ways there were to kill, and which ways held the greatest beauty . . . .

—*UnFound religious tract*

They came to a barrier constructed from something fluid and opaque, like a wall of impenetrable warm milk; and Moliak said, "Wait," while pressing controls set into the wall. His face was composed and focused, but his hands seemed excited. He was still sweating, but there was a confidence in his motions. They were very close to their destination, Billie reasoned. She could read that much when she looked at him.

The barrier dissolved; a single round room was behind it.

Kyle gave her hand a long hard squeeze, then a softer one as if to apologize for any pain.

Cotton was directly behind them. Quencé was ahead, and Moliak too, and everyone moved together. There was an accidental rhythm, a simultaneous next step, and they were into the round room with its domed ceiling and the approximate dimensions of their portal. The walls were white and the floor was white, and set at the exact center was a small glittering dome.

Moliak made for the dome.

He said, "Cotton," with a quiet, steady voice.

The little man came forward, and with a single graceful motion he pushed the pack to the floor and opened its largest flap.

Billie breathed and looked at her own feet.

Moliak said, "Do you need help?"

"No," Cotton replied.

He pulled the autodoc from the pack. Why did they need it here? she wondered. She breathed and looked straight ahead, staring into the eerie dome. It was the size of an igloo and colorless, and she couldn't see anything within it but flashes and occasional streaks of darkness. Was it making a sound? She heard something like the hum of air conditioners, and she could feel the vibrations coming through the floor. Why did they need a robot surgeon? She thought of Jy suffering under its knives and lasers, and she took a deep breath, then held it.

The autodoc made a high-pitched tone.

It unfolded arm after arm, resembling a bristly beetle—a child-size beetle—moving with strength and an impossible delicacy. She watched it move, testing itself. Then it stopped and stood motionless, raised up on its ostrichlike toes.

Moliak gave Cotton a long look before he lay on the floor, flat on his back.

What was happening?

The autodoc sputtered and turned, two arms reaching, and padded hands grasped Moliak's neck and head.
He didn't resist; he couldn't have moved if he had
wanted. He kept his eyes open, very pale and bright,
and then cutting hands reached towards his bald scalp
and paused for an instant before setting to work.

Wysh gasped.

Would you look? said Janice's voice. *What's this?*

There was a moment of blood and some pain, Moliak
arching his back as a gruesome light sliced open the flesh
and the skull before cutting straight into the dying mass
of the brain.

Is he dying? Billie wondered.

She hoped he would die. She willed his death and
watched, Cotton standing over Moliak and Quencé
watching Cotton. Moliak's face turned empty, gray and
soft, and Quencé kept studying the little man without
being obvious or making any motions. Then additional
surgical hands were reaching, the autodoc pushing into
the blood and the ruined tissues, and it found something
and grabbed hold and tugged with a shocking force, like
jerking a stubborn cork from an old bottle.

The corpse flexed and fell limp.

It was Moliak's hard-memory, realized Billie. Under
the blood it resembled a mass of interwoven fibers. She
thought of a robust spiderweb. The autodoc lifted it into
the air and squirted water and cleansers over it, and the
fibers became whiter and less substantial. They were
glossy and miniscule, and mashed together they wouldn't
fill the smallest hand.

"It looks very different from ours," said Quencé.
"Our hard-memory is clunky and old-fashioned next to
that."

Cotton said nothing.

"You have done wonders, Moliak."

"He can't hear you," said Cotton.

Wysh seemed to shudder, making a pained sound.

Cotton couldn't stop gazing at the hard-memory, his
face still and something showing in his eyes. What was
showing? A suspicion? Or was it just a clinical interest?
He was standing with his right side toward the others,

his gloved hand opening and closing and opening again; and Moliak was deaf for the moment. Nor could he see anything. Was that why Cotton was letting his feelings show?

He's suspicious, all right! Look at him!

But then the autodoc plugged a glassy wire into the hard-memory, and a large voice said, "The rest of it . . ."

The rest of what?

The voice said, "Cotton? Give me the other part."

"I will," Cotton replied. He knelt and put a hand into the corpse's shirt pocket, removing the coin-shaped object and looking at it before saying, "Here." It held the piece of Jy's hard-memory.

The autodoc put out another hand, and Cotton set the coin on its round ceramic palm.

Quencé glanced at Billie, then Kyle.

Cotton pulled the corpse away from the autodoc, moving with a dreamy strength, and Billie was smelling something. Something cooked? It was cooked flesh, and her belly hurt. She touched herself and thought about Mr. Phillips, thoroughly dead and so far from home.

She felt lonely and cold.

"Which one of them?" asked Cotton.

"The young one," said the new voice. "Kyle. He's the logical choice." Moliak sounded smooth and electronic and entirely inhuman. "Kyle," he said, "please step forward, if you would."

Kyle took a breath and held it.

"Cotton?"

Billie saw Cotton half step, half leap, and he grabbed Kyle by the wrists and jerked once, then twice again. She felt Cotton's heat for a moment. Kyle muttered something and struggled against the pressure, and he said, "Don't, no," with a soft urgent voice.

Quencé said, "Kyle." He lifted his hands and then thought better of it, putting them down and saying, "Kyle," with the same precise voice. "You can't fight him."

Cotton was tiny and lean and very hard with his veins showing on his bare forearms, and he lifted Kyle from the floor and said, "Listen to me," with a slow, relaxed voice. "In a few minutes, I promise, we won't exist anymore and it will be finished and nobody is going to have an easier time getting there than you."

Kyle moaned, and he was set on the floor, on his damp back.

"Moliak needs your house, Wanderer," Cotton explained. "All right?"

He didn't like this job; Billie could tell.

Kyle tried to speak, sputtering some broken words and starting to weep, then beg, his arms across his chest and his hands wrapped together as if in prayer. Cotton said, "Stop. Stop."

Quencé touched Billie on the shoulder, bent close, and said, "Tell him to be brave. Would you?"

"Kyle?" she managed.

"I'm not," Kyle seemed to say. "Not . . . !"

"Kyle!" barked Quencé.

Billie said, "You have to . . . have to be brave—"

"Or you'll make it harder for all of us," Quencé added.

"Oh, Kyle!" She covered her mouth with both hands, feeling sick.

Cotton looked up and said, "Make him relax," while staring straight at Billie.

She felt Quencé pushing her forward.

"Kyle?" She got on her knees and said, "Please?"

Kyle looked at her and then Quencé. He blinked and his expression was odd, but he lay motionless long enough for the autodoc to find him. It hummed and turned on its toes with the padded hands extending. Kyle said, "All right," to Quencé. He quit trying to fight. Then to make sure he stayed in one place, Cotton put the gloved hand on his chest and pushed him flush against the floor.

"Why . . . why do you want me?" Kyle managed to ask.

"For your meat and hard-memory," said the little man. "When Moliak is in you, you are going to stop feeling any of this—"

"Do you have him?" asked Moliak.

Cotton said, "Yes."

"Is it starting?"

"Yes."

Kyle looked at Quencé again and clenched his jaw as the padded hands closed around him. He grew quite still. He lay motionless on the floor and seemed to give a vague, almost invisible nod. Quencé pulled Billie away from him. Then Kyle stared up at the ceiling, high and rounded, and he blinked slowly and tried to swallow, once and then again.

Billie was standing again.

The autodoc was in position.

It held Kyle and both hard-memories, and its free arms started to extend. There was a whirring sound. A glassy blade emerged from its sheath and pivoted and took a couple tentative swipes at the air. Then Quencé was talking, taking a half-step forward and saying, "What if?" with a firm voice. "What if?"

Cotton turned, his features pinched and angry.

"What do you mean?" he asked.

"What if that isn't Moliak?" Quencé's eyes were steady, almost calm, and he said, "It could be a bundle of circuits and memories and an unFound hiding in the middle—"

"Cotton!" cried Moliak's new voice.

Cotton didn't speak. He regarded Quencé, sizing him up with a hard stare while his gloved hand closed into a fist, a rain of golden drops hitting the floor and evaporating.

"Is something happening?" asked Moliak.

"No," said Cotton.

The autodoc started to cut with the blade and cauterize with lasers, and the incision was remarkably small and clean. It wasn't deep yet. Kyle was crying without sound and kept still, but the tears ran down the sides of his face and his hands were locked together on his belly, knuckles white and flexed.

Billie couldn't feel anything.

She heard Quencé say, "Maybe he is genuine," and she looked at Cotton. He was watching everyone, and he was breathing at an enormous pace. "What does it matter either way?" asked Quencé. "Both ways give the unFound huge opportunities—"

"*What do you mean?*"

Cotton pivoted and stepped closer to the autodoc, his bare hand pulling on his hair. He looked injured or ill with his face twisted and his mouth wide open. Moliak asked, "What are you doing, Cotton?"

"Nothing."

"Trust me!" said Moliak. It sounded like a challenge. "What will the unFound gain? They're divided and bloodied and they have nothing but dead empty earths to invade. Termite Mound is in no danger!"

Cotton kept silent.

"Don't you believe me?"

Cotton stared at the white mass of fibers, and he was in agony. He looked confused and tired, unable to cope with everything that was happening to him—

—and there came a soft sudden tone.

"There's a problem," Moliak reported. "Cotton?"

"What? What?" Cotton pushed his bare hand through his hair, then he used his gloved hand. "What is it?" he cried.

"The sonic probe . . . there's no hard-memory inside him," said Moliak. "It doesn't see any—"

Cotton wobbled but stayed on his feet.

The autodoc withdrew its tools, and Kyle made a wet sound. He took a long breath, and Moliak explained, "He lacks hard-memory. I have nothing to use! Where's his hard-memory?"

"*What?*"

Billie saw Cotton put both hands on top of his head. He seemed baffled and angry and lost. His head turned back and forth, back and forth, as he looked at Kyle and Moliak. He didn't notice Quencé moving closer. He never saw Quencé reach out and grab the gloved hand with a lunge, Quencé's legs driving and his big body shoving Cotton off his feet. Cotton was too light and too startled to resist. His head struck the glittering dome, and he grunted once. Quencé wouldn't release him. He lifted Cotton overhead and drove him down hard, trying to shatter the skull, the little body twisting and going

limp and Quencé gripping the floppy head and jerking
it, trying to shatter the spine with his forearms bulging
and his face turning, eyes wide and his solid voice saying,
"Run! Go! Everyone run—now! Go go go go!"

3

THE BRIGHT is an elaborate pipe built by the
Makers and meant to carry away their sweet
and glorious shit . . . .

—*Graffiti inside portal*

Billie turned and nearly ran. Then she stopped and saw
Kyle on the floor. The autodoc had started to back up,
every arm raised, and Kyle rolled onto his side and
gasped.

"What's happening?" Moliak shouted. "Cotton?
Cotton?"

Billie grabbed Kyle's wrist and helped him to his
feet, and he took a step and then another before collapsing to the floor.

She saw the cut in his scalp, clean and bloodless.

There was a shout and a grunt, then one choked
scream from behind them. Kyle stood again. He had no
color and little strength, and Billie thought of dropping
him. She couldn't possibly carry him, yet somehow she
got under an arm and started forward without quitting,
and Quencé was beside them. He got under the other
arm and stayed with them into the hallway, saying,
"Hurry, hurry," under his breath.

Jy was waiting for them.

Wysh and Xen were farther along, beckoning to
them.

Someone was moving. Billie heard motion behind
them. Where was Quencé? He had vanished. Kyle's
weight jerked her sideways, and he said, "Sorry," with
a ridiculous little voice. He was sprawled out on the floor
again. Quencé? She turned and saw Cotton rushing

them, his face bloody but alive, and Quencé touched a
control on the wall, at the last instant, and the milkish
barrier appeared, magnificent and invincible.

"Go!" said Quencé. "Keep moving!"

Quencé was towing the gray pack. He had stolen it!
He told everyone to get inside the elevator, Cotton was
coming, and he helped Kyle to his feet and stayed with
him. They were down the hallway and ready to leave in
a few moments. They stood along the back wall of the
elevator, and Quencé hit a red button as he staggered
in after them. Nothing happened, and he hit it harder,
and nothing changed.

Jy said, "Locked," with a soft, old-woman voice.

"Moliak used a code, before," Quencé responded.
He punched buttons as fast as possible, and Wysh said,
"It might have been changed," with a despairing shake
of her head. She pulled her silvery hair across her chest
and squeezed it with both hands, then they were listening to someone running fast towards them. It was an
unmistakable sound, and Quencé said, "There," and the
doorway moaned and sealed before they could see Cotton. It felt like an enormous margin of safety, it felt
wonderful, and they were climbing. Billie felt them lifting higher and faster, and she cried out. This was lovely.
Fine and lovely and thank you, Quencé. Thank you! And
Quencé gasped and turned, pressing his back against the
door while bending his knees.

"This is what we will do," he said.

Nobody spoke.

He coughed and nearly smiled before saying, "We
still have to get away from them," in warning. "Cotton
is going to call the elevator back. I don't know any way
to block him. And he has to guess that we'll go straight
for the mag-car, which is why we won't."

He looked at everyone.

Xen made a puzzled sound.

Wysh asked, "Where else can we go?"

"We scatter." He told them, "Take a direction and
move fast and make Cotton's work harder. Give us time.
And in the meantime I'll take the mag-car back the way
we came, as far as I can manage—"

"To the portal?" asked Jy.

"I don't have that much time," he answered.

Billie saw Kyle on the floor, his face like cottage cheese and his knees up against his face and his eyes empty and huge. She kneeled and touched him.

"Someone should pull the pack," said Quencé. "Xen. You have to try to keep Cotton from getting to the food—"

"Why do you need the mag-car?" asked Wysh.

"Because I have to do something." Quencé lifted a fist and with apparent effort he opened it and flattened his hand, showing everyone the coin-shaped disk. "It's what they need most—"

"Oh, Quencé," said Jy. "Very good!"

"I can destroy it." Quencé shook his head and said, "If I could have killed Cotton . . . it would be finished now."

"He's too strong," said Jy.

"He's a damned rock," said Quencé.

"How will you destroy the hard-memory?" asked Xen.

"Do you remember the rift zone we crossed? Dropping it into molten metal should be enough."

Kyle grasped Billie's hand.

She bit her lower lip and looked down at him.

"I'm not a Wanderer," he confessed. "I've never been a Wanderer."

She shut her eyes and opened them again.

"I lied. I'm sorry. I just . . . it's complicated. I don't know what to tell you . . . ."

She watched his face and thought nothing. Her mind was remarkably empty, considering the circumstances, and she couldn't feel anything like malice or fear or anger. Again she shut her eyes, turning and opening them and noticing everyone staring at her. They watched her, not Kyle.

Kyle said, "I'm an idiot."

She felt his hands squeezing.

"I was stupid . . . mean . . . I wasn't being fair."

She sighed and turned to him, and after a minute she heard her own voice. It was calm, absolutely calm, saying, "It's not important," because it wasn't important. Not at all. Compared to everything else, Kyle's lies were just so much noise. "It doesn't matter," she told Kyle, and everyone. Then she rose and took a solid step backwards; and Kyle, who wasn't a Wanderer, watched her hand pull free of his grip.

COTTON

1

ONE FLAVOR is always, always inside my mouth.
I can taste it in the middle of a fight, the
unFound charging and everyone dead around
me. I can taste it when I'm cold and slow, the
air inside my armored lifesuit going dead. What
I taste are the sweating bodies and the food
smells and the old stone buildings and the farts
and a thousand other tastes too small to name,
and all of them essential . . . .
I'm talking about my home enclave.
Wherever I am and whatever I'm doing, I
can shut my eyes and lay my tongue flush against
my old home.

—*Cotton, in conversation*

He waited with the blood drying on his face and the
elevator humming, then it quit humming, too high above
him to be heard anymore; and Moliak made the autodoc
waddle down the hallway towards him, his flat new voice
saying that everything depended on him and it was a lie,

all of it. Quencé had made some clever guesses based on nothing. Happenstance circumstances meant nothing.

"I know," Cotton replied.

The autodoc bumped into one of the arches with a graceless *whump*, sputtered and took a backwards step and then continued.

"What are you doing, my friend?"

Cotton said, "Waiting." He had been living fast for an enormous time, it seemed, and the only rest he had enjoyed were the rare naps he managed for a few moments. They were frothy, dream-rich naps like the sleep he used to find on battlefields. He had been tempted to eat, but digestion would have lowered his metabolism. Something might have gone wrong anytime, he had reasoned, and he didn't dare such a luxury. Besides, he'd had plenty of reserves. Even now he had fat. Cotton grasped himself in a knowing way, estimating what he might need outside.

Quencé had fooled him and nearly killed him, then he'd had the presence to steal the last of their food too.

He couldn't believe he had been beaten by that man.

"Are you there?" asked Moliak.

"Over here," he responded.

Moliak made the autodoc approach his voice, then he said, "You have to find the hard-memory—"

"I will."

"Quencé will try to destroy it."

Cotton thought about the possibilities and decided what was likely.

"Can you believe it? Kyle was a pretender," said Moliak. "He just happened past at the worst moment, and I wasn't paying attention."

"He seemed genuine to me," Cotton allowed.

"It was my fault!" The machine voice was loud but not capable of anger or honest anguish. "We had made our destination, and I was much too eager. I wasn't thinking."

"We have some time," Cotton maintained.

"I hope."

"Nobody knows what we want here, and nobody is

going to find us." Cotton shook his head and gazed down at the autodoc and the stringy hard-memory. "They can't stop us, my friend."

Moliak didn't respond. Every few moments Cotton would punch the red *Return* control, nothing engaging. Several times Moliak wondered aloud if the elevator was returning. "Not yet?" Cotton wished his friend could have kept the same voice. He kept hearing a stranger talking to him, and it made him nervous and concerned.

Again he punched the pad, and it turned green.

"Now?" asked the flat voice.

Cotton said, "Yes."

There was something between them. He could feel it. He could nearly taste it hanging in the stale air. It wasn't distrust or dishonesty or any related ugliness. That's what made the feeling strange. No, it was a kind of sorrow, a grave disappointment shared by both of them. They had planned to do this thing with a minimum of violence and death. They would die and the hostages would die and the Archives would be extinguished, but the Archives were just old-fashioned hard-memories—dusty tombstones with the power of speech—and killing them couldn't be construed as murder.

In the parlance of the military, theirs was a sweet plan.

It was an innocent plan, he realized. To erase a great wrongheaded struggle with one motion . . . it seemed like pure innocence to him. He bristled and shivered and shook his head.

Cotton couldn't say where everything had gone wrong, or why, but he looked at the green light and remarked, "It'll be here soon," for lack of anything better to say. He feared that if he said something that wasn't banal and pointless, he would merely make everything worse. He found himself trying to be extraordinarily cautious.

"I don't care which Wanderer you catch," said Moliak.

"All right."

"Perhaps you should change the elevator's code too."

"I will."

There was a pause, then he said, "Would you bring Jy back to me?" with the voice half hopeful.

"I can try."

There was a humming sound from behind the massive doorway.

Cotton blinked and breathed, wishing he could recover that sense of doing something right and clean—

"Cotton?"

"In a moment," he told Moliak. He flexed his fighting glove, then his bare hand. "The elevator is coming."

Moliak said, "Fine."

There was a hissing and the first tentative motion behind the doorway, and Cotton tensed reflexively.

"Good luck," Moliak offered.

He said nothing.

Moliak's new voice made a rasping noise, then he said, "If I were an unFound—if Quencé had been right— I wouldn't care about getting Jy back down here again. You realize that, don't you?"

"If you were an unFound," said Cotton, "you would have killed me and everyone but one of the hostages. You probably would have done it when we stopped at the poisoned earth and dumped our bodies to lessen the mass inside the portal . . . if you weren't real . . . ."

"Yes," said Moliak. "I would have—"

"I realized it. Just now. It took me this long." Cotton shook his head. "I guess I'm too tired to think clearly—"

The doorway pulled apart, and Cotton leaped an instant later.

"Good luck!" shouted Moliak.

A hundred comforting statements came to mind, but there wasn't time for anything except a blurted, "Thank you." Cotton sensed he had nothing left to waste.

2

WOULD YOU like to hear about my homecoming, my friend?

The enclave greeted me on my arrival, family and friends pressing close to me to share my lucky heat, and of course I used some of my new wealth to buy a feast of sweet meats and rich cakes. Thousands gathered in the public hall, and I suppose they wanted to make me happy. I was odd because I had gone to fight the unFound—the Wanderers had larger, more traditional enclaves for the best Termite recruiting—and I was remarkable for having survived and come home again. They wanted me to have a good time, and they were drunk on meat and excitement, screaming insults at the ugly unFound. They said the unFound were nothing but machines. The most vile cockroach on the worst earth was beautiful and honorable set beside any unFound.

I lost my temper. Like you, my friend, I discovered I had a strange respect for our foes, and I beat one of the closest, loudest complainers to where he was half dead. My audience was stunned, then horrified, and then, once they recalled what I had experienced, they were ridiculously forgiving . . . and moments later, coming through the haze of my anger, I could hear voices shouting, "Pass the platter! Pass the frosted cake!" and I discovered I had no appetite whatsoever.

—*Cotton, in conversation*

The landscape was unnerving. There was the sheer size of the place and its emptiness and the steady unnatural heat welling upward from the strange ground, and there was also the incredible fact that a few pulses of old electrical data could make all of this explode.

Cotton was running.

He manipulated his glove with small finger commands, and it radiated an invisible glow. The subtle tracks of passersby showed as smears and splotches. He could see where everyone had come from the mag-car, and a single set of large feet returned on nearly the same course. He imagined Quencé running. He tried to become angry for what Quencé had done—muddling his mind and nearly breaking his skull—but any anger was mild and tentative. Cotton picked up his pace and pressed against the thin air and the tough gravity, and he told himself to watch for other traps. The big Wanderer was going to fight him all the way.

A sound came from somewhere to his left.

Was it a shout? A warning? It sounded feminine, but he couldn't see anyone. It didn't matter, he decided. Sound could travel long distances here. It wasn't absorbed by the ground or the faint winds, and there was nowhere to hide. There wasn't so much as a gully on this vast hard floor, borderless and uninhabited.

Cotton ran up to the black mag-rail.

The car was gone. He paused and aimed his glove and drove a strong bolt into the metal and superconductors, his bare hand over his eyes and the glare likely visible for a long distance.

Hopefully nothing had noticed. Either an Archive would be nearby, he thought, or there wouldn't be one. He had to be fatalistic, turning and running hard alongside the rail. He made for the portal and estimated the time wasted, the car's velocity, and Quencé's own running pace. He didn't have a Wanderer's hard-memory; he could have used it. Sometimes he felt a fogginess in his head, a sense of weight and grayness, his thoughts coming slower than was right, but his body wrung more fat from his reserves and never slowed. He wrestled with the fogginess and beat it, and when it started coming again and more often he tried to ignore the trouble.

Quencé had come this way. The glove told him that the rail had been used, sensors detecting residual energies and the time estimates becoming more precise.

He started to feel awful, sick and weak and awful.

There was a pain beyond the fogginess, a sharp discomfort cutting through his body, and Cotton was beginning to digest proteins. His fats were nearly exhausted. The proteins were being pulled from every muscle, his heart included, and pain was just the dangerous first symptom.

His legs were tiring.

He had an enormous metabolism, yes. It was tailored to be efficient to an amazing degree, but there were still fatigue poisons making his legs rubbery and slow and stiff.

Cotton shook his head and strode on.

The mag-car was resting dead on the rail, and Cotton lifted the glove skyward and hunted for anything alive. Quencé? He was gone. Cotton scanned the ground and found no trace of him, and for one fuzzy instant he wondered if the mag-car had been a ruse. Quencé could have sent it as a diversion—but no, wait. He leaped onto the rail and over and spotted the familiar tracks shining beneath him. They meant Quencé's sandels and his long stride.

The man was running for the molten zone.

Cotton couldn't remember distances anymore. He couldn't guess how much time was left for him. He could only hurry and consume his body in the process, burning himself to a skelton and then a running shadow, and then, if need be, to nothing at all.

3

SOMETIMES I dream that I am living too fast and eating too well and my flesh glows red with a scalding heat that ignites my fat and muscle into a sudden bluish flame . . . and other nights I dream of being back in battle, a calm descending over me and the dead landscape, and I wake missing the place, my friend. Isn't that odd?

—*Cotton, in conversation*

Every so often Cotton would send a pulse of energy ahead, and he would listen for the echo that meant Jy's hard-memory was nearby.

There wasn't anything for a long while.

Then there was a soft *ping*, tiny and brief, and Cotton started to think about catching the Wanderer. In time? They were approaching the molten zone. Sometimes he could smell the hot metal and taste it in the back of his mouth, but then the breeze would shift and all he smelled was his own foul breath. He was starving. The metabolic pathways were making aromatic wastes, and the wastes clung to him and made him increasingly ill.

There was a motion in the distance.

Cotton blinked and saw nothing.

Again he sent the pulse, and the echo was immediate and clear. He was very close. His heartbeat quickened, and he swallowed twice with his parched throat and tried to sprint but his legs gave him nothing. They were moving as fast as they could manage, and asking for more only made them heavier and slow.

White pains shot down each thigh and calf.

Cotton nearly stumbled, and he realized time was beginning to quicken again. He was turning cold. He hadn't planned on being alive for this long; he should be a blossom of light streaking across this galaxy now. What could he do? None of his tricks helped. He felt as though he were wading in muddy ground, every motion agony and his body ready to fail.

There was the motion again. *There!* Quencé's soaked gray clothes seemed to shimmer and float ahead of Cotton. The big man was picking up his own pace, driving with those long legs.

Cotton leaped.

He got up onto the mag-rail, and he ran along its narrow flat crest. He balanced with his arms partway extended, and he half saw Quencé glance over a shoulder. The man had heard something, or felt nervous. He knew he had almost made it, and he was worrying his luck would turn stale.

The molten zone was approaching.

Cotton saw a red smear ahead, and the heat was worse with every stride.

Quencé gulped air and moaned quietly.

Cotton was close enough, he felt, and he made the long jump from the rail's crest while swinging an arm, landing and driving his elbow into the back of Quencé's skull.

The big man staggered and collapsed.

Cotton was twisting as the metal ground rose up and slammed into his back, the impact driving the air from his lungs, and he gasped and lay still and saw Quencé standing again. Cotton considered using his fighting glove and stopped himself. He needed a Wanderer, an intact and thoroughly legitimate Wanderer, and he opened the gloved hand as Quencé began to run again.

Cotton found the breath and rose and made himself leap. He aimed low and struck lower, knocking the legs out from under Quencé and crashing his own face into the hard warm rail.

He started to think about candy, and he could taste it.

Again he fought his way to his feet, and Quencé tried hitting him. His first swing missed, his second swing connected with Cotton's chest, and Cotton used his legs. He gave a blind kick and somehow connected with the knee, driving through it, and he heard tendons snapping and the very precise splitting of the bone.

The Wanderer screamed and dropped.

Cotton stumbled backwards and gasped.

They stared at each other for a moment, then Quencé pulled the tiny hard-memory coin from his shirt pocket and lifted it to his mouth, hesitated and then swallowed it. He made a sour face when he swallowed, and Cotton screamed, "No!" and slapped him.

"There," Quencé managed.

The man looked miserable.

He said, "There," again, with finality, as if he had done everything possible and had no regrets. He was exhausted but defiant. He gulped the heated air and wiped sweat from his eyes, and he said, "You look tired, my friend," while smiling.

"Do I?"

"Yes, you do." Quencé moved his bad leg, trying

to make it more comfortable. "You might starve before
you can make it back," he added. "You came too far."

Cotton said nothing.

"The Archives . . . they will come see why this mag-
rail broke. And eventually you can expect a rescue party
arriving from the Bright . . . ." He coughed, then declared, "You are trapped."

Cotton took a step backward and made his decision.

"And don't you still need a host for Moliak . . . ?"

There was no other choice left for him.

" . . . because you can't use me, my friend . . . ."

They had had such a lovely plan, Moliak and he.
They would stop the corruption while it could be
stopped, and Cotton would die with some shred of his
morality intact. There were certain taboos he had never
broken, in war or at any time, and that had been a point
of pride for him. Yet now the lovely perfect sweet cleansing plan was turning into something worse than anything
he had faced, even while fighting.

He lifted his glove and almost aimed.

Quencé stiffened.

Then Cotton chose a more decent way. He made a
show of dropping the glove, pretending to change his
mind; and when Quencé started to relax, risking a breath,
Cotton used a cutting beam to lift his head from his strong
body.

The head fell to the side with a useless *thunk*.

Cotton nudged it aside, then cut into the guts until
he found the hard-memory. Then he stood again and felt
a dizziness that wasn't passing, and he smelled the metal
in the air and his own breath, his head rearing back to
stare at the changeless stars, steady and bright.

He used a burning beam on a light setting.

Suddenly all he smelled were the teasing odors of
cooking flesh.

MOLIAK

1

I AM a Founder and I will remain a Founder
and if I do this thing I need to at least try to
make my audience understand me . . . and if
possible, which isn't likely, I want to win an ally
in Jy before it ends.

—*Moliak's private journal*

The eyes came open with a laziness, a certain indifference, and Moliak felt himself fighting to adjust to the
new body and the submerged presence of its Wanderer.
The operation had worked, he realized. They had survived and would finish everything now. He blinked and
lifted a hand and saw the smooth black skin in the air
above him, limp but functioning. He took a breath and
smelled a myriad of distinct odors, most of them stale,
and he grunted with Wysh's voice.

Cotton had found Wysh while returning, their good
fortune on the rebound. He had stunned her and carried
her on his shoulders, bringing her to Moliak; and now
he told Moliak, "I can find Jy," with an angry edge to

his voice. He was grave and rather bitter, saying, "I saw her tracks but decided to come here first."

Moliak said, "Fine," with the unfamiliar voice.

Cotton didn't want to go anywhere. He wanted to be finished. They didn't need any audience but the two of them, and it would be easy to sit where he was standing and watch the end unfold.

Moliak read his friend's thoughts in his face and posture.

Cotton cleared his throat, then he said, "Do you want me to hunt for Jy," without framing it as a question.

Moliak nodded.

The floor seemed to buck and sway.

He had to have Jy with him. If there wasn't any last meeting, any final words at all, Moliak would go into death feeling an emptiness. He couldn't imagine her being somewhere else.

"Please find her," he said with resolve. "Do it now."

Cotton said nothing. He merely turned and left at a fast trot, and Moliak watched his bounce and sniffed the air with the eerily potent nose, the answer obvious. Moliak knew what had happened. Cotton had returned without the pack, yet he was stronger than when he left . . . and it didn't matter. *Forget it!* Moliak stopped his mind and tried to clear it, then focused on Jy again.

Eventually he felt somewhat adjusted and marginally comfortable. He managed to sit upright with every motion odd, clumsy and slow and *wrong*. One black hand made an exploratory grasp of the firm breasts, then it started downwards and quit at the belt line. He pulled the hand away and thought, *No, no. It doesn't matter*. Then he stood and felt the wounded head spinning, both hands clasped to it and trying to steady it, and he touched the dried blood and the neatly sliced skin glued together to heal quickly, without scars.

There was weakness, but it was only bothersome.

The longer Moliak stood upright, the more natural standing felt.

Wysh's personality was nearly extinguished. Sometimes she tried to fight him, but fear and strangeness kept her ineffective. She was a mild distraction at the worst, and at the best she was a string of precious identity codes.

"Take a step," he told himself.

The too-small feet tried to obey, and he didn't fall. That was a positive achievement. He glanced at Mr. Phillips's body and remembered how it had tumbled with its first step. Now he tried more steps and walked to the body and kneeled and pulled the fighting glove from the stiffening dead hand.

It lay rubbery and nearly weightless in his new hands.

Why bother with it? he asked himself. A fighting glove would just make his new fingers even clumsier, provided he needed any hands.

Moliak left the glove on the floor and rose and started toward the strange little dome at the room's center. For the first time, in small bites, he started to investigate Jy's hard-memory. What would he need to do first? Perhaps it would be best to get ready, he thought, in case something were to go wrong all at once.

ENTER THE SECURITY FIELD.

The instructions couldn't be plainer.

With one hand, then the other, Moliak touched the dome and pressed against it. Nothing happened. He might as well have shoved against an entire earth, and he strained and heard a buzz inside his head as a sensor made a probe of his hard-memory—

—and the dome dissolved into nothingness.

He could smell oily air and age as he fell forward. There was an unremarkable round patch of white floor beneath him, and he struck hard and moaned while rolling from side to side.

There was nothing inside; the mechanism had been removed, probably ages ago.

He shut his eyes and sobbed, wondering what was going to happen.

LOOK.

The instruction was confident and even a little impatient.

Moliak opened his eyes and found himself on his back with short brown grass surrounding him, a hard blue sky overhead, and a warm wind blowing. It was a projection. He rose and marveled at its intricacies, while turning in a slow careful circle.

Jy had designed this system.

What was her intent?

The wind gusted, and he could smell the sun-baked ground and the animal wastes mixed with the grass. Someone was speaking to him, using Founder. He heard the voice and straightened, someone asking him, "Who are you and what do you want?"

Moliak turned.

A stranger—a Founder woman—was sitting beneath a sudden grove of tall straight trees. She was wearing the clothes of an old-fashioned scout, gray but more complicated than a Wanderer's garb; and sparkling between them was a shallow pond, muddy and wind-rippled.

"Can I do something for you?" she inquired.

Moliak shook his head.

After a moment he told her, "No, not yet."

"Are you certain?"

"Not yet," he said, "but soon."

2

THE WOMAN TOLD ME TO WAIT FOR-
EVER, AND SHE TOLD ME WHAT I
SHOULD ASK AND WHAT TO DO IF THE
ANSWERS WERE PROPER, FROM A
PROPER PERSON, AND I STAND ON MY
PLAIN AND WAIT TO CARRY OUT THE
COMMANDS SHOULD THEY COME.

THE WOMAN TOLD ME TO BE PA-
TIENT, AND I AM EXTREMELY PATIENT.
AND SHE TOLD ME TO GRIEVE SHOULD
I EVER BE NEEDED. I WILL DO EVERY-
THING AS SHE PLANNED AND AS
QUICKLY AS NECESSARY, AND I WILL

GRIEVE. THE WOMAN WANTS MY
TEARS.

I HAVE BEEN SAVING THEM FOR A
LONG WHILE. THOUGH OCCASION-
ALLY, IN SECRET, I WILL PRACTICE MY
CRYING FOR A MOMENT....
                              —*The waterhole guard*

She vanished.

Moliak squinted at the apparent sun, high and brilliant, then studied his own odd-shaped shadow. What
should he do? He decided to sit and wait for Cotton and
Jy, and he picked a comfortable place. He was under
the trees, the shade not cool but not as brutal as the
sunshine either. He watched the wind move the grasses
and the branches overhead, and from the shadows cast
by the tree trunks he decided the sun wasn't moving.
The projection wasn't complete, or it wasn't intended to
be complete. What had Jy meant with this place? Was
this a significant part of some long-ago significant day?
Yes, of course...it was where she had had her inspiration for the mission. It was a mythical place. He had
imagined the land looking different for some reason; the
barrenness was a surprise and something of a disappointment for Moliak.

What did the strange woman represent?

When he considered her, she reappeared to him.
"Yes?" She was sitting with her back against a tree, and
she was sober-faced and somewhat tense. "Do you want
me?"

"Soon," he replied.

The woman shut her eyes and nodded, and he could
see her big teeth and the wrinkles on her black face. For
an instant he could smell her. She smelled like a Founder
village surrounded by its tended soils and the ripening
grains, and the scent made Moliak ache. He grasped his
wrong-feeling self and squeezed and straightened his
back. The tree behind him was rough, unyielding. He
knew the exact words that would start the irreversible
process, and he came close to thinking them. Then he

stopped himself. He had been examined and found adequate within the parameters of the programs, and nothing remained but to say the words aloud and in a clear voice.

The strange woman shook her head as if hearing his mind.

Again Moliak promised, "Soon."

"Soon," she echoed.

He shut his eyes and expected her to vanish.

Yet she persisted. When he opened his eyes again she was leaning forward, and she told him, "You would come here for one reason," with a toughness. "What do you want?"

"Go away," he remarked.

She vanished.

Again Moliak shut his eyes. Where were Cotton and Jy? He tried to ignore this nonplace; instead he remembered the day when he had first seen Jy standing on the stage, giving her rally, and he had saved her with his sudden applause. Without that rally, he knew, she might never have won his portion of the Founders' earth. She was an old woman with little time left in a perishable cause that would wilt and die without her, in a moment, and it was easy to believe that Moliak, in that long-ago instant, had saved the mission.

He looked at the sprawling grassland and the waves of rising heat and the impossibly blue sky.

"Quit," he muttered. "Stop it."

Moliak was crying. He had been crying for a long while and hadn't realized it, and he started to push at the tears on the unfamiliar face.

Suddenly he was glad Jy hadn't arrived yet.

He couldn't wait. He rose in one motion and pushed the dust from his gray trousers, saying, "I am ready," with his voice too loud. "Now!"

"Fine."

The woman stood to her knees in the ugly little pond, and she started forward with the sucking muds making her work, bugs hanging around her face, and Moliak hoping he had the resolve. He didn't want to see Jy again; he was suddenly afraid. Something made him feel strange and cold. He wasn't certain what he was thinking—they were slippery dark thoughts—yet they existed and were cutting at him while he struggled to focus on what was before him, now . . . .

"What do you need?"

Moliak blinked. The strange woman was speaking to him.

"Do you need something from me?"

"Not yet," he heard himself begin, "no—"

She was gone. She had vanished with his first word, the security machinery having sensed his changing moods. Moliak could see the blacker muds brought to the surface by the woman's feet, and he stepped into the warm water and felt his toes sinking to where it was cool. He stood motionless, eyes narrowed and mouth closed and both arms hanging at his sides, and he kept very still for a very long while. He could wait; he had to wait, he was thinking. Eventually the bugs came around his face, and sometimes they would light on him. He could feel them. He was staring at a distant point, never blinking, but he could feel the bugs' dry wings and soft feet and he didn't brush them aside or even flick his head once.

JY

1

IF THE mission ended tomorrow—if I woke and found myself ordinary again—I would not have any idea what to do with my day.
—*Jy's private journal*

Jy had found a star near the horizon, set in the approximate south, and she had aimed for it. She had walked fast at first, surprised by her own endurance. (Moliak had scrubbed her muscles while she was in surgery; Quencé had told her.) But her new youth had its limits, and eventually she was slowing and stopping to breathe, and every time it was harder to make herself move again. Quencé had wanted them to scatter—a reasonable scheme—but her nerves were shot and her legs were old, scrubbed or not, and she felt a powerful impulse to turn around and go back again, trying to find Moliak and talk him out of this madness.

What was happening to Quencé? she wondered.

She was worried for him and sick with the thought

that Cotton would catch him. Too soon or too late. Either way.

Eventually the moon rose, a swift crescent, and Jy decided to walk toward the moon for a while. She recognized its ancient features; the Founders had never seen any reason to colonize or mine their sister world. It was larger than seemed right, but this earth was swollen and they were closer to it, and of course, it was orbiting fast because of the buried hydrogen. As it rose it became fuller, she noticed. And once she winked at its reliable face, and she caught herself wondering when the Archives were going to dismantle it to enlarge this earth.

Never, she recalled. *They will never have the opportunity.*

After a while she turned again and used the stars to estimate the elevator's position while increasing her pace. She felt a little bit stronger now. This was her only reasonable choice, she decided, and while she walked she tried to imagine Moliak standing with her in that underground room. She wanted to know why he had to do this terrible thing. There were problems, she knew ... yes, horrible failures, yes ... but who was he to decide the mission's fate? Why end everything with one Founder committing murder to extinguish the good smart work of billions?

She wouldn't allow it to happen.

She saw herself screaming at Moliak and begging, using every argument to make him pause and look at himself and be reasonable.

"Why do you do this thing?" she muttered aloud. "My dear, dear friend—"

The round elevator stood in the distance, obvious under the moonlight. She was closing on it when she came upon Billie and Kyle. They were on the glassy ground, Billie sitting upright and Kyle on his back, his head resting on one of her outstretched legs. He seemed to be asleep, and she was staring into the distance. Jy said her name softly, and the girl turned with a start.

"His wound is bothering him," she explained. "In

his head? He had to have help . . . after we left you . . .
I couldn't leave him."

Kyle didn't look comfortable, but his chest rose and
fell regularly.

"He's been asleep forever," Billie reported.

"It's the trauma of the sonic probe," Jy told her,
"but I don't think it will be serious."

The girl sighed.

Jy said, "Everything will end well," without feeling.
She uttered words, nothing more, and she was embarrassed and shaken to hear herself using so little energy,
her reliable spark gone.

"I know we'll be fine," said Billie, and she seemed
to nod.

Jy said nothing.

Billie gazed at her with an honest sorrowful expression, emotions beneath the surface. She was feeling sorrow for everyone's pain and the coming destruction, and
Jy stepped forwards and bent and kissed the girl on her
forehead.

Both of them were crying.

Jy had to step backwards and turn and walk again.

"You're going back there?"

"Yes," she managed.

"Cotton's gone," said Billie. "I saw him leave."

What else had she seen? Jy wondered but didn't
ask, not wanting to know anything more. She found the
elevator open, seemingly waiting for her, and she entered and pushed buttons until there didn't seem to be
any point. Nothing happened and she sat in the back
and waited for an age, trying to practice her speeches
for Moliak. Even in her imagination the speeches were
flat and empty. She heard the words that had worked
endless times and on every flavor of earth, yet here they
felt like empty sounds, contrived and perhaps foolish.

She tried more buttons, then she sat again.

What about Quencé?

Fitting both hands over her face, she tried to rest
and make everything clear once again. How could she
make it clear?

Then there was a light footfall, almost no sound at

all, and she looked between her fingers and saw Cotton standing in the doorway. He was shaking his head as if displeased, and he was showing a bitter little smile.

"You found somewhere to hide," he muttered.

She remained sitting.

He entered the elevator and touched the controls in some new sequence, and the doorway creaked and pulled shut an instant before they started to fall.

2

BUT THE mission will never end tomorrow. I feel quite sure....

—*Jy's private journal*

She saw Wysh standing among the trees, halfway across the room, and Jy stepped out of the hallway and onto the dried grass. Then she could move no farther. Her legs locked, and Cotton touched her. His hand felt as if it had been pulled from a smelting furnace. She was shaking, her hands and feet completely out of control, and she glanced back over a shoulder and saw the flat plains running on and on. The hallway itself was hidden. "I am ready," called Wysh, speaking Founder. "I am ready!"

Jy turned forwards again.

Two women were standing beneath the trees.

One of them seemed to be Wysh, only she stood differently. Her feet were too far apart and her hands were on her hips, man-fashion, and when she dipped her head for a moment Jy saw the telltale patch of clotting foams. She knew what must have happened.

Again she shivered.

"What do you want?" asked the Founder woman. "What can I do to help you?"

Jy recognized everything for what it was—it all returned now—and she remembered designing these systems, intending them for herself. She had believed that it would be her onerous duty to come to one of these places, to go deep underground, and to tell the illusionary Founder woman:

"The mission must end, my friend."

Wysh was talking, only she wasn't Wysh. Moliak was saying the proper words, and Jy started forwards.

"This is sad news," said the Founder woman.

Moliak replied, "I would never have come if I felt there was another choice," and gave a tentative sigh.

Jy circled the little pond. She saw the dead body of Mr. Phillips and the shiny autodoc. Cotton remained behind her; she felt his presence. Her aches and exhaustion had fallen away, and she heard the Founder woman asking:

"What should I do?"

"Nothing!" screamed Jy. "No—!"

The woman watched Moliak without blinking. For her nobody else was real, her programs recognizing only the codes and the hard-memory surrounding them.

Moliak spoke. "I want you to start a fire for me."

Jy shouted, "No!" She charged him and raised her fists without realizing what she was doing. "Will you stop!" She nearly struck him.

Moliak grabbed her wrists and pushed her backward.

Jy stumbled and landed on her butt—smack—on the muddy shoreline.

"What type of fire?" asked the woman.

"A very large fire, please." He used Wysh's voice with precision, then he pulled a hand across his opened mouth.

"You have no right," Jy told him. She rose and said, "This is no justice. This is no answer!"

"No?" Moliak shrugged.

"I will set the fire," the Founder woman promised, "then I will return and ask what I should do with it."

Moliak said, "I will wait," and nodded.

The woman dissolved.

"Don't do this thing," pleaded Jy.

Moliak didn't seem to hear her.

Jy approached him again, saying, "It isn't a solution," with a weak voice. "You cannot—"

"*Why am I doing this thing?*" he blurted, "Do you know, my friend, why this is how I wanted it?"

"Because the mission is ill—"

"Tainted and damned. Yes, you're partially right. Everything is twisted and ill at my end of the Bright, and someone needs to stop it, yes—"

"Then we should work together," Jy interrupted, "and try to heal the mission and begin again somehow."

He merely stared at her.

"What is it?" she asked.

"Imagine that we do heal the mission," he told her. "I don't see any means, but imagine that I am wrong and some stable absence-of-war state is reached and you can continue onward at your end of the Bright. There is still that safe direction. You move and you succeed for another ten earths or a million earths or perhaps tens of millions of earths. The Bright takes you to beautiful places and fine people . . . and then there is someone like the unFound. If the unFound can evolve once, Jy, they can certainly have cousins somewhere. Or perhaps something even worse!"

"Let *me* find them," she said. "I can prove you're wrong."

"My dear Jy, are you listening to me?" he cried. "People almost as good as you have failed. *I have failed.* It was a beautiful mission while it lasted, and it lasted nearly forever. But someday the unFound will be on both ends of the Bright, and they are going to learn about all these earths ripe for the taking . . . and you are going to have to fight them, Jy, or let yourself be set aside while others fight. Can you understand? I am saving you. I love you and have always loved you and I came to finish you before you are ruined like me!"

She said nothing.

"*The Founders were an anomaly from the beginning, Jy. We were the first advanced humans, peaceful and rational, but we have shown ourselves inadequate!*"

She shook her head. She was not inadequate!

"Humanity was blessed, and humanity has failed."

Moliak screeched and shook a bare fist at the false sky. "Now we have to step aside and trust that some great fortunate earth somewhere can evolve a better species than we are. It will have to be a species purer than the Founders, and kinder, and clever enough to deal with scourges like the unFound—"

"Stop!" she yelled.

"—and a superior Jy will be born among them—"

"No!"

"—and she will lead in your place, my friend!"

Jy felt acid rising in her throat.

"Perhaps in a hundred million years," he moaned, "there will be a better intelligence and a better Jy, the perfect mission formed, and *they* will find the Makers—"

She flung herself at him, trying to strike the thick body and the blazing eyes. Jy was swinging with her fists and crying and shouting, and Cotton grabbed her from behind with a solid jerk. He lifted her as if she were feathers, and Moliak was saying, "Put her on the other side of the pond, please." He seemed euphoric. He gestured and said, "I don't have anything else to tell you," and shook his head at Jy.

She struggled without effect.

Cotton circled the pond while carrying her, then paused. There was strange urgent thunder somewhere beneath them. It was beginning, she realized. She quit fighting and listened, and Cotton hurried and put her to the ground and took a long step backward, watching only her.

"Come back here, please," said Moliak.

Jy could barely breathe.

Cotton ran and reached Moliak in an instant, then the ground shuddered and rolled. The pond was sloshing in its basin, and the trees swayed as if in a terrible wind. Jy managed to sit upright and gasp and finally stand, and when she fought for her balance she happened to glance sideways at the Mr. Phillips and notice his hands.

Both hands were bare.

Moliak was screaming at nobody, or himself. "With another billion years of evolution and another billion earths on the Bright," he claimed, "some deserving sweet organism is going reach the Makers and deserve them too! It's inevitable!"

Cotton was holding Moliak's right hand with his gloved hand.

Where was the missing glove?

"*I feel glorious!*" Moliak shouted over the roar.

Then the woman was standing before him, and the quakes diminished. There came an unnerving silence, and she asked, "Should I let the fire burn?"

Jy found the glove curled up and discarded in the grass.

Cotton was staring at the apparition, startled and oblivious to Jy. Jy took a step forward and knelt and placed her left hand into the glove, feeling a dry warmth and a tingle and then a shrinking sensation until it fit snug against her skin. She kept her hand low, out of easy view, and she made a careful fist until she felt the first tentative surge of power.

She recalled how the gloves felt from the illusions, she and Maliak having fought together in them. Her nerves were interfacing with the mechanisms; she could feel them.

The Founder woman was waiting for Moliak's answer. She was crying. Moliak was smiling as if he had practiced the smile for ages, and Cotton kept watching the woman as if expecting some sudden trick.

"Let the fire burn," said Moliak. "Can you let it burn?"

"It could escape," she warned.

"Let it escape."

"Do you want the fire to spread?"

Cotton glanced at Jy, and he squinted as if suddenly concerned. What could he see? Had he remembered the glove too, or was there a suspicious glare at her feet?

"In a moment," said the crying woman, "I won't be able to stop the fire. I won't have the power."

Moliak said nothing, holding Cotton's hand tighter.

"Please," she said, "allow me to stop it."

If he told her, "No," it would be too late. Any negative sound would initiate the final sequence; and Jy would be powerless. She had to act now. She lifted her fist and tried to aim it, and Cotton was glancing at Moliak and then the apparition and back at Jy—

Moliak opened his mouth.

Cotton was trying to lift his gloved hand, pulling it from Moliak's hand but too slowly, his companion clinging to him and grinning while he cherished this golden instant on the brink—

—and a scalding white flame erupted from Jy's glove, streaking across the pond and cutting into the three figures, the real and unreal evaporating in an instant. Cotton was too late. His bolt passed beside Jy and knocked her from her feet while her fist continued throwing fire that burned the trees and the grass, and the pond boiled, and the high false sky and sun turned to the color of fresh soot.

EPILOGUE

QUENCÉ

I KNOW what I must do. I see it very plainly.
—*Jy's speeches*

Quencé was the last of the survivors found. A maintenance robot detected his partly-consumed body and deftly collected all its pieces, hard-memory included, and later the Archives jerked him out of his coma and gave him a temporary mouth and ear and eye. He came awake grudgingly, glad to find himself alive and the earth intact . . . yet the trauma was severe. Quencé growled and moaned, pivoting the clumsy eye and seeing faces everywhere. He was surrounded by high-ranking Wanderers; he knew these people, he realized. They were standing inside a large temporary building set up by the Archives. They must be the Wanderers who were sent after Jy. Were they his rescuers? How long was he in the coma? With a clumsy pained voice he asked about Jy. "Is she alive?" An imaginary stomach was twisted into a knot. "Where is she? Have you found Jy? Where is she—?"

"She's well," said one Founder. "She survived unhurt."

"And Moliak?"

"Dead. He and his companion were killed."

Quencé felt sick and cold, but the knot was loosening.

"Who else survived?" he asked.

"The natives, and Xen."

"Not Wysh?"

"No."

Poor Wysh, he thought. Suddenly he couldn't recall ever having an ill feeling about the woman.

"But is it finished?" he persisted. "Are we out of danger?"

Several voices said, "Yes," at once.

Good, he thought. *At last.*

Then the Founder, grave-faced and determined, started talking to Quencé in a practiced tone. She explained what had happened after Cotton caught him and killed his body, and she concluded with Jy's horrible brave deed at the last instant; then she described at length what changes Jy had already ordered. "As soon as possible, she wanted you aware of what is to happen—"

"What?"

Sweeping changes were coming in response to Moliak's revelations, and Quencé was to have an active role in the future. Jy wanted him to help reapportion the energy produced by the Founders' earth. The sick arm of the Wanderers was to get a sliver of its normal share—enough to maintain ties between the peaceful earths and no more. The worst of the infected earths were to be isolated. It needed to be done as soon as possible. Termite Mound and the unFound earths and the others had to be held in stasis. Only certain Wanderers—trusted Wanderers—would be able to travel to them and between them and come back again.

Quencé tried to nod with his nonexistent head.

The Founder seemed offended in having to explain these matters to him. "Jy wanted you to begin work as soon as your new body can be cultured," she admitted.

"You will work with the Archives, then you can return to us and help us continue the mission. Jy hoped we could find a renewed zeal and a fresh sense of commitment."

Quencé was thinking.

"She will send us more explicit instructions later," said the Founder. "Until then we have to work together in her absence—"

"*Where is Jy?*" he asked.

Somehow he made his temporary mouth loud, almost forceful.

The Founder replied, "Jy has gone."

People nodded.

"Where?" asked Quencé. His eye twisted and twisted, but he couldn't find Xen or Billie or Kyle. "Have they gone back together? Are they traveling to Lincoln . . . or where?"

"Not Jy," said the Founder.

"Then . . . where?"

The ageless black face seemed graver. She took a breath and held it, then she said, "Jy left as soon as she was able, as soon as she could make her wishes clear." There was a second breath. "She went in the other direction, using the courier codes . . . she said she couldn't waste any time."

"*You let her go alone?*"

There was an embarrassed silence.

"What does she expect to do there?" roared Quencé. "By herself—what does she want?!"

It made no sense whatsoever. Quencé wanted to shake his head and grimace and howl. Then he heard a new voice speaking. It was a Cousin with a smooth voice, saying, "Jy went to appraise the situation and do her best to save them . . . ."

Of course.

Quencé knew why she had gone; he had known it immediately.

To save them.

This was her mission and her crushing burden, he understood. Of course she would go there. She wouldn't hesitate.

"I see," he managed.

Nobody was speaking.

"But did she give . . . perhaps she mentioned when she might return?"

No, she had not.

Quencé saw the heads around him shaking.

"We won't see her for a very long while," someone muttered.

No doubt, thought Quencé. *No doubt*.

Then they made him blind and deaf again, and the mouth was pried from him. The Archives and their robots did the work; all of it was new for them, working with the living. They placed Quencé's hard-memory into an appropriate mold into which they poured trillions of totipotent cells, and he was put into a deep sleep while the cells differentiated into distinct tissues and organs and a fully functional body. He began to dream, and eventually he found himself on one of his perfect dream earths. The landscape was emerald green and laced with clear streams and floating cities drifted overhead. He met his perfect lover on a narrow forest trail, and he followed her home and they made love on a bed of perfumed pillows with everything splendid, as always, and he was a tireless bull, as always, and there came a point when he could feel himself coming awake. Invisible cords began jerking at his mind, stealing him—

—but the machinery attending to Quencé wanted him asleep.

It used strong pulses of electricity to keep him dreaming, and his surroundings changed. The bed of pillows became sun-dried blades of grass, and they were outdoors. He and his lover were on a hilltop and both of them were spent now. Quencé breathed and looked down on complicated green fields and a little village with white, white homes, and he almost recognized the place. Where was he? Then his lover said his name, once and softly, and Quencé turned to face her.

Later he would remember the moment and realize that the strangest part for him was his own utter lack of surprise.

He felt none at all.

And again she said, "Quencé," and she smiled, her eyes glinting gold at the margins; and Quencé reached with one hand and stroked the dampened gray fur along her flat fine belly.

KYLE

I HAVEN'T come here to save you. I am here to
save myself and to do it through you.
—*Jy's speeches*

Xen escorted them home. It was a duty and a chore, and
he quit pretending to enjoy any of it after the first few
days. Mostly Xen kept to himself, and that was fine. For
the first ten or twelve days Kyle was content to sit alone
too, watching the slow, almost luscious appearance of
each new earth. They were still racing on the Bright,
but this was many times slower than the first trip together. Every earth would linger, inviting their studied
looks, and there wasn't any danger in the air. A residual
tension worked on everyone's nerves, but it was never
distracting. Kyle could sit and relax and watch the vast
eerie show.

   Billie spoke when Kyle prompted her, and she
seemed pleasant. No, she didn't hate him. No, she wasn't
angry anymore, if she was ever really angry. She claimed
to be distracted, that's all, and she was sorry she wasn't

better company. She sounded like herself when she apologized for her quietness, for her apparent distance. Things were on her mind, that's all. *Things*.

Sometimes Kyle would ask about her thoughts.

She would evade his questions. There would be a sideways glance and a purposeful sigh, and she was entirely polite and never honest.

Kyle apologized whenever he saw an opening, saying it had been his fault and he was sorry she was unhappy. Wasn't she unhappy? She said, "No, I'm fine," and left it at that. Sometimes she sat through the night, alone, and she would carry on conversations with herself. Her voices had two tones, like two distinct personalities, and Kyle would lay awake and listen, never quite able to decipher the words.

Billie was in her own world, he finally decided. Forget her! Just forget her!

Then after three weeks of following the Bright—numberless earths flowing past and none like home—Kyle became sick of the fluid scenery and the strangely built humans and the glimpses of cities and odd technologies and all the other tiresome oddities that were supposed to make him feel honored and alive.

He was sick of the Bright.

He wanted to be home again. It was all he wanted: normalcy, a chance to regain a normal life. Sometimes he would approach Billie just to make her talk about little things. He missed the smells of car exhaust and the sharp flavor of a good hotdog and buying doughnuts in the early morning, glazed doughnuts still warm, and his favorite television shows. Billie knew what he meant; she had grown up with these things and understood, or she ought to understand. Only it was Kyle who did most of the recalling and the talking. Billie's gaze would fix on a point somewhere behind him, her dark eyes glazed, and he wouldn't have any doubts about what she was thinking.

She was angry with him.

She was still angry and would always be angry.

But they had survived, hadn't they? Kyle wanted to shake her and scream, making her see the truth. How could he feel bad about something that had turned out so good?

Xen, in a rare talkative mood, told Kyle, "Without you we might not have won. You helped and we owe you an enormous debt."

"Really?"

He nodded vigorously. "If you hadn't been there to distract the Termite . . . I think we wouldn't have escaped."

"I helped?"

"Both of you helped."

It was interesting to believe he was partly responsible. It would make a fine story to tell, but who would believe him?

"We were fortunate in many ways," Xen concluded. He gave a satisfied nod and smiled, saying, "Very fortunate, and I have to wonder if something is responsible . . . for everything. . . ."

"What do you mean? What something?"

"I do not know," he replied with great authority. "I do not know."

It took them five and a half weeks to go home, half a million earths seen along the way. Kyle was exhausted by novelty and frustrated by their own inactivity—they had never once left the portal dome—and he was sick and tired of Billie's being so quiet, making him suffer for his crime. If it was a real crime. . . .

Wasn't it sweet to be home?

They arrived at night. From the hilltop Kyle could see the city's lighted streets and the lighted buildings and the pulsating red warning light on top of the state capital. A small Wanderer ship was waiting for Xen, floating beside the portal with its staircase deployed. The portal's new guard was a wisp of a person, sexually imprecise, and the soft voice greeted each of them by name and told Billie and Kyle that their ride was waiting. A tiny hand waved towards the parking lot. "It's good to see you back and safe," said the guard, smiling.

Kyle looked at the parkland, then asked, "Does anyone know we're coming?"

"Miss Zacharia requested that nobody would be here." The guard gave a little bow. "If we had told her family and friends she was coming, there would have been a crowd of well-wishers and reporters."

No mention was made of Kyle and his family.

He shrugged his shoulders and tried to forget it. What did it matter? He was home and absolutely safe, it felt wondrous, and where was their ride into town?

Xen was saying his good-byes.

Billie told him, "Thank you . . . for everything," and she threw her arms around the strange little man, squeezing him. His eyes became enormous. He was thoroughly embarrassed.

Kyle said, "Yes, thank you," and left it at that. He didn't even offer his hand.

Then Xen retreated, walking up the stairs and going without a backward glance, and Kyle watched the ship lift away. It was a cool night, autumn here, and he shivered with a gust of wind and turned and realized he was alone. Billie? She was already partway across the prairie, hurrying for the distant car. She was eager to get home, the same as he, and he trotted after her and said, "Wait." She gave him one expressionless backward glance without slowing.

The wind became stronger while they walked, coming straight out of Canada. It was cold and dry, and it was all Kyle could do to keep from shivering.

Billie never spoke.

She hugged herself and walked with her head down, and he bitched about the wind and the walk, meaning it as a joke. "At least Xen could have carried us to the car," he joked. "Don't you think?"

She said nothing.

He waited for a moment, then he asked, "Do you know what I'm going to do? Starting tonight?"

Her face turned; it was impossible to read.

"I'm going to bring out my real clothes and put them on. Just as soon as I get home."

She said, "Good."

What did she mean?

What did *good* mean?

Kyle touched the gray sleeve of his shirt. Their car was straight ahead, waiting as promised. It was a little thing driven by an enormous Wanderer with a fearsome tattooed face. He had a spider's jawed face overlaying his own, and he scarcely spoke while he drove. He was a careful driver, maybe too careful, creeping into the city despite a lack of traffic. Everything passed slowly and felt shockingly familiar. There were the long streets and the shrouding trees in places and more homes and businesses by the minute, and Kyle sat back and smiled to himself.

What did this earth know about Jy's kidnapping?

Had they heard about Moliak?

Xen had explained the situation without giving details. The Wanderers, he said, had admitted to the abduction and the subsequent release of Jy, no harm done. Moliak and the unFound would have to be reported later, after considerable planning and preparation, and that was true not just on this earth but on all the others too.

What could Kyle tell people about what had happened?

Xen made it clear they weren't under any pledge of silence. "We would prefer discretion," he admitted, "but what you say is up to you. You can tell whomever you like whatever you like."

Billie asked the driver to let her off at her house first.

Kyle blinked and turned to her—he was sharing the backseat with her—and he nearly didn't speak. He hated the way she ignored him, but why did he bother? What was the sense in trying?

But habit made him ask, "Can we get together later?"

She looked at him.

"Billie?"

Then she seemed to smile, saying, "If you want."

He discovered he was happy. He was thrilled and hopeful, watching her pretty face and remembering everything good between them. The memories came back to him suddenly, and he gasped and smiled to himself while holding his hands on his lap.

They pulled up in front of her house, and she was out of the car.

"Later," Kyle reminded her.

She waved and started to run. The driver was pulling away from the curb, and Kyle turned to watch Billie's gait and her cute bottom with his face suddenly warm.

"Everything is settled, friend."

The driver was speaking to him.

"We start to move again in another month."

Kyle said, "Do we?"

"The next earth is easy." The driver seemed to nod, then he said, "Its people are simple and scarce. They're practically Cousins."

"An easy earth?" Kyle muttered.

"They're getting rare," his driver observed. "Don't you think they seem unusual anymore?"

"I guess they are."

They pulled to a second stop and the driver sat behind the wheel, waiting.

Kyle looked around after a moment.

"This is the address, isn't it?"

Kyle blinked. "I'm sorry. Yes. Yes, it is," and he climbed out and wished the driver well, and the driver responded in Founder. What did he say? Then the tattooed spider-face was smiling with human teeth, and Kyle gave an imprecise smile and nod before turning and walking away.

His landlord had left a note inside the door, taped to the tired old wallpaper. Kyle owed a couple months rent, but the landlord trusted him because he was a Wanderer and good for the money. But because he was late, if it wasn't too much trouble, could Kyle add ten percent to the total? And deliver it as soon as possible, please?

The roll of money was where Kyle had hidden it.

Kyle had his bag already packed. After pulling the rent money his savings were thin. What to do? He wasn't sure what to do. He could unpack and stay here and find a job . . . maybe. He could work and save more money and remain close to Billie. Suddenly that seemed important; he needed to stay here. A new job and a fresh

life had their appeal. He would begin the courtship again,
doing everything right this time, and this time he would
win her for himself. He wouldn't be a Wanderer, no.
He would be Kyle Stevens Hastings for the first time in
months.

That's what he would do.

It was decided.

At the bottom of his traveling bag were some ordinary civilian clothes . . . only wait, they wouldn't work.
All he had brought were shorts and light T-shirts, and
he would freeze in this weather.

Instead Kyle put on two more of his gray shirts,
vowing to purchase honest clothes soon. He could do it
tomorrow morning. Then he went back outside and made
the familiar walk to Billie's, going fast, and he climbed
the footworn stairs and smiled to himself and knocked.
Then he knocked harder. Where was the girl? Where
did she go? A little light was burning in the kitchen, but
the door was locked. He tried the knob several times,
then banged on it with his fist, making his bones hurt.

Eventually he went back around to the front and
noticed that Janice's car was gone. Was it at the curb
when they arrived? He couldn't remember. Where were
the girls? Maybe they were out celebrating Billie's return, he thought. Just the two of them.

Kyle felt cold enough to shiver.

He went back upstairs and tried knocking again,
estimating the time and getting angrier. Hadn't Billie
told him to come? If he wanted? What were her exact
words? What had she meant?

The bitch.

He thought the words before he realized what he
was thinking.

The fucking tease!

Again he went downstairs and around to the front
yard, and there was Janice. She had just parked her car.
She was crying. He could hear her crying behind the
closed windows. What was happening? What was wrong?

"Janice?"

She turned with a start, then said, "Oh, it's you."

"Have you seen Billie?" he began. "She told me to—"

"*She's gone!*"

The voice was bitter and final.

Kyle stiffened. Gone? What had happened?

"She gets home after being gone down the portal, God-knows-where, no warning, then she rushes up to me and tells me that she needs a ride. Quick. She makes some noise about having just decided. Just two minutes before, finally, and she can't wait—"

"Decided what?"

"I don't even know where she's been! Somewhere down the Bright, that's all. Some big ugly Wanderer came and told me she was healthy and fine and coming home . . . but I didn't know when she'd show and here she is, *poof*, and she wants me to take her somewhere. She didn't trust herself to wait."

Kyle took a breath and held it.

"She was like a crazy woman," said Janice.

"Where is she?"

"I've got all these messages to deliver. I've got to tell her folks, and everyone—"

"*Where is she?*"

Janice blinked and came towards him, coming from the car and clinging to him with her breasts against his cold chest and her sobs awfully loud and overdone and couldn't she stop? This was ridiculous.

"Where did you take her?"

"She isn't back two seconds," said Janice, "and right away she has to go back to the portal again. Right away. So she can make the pledge, or whatever it is you people do."

Now Kyle understood what Billie had meant.

Can we get together?

If you want.

Only it would be a longer trip than walking two city blocks. She was demanding a huge journey and a staggering commitment, and Kyle knew the answer without the slightest doubt.

No.

Not now or ever, no. Kyle couldn't . . . he couldn't

even think about doing such a thing. Just thinking about it made him crazy. *What a stupid thing to do!*

Janice sniffled and said, "You're freezing. Come inside and I could make coffee or something."

Kyle breathed.

"You can tell me she did the right thing, and all that stuff."

He looked at her and heard himself say, "No," with a weak voice. "Later. I can't . . . I'll come by later . . . ."

She let him go and turned and left. Not a word . . . .

Kyle retreated to the street, struggling with his thoughts and paying little attention to where he went. He ended up in the open, standing beside the compacted gravel bed of the railroad tracks, and he remained motionless for a very long time. Then there was a noise, distant but urgent. He fell from his trance and heard the horn of a coal train and shook his head, then he climbed the gravel slope and straddled the first rail.

In the west was the sharp blue-white light of the locomotive.

For an instant Kyle contemplated waiting here. He imagined himself on his back with the rail sticking into his waist, and the thousands of tons of metal and coal would roll over him and cut him in two, and wouldn't that be fine? Wouldn't it be?

But he couldn't make himself wait.

The wind was cutting through him. He was shivering and exposed, and maybe he would like to be dead, yes. But he didn't like being cold.

Wasn't that odd? he thought.

He was too uncomfortable to wait here and commit suicide. He slid down the slope, the gravel rattling with a dull ceramic sound, then he walked back to his apartment and got his travel bag and the old bus ticket. Then, since he was no longer a Wanderer, he took back the rent money and made himself a slippery promise to pay the landlord when he had something extra; and he left for the bus station, walking fast, then trotting, the wind pressing from behind him and Kyle working to stay warm.

JY

FOR THE sake of our own salvation, for the time being, what we need to do is think of the Bright as being an enormous, convoluted ring. There will come a day when both groups of Wanderers will meet each other, the ring circumnavigated ... and it is vital, absolutely vital, that the groups still be able to recognize each other as humans. We will be siblings and decent souls and friends long missed. . . .

For the time being the Makers and their grand answers are much, much, much too much to expect.

—*Jy's speeches*

She held the rally, like so many, inside one of the abandoned unFound bunkers. It was a long drop beneath the earth's battered crust, a titanic affair with carbon-fiber and composite walls and recycled air and permanent furniture scattered across the largest stretch of ceramic floor. Jy's audience began as a good-sized collection of soldiers and others. There were Wanderers among them, a few novices, and the rest were primarily Termites. There were several hundred in attendance. It was an enormous crowd considering they were all volunteers.

This was the farthest earth still in Wanderer possession.

There had been fighting at the next earth, but Jy had ordered the cuts in energy that had brought a sudden unplanned retreat. Exposed soldiers needed too many supplies; there was no choice. The various commanders, angry but helpless, brought back the units and counted the dead and tried to ready themselves for any unFound tribes who smelled weakness and could reinvent the portal technologies.

The only unFound here were among the comets, never seen.

The little planets and moons were gone, excepting this earth, and the ruddy cool sun shone down on the unFound artifacts.

It was nearly dawn on the surface.

Jy had been speaking for eight hours, rarely pausing, telling her audience about the wrongness of their acts and the golden purpose of the Wanderer mission and what she envisioned for them from this point on.

It was a typical audience, she reflected.

Each of them was a killer, in intent if not deed. They had been conditioned as killers, and they were quick to anger and slow to agree with anything Jy would tell them. Common wisdom held her responsible for their losing ground to the unFound. Even the highest-ranking Wanderers resented her presence and her nagging moral tone. This was their fight, they felt, and they would win it. Jy had not been an effective force in their lives for a million years, if ever; she was an archaic myth out of the Wanderer past; she was useless and silly and wrong.

The audience began to shrink from the outset.

In ones and twos and sometimes larger groups, the bored soldiers decided they had heard enough. They would rise and leave, shaking their heads and sometimes glancing towards Jy, perhaps wondering if her security shields were strong enough to withstand a blast from a fighting glove.

She had talked through the night, working on those who remained, and she scarcely felt the hours.

Her body was young again. She had dark brown fur and strong muscles strung on solid bone, and she was the picture of vigor and tenacity as she strode back and forth on the little stage made for her by a few loyal followers—the reborn Wanderers and the others she had gathered to date.

Only a few dozen faces remained when she started to talk about the future. It was a typical audience, judging by the attrition rate. People sat about the room in scattered knots, and she knew better than to try coaxing them closer. She was using holos to show them various futures, and every little while she would ask the same question aloud:

"How do we cope with the unFound and secure the mission too?"

She showed them powerful starships accelerating away from the damaged sun, slipping through the comet belt and scattering throughout the galaxy.

"Is it reasonable to believe that the earth and only the earth can be a gateway to the Bright?" She paused and gave them a slow sober gaze. "I know your response. 'Jy,' you want to say, 'people have hunted for other gateways. Tens of thousands of colonized worlds have been examined.' But I remind you of the obvious, my friends. There are perhaps tens of millions of habitable worlds in this one galaxy, plus thousands of billions of worlds too small or too large for normal scrutiny. I admit this is daunting. The numbers do frighten, and perhaps every search will fail. But why would the Makers have only one gateway? What if we can find a single asteroid or an icy moon where the Makers left their mark? What if we can step sideways here and slip past the unFound entirely? Isn't it worth the attempt?"

There were a few hopeful nods mixed with grumbling sounds.

Jy changed the holo, filling the room with a piercing image of the Bright itself.

"We should focus our energies and intelligence on the Makers' work," she told them. "What might we learn about the Bright? Is there a better way to utilize it? Perhaps we can find some means to skip ahead two earths at a time, or two thousand earths, or perhaps steady motion can be achieved and this room could be transported to some Maker nexus in a matter of moments, every puzzle ready to be answered...."

Her audience allowed there was a remote possibility. They were too fatigued to insult her wishful thinking or to mention the abundant research that already said otherwise. They merely nodded and sat on their hands.

Jy changed the holo once again.

A green earth floated overhead, and while people watched the familiar continents split and slid across its face. The fragments collided and stuck, mountains rising and oceans changing, and the image created a sense of deep, deep time.

"If both options fail," she allowed, "we have one and only one choice left for us. We will wait. We won't fight the unFound, and if they come we will isolate them with shields and other defensive means to the best of our ability—"

This brought *boos* from the back and harsh dry coughs.

"—and we can wait here and nourish the mission, biding time, because the restless forces of natural selection will someday make the unFound extinct. *We will outlast them!* Someday we will send scouts ahead, perhaps for the first time in a million years, and they will come home to report that our enemies are now docile, calm, and even peace-loving...."

A large portion of the shriveled audience stood and left. It was typical. Soldiers and Wanderers shook their heads, kicking furniture aside. Wait and do nothing? they thought. It was a ludicrous idea... *imagine such an option!*

And while they slipped through the narrow unFound doorway, Jy, using her famous nagging voice, shouted, "Why not be patient? Have you no faith in the human spirit? To do one great thing right . . . is a billion years too long to wait? I ask you! Is it?"

She had talked for eight hours, and her audience was a mere handful of the original close-packed crowd. It was a good night because more often than not nobody remained at this point, and Jy was free to sleep badly, as usual, and study whatever communications had come from the Other Side.

Not this morning, however.

She had five true candidates sitting before her. They seemed eager to be included among her slow-growing ranks. She smiled at them and asked them to come forward. Were they earnest candidates? she wondered. Most likely one or two were agents planted by her shadowy foes, and she would have to remain alert to nuances, doing her best to filter out those who could never be trusted.

Jy was learning quickly about trust and duty, particularly as it was perceived in this place. Moliak had merely hinted at the violence possible and the depth of the illness—

—sometimes she wished for help.

She would think of her entourage and the various Founders and Cousins whom she had trusted for ages, and people like Quencé with their potent skills. Why not bring them here? she would ask herself. She could make the appropriate orders and find talented, absolutely devoted helpers like dear Quencé . . . and the healthy arm of the Bright would be weakened as a consequence; what was her burden would become theirs too.

Quencé sent her occasional communications.

He described the work he was doing and the long-term plans; everything was going well at the moment. He made a point of asking about her—perhaps too much of a point, she felt—and sometimes Jy had the distinct impression, between his careful words, that he was thinking things that were more than a little remarkable.

Quencé's holo image would stare straight at Jy.

The stare had a way of unsettling her . . . and she

would shake her head and think of other issues. There was too much to be done. This earth and several dozen more earths needed her attentions and rigid convictions. And no, she wouldn't bring anyone to help. This was her task and her responsibility, and the ill were going to cure themselves with their own strong wills.

That is what she explained to her little collection of Reborn.

It was how she finished the rare successful rallies.

Jy described her abduction and Moliak's scheme, telling the entire story with her practiced voice, and she told how it had come to a point where she and Moliak and Cotton stood on the false savanna.

"I killed them," she admitted. "I murdered both of them. For a thousand millenia I was the ceaseless advocate of peace and reason, and I murdered them purposefully and gladly."

A pair of Termites watched her, and a Cousin, and two Wanderers from unfamiliar earths. They nodded with her confession, unsure of its purpose. Of course she had murdered, they thought, because it was in self-defense. There was never a clearer incident of self-defense, at least in their own experience. What was there to forgive?

She stared at them, and she waited.

At last one of the Wanderers, a tall muscled woman with a serious countenance, remarked, "You seem angry with yourself, Jy, and I don't understand. You had every cause to do what you did. You acted responsibly. A person in your position would be damned if she didn't kill them."

"I agree," Jy responded. "In principle, yes, you are right."

The tall woman waited.

Jy held up her left hand, showing everyone the glove she had worn since that fateful moment. It was an unFound fighting glove drained of its energies, and in the bad light it appeared dull and cold.

The woman couldn't hold her tongue anymore.

"Why grieve," she asked, "over Moliak and the other one? I mean, you were within your rights. You lived to begin again. You did what was best, and you say it yourself!"

"But why did I do it?" Jy asked in turn. "Why did I act as I did?"

The woman blinked and appeared mystified.

Jy said, "Listen," and leaned forwards, creating the mood of a secret about to be shared. "Remember how Moliak screamed at me, telling me the human species was not worthy, and someday another species led by another Jy would begin the mission over again—"

"Yes, but—"

"Realize something!" she said. "I did not kill Moliak and Cotton to save anyone's life, nor did I want to save the mission." She was beginning to cry. She couldn't have stopped the crying if she had wanted, and she let them look at her suffering face, telling the mismatched group, "I murdered them because I was protecting my fame. It is that simple. I didn't want any other Jy to take my place. *Do you understand?*"

Nobody spoke.

"And that is why I come here as I have, alone." She moaned and rocked back and forth, telling each of them, "Like you, I am a criminal. Like you, I want to hunt for some way to make myself whole again. Like you, I am a soiled human. Like you . . . like all of you!"

BILLIE

> TODAY I saw an earth I didn't recognize, and it
> was mine.
>
> —*Billie's private journal*

The ceremony was small and quick and rather informal.
It was attended by two of Billie's teachers and the customary Founder, a jolly little male who liked to tell bad
jokes, plus a few people who happened to live in the
area. The ceremony was held at the approximate site
where she and Janice had lived, and when they were
finished Billie asked the nearest teacher if she might take
a brief walk and see what there was to see.

The teacher, a Sasquatchlike woman with an easy
humor, told Billie, "You can do what you wish, my dear.
You're no longer a submissive young novice . . . are you?"

She had been a novice for centuries, and the change
was hard to accept. She wasn't a novice anymore. She
was an extremely low-ranking Wanderer, newly made.

"Go on, Billie. Go!"

She took her walk. It was summertime, late summertime, with the bluestem and Indian grasses growing shoulder high, wildflowers here and there, and nothing obvious left of the lost city. Billie could see some vague markings that might mean buried streets, and some squarish little marshes might be the flooded remains of old basements. Otherwise the country was a wilderness. The grasses ran to the horizon, bending under the ceaseless wind, and in the distance she could see blackish dots that were grazing animals of imprecise shape and origin.

The people of this earth—Billie's earth—had migrated into space.

It had happened at a remarkable rate.

Billions of people lived throughout the sky. The moon was a swollen green crescent, and there were new moons made from captured asteroids, hollowed and filled with cities and traveling in swift low orbits. The colonists already were reaching the closer stars, the spawn of this earth thriving; and their old cradle was parklike and healthy and mostly uninhabited today.

Billie wasn't thinking about any one thing when she came to the raised ground that had been the railroad bed. She climbed through anemic grasses and reached the flat crest, then she pulled a little book out of her trouser pocket. She wanted to sit and read, if only for a moment. She could see her surroundings better from this place. And while she hunted for comfortable ground she came across a young man sitting cross-legged in the grass, smiling and watching her.

Billie asked, "Can I help you?"

His smile grew larger. After a moment he asked, "Do you know what?" in a dialect of English, and he rose. He was a blend of races, pleasant-faced and rather handsome, and he had a quick smart voice. "Do you?" he repeated.

"What should I know?" she responded.

That made him laugh. From the belt of his trousers he removed a folding knife, and he withdrew the long ceramic blade and grinned again and knelt in front of her, digging at the ground.

Few people lived in this region anymore.

Judging by those who attended the ceremony, they

were primarily religious groups with an interest in self-reliance and the isolation afforded by the holy earth.

Billie wondered where the young man lived.

"What are you doing?" she asked.

He pulled the knife from the fresh hole, inserting a finger and nodding while telling her, "You can dig down and find them."

"Find them?"

"The old wooden ties. The train ties."

Of course. She nodded and asked, "They're still there, are they?" and took a half step backward.

The man gave her an odd look and stood, saying, "The trains don't run anymore, but their ties are still here. All of them the same size and shape and made from the same kind of wood."

She waited.

He folded his knife and put it out of sight.

She said, "You're right," and smiled.

He was staring at Billie. She didn't know what to make of his intense expression or his little speech about ties.

"Do you think a lot about the old trains?" she finally asked him.

"No," he responded.

"No?"

"That's not what I think about, no."

She waited, then asked, "What do you find interesting then?"

"You'll never find them," he stated.

"Who?"

"You know who I mean."

She did understand. *The Makers, yes*—

"Whatever they were once," he said with force and conviction, "they've gone on somewhere by now and changed and the Bright is something left over and you'll never get close to them. You can't ever catch them."

Billie took a deep breath.

She smiled.

Then she nodded, admitting to the man, "I have days when I believe just what you believe." She took another breath. "But then I have other days too . . . .

ABOUT THE AUTHOR

ROBERT REED was the grand prize winner of the 1985 Writers of the Future Aware (for "Mudpuppies," written under the name Robert Touzalin), and was a finalist for the John W. Campbell Award for Best New Writer. His short fiction has appeared in *The Magazine of Fantasy & Science Fiction*; *Isaac Asimov's Science Fiction Magazine*; *Universe 16*, and many other publications. His novels include *The Leeshore, The Hormone Jungle, Black Milk*, and the upcoming *Down the Bright Way*. A graduate of Nebraska Wesleyan University, he majored in biology with an emphasis on ecology. His hobbies include baseball, movies, and marathon running. Reed lives in Lincoln, Nebraska.

BLACK MILK

Ryder's gang is just like any other gang of sub-
urban kids. They do what all kids do: build tree
houses, hunt snakes in the woods; boast, trade
secrets, and argue. Ryder, the sensitive day-
dreamer; Cody, the tomboy; Marshall, the know-
it-all; Jack, the mischief; and Beth, the pretty little
girl with the sweet singing voice. Everyday kids
. . . except . . .

They are members of the first generation in a
new world of genetically tailored individuals, all
created by Dr. Aaron Florida. Marshall's parents
designed him to be a top scientist; Cody's two
mothers have a girl who can do anything a boy
can—only better; Ryder's mother and father have
a son possessed of a perfect memory. It is
through Ryder's perceptions that the story of
Black Milk unfolds.

Here is an excerpt from Black Milk
by Robert Reed,
on sale now from Bantam Spectra:

People don't think like I think.

Most people barely recall past times, and their memories are forever infected with wishful thinking and impenetrable holes. But I have my way of focusing—concentrating hard on things stored within me. To me a memory can be more real and true than the things of the moment. Memories are reality cured and conditioned into a hard, clear stuff that can be examined with care from every angle and with every sense, new details always lurking, always close.

I have an early memory of the parkland, for example.

We had just moved to the city, and our neighborhood was full of new houses and young families. Mom and Dad walked me down to the old streambed that was soon to become the bottoms. Big bulldozers were gutting out the trash and eroded earth, making room for a modern, efficient sewage treatment scheme. My folks had been reading about it. They spoke of big perforated pipes and special cleansing sands, understanding almost nothing. Mom said, "It's Florida's park," and Dad said, "Florida *is* this town." I wasn't four years old, and a lot of the words were strange to me. They were so much noise. What I noticed most were the huge and magnificent bulldozers with their robot brains and their high, empty seats where people would sit and drive, should the robots fail. I felt their throbbing and clanking, the sensation frightening and fine; and I stood safe between my folks, Dad talking about the dozers now and their invisible riders, and Mom confessing that the dust was bothering her, so couldn't we go home now? Please?

We walked through the future pasture. I remember more weeds than grasses, and the weeds had a rich stink that lingered on my clothes and skin. We crossed a newly made street and followed a second street up to our house, blue and bright and sandwiched between the other colored houses. I went upstairs to my new room and sat on the stone floor, a big sheet of old-fashioned paper between my legs and a lovely black crayon letting me make lines. I didn't understand tailoring. My idea came to me from a simpler, childish source, and it had nothing to do with genes and splicing.

I remember drawing hard and fighting my clumsy young hands, concentrating on little details. I did the bulldozer as well as I could manage, then I looked in a mirror and made a snarling face and drew it too. Then I went downstairs and found Mom. "Look look look," I said.

"I'm looking." She was sitting on our new couch, my drawing in her lap. She said, "Goodness."

I said it was Dozerman. The dozer was below, the man on top. I was on top. I was the man, I explained. "Dozerman! Dozerman!" I'd drawn it the way I saw it in my head, minus the shakes of my hands and the limits of my crayon. Mom watched me chug-chug around the room. I imagined myself with the funny Dozerman wheels, and I told her I'd grow up the same way. "Dozerman!"—powerful and loud, digging and pushing all day, all night, its big super-loop batteries brimming with juice and no need for food or water, or anything—

"All right, dear. Stop." Mom stared at me, folding the drawing in half and tucking it out of sight. "No more," she said. "What you should do is go upstairs and rest. You must be tired. Aren't you tired?"

Dozerman doesn't get tired. I tried telling her so.

"But you're not him, are you? Are you?" She shook her head, saying, "So stop, please. Would you? Ryder? Would you stop now please?"

When I was very young and my folks were talking—at the dinner table, watching TV, or anywhere—I'd catch them forgetting something or telling a story wrong. I would correct them. Of course I meant nothing bad, and I certainly didn't wish to seem proud or to belittle them for their failures. I didn't even understand at first. Couldn't they summon up the past? Did they blink at the wrong moments? I wondered. You put your keys there, Mommy. No, up there. Mr. Evans said the house was on Weavehaven, Daddy. And who cut down that tree? The one by the green house. The green house that was yellow last year, Daddy. Mommy. You remember! We drove past it when it was Christmas and they had all the fake Bambis pulling Santa across the yard. We went down this street and turned, and Daddy said, "I feel snow in my bones, Gwinn. Maybe when we're home we can melt it together," and it snowed three inches that night. It did—!

My memory grew as I got older, and I began to have spells.

My capacity to focus was the culprit. Just as I could look inside myself, I could watch the world without and lose myself at times. Once when I was five I climbed a high stool to look at water boiling in a big pot. I'd never gotten lost in such a thing before. The clear water churned and popped, the bubbles skating along the bottom, and growing, and then rising free with such violence that my heart was left pounding and my chest felt tight. Mom was beside me after a while. She took my arms and face, saying, "Oh, what is it? Ryder? Ryder?" Couldn't she see the water boiling? How could she miss such a wonder? I tried to answer her, but I couldn't speak. I was completely lost, oblivious to the scalding steam and my bright burns. And she was terrified, of course. She told Dad so later. Another damned trance, and she didn't care what the doctors said. I was hallucinating! These weren't *discrimination* problems, or whatever they were calling them this week. It was just boiling water, for God's sake! And while I listened I grieved for her and for Dad. I did. That was the moment, precise and undeniable, when I understood that my folks were, in some fashion, blind.

Then I was six years old, and a certain teacher came home with me. The meeting had been arranged and my folks were waiting in the living room, wearing good clothes and smelling of soap. "Go play in your room, Ryder." Mom spoke with her voice slow and tight, her face strange. "Shut your door so we don't bother you. All right?"

I went upstairs. My room was cool and dark with the shades drawn, and my door didn't quite fill its frame. The stone floor served to reflect sounds through the gap at the bottom. I heard talk from the living room. I focused on every sound.

"We're glad to meet you," said Dad. "Can I get you something?"

"A soft drink," said the teacher.

"What can we do for you?" asked Mom. "Is anything wrong?"

"Oh, no. No." The teacher was a fat woman, and old. She was wearing a huge bright dress and paint on her face, and no one liked her. Not at school, at least. The kids called her a witch and worse, and the other teachers said hard things when they thought no one was in earshot. I lay on the floor and thought about the things I'd overheard, the voices like angry bees in my head. "Manipulative," they said. "Two-faced."

"I was studying Ryder's files," she explained, "and I thought this would be a good time to meet his parents. That's all."

"It's good meeting you," said Dad.

"A very special boy. Unique, I think." She wondered, "Where, if I might ask, did you have the refinements done?" Refinement was the same as tailoring. She said the word slowly, as if it was three words.

"In California," Mom told her. "In a Florida clinic."

"An interesting coincidence, your moving here. Dr. Florida's home—"

"A business decision," Dad mentioned. "This is one of the fastest growing states, after all."

"Quite reasonable of you, yes," said the teacher. "Let me thank you for letting me visit, first of all. And I want you to know that we at the school, and myself, want to do our utmost to help your son master his talents and smooth over those points where he might have troubles. I want you to feel assured that all of us wish the best for him, and everything from adapted personals to private tutors will be done on his behalf."

There was nothing. Then Dad said, "Well, thanks . . ."

"Are there any questions about his prognosis?" she wondered.

"More of the same," he said. "It's something like autism, they tell us. His difficulty coping with the environment, choosing what to watch and what to ignore. He has these trances—

"He's very sensitive," said Mom.

"Oh, yes," the teacher agreed. "Autism has its similarities, yes. But an autistic child would be helpless. Ryder is not. With training and hard work, Ryder should be able to carry on normally. Maybe he'll lack some abilities. He does pay a cost for having such a powerful memory . . . the brain being finite, after all. But we shouldn't grieve for him. I know I don't grieve. When he's like me, old and gray, he'll only have to concentrate for a moment to remember youth." She laughed and said, "That seems like a precious talent to me." She said, "Maybe I do envy him. A little bit. If I could remember being twenty again, if I could," she laughed loudly for a very brief moment.

Then no one spoke.

Finally Mom said, "You're very kind," with a certain voice.

Dad said, "Gwinn? Don't be—"

"What?" she asked. "Isn't this rather patronizing? I don't like being patronized, and I'm not sitting through it."

"I'm sorry," said the teacher. "I just hoped—"

"Lady," said Mom, "it's difficult to have such a son." She was angry in a quiet fashion. She said, "We wanted a fine healthy boy, Kip and I. We're ordinary people, yes, and I for one take pride in that fact. I don't mind admitting it. I am not gifted. I can't juggle enormous math problems in my head, or paint great paintings, or call myself a beauty. Not even on the old scales. I'm part of the last honest generation . . . the good and decent people who were brought up to accept their shortcomings. . . ."

"Gwinn?"

"Let me talk, Kip. Please?" She said, "We had the tailoring done, and I guess I am glad for the bulk of it. We made certain that Ryder would be healthy and long-lived and we got what we paid for, yes. But there was this self-serving bastard at the clinic. I'm not blaming Dr. Florida himself, I know better than to do that in this town. But this one man was a demon. Smug. Smart and proud of it. He had his lab coat and his charm, and he seduced us with nonsense about every child being born with enormous talents. Awesome brains and other bankable skills, and we would be unfit parents if we settled for a plain-label boy. That's how he put it. A plain-label boy. And both of us were a little bowled over by him. He told us how a few synthetic genes could be sewn into the fertilized egg—tiny, potent brain enhancers—and we'd make it possible for Ryder to compete in the world—"

"Darling?" said Dad.

"What?"

"What if someone overhears? Don't you think—?"

"What? I'm talking honestly. We spend too much time and breath hiding things as it is," she told him. "When he's old and gray, like she said, he can remember this with everything else. Maybe he'll understand." She sighed and told the teacher, "I'm sorry. I sound bitter, I know, but I've got reasons. I love my son very much, I do, but he can't simply walk home from school. He's always finding distractions. Diversions. An ordinary leaf, and he'll sit on the ground and study it, and then the next leaf, and so on. Then it's after dark, and I'm worried sick and I have to come out and find him. Do you understand? I find him on someone's lawn, and he's holding leaves up to the streetlights . . ."

"I do understand," said the teacher.

Mom said, "How many times has it happened, Kip? We're talking to some friends or business associates, whoever, and poor Ryder corrects us on this point. On that point. A little boy, and he tells people the most remarkable things, embarrassing things, and everyone knows it's true because they know him—"

"He's not vindictive," said Dad.

"Am I saying he's vindictive?" She paused for a long moment, then she said, "I'm angry because I didn't pay someone for the privilege of having such a child. Special or not. It's not fair, and I realize there are legal rulings that keep us from lawsuits. We signed plenty of papers and clearances and tied our own hands. And yes, maybe I do seem rather simple-minded to you. Shortsighted and all. But I can't help it and I've given up trying to stop myself—I am no saint—and so there. I guess I've said my piece. So thank you."

No one spoke.

Then the teacher said, "Genetics are difficult. At best." Her voice was soft and slow. "Even now they can't predict all the effects from a single novel gene. Particularly the synthetics. A gene meshes with many thousands of genes, and who knows? Who knows?" She paused, then she said, "I don't know." She said, "I see it every day, this new world, and you're right. Not everything is perfect. I see geniuses who aren't smart enough for their parents, and children sculpted according to whims and fancies. We've got synthetic genes and famous genes, and what bothers me most is the parent who can't accept the fact that every child, gifted or not, is a child first. Immature. In need of help."

"These have to be tough times for kids," said Dad. He sounded agreeable and quite sober.

"And yet, you know, the children themselves are such inspirations," the teacher said. "All my life I've worked with the youngest ones, and I've seen the changes. Years ago they would pick on one another for being odd. You know . . . different? I'm sure you remember the horrors. The funny-looking boy was tormented. The ugly or smart girl was friendless. That sort of crime doesn't happen so much anymore—"

"Everyone's smart," said Mom. "And pretty."

"Maybe that's part of the answer," the teacher admitted. "Sure. But there's nothing homogeneous about my kids. There are plenty of chances for viciousness, for in-groups and out-groups. Yet they seem to tolerate the differences. Indeed, if anything, these children nourish a strange, resilient independence . . . based on their own special skills . . ."

"How many children do you have?" asked Mom.

"I see about a hundred every day—"

"I mean you yourself. Have you been a mother?" she wondered. Her voice was wearing an edge.

Dad said, "Another drink?" I heard him moving, his voice turning quiet. Soothing. "It's awfully good of you to come." He was trying to lessen the tension, saying,

"We must seem pretty ragged to you, but under the circumstances—"

"Don't mention it. Please," said the teacher.

"Still and all." His voice got louder. "Whatever happens, we do wish the best for Ryder. Always have. We thought we were helping him with the tailoring. The refinements. Because it's tooth-and-nail out there. We wanted him fit to compete for the jobs and the promotions." He paused, then he said. "Think of our position. In a very few years my wife and I will be facing the first of Ryder's generation—their brainpower, their good looks and confidence—and I can confess to feeling nervous." He said, "The tooth-and-nail business of business." He said, "We took our chances and the poor kid suffers for us having done it. And so we make ourselves suffer too. Don't we, dear?"

Mom said, "Kip."

"Sure you don't want another drink?" asked Dad.

"No thank you," said the teacher.

"Where are you going, dear?"

"Downstairs," said Mom. "You mentioned work, and it occurred to me that I might do some. All right?"

No one spoke.

Mom said, "I am sorry. I just want something accomplished today. If you don't mind."

No one spoke while she went downstairs, then Dad said, "Gwinn is a little touchy, that's all. She takes it personally when Ryder does some strange thing or another. When he starts to stare at one of our friends with those big eyes—"

"I should be honest," the teacher announced. "I do have a second agenda today. A request, if you will."

Dad said, "All right."

"A series of studies and papers on Ryder might just help find and treat children like him. And maybe we can learn how to avoid the same mistakes again. For those who wish to consider them mistakes." She paused, then she said, "As I understand it, no one is certain why his ordinary genes and the synthetics merged like they did."

"No one's told us how," said Dad.

"I'm in a unique position, you see. I've access to facilities and I've got the essential training, and so with your permission—"

"I don't believe so."

"Could you tell me why?"

"First," said Dad, "Gwinn wouldn't allow it. And second, neither would I."

"I see."

"It's something we decided long ago. Label us however you wish, but the truth is that we appreciate our quiet lives. We don't want notoriety. A kid like Ryder, with his talents, could become an enormous novelty act on TV. You know what I mean. The public would want to test his memory by every goofy means, and that wouldn't be best. Not for him. Not for us. So I'm sorry, but no."

"Well," she said, "if publicity is the problem—"

"A John Doe? I think not," said Dad. "That doesn't sound appealing. Besides, there's no way you can guarantee our privacy. Is there?"

She said nothing for a good long while. I imagined her sitting on a chair in the living room, filling it, and Dad sitting opposite her and leaning forward with his bony elbows on his bony knees.

She said, "Perhaps I should mention other terms."

"I don't follow you."

She said, "A cash incentive. A gift for the good of the boy—"

"No."

"But you can't—"

"Lady," he said, "let's call it quits." I could hear Dad standing and moving to the front door. The teacher followed. She breathed like fat people breath, quick and shallow. We didn't have fat kids at school, I thought. All of us made our food into heat and motion. "Your intentions are splendid, and thanks," said Dad. "But I ask— I insist—that you leave and forget this conversation." His voice wasn't angry or sad or anything. It was flat and plain.

"I'm sorry if I offended you."

"I'll live." The front door opened, squeaking, and he said, "It was nice of you to take the trouble," with that flat voice.

She said, "You shouldn't be ashamed of him."

"You think we are? You haven't been listening, lady."

She said, "Give him my best," with anger seeping out between the words.

"Sure."

"I can tell," she said. "You *are* interested in the offer."

"A little bit, sure. We could always use the cash flow." Then Dad said, "The thing about being ordinary is that we're weak and we don't have any illusions. And no denials either. I admit it. We're subject to temptations." He made a small, harsh sound, and I imagined him shaking his head. "Maybe there'll come a day when Florida, or someone, learns to tailor out those traits. You suppose? A dose of this, a shot of that, and *poof*! Instant character. Neat and quick."

We were eating that night, sitting at the kitchen table and the teacher gone. No one was talking. No one could think of anything to say, their mouths full and their plates steaming and the forks going *click-click* when the peas ran away. I was thinking about my peas. I was studying their wrinkled faces, each face different in tiny vital ways. I was watching the tines of my fork come down on them and stick into their firm green meat, or cause them to jump and run away. *Click-click*. And Mom said, "Ryder? Ryder. Don't you want to know what she said?"

I blinked. "Was it good?" I asked.

They glanced at each other. "Absolutely," said Dad.

"Why? Did you think you were in trouble?" Mom started to watch my peas too. "Have you done something wrong?"

"I don't think so."

"You haven't," said Dad. "Don't worry."

"Is she a nice lady?" asked Mom. "This teacher?"

"I don't know. She's okay."

"What do people say about her?" she asked. "Do they like her?"

"Not really."

"Not really?" She halfway smiled and said, "Go on. Eat."

But I couldn't. All at once a question came into my

head, and I thought of how I might ask it. What would be the best way? I pondered and then cleared my throat, looking at Dad and wondering, "Dad? Who's the best person in the world?"

"The best person?"

"Is there one? Anyone?"

"I suppose there must be," he admitted, shrugging his shoulders. "Why do you ask?"

I remembered older kids talking on the playground one day. I saw their faces and heard their self-assured voices, then I blinked and said, "These kids told me it was Dr. Florida. He's the best."

"A good candidate," he decided.

Mom said, "He's not perfect," with that edge to her voice.

"And who is perfect?" asked Dad.

She looked at me and said, "I'm sure he's a decent fellow. Probably better than all of us. Now eat your peas."

I caught three peas and chewed them to slime, then squished the slime between my teeth. I started to daydream, imagining the doorbell ringing and Dad going to the door, finding Dr. Florida standing on our porch. He was so very tall, smiling like he smiled on TV, and he said, "Good evening," and put his hat in his hands. "I hope I'm not intruding."

"Of course not, no," said Dad in my daydream.

Mom smiled and said, "Come in, sir. Please."

We gave him a plate and good shares of everything, and he took off his raincoat and sat opposite me, looking at me, his smile never wavering. He was friendly all of the time. People said he was a saint, I remembered, and a great genius too, and we couldn't have invented a better person to be so important. I remembered one adult saying, "If someone has to hold the world in his hands, who better than Florida?" Father-to-the-World. He ate his imaginary dinner and spoke with my folks, then he helped clear the table and followed me upstairs. He came into my room and said, "Ryder, you're such a good fellow. I know it." He touched the back of my head, rubbing my hair, and told me, "You're fine as you are, Ryder. Believe me."

I did. It was all imaginary, but it felt so wonderfully real.

"I'm proud to have played a part in you," he told me. "Don't count me with the others. I understand you."

Here was the man who made the tiny, tiny genes that fit inside me, and inside all of us. He was brilliant and richer than kings, and in some sense he was father to my generation—all of those lean and strong and smart kids—and I could practically see him in my room. With me. Me—!

"Ryder?"

"Ryder? Son?"

"Ryder?"

—and I blinked, shaking my head, having to bring myself back to the real and now.

Ryder, Cody, Marshall and their friends become deeply involved with Dr. Florida's plans for his brave new world...and what they discover will change their lives forever. **Black Milk** is a work of powerful imagination and storytelling technique, a captivating and chilling tale of a very possible near future.

Black Milk is on sale now from Bantam Spectra.

For the summer's best in science fiction and fantasy,
look no further than Bantam Spectra.

SPECTRA'S SUMMER SPECTACULAR

With a dazzling list of science fiction and fantasy stars, Spectra's
summer list will take you to worlds both old and new: worlds as close
as Earth herself, as far away as a planet where daylight reigns
supreme; as familiar as Han Solo's Millennium Falcon and as alien
as the sundered worlds of the Death Gate. Travel with these critically
acclaimed and award-winning authors for a spectacular summer
filled with wonder and adventure!

Coming in May 1991:

**Star Wars, Volume 1:
Heir to the Empire**
by Timothy Zahn

Earth
by David Brin

King of Morning, Queen of Day
by Ian McDonald

Coming in June, 1991:

**The Gap Into Vision:
Forbidden Knowledge**
by Stephen R. Donaldson

Black Trillium
by Marion Zimmer Bradley,
Julian May and Andre Norton

**Chronicles of the King's Tramp
Book 1: Walker of Worlds**
by Tom DeHaven

Coming in July 1991:

**The Death Gate Cycle,
Volume 3: Fire Sea**
by Margaret Weis and
Tracy Hickman

**The Death Gate Cycle,
Volume 2: Elven Star**
by Margaret Weis and
Tracy Hickman

Raising the Stones
by Sheri S. Tepper

Coming in August 1991:

Garden of Rama
by Arthur C. Clarke
and Gentry Lee

Nightfall
by Isaac Asimov
and Robert Silverberg

Available soon wherever Bantam Spectra Books are sold.

AN217 -- 4/91